DEADLY GAMES!

BOBBY NASH

Jere —
GAME ON!
Best —
Bobby Nash
1 19

BEN
BOOKS

First BEN Books Edition
2011

DEADLY GAMES!

© 2011 Bobby Nash
All Rights Reserved.

First Printing.

ISBN: 0615553435
ISBN-13: 978-0615553436 (BEN Books)

Book Production, design, and cover by Bobby Nash.

Special Thanks to Kurt Allen.

Printed in the USA

Publisher's Note:

Published by BEN Books, PO Box 626, Bethlehem, GA 30620
http://BEN-Books.blogspot.com

Dedicated to my wonderful parents, R.O. and Margaret
Nash for their continued support and encouragement.
And to my brother, Wes, who keeps me on my toes.

Francis Chalmers moved quickly down the corridor.

As warden of one of the nations most heavily guarded prisons, Chalmers was not used to doing anything faster than he felt like. Anyone who didn't understand and respect that simple fact of life could expect a lightning bolt to the backside. In here he was god and everything happened at his speed, not the other way around.

At least on most days.

Warden Chalmers ran a tight ship.

But today was anything but an average day.

Today, he was in a hurry, but not because he wanted to be. No, today the situation warranted speed and decisive action.

So, naturally, everything that could have happened to slow him down did. Murphy -*you know, the guy with the law*- always paid a visit when time was of the essence. Still, for all the urgency of the moment, the warden's wide girth -*and being completely out of shape*- kept him from running full speed down the corridor. He was intimately familiar with the route. Twice a day every day for the past six years he had walked this same route and checked on the prisoner living in isolation and segregated from the other inmates.

Though usually with much less urgency.

The warden stopped just outside the all too familiar cell in a secluded area of the prison that was set aside for some of the more dangerous inmates. Taking in a deep, calming breath, he looked tentatively inside. He had known that a day like this might eventually come, but he never believed it would be this soon. Plus, he expected to be happier about it. He could not help but wonder, *Why aren't I happier about this?*

With surprising hesitancy, the warden stepped uneasily inside the cramped cell.

"My God!"

One of his uniformed guards, Dennis Truchess, was already inside the cell. He had discovered the body while making his rounds. He turned as Warden Chalmers entered, holding a large manila envelope in his left hand. Boldly scrawled across the front of the envelope, probably written with a thick, black magic marker was a name.

The warden was not surprised to find the name was his.

FRANCIS CHALMERS

Chalmers noted that only his name was on the envelope.

Not his title.

Just one final example of the contempt his prisoner felt for him. He refused to admit anyone held any power greater that his own. Chalmers knew from firsthand experience the perverse fascination his prisoner -*now former prisoner*- had with playing mind games. He had a devious mind, dark and twisted, but very intelligent. Dangerously so, in fact.

So it came as no surprise that, even in death, Darrin Morehouse would find a way to lash out at those he deemed as enemies. Francis Chalmers knew he was counted among the growing list of men and women that Morehouse blamed for his capture and incarceration. At times, the warden was almost proud to be on that list. Truly, he was counted among good company.

He could only wonder what game the scheming Darrin Morehouse planned to put them through this time. *To pull off a plot against your enemies from beyond the grave. Only a madman such as he would dare be so bold,* he thought.

"Sir?"

"Hmm?"

Remotely aware of the attending guard in the small cell, the warden reached for the offered envelope from Officer Truchess without a second glance, but he did not take it. His eyes fixed on the object above him.

"Warden Chalmers..." the guard began, but a look from his superior stopped him in mid sentence.

After a moment the warden simply nodded at the man's unspoken question.

Truchess assumed that the warden was simply in shock. It was a natural assumption considering the tense relationship between the warden and the former inmate that occupied the cell where they now stood in stunned silence.

It was Officer Truchess that finally broke the stillness. "I've placed a call to the morgue," he said cautiously. The last thing he wanted to do was upset the man, but he also knew they couldn't simply stand there all day staring at the body hanging from the light fixture.

The warden nodded slightly and the guard hoped that meant his boss understood.

"They'll be here any minute to take him down," he added.

A moment passed. Chalmers still said nothing.

"Sir?" Thruchess pressed again, concern visible on his face.

The warden continued to look up at the body hanging from the ceiling. Beads of sweat had popped up on Chalmer's brow and Truchess was concerned the man was going to have a heart attack.

From the angle of the body, Chalmers could not clearly see the face of the dead man. Not that it mattered. The warden knew exactly who it was. What it was. Part of him was thrilled that it was finally at an end, but another part wanted that man to suffer an eternity within this eight-foot by eight-foot cell.

"Bastard got off easy," the warden swallowed, catching a lump in his throat.

"Yes, sir," the guard agreed. "He did."

"He, uh, left this for you, sir," Truchess said as he placed the large envelope in the warden's still outstretched hand.

Chalmers accepted the envelope, gazing at it as if he had only then noticed its presence. He unclasped the metal clip at the back and carefully lifted the flap away to peer inside. With the envelope open, Warden Chalmers poured the contents out onto the cell's single unkempt bed.

The items slid out into an unorganized pile on the disheveled bed. Envelopes.

Eight of them in fact.

Eight small white envelopes had fallen out of the larger one. Each had a name written on it in the same bad penmanship that Chalmers recognized as belonging to the prisoner who lived in this cell. The prisoner always wrote in all capital letters, which made the warden think that everything he wrote looked like it was being screamed.

He scanned the names and recognized all but one of them.

JOHN BARTLETT
BENJAMIN WEST
VIVIAN MOREHOUSE
LAURA SELLARS
NATHAN HUGHES
MICHAEL COOMBES
FRANCIS CHALMERS
PHILIP JASON HALL

Only one of the envelopes had an address on it. The envelope was addressed to Philip Jason Hall, attorney at law in Atlanta. A sticky note was affixed to the front of the envelope. In the same scrawl it read: *LAST WILL AND TESTAMENT OF DARRIN MOREHOUSE. IN THE EVENT OF MY DEATH, DELIVER TO MY ATTORNEY AT THE AD-DRESS LISTED.*

The eighth was not someone the warden knew, but the larger envelope was addressed to him via a law firm so it didn't take much to put two and two together.

There was a simple, tri-folded piece of paper with the envelopes. Chalmers bent over and retrieved it from the pile of envelopes and unfolded it carefully, as if afraid it might explode. Knowing Morehouse's twisted mind as well as he did, it was a distinct possibility. He let out a breath when he realized it was simply a letter.

"For Warden Chalmers," he began reading aloud. "In the event of my death."

Chalmers and Thruchess exchanged a look before Chalmers read the letter. He read it twice just to make sure he wasn't missing anything. The letter contained a list of instructions to be carried out in the event of his death. The envelopes were to be delivered, unopened to his attorney, Philip Jason Hall care of the law firm of Johnson, Murdoch, and Lower.

Apparently, Morehouse had one last game he wanted to play. One final *hurrah* as he shuffled off to the hell where Chalmers hoped his mortal soul would burn for eternity. The prisoner had visited with other attorneys since his incarceration, but Chalmers could not recall Mr. Hall being among them. He would check the sign in logs to verify that, but when it came to Darrin Morehouse, the warden stayed up to date on his activities.

"Damn," the warden said, thinking aloud. "What game does that madman have planned for us this time?" It was a fair question. In death, Darrin Morehouse could very well be as dangerous as he had been in life, if not more so. Now he had nothing to lose. *How do you bring a dead man to justice*? he wondered.

"Damn," he muttered again, shaking his head.

What more was there to say?

"Lock this place down," he ordered the guards. No calls in or out without my written permission. I want this cell searched top to bottom then sanitized. Cover all the bases, but do it with as few people as possible. The less who know about this the better we'll be able to contain the fallout."

"Yes, sir."

"If he truly hung himself, then that's great. It just means there's one less scumbag in the world I have to put up with and I'll drink a toast to the bastard shuffling off of this mortal coil." Chalmers' expression darkened. "However, if he didn't do the deed himself than that means someone helped him. And while, personally, I'd love to give that person a medal, I can't abide it in my prison. If someone killed him then I need to know that too."

"Yes, sir," Truchess said as he clicked on his radio.

"We keep this quiet," Chalmers reminded his men before Truchess could make the call. "Am I understood?"

The guards nodded.

"I mean it," the warden said, his threat imminently clear. "Not a word. If the press gets winds of this it'll be both your asses, you got me?"

The guards nodded again, this time a little less enthusiastically. It wasn't often that the normally friendly warden pulled rank like this, and he certainly never leveled these types of threats to his guards, which only drove home just how serious the situation before them was. Morehouse's death was a powder keg and if they weren't careful it could very well explode beneath them.

"Good. Let's get to work." Chalmers took one last look around the cell before leaving it. He had to hurry back to his office.

"I've got to make a phone call."

As he headed back to his office he could hear the voice of the dead man in his thoughts. It was something he had heard the man say many times before, yet somehow it seemed to fit the current situation. Morehouse was a schemer. Perhaps he had been planning this day for some time. Chalmers was not certain, but nothing Darrin Morehouse did surprised him anymore.

Or so he thought until today.

The warden did not know how or why, but something told him that his headaches were just beginning.

Darrin Morehouse's voice echoed in his memory.

Let the games begin.

DEADLY GAMES!

CHAPTER 1

Six years earlier.
How it all began.

Fulton County Courthouse
Atlanta, Ga.
December 21

The circus was back in town.

Cameras surged as reporters jockeyed for position on the steps of the Fulton County Courthouse building, each one vying for that perfect angle, the one shot that would catch and hold the attention of their viewers. Despite the bone-chilling thirty-four degrees and light drizzle, the crowd outside continued to grow as the moment grew closer.

Fabian Alexander shrugged off his warm coat, which his shivering assistant then cradled to her chest in an effort to salvage any leftover body heat. She knew that the reporter must have been freezing, but she also knew the man. It was always better to look good than be comfortable.

"You ready?" Alexander asked as he straightened his tie and flicked a piece of lint from the front of his tailored sport coat.

"We're live in," Mike Greenway, the cameraman said between chattering teeth. "Four... Three…" He mouthed the words *two* and *one* before the reporter started speaking.

In his ear piece, Alexander heard the anchors in their nice, warm broadcast booth introduce him. "We go now live to Channel Ten's own Fabian Alexander who is on scene outside the Fulton County Courthouse on this frigid December morning." She turned to look at the monitor where the reporter waited on the scene. "How are you doing out there, Fabian? Are you staying warm?"

"It is very cold outside the Fulton County Courthouse today, Monica," he started. "But you're right. It has been a very busy morning here. Today, in what is being referred to as a bold move by the Atlanta Police Department, suspected head of a large, and as yet unnamed criminal syndicate, Darrin Morehouse was arrested and charged with a list of charges ranging from murder to conspiracy to commit murder."

The television monitor switched to file footage that had been shot earlier of the accused, Darrin Morehouse, at one of the many political fundraisers he attended.

"From what we've been told, John and Monica, it appears that the District Attorney will indeed be, as they say in the movies, throwing the book at the man. Information received earlier tells us that this extensive investigation into Mr. Morehouse has been ongoing for the last three years."

One of the anchors interrupted with a question. As much as the reporter hated it when the guys in the booth did that, he knew it was good for the show and he rolled with it even though it meant standing out in the freezing cold for another minute. "Has the district attorney's office given any indication of which specific charges they plan to bring against Mr. Morehouse?"

"Not yet, John," Alexander answered. "The Atlanta Police are being tight-lipped about this case for the moment, but we expect to hear from a police department spokesperson before long. We will, of course, keep you up to date on any further progress. For Channel Ten Up To The Minute News, Fabian Alexander reporting. Back to you in the studio."

"And we're clear," Greenway said as the light winked off his camera.

"Thank God," Alexander said as he retrieved his coat and put it on. "It's fucking freezing out here."

"Coffee?"

"It's too early in the morning for stupid questions, Angela," the reporter said. "Just get me the damned coffee." He scowled. "Quicker is better."

"Yes, sir," she said and ambled off toward the Starbucks across the street.

"I swear, that girl is worse than useless," he complained as he got into the news van that was only slightly warmer than the frigid temperature outside. What little warmth there was inside was a welcome feeling. It wasn't long before he felt a tingle creep back into his fingertips.

"Yeah, but at least she's hot," the cameraman said with a knowing smile.

"If only that's all that was necessary to do her job," Fabian sighed. "Anyway, as soon as I defrost we can shoot the coverage. I want some face time with Bartlett before our next pickup."

"He's not going to like that."

"Do I look like I fucking care what John Bartlett likes?"

"Not especially," Greenway said, still smiling.

"Just keep an eye out for him. We move as soon as he exits the building."

"Will do."

# # #

5th Precinct, Atlanta Police Department
Atlanta, Ga.
December 21

Fabian Alexander was freezing.

Once again without his coat and gloves, he stood outside for the live report. This time in the rain, although an umbrella covered him, albeit off camera and held by his assistant as she stood perched on a ladder just out of frame.

"As you can see behind me," he said, pointing toward the throng of police officers escorting their prisoner inside. "Police are taking Darrin Morehouse inside the Atlanta Police department building behind me in handcuffs. Morehouse, a prominent citizen and local businessman who is often seen at charity events around the country, was arrested last evening by Atlanta Police Officer John Bartlett. The lead detective in the case, Lieutenant Bartlett has served with distinction on the Atlanta Police Force for just over ten years. Three of those years were spent gathering evidence against Morehouse. Lieutenant Bartlett had this to say to our cameras..."

The monitor switched from the freezing reporter to a handsome man in his late thirties, maybe early forties. He had a face that the camera loved.

"All I can say at this time," police officer John Bartlett started, "is that we have a very strong case against Darrin Morehouse and that I am personally working very closely with the District Attorney and we will put this criminal behind bars where he belongs. That's all. No more questions."

The camera light winked back on and Fabian Alexander continued. "Lieutenant Bartlett was one of two individuals primarily involved in bringing the Morehouse to trial. The other is Benjamin West. Mr. West, whose name you might recognize works as a photojournalist with the Atlanta Journal and Constitution, admitted in an earlier interview that he had become an unwitting pawn in a revenge plot against Detective Bartlett by the accused, Mr. Darrin Morehouse. We hope to have an interview with Mr. West tomorrow on Channel Ten Up To The Minute News at ten."

"And we're clear."

Fabian Alexander pulled his overcoat back into his place, shaking his head as his camera man stepped over to help his assistant off the wet ladder. He had watched as the fool had fawned over her all day in a feeble attempt to score some brownie points. Part of him found it amusing, knowing that the cameraman stood less than a one percent chance in hell of getting in her pants. Another part of him felt sorry and wanted to tell him that the only way to get in her good graces was to have some sort of power or influence that could help her career. The fact that she had already boned most of the male producers at the station was evidence of that.

Mike Greenway was many things, but powerful and influential he was not.

Yes, Alexander felt sorry for Mike until he remembered that he really didn't care for the man so he decided to just sit back and enjoy the show.

#

Fulton County Courthouse
Atlanta, Ga.
December 23

The media circus surrounding the Morehouse trial continued on Monday.

As soon as the national news got in on the act the city bulged with reporters and activists from around the country, a few even flying in from other countries to film the craziness that had become the Morehouse trial.

Reporter Alanis Cooper replaced Fabian Alexander as the face of Channel Ten at the proceedings as more seasoned reporters began vying for more face time than their rookie counterpart. Although Cooper was more experienced than he in terms of broadcast years, she did not resonate with the viewers quite the way Alexander had.

Although Fabian Alexander loathed the thought of sharing his story, he was happy to spend the day inside where it was warm. Especially once the light snow began to fall. Snow in December was something of a rarity in Georgia. He knew that is would probably be ice by tomorrow and all of the reporters would be doing remotes in the freezing cold as the city ground to a halt and the winter weather became the top story. It was sad, but all it took was a hint of snow and the state of Georgia went into panic mode, buying bread and milk and closing schools and businesses before the first flake was spotted. It was comical because even in the worst snowstorms that hit Georgia, the roads were passable by the afternoon. Yet, every time the people panicked.

Cooper handled herself well, but this early in the trial there wasn't much that was actual news that had not been reported on already.

"Superior Court Judge Nathan Hughes today refused bail for the defendant in the Darrin Morehouse trial," Cooper said as if she had just announced the winner of a Presidential Election. "Morehouse, the fifty year-old Atlanta native and suspected head of an as yet unnamed alleged criminal consortium has been in police custody since December 19th. A police spokesman announced today that Morehouse's arrest was only the beginning. During that press conference we were told to expect more arrests for Morehouse's suspected 'cronies in crime,' as the police commissioner had dubbed the still as yet unnamed suspects in this court case that grows more interesting by the day. Only time will tell if these promised arrests do indeed happen as police officials promise."

The reporter turned to point toward the courthouse behind her.

"Inside the courtroom Morehouse's attorney, Laura Sellars, has thus far bested the District Attorney at every turn. Our experts tell us that the District Attorney's case is not going well, but also reminds us that it is still very early in the proceedings and that such a hot topic trial as this one can turn on a dime. Police sources close to the investigation who wished to remain anonymous, told us earlier today that once the next batch of arrests were made it would be a whole new ball game. Guess we'll have to wait and see what the prosecution has up its sleeve. Court resumes at ten a.m. tomorrow. Live from the steps of the Fulton County Courthouse, this is Alanis Cooper. Stay with us here at Channel Ten for more on this fast breaking story. Back to you in the studio."

# # #

Channel Ten Studios
Atlanta, Ga.
December 23

Edwin Mathis smiled for the camera.

As host of The Atlanta Forum Hour Featuring A Weekly Talk and Discussion Segment Called *"Focus On Atlanta,"* As host, Mathis sat in the center of a semicircle arrangement of chairs where his guests would sit after the commercial break. On each side of him were two chairs, with room for one more on each side if necessary depending on the number of guests featured that evening.

Tonight, he had gathered four guests for his program dedicated to studying the intricacies of the case of the State of Georgia v. Darrin Morehouse. His first guest was former Fulton County District Attorney Jameson Underwood. The former DA was there to comment on the strategies being played out by the District Attorney arguing the Morehouse case. His second guest was Parker Hunt, a defense attorney with offices in Los Angeles and New York. His firm only handled big cases. He was there to provide a strong counterpoint to the former

DA's argument. The ratings always went up when the panel got into a heated discussion so Mathis and his producers always looked for panelists with strong viewpoints and a penchant for exuberance. The other guests included retired police detective Peter Mace and Angela Adams, a former reporter for the AJC who was currently between assignments.

Granted, none of the panelists had any knowledge of the case beyond what had been reported on the news. Not that this lack of first-hand knowledge dissuaded them from putting forth their opinions on the matter. He and his producer had discussed the possibility of bringing in Channel Ten's own Fabian Alexander, who was probably the most knowledgeable Channel Ten employee in regards to this particular case. After a heated back and forth argument, it was decided not to invite the reporter on the show, mostly at Mathis' request. The producer did not understand the host's reluctance to use the man since he was available to them, but he capitulated nonetheless. Despite the absence of Fabian Alexander, Mathis' producers found a perfectly good mix of guests, each with expertise in the areas of interest happening in the case. And they were all rather opinionated and had no trouble arguing their point of view ad nauseum.

It was bound to be a stellar show.

The producer signaled that they were on and Mathis leaned forward in his chair to address the camera. "Tonight on 'Focus on Atlanta' we take a look at the life of Darrin Morehouse. For those not familiar with the case, Darrin Morehouse is a local Atlanta businessman accused of heading up a substantial criminal syndicate in our fair city. With his trial slated to begin soon we are going to take a look at his distinguished life, career, and his previous commitment to the community. We'll be back with our panel of experts to discuss the hot button topic after these messages."

# # #

Fulton County Courthouse
Atlanta, Ga.
January 7

With the dawn of the New Year, Fabian Alexander returned to the steps of the Fulton County Courthouse. As his approval rating with viewers soared, the producers at Channel Ten began increasing his on camera time, much to the annoyance of Alanis Cooper, who now found herself with less and less screen time.

The behind the scene politics at Channel Ten had become more tense than usual, which was saying something. If only the viewers could see the soap opera bickering and backstabbing that happened when the cameras weren't watching the ratings would no doubt increase. In fact, though none of the anchors or reporters were aware of it, the segment producer had pitched a reality show to the networks that would follow the reporters around. The networks were concerned that showing the foibles of the on air talent might have a negative impact on viewers who were supposed to trust the news as reported by these people.

Cooper had threatened to break her contract and walk because she was unhappy with her change in assignment. More over, she was not happy playing second fiddle to Fabian Alexander and she wasn't shy about sharing her feelings with everyone. She had used the breaking her contract tactic for years to get her way and it usually worked.

This time, however, management called her bluff. They were willing to break her contract rather than argue the point. Fabian Alexander's growing popularity made it easy for the management to stand their ground.

Cooper backed down and handled the story she had been assigned, but she made sure everyone knew how unhappy she was about it. Until Channel Ten management put a spot to it, readers of her online blog were treated to a daily spewing of vitriol against her employer, her producers, and most especially the wet behind the ears punk she considered her chief rival.

"Trial begins today in the case of The State versus Darrin Morehouse," Alexander started. "The defendant's attorney, Laura Sellers, seemed convinced at a press conference held earlier this morning that her client would be cleared of all wrongdoing and would be released."

"In her words," he started as he held up a piece of paper in front of him so the camera would pick it up. There was a statement from the defense team that he had been asked to read. "Mr. Morehouse is a pillar of the community, a businessman, and a family man." He stopped looking at the paper and focused once more on the camera. "District Attorney Michael Coombes counters that Morehouse did in fact commit the crimes with which he has been charged and insists that his office has undeniable proof to back up their charges and that they will bring this evidence to light when the state presents its case."

Alexander walked up the steps toward the door where other reporters were also doing their pick ups. The camera followed. "Despite the forecasted winter weather advisory now in effect for Atlanta and surrounding areas, the trial is expected to heat up for several days as the District Attorney presents his case on the other side of these doors."

He pointed to the guarded entrance at the top of the stairs.

"Reporters have not been allowed inside the courtroom for this trial with the notable exception of photojournalist, Benjamin West. West, as you may recall, is one of the key witnesses for the prosecution along with Atlanta Police Officer John Bartlett. We will continue our live coverage from outside the courthouse. Please keep it here on Channel Ten News. Back to you in the studio."

# # #

Fulton County Courthouse
Atlanta, Ga.
January 10

Alanis Cooper opened the midday news with an update on the Darrin Morehouse trial. As Fabian Alexander's popularity continued to rise, the veteran reporter found herself being relegated to the noon news while Alexander worked the more widely viewed nightly news. She had started drinking heavily back in December and her family and friends were starting to worry. As were her producers.

"Today in the Morehouse case, Atlanta Police Officer John Bartlett took the stand for the first time. He made mention several times of how the accused loved to play games and how he and Photojournalist Benjamin West had almost died as the result of those games. This heated trial continues tomorrow. Tune in for hourly reports by our Channel Ten News anchors and a full report tonight at Five, Six, and Ten o'clock."

All smiles, she moved on to the threat of yet another impending onslaught of wintry mix coming into the Metro Atlanta area.

#

Channel Ten Studio
Atlanta, Ga.
January 13

"Today, the prosecution in the Morehouse case dropped a surprising bombshell by calling Vivian Morehouse to the stand," Alanis Cooper reported from the anchor desk at the Channel Ten studio in Atlanta.

"Sources inform Channel Ten that Mrs. Morehouse has allegedly turned states evidence against her husband. Mrs. Morehouse's attorney would offer no comment on whether a plea had been reached with the District Attorney, but our legal advisors can think of no other reason for Mrs. Morehouse to take the stand as spousal privilege would have prevented her from testifying against her husband in this trial. This could be a crushing blow for Morehouse's defense. However, Defense Attorney Laura Sellars told Channel Ten News that it is only a minor setback and that they are prepared for it.

Only time will tell how accurate her assessment is."

#

Channel Ten Studio
Atlanta, Ga.
January 15

Fabian Alexander was all smiles on his first day behind the anchor desk at Channel Ten News' evening newscasts, airing at five and six p.m. While this meant that he would no longer report from the field, he would get more on screen time, which was never a bad thing as far as his career goals were concerned.

After coming out of a remote with Alanis Cooper, who had happily picked up the location shoots that he had been doing, he added, "The prosecution rested today in the trial of alleged criminal mastermind Darrin Morehouse. The trial will resume in two days."

#

Fulton County Courthouse
Atlanta Ga.
January 24

Alanis Cooper showed no emotion as she repeated the verdict that had been read just moments before inside the courthouse.

"Guilty," she said, pausing to let the word sink in before repeating for effect.

"Guilty.

That was the verdict today in the trial of Darrin Morehouse. The suspected leader of a criminal empire, Morehouse was sentenced to life in prison today. District Attorney Michael Coombes, attributed this victory to solid testimony by Atlanta police officer John Bartlett and reporter Benjamin West, but it was the surprising testimony of the defendant's wife that had the strongest impact on the case. Vivian Morehouse refused to comment publicly about the fate of her husband and his businesses. She was escorted out of the courtroom under guard and did not make any statements to the press."

"However, in a Channel Ten exclusive, both Officer John Bartlett and photojournalist Benjamin West were on hand today and offered their opinions of the verdict on the steps of the Fulton County Courthouse."

The camera switched off as the monitor showed the prerecorded question and answer session.

"Mr. West! Mr. West, can you comment on the verdict?"

Benjamin West stopped on the steps of the courthouse as the reporters swarmed around him like bees around honey. "I am just grateful that this is finally over," he said once the reporters stopped shouting to get his attention. "The past few months have been a burden on all of us, but we can feel secure in the knowledge that justice was served and the good guys won one. Thank you. I have no further comment at this time."

Not content with the response, Alanis Cooper blocked the journalist's escape. "Just one thing further, Mr. West. Did Darrin Morehouse threaten you in any way during the trial?"

The comment brought Benjamin West up short.

The reporter noticed a muscle twitch in his cheek and knew she had him.

"No. He did not threaten me during the trial. He did, however, try to kill us just prior to his arrest, if that counts for anything. Now, if you'll excuse me, Miss Cooper."

He pushed past her and for a moment she considered following until the State's star witness, Officer John Bartlett, exited the court-house. Bartlett was not known for his willingness to speak to the press, but he had a prepared statement.

The reporters ran up the stairs and shoved microphones at the police investigator.

"I have a statement, but will not be answering any questions," he said, quite certain that they would hurl questions at him regardless. He really hated reporters, but had promised his captain and the DA that he would keep his temper in check.

After clearing his throat, Bartlett began. "I'm just glad it is over. Darrin Morehouse was - is - a dangerous man. I, for one, am happy that he is off the street and behind bars where he belongs." He paused as if finished before looking directly at the cameras instead of at his notes. "Darrin Morehouse liked to play games," he said sternly. "This man took a perverse thrill from the suffering of others, but the games finally caught up with him. Darrin Morehouse was snared by one of his own traps and now he has to live with the consequences of his actions."

"As for me..." he started and took a deep breath.

"As for me, my game playing days are over."

# # #

Channel Ten Studio
Atlanta Ga.
January 25

"My game playing days are over."

"With those words, Atlanta Police Officer, Lieutenant John Bartlett left the Atlanta Superior Courthouse for the last time as a member of the Morehouse case." Once again behind the Channel Ten anchor desk Fabian Alexander delivered the final summation of the trial of Darrin Morehouse, the news story that had launched his career.

"That was yesterday," the anchor said.

"Today, Darrin Morehouse was remanded into custody at an as yet unannounced maximum security prison. The name and location of that prison has not yet been released for fear that a rescue attempt by Morehouse's alleged criminal conspirators might be made to free him from police custody."

The anchor paused as if lost in his thoughts. He shuffled uncomfortably in his seat. "On a personal note," he continued after a moment. "This trial has been a long, hard battle for all parties involved. Having been here since the beginning, I can identify with Detective Bartlett's final statement to our reporter yesterday when he said..."

The tape cued up and once again John Bartlett uttered the words that would follow him for the rest of his career.

"My game playing days are over."

CHAPTER 2

Today.

The Rusty Mug Pub was widely known as a favored hangout for the city of Atlanta's Law Enforcement Professionals.

Simply put, The Mug, as it was affectionately called, was a cop bar.

From the outside, the Rusty Mug Pub looked like a relic from a bygone era where everything had a rustic, old home feel. The wrought iron grating running along the outer edges of the concrete tiled sidewalk was older than most of the bar's patrons. The walls were made up of deftly placed red bricks made from red Georgia clay. The bricks had probably been manufactured not far away from the very spot many, many years earlier. Who knows, perhaps maybe even before Sherman's famous fire sale all those many decades past. The place looked like it should have been on a historic tour line instead of serving as a local dive.

It was the kind or place Norman Rockwell would have painted in his day.

And thanks to the clientele, it was a place where everyone truly knew your name and one place no one would ever dare think of robbing.

The Mug was a beautiful place on the outside and the patrons loved it, but the inside told the true tale. On an average night thick smoke would fill the air and the smell of alcohol and cheap cologne would mingle with the smoke from at least a dozen cigars, forming a fragrance unique to the Rusty Mug. The Mug was one of the last public places in the area where public smoking was not banned. Okay, technically, it was banned there as well, but who was going to call the cops when they were the ones doing the smoking? *Don't ask, don't tell* was the rule when it came to smoking at the Rusty Mug Pub.

And then there were the stories. Oh the tales of bygone glory days.

People would talk for hours on end. Stories about stalwart heroes, vile villains, and beautiful damsels in distress were the norm, even though many of them -if not al-) were blatant fabrications. At the least the stories were cleverly exaggerated, weaving intricate plots along with colorful characters that rivaled anything penned by many a professional writer.

Many were the nights that the Rusty Mug Pub would bring about good fiction.

That came later in the evening, after the sun had set behind the city's many skyscrapers. But during the day, the pre-lunch crowd consisted of only a small handful of patrons. Which wasn't so unusual for the 11:45 a.m. on a Thursday.

Most sat at the bar, but a few of the regulars sat in the booths. Some played cards while others read. Many of the regulars were retired Atlanta PD who came in just to give themselves something to break up their day. The occasional off duty officer out for a mid day belt or some retirees coming in to relive the good old days in the quieter, familiar setting of midday. A couple of the old detectives got together a few times a week and worked on cold cases just to give themselves something to do. Or just to get out of the house for awhile.

There were other reasons to be bellied up to a bar before noon on a slightly chilly Thursday in October. If one thought hard enough, he could probably even come up with believable excuses.

Inside the Rusty Mug Pub, police lieutenant John Bartlett was sitting at the bar, nursing a beer that had stopped being cold about twenty minutes ago. Piled next to him on the wood grain bar was a small stack of file folders, each crammed beyond capacity with neglected paperwork that he should have been working on instead of sitting behind a bar during the day. His mail was also lying there in a heap. It had been nearly a week since he had stopped by the Post Office to pick it up and there was no telling what was in there. Mostly bills, he assumed. *Probably past due by now.* Not that such things really mattered to him anymore. Since his wife left him he could care less if the house fell apart or caught fire. Part of him wanted to sell it, but the sentimental part refused to part with it on the off chance that one day she decided to come back.

Now that he had retrieved the envelopes, he just couldn't muster up the energy or desire to open any of them. *Most likely bad news anyway,* he suspected. *Not that I'm a pessimist or anything.* He took another sip of his warm beer and grimaced.

John Bartlett had sought out the Rusty Mug Pub for one particular reason. He and the owner, Mac Sperling, were very good friends. Lieutenant Sperling had been a police officer for nearly twenty years until he was injured in a drive by shooting about eight years earlier. Luckily, Mac survived, but he lost most of the mobility in his right leg. That injury was more than enough to have him pulled from street duty and placed behind a desk. To this day he still walked with a pronounced limp, but he remained positive. "At least I can still walk," he liked to say whenever anyone started to feel sorry for him.

His superiors offered him a promotion and the dreaded desk job, but Mac Sperling was a beat cop. If he could not be on the streets, he wouldn't be happy. Rather than becoming saddled with a desk job he knew he wouldn't like, Mac opted for early retirement. He bought the bar less than a year later with some *mad money* he'd stashed away, changing the name from the unimaginative *Carl's Place* to the more interesting *The Rusty Mug Pub* shortly thereafter.

And the rest, as they say, is history.

Mac was always there to lend a helpful ear to John Bartlett, not to mention any other person, law enforcement officer or not, that needed to talk. Mac was an excellent listener, which turned out to be an extremely good quality for a bartender. *Not such a bad thing for a police officer either*, John thought.

Mac had helped him through some tough times in the past. The first time John shot a suspect had been emotionally draining, but it was nothing compared to what he went through when Elisabeth left him. Their marriage had been anything but perfect, but John was committed to making it work. He thought she was too until one day he came home and she was gone.

He never heard from her again.

John almost lost his mind. The only thing that saved him was burying himself in his work. If not for the job and friends like Mac, he might not have been able to pull himself back from the brink. He still missed Elisabeth and from tie to time thought about trying to track her down. Each time he stopped himself. He decided that if she ever wanted to talk to him then she knew how to find him.

After the crappy day that he had endured, *and it's only just getting on noon for Christ's sake*, Bartlett needed a friendly face and some sage advice from an old pro like Mac.

Unfortunately, Mac was not at work today. He had taken the day off, a rare occurrence indeed, to spend some much needed quality time with his son, Shaun. Mac had been absent for most of the boy's formative years, which was a fairly common occurrence in their line of work. If he had children, John assumed his situation would hardly be different, as the job demanded more and more. At least, Mac was finally able to make up for lost time while his son was still willing to accept him. His friend was lucky. Not everyone in his situation was so fortunate.

John would just have to wait before he could tell his friend about his day. Sure, he could have simply called Mac on his cell, but he did not want to disturb father and son bonding time. He had considered leaving since Mac was out, but, honestly, he had nowhere else to go.

Over the bar, a TV newscast anthem faintly broke through the idle chatter around The Mug as the anchors were introduced by a deep, professional, James Earl Jones-ish voice. The noon news, just like the evening news, always started with a big story. Normally, John might give the news broadcast a second glance if for no other reason than simple curiosity. Wondering, *What would be today's big story?*

But not today.

No, today he had a pretty good idea what the lead story would be.

The anchor for Channel Ten Noonday News, Fabian Alexander, began the broadcast with a welcome to his friends in the city of Atlanta. The same cheesy greeting he had given every day since he was promoted into the anchor spot a few years back. Bartlett did the math in his head. *Going on six years.* He tried not to grimace at the anchorman's less than genuine personality. Perhaps he only thought that because he had gotten to know the man during the course of his career.

John did not like the media and he truly had no love for reporters like the one on the TV screen. Ironically enough, they loved him. Everywhere he went, every turn, every motion was captured on film and transmitted for all the world to see. *They haven't left me alone since we nailed Morehous*, he groused. He often repeated this complaint whenever the press came around.

Fabian Alexander was one such media personality, and Bartlett had no great love for the man, but he was by no means the worst. No, there were other so-called journalists out there that he disliked even more than the arrogant television anchor. There was one in particular, but John tried not to dwell on the subject because thinking about it only made him angry.

The anchor began the broadcast with a big lead in as usual. It was a story about a courageous act that *"local hero; City of Atlanta Police Department, Detective John Bartlett"* had performed earlier in the day.

John assumed they liked to pull out the *"local hero"* angle to attract viewers. He did not consider his actions as heroism, quite the opposite actually. He considered it to be just doing his job, but the reporters chose not to see it that way.

Just doing my job wasn't sexy enough for the news.

Looking at the monitor above the bar as he downed the last of his warm beer, Bartlett groaned as video images of him entering a run down looking brownstone, just three hours earlier this morning, were shown. With the camera angles used and the quick, choppy editing, what little footage of the morning's incident looked like something out of a big budget Hollywood action flick. Such tricky with the video only added to the *Hero Cop* tag that had been attached to him since Morehouse.

The bartender, noticing Bartlett and a few of the Pub's regulars watching the television set turned up the volume with the remote control he kept hidden in his shirt pocket. Just one more way of serving the customer.

He had been tuning out the drone of the television until he looked at it. Once he noticed the familiar presence on the screen he could no longer ignore it. Fabian Alexander's on air voice broke the silence. He was in mid-spiel. "--saving the lives of both mother and child. We were unable to reach Lieutenant Bartlett for comment, but his superiors at police headquarters were more than happy to praise the heroic efforts of this courageous officer."

"Oh, please." John simply shook his head while listening to an on-the-scene reporter whom he did not personally know drawl on and on and on in a never-ending string of well known television cliches. *'Heroic efforts.' 'Courageous officer.'* He knew that, if he kept listening the words *'racially charged'* would make their way into the report somehow.

"Give me a break," John mumbled.

It sounded like they were talking about someone else.

Unfortunately, knowing Fabian Alexander as well as he did, there was little doubt tonight's evening news would feature a follow up on the life and career of John Bartlett, Atlanta PD. Every time he made the news, Alexander pulled out that old sound bite from the end of the Morehouse trial and replayed it over and over again. *"My game playing days are over."* He had regretted the words the moment they left his mouth. And now, six years later, he still regretted saying it.

John's attention was drawn back to the TV when the image on the screen shifted from the anchor to show his boss at the scene after the suspect had been taken into custody and rushed him off to the hospital under guard. John had conveniently exited stage left before anyone could shove a microphone in his face.

His boss, Captain Miller loved the spotlight. The spotlight did not return the favor. John would have been glad to give the media frenzy that clung to him over to his boss. However, John guessed that after a minimum of two days of endless hounding by reporter after reporter, even Captain Miller would lock himself away in his office, never to be seen again. *If only that option were available to me,* John wished.

The captain continued. "The suspect, one Philip Carteros of Atlanta, reportedly opened fire on Lieutenant Bartlett as well as a minimum of six hostages whom he had taken earlier in the morning in the apartment building behind me. As ranking officer on the scene, Detective Bartlett went into the building to communicate a peaceful solution to the situation before the suspect could kill any of his hostages."

"Captain, is it true that Detective Bartlett shot Philip Carteros?"

Miller paused as if to search for a proper response. He cleared his throat before continuing. "The suspect fired on my officer and, as he has been trained to do, defended himself. Detective Bartlett had no other recourse available than to return fire," Captain Miller said, looking directly into the camera. It was a rehearsed speech and John knew it. Hell, half the city could probably tell. Captain Willie Miller was rigidly stiff and spoke in choppy sentences as he pretended not to read his lines off of a cue card he had hidden just out of the camera's view. Bartlett always knew his boss had a bright future ahead of him in politics.

Captain Miller concluded his statement in his customary way, saying, "The department stands behind Detective Bartlett one hundred percent. Now, if you'll excuse me, we have a lot of work to do and I should get back to it. Thank you."

"Well that's good to know," Bartlett said with a smirk. He knew he wasn't in any sort of trouble with the department or his captain. If he were he would be sitting at the station instead of nursing a beer at the Mug. There would be an official IAD investigation, but that was standard procedure with any officer involved shooting. He had no doubt Internal Affairs would clear him.

The image of Captain Miller faded out quickly, only to be replaced a scant millisecond later by Fabian Alexander in his position behind the anchor desk, a large, green numeral 10 positioned behind him in bold, three dimensional lines. "The suspect mentioned by Captain William Miller, one Philip Carteros of Atlanta, age 34, is currently at Grady Memorial Hospital in stable condition, but under the strictest police guard until he can be safely moved to one of the local police stations for processing. Channel Ten's Monica Kennedy is standing by at Grady Memorial and we will, of course, keep you posted on Mr. Carteros' condition later in this broadcast."

The anchor continued to talk, but John had heard enough and his attention moved elsewhere, turning toward the glass on the bar in front of him.

The glass was empty.

His life was empty.

If he'd had the strength, he would have laughed at the irony, but he was tired. This morning's shoot out, which was far more involved than the news had made it out to be, had sapped him. *Maybe a few hours of shuteye will help*, he thought even though he doubted it would. He'd not had a truly good night's sleep since Elisabeth left. Sometimes he wondered if he would ever get a peaceful night's sleep again.

It was at that moment a familiar waitress walked up next to him, leaning with her elbows behind her on the bar. She tilted in close to

John, so that he could hear her soft voice. "Looks like you get to be a hero again, John." She knew how much he hated the spotlight, but she could not let the opportunity to get in a good zinger pass her by. Thankfully, he knew she was only teasing.

"Yea, me," John said with as little enthusiasm as possible.

The waitress placed another bottle of beer in front of him. He hadn't ordered another and he looked at her curiously, wondering.

"What's this?" he asked when no explanation was apparently forthcoming.

"It's on me."

He gave her a quizzical look, eyebrows raised. "Why, Stella, I must say this is a surprise. I've been coming here for years and I do believe this is the first time you've ever bought me a drink. What's the occasion?"

She flashed her winning smile. "What can I say, you're the only super hero I know."

"Gee thanks. I'm almost touched at your sincerity." He paused to take a sip of his beer. It was nice and cold, frost still on the bottle. "And I *am not* a super hero!"

"Well," she said in mock annoyance. "Take away the camera crew and the mob of reporters and John Bartlett is a human being after all."

He gave her a wink. "A scary thought, huh?"

She shrugged. "Maybe a little."

"Just don't spread it around, okay? I've got a reputation to protect."

"Your secret is safe with me, officer," Stella said, returning the wink.

Bartlett smiled in spite of himself.

"Come on, John," she prompted. "Doesn't it feel good to be labeled a hero? I mean, you do your job day in and day out with little or no fanfare. Usually, the news only reports on the mistakes."

"Yes they do." He took another long pull on his beer.

"So, it must be gratifying to get a little respect for it every now and again." She turned to the bartender to enlist his help in making her point. "Wouldn't you say, Ernie?"

Ernie, a new bartender that Mac had hired about a month before wasn't as much of a conversationalist as the Mug's owner, or apparently, the waitress. Ernie let out a fake laugh before returning to his work wiping off the bar. "Leave the customers alone, Stella," he told her. Ignoring the bartender, the waitress simply shrugged off his *suggestion* and turned her attention back toward Detective Bartlett.

"Besides," she continued, "it gives all of us little people hope when the good guys win one."

"If you say so," John said. "Too bad we win so few of them."

"Oh cheer up. Tomorrow's Friday. You can gear up for the weekend. Maybe those bosses of yours that are so very proud of you will see their way clear to give you the day off."

"Yeah. That'll happen. My luck doesn't work like that, Stella." He sighed.

"Maybe it's time for your luck to change," she told him. "You shouldn't be so... you know... Mr. Glass is half empty. You should try to be more sure of life."

"I guess my glass needs a refill, huh?"

"Ha. Ha." Stella showed no enthusiasm and made no attempt to hide her annoyance at his self-deprecation.

John simply shrugged it away. He was in no mood to be optimistic. He was even less interested in having someone try to cheer him up.

"Have a little faith," she told him.

"I have faith. I *know* that the worst is yet to come. That's why I'm here." He looked down at the drink she had only seconds ago placed on the bar in front of him. With one gulp, he downed a sizeable amount. It was good and cold. "I prefer to be drunk when the other shoe falls," he added for emphasis as he clanked the bottle down on the bar.

As if on cue, the outer door opened and the bell above the door jingled. Bartlett turned slightly to see who had entered the bar. A younger man walked in and he immediately recognized the new arrival. His arrival wasn't, but it wasn't anyone Bartlett had any desire to see.

It was Benjamin West.

Oh crap.

Benjamin West. The one newsperson John Bartlett disliked more than Fabian Alexander.

"Ah, shit," John said under his breath.

"I beg your pardon?" the waitress asked.

Bartlett did not answer, turning back toward his beer as the new arrival walked across the floor straight toward the bar. West took a seat next to Bartlett without asking. Then, the new arrival pushed aside the officer's case files and stack of mail.

John looked up at the waitress with tired eyes.

"Stella, I'd like you to meet the other shoe."

CHAPTER 3

Benjamin West grinned at Stella as he said hello and introduced himself.

West was certainly suave. His boyishly rugged good looks were not lost on her either. She felt heat rise in her cheeks as she shook his hand. His grip was strong, but somehow tender at the same time. She could easily see why some of her girlfriends *oohed* and *ahhed* over this man.

The Rusty Mug Pub waitress would have to have been blind, deaf, and dumb not to feel the tension in the air between these two men. She didn't know much about either man aside from their respective reputations and she was beginning to think that was a good thing.

John Bartlett was a semi regular at The Mug and was a friend of the owner, Mac Sperling, himself a retired police officer, as were the majority of the customers inhabiting The Mug at 12:15 p.m. on a Thursday. He was also touted as a hero cop who had become the media's favorite subject over the past five years or so.

Benjamin West was a local celebrity in his own right. He was a photojournalist for The Atlanta Journal & Constitution. He'd come to work for the AJC about six or so years before and toiled in obscurity until he got tangled up with Detective Bartlett and a high profile case he'd been working on.

"Stella, I'd like you to meet the other shoe," John Bartlett said by way of introducing the brash, young reporter.

The reporter smiled at her and she took an instant dislike to him. For all his charm, she felt something untrustworthy in those baby blues of his. Stella suddenly felt an overwhelming urge to be elsewhere. "Uh huh. A pleasure to meet you, Mr. Shoe."

"Ben West," he said, offering his hand.

"Nice to meet you," Stella said. "I'll just be going... uh... over there so you too can talk." She pointed toward the other end of the bar before beating a hasty retreat.

Bartlett tossed her a slight wave as she walked away from the two men, wishing he could escape as easily as she had.

"You certainly have a way with people."

West waved as well, but Stella either did not see him, or she simply chose to ignore him. Probably the latter, he assumed. "Charming woman," West said to no one in particular as he watched Stella move to a table in the far corner. "Are you two...?"

"No."

Benjamin West made a small, silent motion toward the bartender who immediately dropped a fresh, cold beer on the bar in front of him.

"Thanks. I'm gonna need another," he said with a half grin. "And bring my friend here one as well. He's going to be needing it."

"I didn't think you were much of a drinker, West," Bartlett asked, finally breaking the awkward silence that often settled between them. For two men who had each saved the others life more than once, they had a hard time just being in the same room together, much less carrying on an adult conversation.

"Only on special occasions," West said, grinning the entire time.

"Oh. And what's so special about today?"

Another moment of pained silence passed between them. The two men just looked at one another, West's jaw nearly falling open to the floor. Bartlett's look consisted primarily of fatigue, annoyance, and just a touch of anger. The young reporter always brought out the worst anger in the police lieutenant, no matter how much Bartlett tried to keep it reigned in West's presence. The last thing he wanted was to give West the satisfaction of knowing how much he got to him.

"You don't know, do you?" Benjamin West said, trying to hide his surprised look, unsuccessfully. The man was a terrible actor. He could lie with the best of them, but his acting abilities left a lot to be desired. Except for that one time when one of Morehouse's men thought he was an out of town buyer. He had surprised Bartlett that day. It had been the first major break in the investigation.

"What do you want, West?" Bartlett said with a shrug, uncertain of what this man could possibly be talking about and really not in the mood to care. "It's been a rough morning and I'm too damned tired to play guessing games today."

"Well I'll be damned," West said as he slapped an open palm on the bar. "You really don't know, huh? How about that?"

Bartlett, trying to hold in his ever-increasing anger, leaned over toward the irritating photojournalist sitting next to him. "Look, West, you have exactly three seconds to tell me what the hell you want before I rip your fucking lips off. Got it? I've had a really rough day and I don't think I can possibly handle any more bullshit. So, tell me what your problem is and then get the fuck away from me, okay?"

West pulled away from the angry man's grasp. He was not a stupid man. There was just enough menace in Bartlett's tone to tell him that today was not the day to push his luck. West knew when to press his advantage and when to back off. This was definitely a time to back off, way, way off from the sound of it.

"Touchy," he said, trying to retain his self proclaimed reputation for bravery. "I see that being in the spotlight hasn't changed you any."

"Don't forget that I have a gun, West."

"So do I."

"West..."

"Okay. Okay. It almost gives me great pleasure to be the bearer of this news. I can't believe you haven't heard." Taking a deep breath, Ben West decided that the best way to deliver this news was to say it flat out. *Quick and painful.* Like ripping off a bandage.

"Okay. Here it is. Straight up. No bullshit."

"Yeah?"

"Morehouse is dead."

The words slapped John Bartlett across the face like the proverbial ton of bricks. Stunned, he could not find any words to express what that simple little statement meant to him. He thought for a moment that he had heard the man incorrectly.

"I beg your pardon?" he said, eyebrows raised.

Ben threw his hands playfully in the air as if confetti were about to fly from his hands. "Surprise!" he added for effect.

For a few brief seconds there were no words spoken. Bartlett was having a hard time processing the news he had just been given. *Could it really be true?* He wondered.

"H--how? When? Where's the body? I have to see it. I won't - can't- believe it unless I see the body with my own two eyes."

"I know how you feel." West pulled out a small white envelope from his jacket pocket. His name was boldly emblazoned on it, written very messily with a black magic marker. Bartlett noticed immediately that there was no return address or postal code. The envelope had been hand delivered.

"Is that…?"

"Looks like the man addressed them by hand," West answered before Bartlett could fully form the question. "Yeah, I noticed that too. It was easy to compare it to some of the other letters I've received from the man since he went in the slammer."

"Yeah. I received my share of those too," Bartlett said. "Stopped opening them after awhile. I figured, what was the point? Why give the son of a bitch the satisfaction of getting under my skin?"

Bartlett looked at the envelope as Benjamin West began tapping it on the edge of the bar. It made a small *thunk, thunk, thunk* as it hit the polished wood grain.

The sound was suddenly loud over the other noises of the bar.

"I didn't want to believe it either, then I got this," West said in reference to the envelope. "I'm still not sure I believe it."

"What is it?"

"It appears that I have been included in the will."

"The….

will….?"

"Can you believe it? The son of a bitch put me in his will." Then, Benjamin West tossed the envelope on to the bar where it slid until stopping against the half empty bottle in front of Bartlett. The heavy black scribbled letters of Benjamin West's name in Morehouse's handwriting emblazoned against the white of the standard letter sized envelope.

Bartlett could only stare at it for a second. Then, as if remembering something suddenly very important, he reached hurriedly past West for the stack of mail the reporter had shoved aside only minutes before. A second later he held a small stack of envelopes of various shapes and sizes.

His mail. He had not had a chance to open his mail yet.

Oh, don't tell me... Bartlett thought as he flipped through the stack.

Quickly shuffling through the small stack of correspondence of various sizes, he tossed envelope after envelope over his shoulder and onto the floor of the bar. He was making a heck of a mess. Not that he seemed to mind.

The bundle of mail contained the usual assortment. *Bill. Bill. Bill. I may be a winner... blah, blah. Bill. Letter from Mom. Junk. Junk. Sales paper. Junk. Jun...*

"Oh shit."

"Let me guess," West started, "Publisher's Clearinghouse says you owe them ten million dollars."

Bartlett did not answer.

"And some change..." West continued joking unbidden.

Still, Bartlett said nothing. He was too stunned to speak.

"Am I close?"

Finally, the blood began pumping again and reanimated John Bartlett's body. "I've been to busy to go through my mail," he said as he ripped open the envelope. He stared wide-eyed at the formal documentation enclosed. "Damn. I don't believe this. I just don't freakin' believe this."

Bartlett stared at the envelope that was emblazoned with his name on it. As with West's envelope, there were no visible signs that it had gone through regular postal machines. There was no return address either. It had been written in the same badly scribbled handwriting as the one Benjamin West had just tossed onto the bar. As with West's letter, John recognized the handwriting as being Darrin Morehouse's, but he would have it checked at the lab to make sure.

Bartlett let the envelope drop to the bar where it landed next to the reporter's similar message. "This is turning into one shitty day," he said as he stared at the two pieces of mail lying there next to one another.

"And it is only just beginning, my friend."

Bartlett rubbed the bridge of his nose with two fingers. Suddenly he had contracted a severe headache and his eyes felt like they were ready to pop out of his head. That seemed to happen a lot whenever Benjamin West or Darrin Morehouse sauntered into his life. The two seemed to go hand in hand.

He had thought, hoped really, that there could never be another situation where all three of them would be involved with one another again.

Now, that just felt like wishful thinking.

"You just had to say that didn't you, West?"

"All part of my charm," the journalist said as he retrieved his envelope from the bar and slid it into his jacket pocket.

Fifteen minutes passed in relative silence save for the occasional stupid remark from West. Sometimes Bartlett wondered if West said half of the things he did just to see if he could get a rise out of him. If so, he succeeded. The reporter had an uncanny ability to piss him off with very little effort.

Finally he'd had all of West he could stand. Bartlett got up from his place at the bar, tossing a few bills onto the wood grain to cover his bill and a fairly generous tip for Stella, scooped up his pile of mail from the floor, and headed toward the door.

Benjamin West also got up, paid his tab, and followed the police officer toward the exit.

"Let the games begin," he said as he reached the door.

"One more, West, and I swear to God I'm going to shoot you."

Those were the last words Stella heard either men say as John Bartlett exited the Rusty Mug Pub with Benjamin West scurrying close behind.

CHAPTER 4

Sure enough, John's Bartlett's guess had been right.

As he watched the eleven O'clock news that night, Fabian Alexander followed up on the story about his shoot out with Philip Carteros earlier that day with a special report that looked back at the Morehouse case and the history of Atlanta Police Detective John Bartlett.

# # #

"Good evening. I'm Fabian Alexander."

Once again seated behind the anchor desk at Channel Ten's News Studio for the nightly expanded edition of the news show, Fabian Alexander's segment called *A Look Back*. He despised the title for its sheer simplicity and had tried numerous times, despite protests from his producer, to have changed, aired every evening after the six p.m. news. He had thirty minutes to fill every night, which wasn't as easy as you might think. The show was then rebroadcast at eleven thirty p. m. and then again the next morning after the Channel Ten Happy Mornings show and before the game shows started.

This particular episode was a recutting of a story that had aired the year before on the fifth anniversary of the Morehouse verdict. A few minor edits intercut with new footage of the anchor was all it took to bring it up to date.

"Welcome," he said, not mentioning the hated title of the broadcast as he moved directly into his introduction to an audience that knew his name well. If the ratings climb was any indication, Joe Q. Public liked what they saw.

"I'm Fabian Alexander. Join me as Channel Ten *Up To The Minute News* takes a look back six years to the largest criminal court case in Georgia's history. Today, I, along with our usual panel of experts, will take a hard look at the case itself. We'll revisit some of the key players in the drama that led up to and followed the trial and sentencing. Plus, we'll find out what lasting effects, if any, Darrin Morehouse's conviction and incarceration have had, and will have, on the city of Atlanta."

John Bartlett's now famous closing statement played on the large screen behind the anchor's head. "My game playing days are over," the officer's tinny, recorded voice intoned.

With those words, Atlanta Police Officer, Lieutenant John Bartlett left the Atlanta Superior Courthouse for the last time as a member of the Morehouse case," the recorded voice of the anchor said. File footage of Fabian Alexander's coverage of the Morehouse verdict a year earlier was replayed for the audience. "That was yesterday. Today, Darrin Morehouse is being remanded into custody at an as yet unannounced maximum-security prison. The name and location of that prison has not been released for fear that a rescue attempt by Mr. Morehouse's alleged criminal army might be made to free Darrin Morehouse."

As the tape ended, Fabian Alexander returned to the screen in the present. "Those comments, made by both Detective Bartlett and myself, happened six years ago. My how things have progressed. But have they really? Channel Ten has unofficially reopened the Morehouse case in an effort to resolve many of the nagging issues that still linger all these many months later. Did the Atlanta Police Department play by the rules? Was there really evidence tampering as Mr. Morehouse's lawyers have recently attested? Did renegade cop, John Bartlett exceed his authority and unlawfully apprehend the alleged crime lord?"

"Our I-Team has uncovered evidence of police cover-ups in regards to other cases currently in litigation. This begs a deeper look into the case of Darrin Morehouse and Lieutenant John Bartlett. I'd also like to note that Detective Bartlett received his lieutenant rank as a result of apprehending Darrin Morehouse. Coincidence?" he asked pointedly in that way anchors use to tease an upcoming story. "Or did this young police officer find a fast track to promotion through guile and misdirection?"

"While we can only speculate at this time, here's what some of the key players had to say, one year later."

A disheveled Benjamin West appeared on tape, apparently having been caught off guard by the reporter and camera crew somewhere in Buckhead. "Of course Morehouse is -*expletive deleted*- guilty. I was -*expletive deleted*- there, remember? Trust me when I say that the supervising officer did his -*expletive deleted*- job! And he did it properly and within the letter of the law."

"So you believe John Bartlett acted appropriately?' Alexander asked from the anchor's desk, even though he had not been the one firing questions at Benjamin West when this had been taped.

"Yes. I do," Benjamin West said as he stalked away from the camera crew that had ambushed him outside a trendy Buckhead eatery.

District Attorney Michael Coombes appeared next, having been similarly unprepared for Fabian Alexander and his camera crew with a fondness for extreme close up shots. Unlike the West interview, Alexander was indeed on hand to question the District Attorney.

"I cannot comment on the case while it is in the appeals process," the DA said diplomatically as he hurried away from the cameras, which were stopped at the door to his office building by two hulking security guards.

"We tried to contact the other key players in the case against Darrin Morehouse for comment. Unfortunately, Vivian Morehouse, the convicted criminal's estranged wife, Laura Sellers, his attorney, and presiding judge, Nathan Hughes were unreachable for comment."

"When asked to comment on the case, arresting officer, Lieutenant John Bartlett had this to say:'"

"Can't you people leave me alone?" Bartlett shouted at the camera crew who ambushed him outside his home early in the morning as he stepped out to pick up his newspaper. "No -*expletive deleted*- comment! Jesus!"

Fabian Alexander could not hide the small, perverse smile from his thin lips as he leaned back in his comfortably plush chair and exquisitely tailored suit. He looked over his stippled fingers at the camera. To those who knew the man, there was no secret of his contempt for the officer. What those in the know understood, what was also apparent to the reporter's audience, was that Fabian Alexander's dislike for John Bartlett very nearly mirrored the police officer's dislike of the reporter.

And Fabian enjoyed publicly pushing the cop's buttons every chance he could. The more public the better. The more he ruffled Bartlett's feathers, the better the reporter liked it.

And his audience ate it up. Nothing brought in ratings better than knocking a well-respected public figure down a peg or two. The only thing that worked better on screen than spotlighting heroes was knocking them off the very same pedestal you helped put them on. And Fabian Alexander was a master at pedestal tipping.

"We'll be back with our panel of experts as we delve into the case of The State vs. Darrin Morehouse right after these messages."

# # #

"And we're clear," the camera operator said after the red light winked off.

The anchor began shuffling his papers when his producer, Katherine Deplana stopped by the desk with new pages. She had been with the station for years, having started out as an intern before becoming a production assistant and working her way up until she eventually became a producer. He knew her pretty well and they had gone out once or twice, though nothing serious ever developed between them since they were both married to their jobs and had little time for anything else in their lives.

"Coming to wish me luck or give me a pep talk?" he asked playfully.

"Neither," she answered. "Just wanted to drop off a few updated pages and remind you to keep a reign on your mouth regarding Bartlett. If you can't back up whatever you say tonight with cold hard facts then keep it to yourself. The last thing we need is another lawsuit or a call from the mayor's office. Keep that mouth of yours under control. Got it?"

"Yes, Katherine," he said. "I'll be a good boy."

"See that you are."

"One minute, people," the segment producer declared.

Katherine Deplana walked away. She could feel the anchor's eyes on her the entire way. If she would let him, Fabian Alexander would do his damndest to sway public opinion toward crucifying not only John Bartlett, but also the entire Atlanta Police Department. She had been reigning him in on this subject since the Morehouse verdict five years earlier. In truth, she was getting tired of telling him to back off. If only he weren't so popular with their target audience, she probably would have tossed him out on his ear years ago.

"Fabian, we're back in… three… two…"

#

Lying alone in bed, John Bartlett blew out a breath before changing the channel to see if he could find something - anything - else to watch. He stumbled across a M*A*S*H rerun followed by a Star Trek: Deep Space Nine rerun about time travel. He fell asleep before Sisko and Dax could find the Tribble with a bomb inside it, but dreamt that he and Elisabeth were being buried alive by thousands of little fur balls and they couldn't get to safety.

He woke up an hour later in a cold sweat.

CHAPTER 5

John Bartlett was in a mood.

He jerked open the double doors of the station house of the fifth precinct of the Atlanta Police Department and quickly made his way inside. By the time he reached the squad room, he was at a brisk walk.

"Hey, Johnny," yelled Pete Kennedy, one of the department's detectives and biggest *class clown* the force had ever seen. If there was a bad pun to be made or an off-color joke to be told, Pete Kennedy told it. If there was a less than tactful jibe or comment, you could expect Pete Kennedy to make it. He was a good cop so the others simply learned to tune him out. "Saw you on the tube last night," he said with a laugh. "You putting on some weight? 'Cause you looked a little puffy on my fifty inch plasma."

"Bite me, Petey," John answered simply, knowing the detective would not take the insult seriously, but he did not stop to hear the man's rasping laughter. Bartlett had only one destination in mind and it was within his line of sight. In the mood he woke up in, nothing was going to get in his way.

Captain Willie Miller was right where John expected him to be, sitting in his office. As usual, he had the phone stuck to his ear and the door closed, blinds drawn to tiny slits. The officers of the fifth precinct had a running joke about their captain. Whenever someone would ask after the whereabouts of Captain Miller, they would all ask, *"Captain Who?"* It was a small joke, but everyone on the floor seemed to get a charge out of it. Well, everyone except for Captain Miller.

Although to his credit he did try to laugh along.

Lately it seemed as if the only time he ever emerged from his small, cramped office was when one of his superiors showed up on the floor or when the television cameras were on the scene of one of his officer's cases. Such had been the case with Bartlett's hostage situation earlier that very morning. Captain Miller bolted toward the door when one of the uniformed officers called in a report of a channel ten news crew van fast approaching the scene.

Captain Miller did love the spotlight.

John passed by his own desk, it still looked cluttered, just as it had been when he left that morning. So much paperwork, so little time to sit and do it. His partner, Detective Shan Lomax, was sitting at the desk across from his own. Shan's desk was in a similar state of disarray, but at least he was making an attempt to knock out some of his paperwork.

Shan had only been with the Fifth Precinct a little less than a year. A good ten months of that had been spent as John Bartlett's junior partner. Lomax wasn't a rookie, but he had transferred in from a small suburb of Pennsylvania and life in Atlanta was quite the culture shock to his system so the captain had teamed him up with the more experienced Bartlett.

He and Bartlett got along really well. The senior partner had his moody moments, but Shan took them in stride. He knew he wasn't always so easy to get along with either and had his little quirks. Several of his colleagues both in Pennsylvania and in Georgia had commented on his penchant for quoting lines from movies. Many of them found it annoying so he was trying to keep a lid on it, even though it was an unconscious thing. As for the rest of the precinct, Shan got on with them pretty well too. Although he had since learned to live with it, it took some getting used to all of them calling him *Shane* instead of *Shan*, which someone told him was *just a Southern thing*, although they had pronounced it as *thang*. Pretty soon he soon started answering to it as if he had all his life. He even gave up trying to correct those who got it wrong. Thankfully, his partner was one of the ones that got it right.

"John?" he asked when he saw his partner walk past him toward the captain's office in quite a hurry from the look of things.

Lieutenant Bartlett turned at the mention of his name. "Hey Shan," he said. "Can't talk now, partner. Got to go see the captain."

"What's up, partner?" he asked, careful not to do his John Wayne rendition. "Anything I can help with?"

"Morehouse."

Shan let his face droop.

"What now?" he asked. Shan Lomax had not been with the Atlanta Police Department when Darrin Morehouse began his reign of terror against John Bartlett and Benjamin West, but he had heard plenty of stories about it from his partner and a few of the other detectives involved with the case. It was a pretty big deal around the station house, even though his partner tried to downplay the *hero* aspect of it as much as possible. Shan knew it made him uncomfortable, but they guys kept bringing it up, especially if they had visitors on the premises.

John didn't like to talk about the past much, but Shan knew it was still a sore point. The case had been a tough one. Not only did Bartlett's marriage break up during that time, but a good friend of his had been killed by one of Morehouse's goons. Shan could see the tension in his partner's eyes any time the subject was broached. He acted as though it didn't bother him, but early in the partnership they had discussed the matter at length over beers and pizza. John was more than happy to never speak on the subject again, but he answered all of his new partner's questions and dispelled many of the more sensational details that had somehow become attached to the tale. These details, while entertaining, had elevated the story to the status of something he might read in a Marvel Comic.

Shan had told him it would make a good movie, to which his partner groaned loudly before ordering another beer. The last thing he wanted was fan the flames of the story, but between Benjamin West's novel refusing to fall off the bestsellers list, Fabian Alexander's weekly retrospectives, and a TV movie in production, it wasn't destined to happen.

And Morehouse himself had not made things easy either.

Even from prison the convicted felon managed to find new and exciting ways to harass Bartlett via long distance. Shan knew it bothered him, but never pressed the matter. John Bartlett was rather private and closed off. Shan knew better than to push. He figured his partner would confide in him if and when he was ready.

"He's dead," Bartlett said.

"You don't sound overly thrilled about it," Shan said, confused. "I thought you'd be dancing a jig when this day rolled around. I know what that man did to you."

"I know," Bartlett added. "I just wish the games would die with him, you know?"

"Not really," Shan said as he stood from his desk and walked over to his partner, slowing his procession to the captain's office. "What else has happened, buddy?"

Bartlett pulled the envelope from his inside jacket pocket and handed it reluctantly over to his partner. "The bastard named me in his will."

"He what?"

"That was my reaction too when West told me."

"West?" Shan asked. "Ben West? I thought you two weren't speaking."

"So did I. Just one more thing I have to *thank* that bastard for."

"Nothing brings people together like a funeral, eh?" Shan joked.

The look on his partner's face told him he didn't think it was all that funny. Benjamin West and John Bartlett got along like oil and water. Both men were more alike than either one of them would ever admit, which was probably the main reason they didn't get along. John tended to think things through, carefully planning out his moves before making them. West, on the other hand, seemed to leap first and worry about the rest later. That was Shan's initial impression of the reporter. He didn't know him well enough to make more than just a casual observation. Despite their dislike of one another, Bartlett and West had made a good team against Morehouse. Shan was often amazed they made it through the ordeal without killing one another.

Since the Morehouse trial, John tried to steer clear of all reporters, but specifically Benjamin West and Fabian Alexander. If there was one thing they had in common, neither Bartlett nor West cared much for Fabian Alexander.

"He hated you, why put you in the will?" Shan asked. "He's got to be up to something. What's his game this time?"

"I tell you, Shan, that's what I aim to find out." he chucked a thumb over his shoulder in the direction of the offices lining the rear wall of the bullpen. "Look, I got to go see the Captain. Has he gotten back from the press conference yet?"

"Yeah. Came in about twenty minutes ago and made a beeline for his office. We haven't seen him since so he's probably still in there."

"Thanks. I need to fill him in."

"Need some company?"

"Nah," he said. "I can handle this."

"You sure?"

"I don't have much choice now do I?"

"Guess not. If you need anything, you know where I'll be." He pointed awkwardly toward his desk.

"Thanks, Shan. I appreciate it. We'll talk after I finish up with the captain."

# # #

The name on the glass door was stenciled in all caps, CAPTAIN WILSON J. MILLER.

However, to everyone on the floor, the department head was named *Captain Willie* or the less flattering *Captain Who*? He was not the greatest supervisor in the world, although he had his moments, but Willie Miller was a good man. He had a very unspectacular career that spanned thirty years with the police department. He didn't make waves so he stayed under the radar. The captain had staying power, but not much else. At best he was just there, a fixture just like any desk, chair, stapler...

John Bartlett and Willie Miller got along all right. They were not friends per se and they never saw one another outside of the office, but they were civil to one another and rarely butted heads these days. Over the years they have had their fair share of showdowns, but at the end of the day they understood one another. Once John learned the best way to relate to his captain it helped to keep things professional between them.

Bartlett rapped his knuckles against the glass door and Captain Miller looked up from his desk without missing a beat in his phone conversation. He motioned for John to come on in. John did so and closed the door behind him gently. Captain Miller was still on the phone, a position that John often noticed the older man in.

He didn't know who was on the other end of the phone line, but

Willie was doing a fair amount of kissing up so it had to be someone higher up the food chain. Probably the Chief of Police the way he was carrying on, but there was no way of knowing for certain. In truth, he had a few other thoughts on his mind that required his full attention.

"Yes, sir," Captain Miller said into the phone. "I understand. Listen, one of my detectives just stepped into my office so I'll have to let you go." He smiled at Bartlett for giving him the excuse of making whoever was on the other end of the phone know that his detectives still came to him for help on cases. "Yes, sir," he continued. "I'll call you back with those figures in an hour. No, thank you, sir. Good bye."

Hanging up the phone, Captain Miller sighed. "They all want something," he said quietly, but Bartlett heard him as was probably the captain's intent. It seemed that Miller always wanted his officers to feel sorry for him. If he sighed out loud, it was a good bet that he wanted sympathy, although these days he didn't get too much of it from the men and women under his command. They had all grown tired of the man's ploys for attention.

Captain Willie Miller was all but ignored in his own squad room. Maybe that's why he craved the spotlight of the TV cameras as much as he did. The news hounds paid attention.

"I thought you were taking the rest of the day off," he said when he finally looked up from the stack of sticky pads he had scattered across his desk. He wrote notes on them and placed them everywhere.

Bartlett wondered if half the time, Captain Miller even remembered what half of them were written for.

"I have a problem, Captain," Bartlett said.

"What can I do for you, Detective?"

"It's this Morehouse situation again," he started.

He had the Captain's full attention now. "He threaten you again, John? He's been warned that--"

"No. No. Nothing like that."

Bartlett, as well as a few other key witnesses responsible for Darrin Morehouse's arrest and imprisonment had received death threats over the past couple of years in addition to the letters. Morehouse had been manipulating the threats from his prison cell, but there was no way to prove it. The Captain met with the District Attorney and Warden Chalmers about the threats and the prisoner was warned to put a stop to it or there would be consequences. Although Morehouse denied any involvement with the leveling of threats against anyone, he sat there with a smug grin on his face that more or less screamed his complicity in the threats. The grin was his was of telling them, *Yeah, I did it. What are you going to do about it, throw me in jail?*

Not one to hold his anger very well, Bartlett had to resist the urge to barge into the prison and beat the man into submission. It was no easy feat.

"You don't sound too sure," the captain said.

"Uh, no. He hasn't threatened me. Not this time," Bartlett answered. His assumption that word had not filtered down to the Captain yet about Morehouse's apparent suicide were confirmed by that one simple question. Somehow, the news had been suppressed so that only those involved with the reading of the will were informed. He wondered how Morehouse, or his people, had managed that little feat. Morehouse was a rat bastard, but he was also a public figure. His death would be big news.

Maybe someone else is manipulating things.

"He's dead, Captain," Bartlett said, without any emotion showing through his features.

"Dead, dead?"

"Hung himself in his own cell if you can believe that. Guards found him a few days ago. Graveyard dead."

"And you've confirmed this?"

"Just got off the phone with Frank Chalmers over at Westmore a few minutes ago. He confirmed it. Said he saw the body with his own eyes. There was no pulse. He checked. Twice."

"So what's the problem, John?" As usual, the Captain was trying to wrap things up so he could get back to his work or whatever interoffice memo he was typing that day.

Something had not been sitting well with Bartlett since West broke the news to him about Morehouse's suicide. Darrin Morehouse had told him a few years earlier that he would make the police officer and his compatriots pay for what had happened to him. With most men he had put away, this would seem like bluster, but with Morehouse there was a bit more weight behind the thinly veiled threat. The man was very committed to this cause and despite Francis Chalmers' best efforts, he had the resources at his disposal to make things happen.

It just didn't seem right to Bartlett that he would take his own life when he had so much unfinished business left to take care of. Maybe the answer to that would be revealed at the reading of the will.

Maybe, but somehow he doubted it would be that simple.

With Darrin Morehouse it never was.

When he had been among the living, Morehouse had been the ultimate game player. Everything was a game or a gamble to him. Bartlett had even witnessed him use the flip of a coin to decide whether or not a man died like the old Batman villain, Two-Face. Heads he lived, tales he died. Benjamin West had been damned lucky that day.

Morehouse had a specific reason for everything he did and those reasons usually spelled trouble for those who got on the wrong side of him like John Bartlett had. Like Benjamin West had. And Warden Chalmers, District Attorney Coombes, or even Morehouse's estranged wife, Vivian Morehouse. They were all on his shit list and probably represented only a small percentage of people that Darrin Morehouse held a grudge against.

Bartlett had a feeling that things were far from over in terms of Darrin Morehouse. Far from over indeed. "The problem is this," he said as he tossed the envelope across the desk to his superior officer, dislodging three sticky notes from their respective positions. On any other day, dismantling part of the great Miller Filing Matrix would have brought some measure of joy, but not today.

Captain Miller picked the envelope up and stared at it a moment as if there were clues to its purpose. "What is this?" he asked without attempting to open it. Why should he do any investigating on his own if his detective could explain it to him? That was, part and parcel, Willie Miller's philosophy. *Why do it yourself when someone can do it for you?*

Agitated, Bartlett took back the envelope from his boss and opened it up, pulling the contents out and unfolding them in his lap. "Morehouse has named me in his will."

"You're kidding?" Captain Miller gasped.

"I wish. I have been requested to report tomorrow afternoon to a formal reading at a nine hundred acre estate that belonged to one of Morehouse's dummy corporations just outside of Sommersville."

"Is that the same place where--"

"Yes, sir. That's where we finally arrested him. The GBI tore that place apart looking for evidence against him, but they didn't have much luck." He pulled a small notebook from his shirt pocket and flipped it open. "I did some checking and the property was put on the auction block after trial. It was purchased by a development firm called Hard Labor Development Partners Inc. There's not much on them, but if I had to guess, and at this point that's all I can do, I'd say that Hard Labor is another of Morehouse's shell companies, especially considering the name. I'll dig into it further, but since they're hosting the reading of the will I pretty much think it's a lock they're connected. Guess I'll find out when I get there."

"You're going?" Captain miller asked skeptically, as if he was sure he couldn't have heard him right.

"I've got no choice, Captain. It came with a summons. I've been called as a hostile participant." Unfolding the summons, he read it aloud, paraphrasing for Captain Miller. "I have been required by the will probate court to appear at this formal hearing or face contempt charges."

"Can they do that?" Captain Miller asked.

Bartlett simply shrugged. "Beats me," he said. "Guess I'll find out when I get there, won't I?"

"Damn," Captain Miller said.

"Don't sweat it, Captain," Bartlett said. "This is just the carrot. He knows there's no way I wouldn't be there. And he's right."

"Oh, it gets better," Bartlett said.

Captain Miller sighed.

"It seems that the body is missing."

"Missing?"

"Yep. I talked with Francis Chalmers. He watched Morehouse's body being put into the ME's van," Bartlett started. "Unfortunately, once it reached the ME's office, if it ever actually got there, it was conveniently misplaced."

"How the hell to they lose a body?"

"Your guess is as good as mine. My guess is it's all part of some stupid game he's pulling. I'm sure the body will show up eventually."

"What does that man have planned for you?"

Bartlett scratched his chin. "I have no idea, but I guess I'll find out tomorrow."

Captain Miller pointed at the summons in his hand. "How did they get that to you?"

"It was in the mailbox," Bartlett answered. "Morehouse's lawyer," he flipped through the notepad and read off the information he had scrawled there. "An attorney, Philip Jason Hall, had it delivered it to me shortly after Morehouse's body was discovered. I have not had a chance to open my mail until today, but I ran into Ben West earlier. He was summoned as well. That puts my guard up another notch, if you know what I mean."

"I see," the captain stated. "What do you need from me?"

"I don't know." Bartlett let a small laugh escape from his throat. "If I'm not back by Tuesday morning, promise you'll send the troops out to look for me."

"I can probably handle that."

"Good."

"John, you want me to send someone with you? I could reassign the case Shan is working on and let him go with you."

Bartlett waved off the suggestion. "Nah," he said, dragging out the vowels. "I'll be fine, besides I doubt they are going to let anyone in that isn't expressly mentioned in the will. I'll be all right and Warden Chalmers will be there too. Plus, there is always West in case I get in a bind."

"You sure you can trust him?"

"West? Yeah. He's an arrogant prick, but when it comes to Morehouse we do have some common ground. It'll be okay."

Bartlett tried not to grimace when mentioning the journalist's name.

He failed.

# # #

"Are you out of your fuckin' mind, John?"

"I don't think so. Why do you ask?"

"Funny. I'll make sure they put that on your tombstone."

Shan Lomax and John Bartlett had made their way from the crowded police station to a more suitable place to talk. Grant Park was fairly secluded during the day like this. The kids were in school and most of the denizens of the city were at their respective jobs, leaving the tranquility of the park to the two troubled detectives and a handful of office workers that came out to jog on their lunch hour. Even the squatters were invisible today.

"Look, Shan, I appreciate it, but what can you do, huh? I have to do this. If I don't put this to rest, I'll be wondering for the rest of my life. I don't want to be haunted by this son of a bitch now that he's dead. He was more than enough trouble when he was alive."

He shrugged. "Besides, I'm damned curious."

"I know that this is rough on you, pal, but you have to face the real possibility that this is some kind of trap. Just don't get too curious. This could be Morehouse's final revenge from beyond the grave," Shan said in a voice reminiscent of an old scary movie.

"Now who's being funny?" Bartlett asked his partner.

"Yeah, well, Vincent Price I ain't." Shan extended his right hand to his friend, palm open.

"I'll leave the drama critique to the professionals."

"Is there anything I can do on my end?" Lomax asked.

"See if you can dig up some information on Morehouse's body. It disappeared somewhere between the prison and the ME's office. There's something fishy there."

"I'll look into it, partner."

"Thanks," Bartlett said. "Just find that body. I won't be completely convinced this is over until I see it with my own two eyes."

"I'll do what I can. Just promise me you'll at be careful, John."

John Bartlett grasped his friend's hand giving it a firm shake. "Aren't I always," he answered.

"Do you really want me to answer that?"

"Not really."

"And keep your cell on. I'll call in and check on you just to make sure everything's okay. Okay?"

"Yes, mother. I'll have my cell with me, but it will be off during the reading. I'll call you as soon as that's finished."

"That'll work. You don't want me to have to come up there and find you."

Bartlett laughed. "I'll see you when I get back." Then he turned away from his friend and walked away.

Shan Lomax watched his partner until he exited the park and was completely out of sight. "Be careful, Pal," he said, knowing that John could not hear how worried by this latest turn of events he actually was.

"Watch your back, pal."

CHAPTER 6

"Sarah?"

"In here, Benny," came a woman's lilting voice from somewhere inside the crowded loft apartment. Boxes were stacked all over, a constant reminder that most of his belongings were still in boxes. He kept planning to make time to unpack, but there was always some story or another that he had to chase. Smiling as he entered, Benjamin West stepped over half empty packing crates and rolled up balls of newspaper lying scattered around the area marked off as the living room. At least that's what it would become once the fifty inch plasma was installed and the new sofa, loveseat, recliner, coffee table, and end tables they'd ordered arrived next week. Several partitions served as walls to block off separate rooms. He could only guess which one Sarah had started working on first.

"Yoo hoo, Sarah? Honey?"

"In the studio," she answered.

Of course, he thought. *Where else would she be?*

Navigating his way down the makeshift hallway, Benjamin moved into the area Sarah had claimed for her studio. This was her private space. He watched as she placed one of the many potted plants she loved around her work area.

"Hi honey, I'm hoooooome," he sung out excitedly from the entrance.

Seeing him swagger in, she smiled, even after hearing the same lame entrance line for the past two days since they'd moved into the apartment, their first together.

She smiled and that was all it took to make him happy. Sarah's smile could light up any room. She had a presence that Benjamin found intoxicating. She held her arms apart, motioning for him to take in her assembled work area. "What do you think?"

The room had three different paintings that Sarah called "*works in progress*," a desk, chair, bookshelf, and a rolling microwave cart that she used to move her equipment and painting supplies around the room. There were also various objects off in one corner in a pile that didn't look like much to Benjamin, but would serve as still life models at some point or another for one of Sarah's paintings. The room really reflected an artist's studio. The midday sun shone in bright through the window where it would be at her back while she painted, which is why she chose that spot for the studio to begin with.

Knowing Sarah as well as he did, he assumed she had planned the look of this room to a T, probably before ever stepping foot inside the loft apartment for the first time. She was definitely a planner by nature. Everything was where she wanted it to be and nothing was haphazard, despite initial appearances to the contrary. *A place for everything and everything in its place.*

She was the complete and total opposite of her boyfriend, the slob.

"Very nice," he told her.

"Thank you, dear," she answered with another smile.

Taking three steps across the room, Ben embraced her firmly and kissed her. For a moment they seemed to lose themselves in one another's embrace until finally they had to come up for air.

"Hi," he said again.

"Hi, yourself," she answered, all grins. "You're home early. What's the matter, crime take a break so all reporters could come home and help their girlfriend's unpack?"

"I wish," he told her. "I..."

She did not give him a chance to continue.

"Come on. I want to show you something."

Grabbing him by the hand before he could protest, Sarah pulled

Benjamin down the hallway to another room on the opposite end of the loft from her studio. This one was smaller than her room, but it had a charm all its own.

He stared at it and, uncharacteristically for him, was speechless for a moment.

"Wow!" he finally said.

"You like?" Sarah asked, already knowing the answer.

"When did you have time to do this, honey?" he asked her as he let her lead him into the office she had created for him. This was now designated as Ben's space, complete with a hand painted sign that said *BEN'S OFFICE* hanging on the wall next to the window.

"What do you think I've been doing for the better part of the last two days?"

"I love you," Benjamin said, not answering her question.

"And I love you too, you big jerk."

"This is great," he said as he moved deeper into the office. His desk, computer, two white dry erase boards, bulletin board, light table, drafting table, and an empty bookshelf were all neatly arranged just as they had been in his old apartment. The desk was positioned next to the window just the way he liked and the window overlooked a small wooded area behind the apartment. With the sun hitting the other end of the apartment, the office had a darker, homier feel.

Again, just the way he liked it.

Several unopened boxes were sitting near the bookshelf. Sarah pointed at them. "I'll let you unpack your books and put them where you want them. Other than that, the room is as ready as it can be. Now you have no excuse not to sit down and work on that new novel you keep threatening to write."

"Yeah," Benjamin said as he ran a finger along the top of his old desk and the computer that sat upon it. He had been trying to pen a follow up novel to *Deadly Games!*, but so far inspiration had eluded him. After several false starts he decided to take a break and see if anything sparked his muse. So far he muse had been eerily silent.

She could tell that the room was satisfactory to him, even though his personal space was a little smaller than her studio. If he had reservations about that, the smart boy that he was, he kept them to himself.

"You are a wonderful woman," he said to her as he took one last look around the room.

"Why thank you, Mr. West. So kind of you to notice. Want to see what else I've done today?"

"There's more?" he asked.

"Of course."

"What are you, Wonder Woman?"

"Close."

"When do I get to see you in your outfit then," he asked jokingly as he followed her once more down the hallway. "Because, you know, I'd pay real money to see that."

She simply laughed in that way she did when he thought he was being funny, but she didn't necessarily agree. Their senses of humor were one of the few things they were polar opposites when it came to it. Still, he kept cracking jokes and she kept ignoring them so it worked for them. Seconds later, they were laughing together as she lead him up the steps to the assembled bedroom.

"*Ta da,*" she announced as they stopped at the top of the circular stairwell.

"Oh, baby. It's perfect."

Sarah shrugged. "I do what I can."

"You're perfect," he told her.

"Also true," she agreed.

"And modest to a fault no less."

"True as well."

"Any other qualities you'd like to share with me, Ms. Wonder Woman?"

"Absolutely," she answered. "But first, why don't you tell me what's bothering you."

CHAPTER 7

Philip Jason Hall was working late.

As an attorney, he represented the late Darrin Morehouse's estate. It was his duty to make sure that everything in the will was carried out according to the deceased's wishes. To that end he had delivered a total of eight letters as specified by his client's express wishes. He had even left very specific notes on how to deliver them, which was odd, he had to admit, but not as out there as some of the guidelines previous clients had left for him. Never in all his years working for the bar had he ever had a client come to him with such fully planned instructions. Every detail had been written down with step by step instructions. Even the most mundane activities had to be followed to the letter.

His job was to dispense with the reading of the will and then to follow the instructions therein, of which there were many, to the letter. His client had laid out a multitude of intricately explicit instructions to be followed. He took great pleasure in writing up such elaborately intrinsic rules for each of the individuals named in the will. While it made Hall's job a little easier in one respect, the client's demand to keep sections of the will secret, even from his attorney, tied his hands. It was unprecedented in his experience, but as strange as many of the instructions seemed, Hall's only concern was that his client's check did not bounce.

Even in death, as much as he had been in life, Darrin Morehouse was not a very trusting individual. Therefore even his trusted attorney, Mr. Hall had no idea what surprises lay inside the large manila envelope that had been delivered to his office a mere two hours he had been informed via telephone of his clients untimely demise at his own hands.

The only information that Hall had been given before receiving the *bad news* was a list of names and instructions that several white envelopes would come to him after the death of Darrin Morehouse. He was expressly ordered to see to the delivery of said envelopes to the proper parties. His client did not want these envelopes handled by the United States Postal Service, a condition that had sent up some red flags with Hall.

After an intense phone conversation with one of his client's most trusted associates, he decided that there was no danger to himself or anyone else and withdrew his objection. He knew of his client's reputation, of course. Like everyone else, he had been glued to the Morehouse case six years earlier. As a result, the names on some of the envelopes were no strangers to him, even though he did not know any of them personally.

John Bartlett.

John Bartlett was the Atlanta Police Officer that arrested his client. His client alleged that Detective Bartlett had fabricated most of the evidence against him. Since there was no proof that backed up his client's claim of evidence tampering by the officer, no official investigation was launched, which really didn't surprise him. Hall's experience working criminal cases early in his career had instilled in him a complete lack of faith in the police. He wouldn't put it past the police to cover their collective asses by burying any such evidence if it did exist. It was possible his client was right about Bartlett, but there was nothing he could do about it. If Bartlett was dirty there was no evidence to prove it.

Benjamin West.

Benjamin West was photojournalist with a well-known and public bias against his client. West had helped John Bartlett entrap his client six years earlier. After Darrin Morehouse's incarceration, West wrote a novel based on his experiences before, during, and after the trial called *Deadly Games*! Part fact, but mostly fiction, the novel spent an impressive six weeks on *The New York Times Bestseller List*. After reading the book, Hall wondered how much was fiction and how much of it was actual fact. Some of the situations in the book were rather farfetched so he suspected that the majority of it was simply the work of a creative writer.

Vivian Morehouse.

Vivian Morehouse was his client's ex wife. For reasons that were never explained, she turned against her husband during the trial. Her *betrayal* -his client's words, not Hall's- gave the prosecution the evidence they needed to convict his client. For reasons he could only speculate on, Vivian Morehouse waved spousal privilege and testified for the prosecution against her husband. He was curious to see what kind of woman fell in love with a man who had the alleged criminal background like his client.

Laura Sellars.

Laura Sellars had been Morehouse's lawyer during the trial. From what he had read of the transcripts, she had done a decent job, but not good enough to get the acquittal her client hoped for. Sadly, the loss of such a high profile case had all but ended her career, one that had been on the fast track before being assigned the Morehouse case. Based on his research, Hall had doubts that she would ever regain her former status.

Nathan Hughes.

Nathan Hughes had been the presiding Judge during the original case. Hall had never stood before him, but he had heard of Judge Hughes. The man had a reputation for being a crotchety old bastard, but also of being fair and impartial. Hall saw nothing to indicate any bias on the Judge's part like his client claimed, but thankfully arguing that was not his concern.

Michael Coombes.

Michael Coombes was the district attorney during the Moreshouse trial, a position he retained to this day. His victory for the prosecution in the Morehouse case had set his career ablaze. A talented attorney, Hall was looking forward to meeting him. He just wished it could be under better circumstances.

Francis Chalmers.

Francis Chalmers was the odd man out on the list. None of the research into the original case showed a connection with Chalmers. As near as Hall could tell, the warden and his client did not meet until he arrived at the prison to serve his sentence. There were reports of tense moments between the two men, but nothing that was serious enough to warrant sanctions or an investigation. Warden Chalmers' record was exemplary.

Hall delivered the letters to each one of them.

By hand.

The strange part was that his client did not want him to speak with any of the recipients when he dropped off the envelopes, which made his job a bit more difficult, though not impossible.

Within twenty four to thirty six hours, all six envelopes had been delivered as instructed. The seventh envelope had been "hand delivered" to Francis Chalmers by the deceased himself. At first he had questioned why he could not put his firm's return address on the envelopes in case any of the recipients needed to speak with him. Upon speaking at great length with his client's associate in charge of the arrangements, Philip Jason Hall decided that it was in his best interests to simply do as he was instructed and to not inquire further.

So he did not question why prominent figures that had helped put his client in prison were being named in Mr. Morehouse's will. Being a good little lawyer, he decided to mind his own business and do what was expected of him as an officer of the court.

So, after seeing that all the "*invitations*," as it were, had been delivered, he sat back and waited for the reading of the will, which would happen a few days later.

Normally, he would move on to another case before revisiting this one, but his client had paid him very handsomely to keep his schedule clear and he had done just that. If Darrin Morehouse was willing to spend good money to keep his schedule open then he was all too happy to comply with those wishes.

Once the check cleared, of course.

CHAPTER 8

Sometimes Vivian Morehouse wished she had never met her ex-husband.

The former Mrs. Darrin Morehouse thought, *although hoped might have been a better word*, that she would never hear her ex-husband's name spoken aloud again. It was just too painful. The memories were too fresh, her emotions too raw.

She should have been so lucky.

If it wasn't the media pestering her for an interview for one of their damned one-sided retrospectives, it was seeing John Bartlett on the news, or seeing Benjamin West's name in the newspaper. Each time she saw them all of those hideous memories flooded back in on her, threatening to drown her in sorrow and depression.

But that wasn't the worst part. No, the thing that made her afraid to leave the house was that godawful made for TV mini series FOX had made around the time of the trial that played over and over again on cable, usually on Lifetime or Oxygen. In the movie, *Lethal Games: The Darrin Morehouse Story*, Vivian had been portrayed as a soulless money hungry whore out for her husband's money while sleeping with every young stud she could coax into bed. It saddened her greatly to know that this TV version of her was the impression the world had of her. She couldn't believe the way Valerie Bertinelli had portrayed her in the movie, even after the actress met with her so her performance would be "as honest and real as possible." She gave her word that the performance would be accurate.

It wasn't.

Vivian felt betrayed by all quarters.

In fact, the sham marriage portrayed in the film, *a term she used loosely* could not have been farther from the truth.

Theirs had been a fantasy courtship.

Darrin had wined her, dined her, and swept her off her feet. A kind, loving man, he took her to the stars and back again. He was very handsome, energetic, and so full of confidence. Plus, he was an excellent dancer. A trait so few men Vivian ever met had mastered.

Outside of that, all Vivian knew of the man she agreed to marry was that he referred to himself as a *"self made man."*

Even though she was unsure of what that meant, she had admired that about him at the time. He had spun elaborate sad stories of his childhood where his poor parents were unable to feed the family and keep a roof over their heads. Now, she wondered if any of it was true.

Naturally, she was curious about her husband's business but chose not to press the issue. She never inquired about his activities. After all, it was "his" business and she felt it certainly was not her place to pry, assured in the knowledge that he would tell her what she needed to know if and when she needed to know it.

Later she would realize how naive she had been in her younger days.

She started to notice little things in the years after the marriage. She tried to ignore the evidence piling up before her, but some truths were hard to ignore. No matter how hard one tried.

Not that Vivian Morehouse had ever cared about doing the right thing, she just became convinced that the man she had fallen in love with was indeed capable of becoming a monster. She didn't think he would try to kill her, but the doubt was there. She no longer trusted him and it soured their relationship.

Vivian Morehouse was not a stupid woman. She had a business degree from Brown University. Although her husband did not forbid her from working, he preferred that she be available whenever he needed her. She decided to stay home and spent her free time helping local charity organizations.

After the initial allegations about Darrin's alleged criminal ties, some small, little voice in the back of her mind concocted a plan. She put together an insurance policy, if you will, and it whispered this contingency every time Vivian Morehouse turned out the lights while a man she no longer trusted lay next to her.

After a time, she decided that the little voice, which she assumed was her conscience, was right. It was time she planned for the future. She had to be prepared for the inevitable day when her husband would turn against her. It started by siphoning off funds into a private account that only she had access to. She would need resources if she decided to go against him. Until then she would simply bide her time. She was patient. She could wait this out.

Ironically enough, it was Vivian that eventually turned on her husband instead of the other way around, as she had always feared. She knew it was only a matter of time and decided to make the first move. Neither Darrin nor his lawyers saw it coming.

It was not out of fear for her life that she turned on him. No, Vivian betrayed the man she had devoted herself to simply as an escape from a life that she no longer cared for. She needed an out so she found one and the District Attorney's Office was all too happy to accommodate her. All she had to do was refuse to claim spousal privilege and testify. Things had not been as comfortable during the last few years of her marriage to Darrin and this was her way out because she could not -*would not dare*- ask Darrin for a divorce. To do so would court disaster.

Or so the scared little voice told her.

Then, the police began their investigation of her husband's illicit activities.

Vivian thanked her lucky stars that she had planned ahead. Especially after charges were filed against her as a possible accomplice in Darrin's plans. Her husband had placed several prime pieces of real estate in Vivian's name. She had no knowledge of this, of course, but the police refused to believe her. And Darrin was so busy covering his own ass that he did nothing to help her. If he had tried to help, if he'd just lifted one damned finger in her defense, she very likely would not have turned on him as she had.

Well, she decided, if no one else would stand up for her, she'd damned sure do so herself.

Her husband was going to let her twist in the wind alone, so

Vivian Morehouse turned over the evidence she had been collecting to Lieutenant John Bartlett of the Atlanta Police Department. It was her information that had turned the tide in the officer's investigation.

She knew he hated her for her part in his downfall, but by that point she no longer cared what Darrin Morehouse thought of her. He could rot in hell for all she cared. One of his spineless lawyers delivered divorce papers to her door during the trial. He was making a clean break from her, leaving her with nothing.

Or so he believed.

Despite the portrayal from that damned made-for-TV movie, Vivian was not a stupid woman. Experience taught her to act the part when necessary, however. She was so often underestimated and used that to her advantage. After stumbling upon things that were registered in her name, she immediately, and very carefully, began moving them to new accounts. She was quite clever. Neither Darrin nor any of his cohorts were the wiser.

At least not before it was too late for them to do anything about it.

If she had not volunteered information, Darrin Morehouse would never have seen the inside of a prison cell, but she did turn evidence over and he did spend time in prison. Five years of a life sentence before taking the cowards way out and committing suicide. She had always thought him to be a smarter, braver man than that. In some strange way, she was actually disappointed in him.

She had been wrong about him before, but her former husband just did not seem the type to take his own life. He would have seen it as the coward's way out and Darrin was many things, but a coward was not one of them.

Now that he was dead there could be closure in her life. She wanted nothing more than to forget the name of her hated ex husband, to close off her past, and look toward a possible bright future with a clean slate. *Along with the bastard's money.*

Then a white envelope arrived at her door.

The handwriting on the envelope's face was unmistakably that of her former husband, but there was no return address and no postage on the envelope. *So how did it get here?* She wondered. She had not heard a knock at the door or anyone ringing the bell. Surely, whoever delivered it would have tried the doorbell instead of simply sliding it through the mail slot in the front door. As soon as she recognized the handwriting on the aforementioned envelope, the tears came.

It would be the better part of an hour before she could summon the courage to open the envelope and read, in explicit legal jargon, the events of Darrin's apparent suicide, something she had a great deal of trouble believing. Her ex husband was many things, but he was not a coward. Suicide seemed so... so... beneath him. She wasn't sure how to process the news.

And, as if that weren't enough of a shock for one day, the fact that she had been named in his will threw her for an even bigger loop.

Directions for attending at the reading of the will were also enclosed as well as the name and number of the attorney handling the will in case she had any questions.

She had questions, but she doubted that the lawyer could answer them. *Why was she, one of the people Darrin hated most in the world, mentioned in his will? Was this another of the man's sick, twisted little games?* And just simply, *why?*

Haven't I suffered enough at his hands?

CHAPTER 9

Michael Coombes couldn't believe his eyes.

Going over the summons to appear at the reading of Darrin Morehouse's will for the third time, he fought down painful memories from years earlier. He had served with distinction as District Attorney in the metropolitan Atlanta area since 2000. His record was something for which he could be proud and he was. He had done a fine job for the city and for the law. He took his work very seriously, but managed to keep his life beneath the scrutiny of the press.

And then he heard the name Darrin Morehouse and suddenly everything changed.

The Morehouse case had not been his first case, obviously. And it certainly had not been his greatest and it had not been his last. The one thing that particular case had done was make District Attorney Michael Coombes a prominent public figure. Seemingly overnight he had become a local celebrity, almost to the point of being unable to do his job.

Everywhere he went, every move, every gesture, it was all captured on film by one reporter or another. Every time he stepped outside his office, his home, or his car, someone shoved a microphone in front of his face. After a time, he came to view them all as having the same face. A fake face with plastered on features. It became an ordeal for him to leave his home for fear of becoming vulnerable before the hounds.

The rigor of it nearly drove him insane.

Then, after receiving some sage advice from an old and dear friend, Michael Coombes learned to tune out the garbage -*the bullshit, as his wise friend referred to it*- and use the media as a tool. It could be a nuisance or a weapon and he chose to use it as a weapon that he could shape and mold into something useful, a weapon to rally support to the cause for which he fought. And that cause was swift and blinding justice.

With his newfound voice in the community, Michael Coombes became the personification of the law in Atlanta, at least for a time. After the trial ended and the controversy surrounding Darrin Morehouse had been laid to rest, the District Attorney became less important as a lead story. Controversy was a small step away from danger.

"The public thrives on danger," he overheard one reporter comment once.

Without the danger there was no story.

The spotlight dimmed on Michael Coombes, but it did not fade completely. He remained very much an adored civil servant. He was still every bit as much the champion of the people as he had been during the televised circus that surrounded the big trial and he expertly wielded that notoriety when he needed to do so. The biggest change in his life was one that he did not miss at all, the absence of television news crews with their cameras and microphones waiting around every corner. It was a refreshing change to go to the bathroom without wondering if someone were outside his window watching him take a piss.

Quietly, in the private places Michael had never opened up to the public, he secretly missed the excitement. He had complained about the continued presence of the media during the trial, but after it was all over and they were gone everything seemed to change.

Eventually he got used to their absence again.

Now, the cameras only showed up on rare occasions. There were still trials that would garner media response and the DA's adrenaline would pump back up as the thrill of the fight would well up inside him once again. His thoughts had not turned toward Darren Morehouse in a number of years and he was fine with that. If he never heard the man's name again that would have been just fine with him. His life and career were both finally running straight and true. He could live without the spotlight.

And then that damned letter arrived.

Sighing, he once again read the name of the attorney in charge of the disposition of the will.

Philip Jason Hall.

The lettering on the enclosed business card was painstakingly perfect. *It must have cost a fortune to print*, he thought as he studied it closely. *Much nicer than the ones my secretary prints out on the computer for me*, he added with just a hint of jealousy.

He read the name on the card, but the attorney's name was unfamiliar to him.

Fuck! The thought was as angry as he could make it. Lately, he was trying not to use such language aloud, a pleasant side effect of working on watching his language in front of his impressionable young daughter who had a habit of repeating whatever new word or phrase she happened to hear. Coombes knew that he would have to reign in his potty mouth the day he heard his little princess tell her mother to "*shut her fucking mouth!*" It didn't take a detective for his wife to figure out where she had picked up that little gem and she made sure it never happened again.

"Doris," he called to his secretary. "Cancel all my appointments for the next two days, please. Oh, and tell Judge Aldridge that I'll have to postpone our lunch and convey my apologies."

"What reason shall I give him?" Doris's raspy voice, twinged by decades of chain smoking, a habit she was trying to kick, by the way, asked through the intercom.

He seemed to think about that one for a moment. What could he say that would sound appropriate? *I'm going to the reading of a psychopath's will? A madman who threatened my life on more than one occasion wants to thank me with an inheritance check? Yeah. Who would believe something as ludicrous as that?*

"Tell everyone except Aldridge I've been called out of town unexpectedly on urgent business. Tell the judge it's unavoidable and I'll call him a couple days to reschedule lunch." That sounded as good as any other excuse.

"Yes, sir."

"Also, see if you can track down John Bartlett. I need to speak with him right away."

"The cop?"

"Yeah. His private line is in my file. Interrupt me if you have to once you have him on the line."

"Very good, sir," Doris said as she began clicking her way through the overflowing address book on her computer. Despite her bosses' skill as a prosecutor, he was completely useful when it came to all things digital. She had more than once commented on how someone his age could be as computer illiterate as he was beyond her. She had been amazed when he mastered the cell phone and longed to see the reaction on his face when the blackberry she ordered for him arrived the following week.

"Oh, and, Doris," Michael shouted from inside his private closet. "See if you can get my wife on the phone. I really need to talk to her as soon as possible."

"Yes, sir."

CHAPTER 10

Patience was not one of Judge Nathan Hughes strong suits.

Comfortable with his station in life, he was unaccustomed to waiting for anything at all. He had to be seated immediately upon entering any restaurant or theater. He wanted the best. As his reputation preceded him, he usually got it.

For twenty-three years he had presided over the Fulton County Superior Court. Not all of those years had been exciting, but most were memorable. Although he wasn't always considered a nice or friendly person, it never really bothered him. *One does not sit on that bench to be liked*, he had been quoted as saying on more than one occasion. *One sits up there to uphold the law*. And he did a fine job of it, too. If you asked him, he'd tell you the same thing.

Six years back Judge Hughes had presided over the case of The State v. Darrin Morehouse. That case had been one for the record books. A media circus, it garnered not only local, but national attention. None of which mattered one iota to the Judge. Quite the contrary, he found it fired up the legal eagles on both sides, making for more passionate, fevered debate, which her preferred over the usual stale legalese he had to listen to on a daily basis.

And fire them up it had.

Attorneys for the plaintiff and the defendant fought tooth and nail in pleading their case. Playing not only to the jury, but the television cameras the judge had allowed inside the courtroom as well. Court TV had been a mainstay of the trial.

Hotly contested debates and fiery cross-examinations kept the interest in the case up. Media consultants and legal experts argued the points of the case in the court of public opinion nightly on the cable news shows as well as the Internet. It also served to keep the Judge, himself, awake during some of the more drawn out witness examinations. However, the down side to heated arguments was that it extended the trial.

The attorney for the accused, Laura Sellars relentlessly picked at the lack of evidence against her client. She tried to convince the jury that the police department in general, and Lieutenant John Bartlett in particular, had a personal vendetta against her client. This vendetta resulted in extensive charges being brought against Darrin Morehouse. The Defense hinted at, but never outright accused John Bartlett of evidence tampering. Miss Sellars smartly towed a very fine line in that regard. One misstep and the judge would have cut her off at the knees and shut down her line of questioning.

She attempted to paint a picture of an innocent man being hounded by the authorities without a shred of evidence to back up their claims of the crimes he had allegedly committed. She repeatedly stressed that her client only wanted to provide for his wife and his community. It was a complete crock of bull and everyone knew it. The judge wanted to toss the book at the man after the first day of the trial, but fortunately for the defendant, the law had to be obeyed and everyone, including a sleazy scumbag like Darrin Morehouse, was entitled to a fair trial.

District Attorney Michael Coombes, hammered at the character of the accused. He wanted to put him put away as much as the judge did, if not more. Nathan Hughes very quickly became impressed with the young DA and decided to have a long talk with him after the trial ended. Eventually, the two men became friends, with Judge Hughes serving as a mentor to Coombes, after a fashion.

The trial dragged on and there seemed to be no end in sight. After a while, the Judge simply wanted it to be over and began pushing the prosecution and the defense to get on with it and speed things up. He had grown tired of the same arguments from counsel day after day after day. What had started out as a quest for justice became a bad soap opera that Judge Hughes just wanted to end.

Eventually, he got his wish.

After the case ended the Judge moved on with his life and rarely gave the famous case and verdict a second thought. He was a man who looked forward, never back. He believed that looking back was what old men who had nothing left to contribute did. And although he could not deny his age, the last thing he considered himself was old. And he knew he still had a lot to offer this world.

Now, six years later, the case had returned to haunt him.

The difference was, this time there were no arguments to be made or heard, not decision to make, only a plea. A simple request for the presence of the Judge that pronounced sentence against a man who had bent the law to his own ends for far too long. The judge had tried to be fair, but he regarded Darrin Morehouse in much the same way as the District Attorney. The man was evil and he deserved to be locked away so far under the prison as to never see the light of day again for as long as he lived.

Which, unfortunately, turned out not to be a very long time.

More was the pity.

Today was turning into one of those rare days where thoughts of retirement started to sounds like good ideas. He had been getting the urge to pull the pin, as his law enforcement brothers referred to retiring. The judge had certainly been eligible for a few years, but he didn't know what to do with himself if he wasn't on the bench. He didn't know how to not work. And now that thoughts of calling it a day entered his thoughts he felt guilty because they had come too late. There was no one left to share his golden years with since the Cancer took his beloved Emily three years earlier.

Judge Hughes Stared at the letter, reading it a third time before tossing it onto the billiard table in his den. Ever since he was a boy, Nathan had wanted a billiard room in his home. His family certainly could not have afforded such a thing and when he joined the service there was no room in the barracks. Once he finally made a decent living to where he could afford it his wife, *God rest her soul*, wouldn't let him. As much as he loved that woman, he converted the den three months after her funeral. This led to some tense arguments with his children and grandchildren, but in the end he got his way.

He was a man accustomed to getting his way, after all.

Only Emily had been able to thwart his plans and now that she was gone he planned to do things his way, no mattered how upset it made his kids.

He poured himself another belt of single malt scotch from the decanter on the bar. It was his fourth since he had first read the letter an hour earlier. A flurry of phone calls followed until he finally found someone who could confirm the news. Warden Francis Chalmers verified that Darrin Morehouse had taken his own life, hung himself by using his bed sheets as a makeshift noose.

A follow up call to District attorney Coombes confirmed another of his suspicions.

"You got one too?"

"Yeah," the tired voice of Michael Coombes sighed into the phone. "I've got a call in to Bartlett. I'm trying to find out if it's legit or somebody's idea of a joke."

"It's legit."

"You're sure?"

"Just got off the horn with Chalmers over at Westmore. He verified everything."

"Damn."

"So what do you think?"

"I don't like it, Your Honor. There's something about this doesn't feel right to me. I mean, do you really think he wants to drag us all the way out there just to get the last word?"

"I don't know. I've heard of some strange last requests in my day," the Judge said with a *harumph* of laughter. "But we are talking about Morehouse so who knows."

"You talked to John yet?"

"No. I tried calling him at the station, but he was out. I don't have his home number."

"I do," Coombes said. "I tried his home and his cell. Straight to voice mail. He's probably on the job. There was something about him on the news today."

"Keep trying. If we got these, I'm sure your buddy Bartlett did too."

"You sound worried, Nathan," Coombes said. It was one of those rare moments where he called his friend by his name instead of Judge or Your Honor.

"You know me, Michael. I never worry."

"Yes, sir. I know."

"Doesn't mean I can't be cautious though."

After exchanging pleasantries, Judge Hughes hung up the phone and returned to the letter lying on the billiard table, propped up against the racked balls. He plucked the letter from its perch and read it once again. Everything appeared on the up and up, but he couldn't help but feel a sense of unease even as he wadded it up into a ball and tossed it toward the trash can next to the bar.

As he broke the balls apart and watched them dance around the table, the feeling remained. And no amount of scotch, not even the high dollar stuff he was drinking, could make the feeling go away.

Not that it stopped him from trying.

CHAPTER 11

Laura Sellars wanted to scream when she read the letter.

Although she no longer worked for the same firm as she had six years earlier, she had been Darrin Morehouse's attorney during his highly publicized criminal trial.

Emphasis on 'had been.'

At the time, she had been a junior partner in the law firm of Johnson, Murdoch, and Lower. The firm had been in service to Mr. Morehouse and his associates for many. She had once noted that her bosses actually appeared to fear for their lives should they lose and Morehouse be sentenced. At the time she thought it was simply her overactive imagination running wild.

She put the thought out of her mind until the senior partners placed this very big trial in her lap. With the wealth of experience at Johnson, Murdoch, and Lower, Laura Sellars was surprised beyond belief that the task of defending such a large client fell to her.

Still, an assignment was an assignment and Laura put her all into the case. It seemed hopeless at first and a small voice kept tapping away at the back of her mind, asking why the more experienced lawyers at the firm were not handling this case. The other attorneys at the firm offered support and she received all the help she asked for at the office. However, when it came to the trial, she was on her own.

Another attorney at Johnson, Murdoch, and Lower, Jacob Danner, sat second chair, but took no opportunity to approach the Jury or the Bench. She quickly realized that he would be of little help to the case, as he never voiced an objection to anything the District Attorney threw at the client. He was barely there, nothing more than seat filler.

Defending Morehouse was a daunting task and she silently feared that she would lose. With the evidence the police had on her client she would be hard pressed to find a jury anywhere that wouldn't convict the man. He was guilty, of that she was reasonably sure. After meeting the man she was to defend, she was obvious to his guilt. Mr. Morehouse made no attempt to deny his crimes. He let her know up front that he would not be going to jail. He said it with such earnestness, such sureness.

The threat was implicitly clear.

She had little doubt that her client was guilty. Unfortunately, her job was to convince twelve seemingly intelligent individuals otherwise. Not an easy task under the best of circumstances, it was going to be even more difficult without the backing of her co-counsel.

If she could win such a difficult case, she thought, then her career would be on the fast track to the top. On the other hand, if she lost, what would happen to her? Would Johnson, Murdoch, and Lower let her go, no longer requiring her services? Would she ever work as a lawyer again?

These thoughts, as well as others like them, filtered through her brain until the first bang of the judge's gavel. At that moment real terror began gnawing at her.

As soon as she stepped into the crowded courtroom, Laura Sellars knew that she was in way over her head. She knew she was good at her job. She knew the case inside and out, backward and forward, and from every conceivable direction the prosecution might attack. She knew how to present a valid defense and how to handle a jury. Unfortunately, she also knew that her client was as dirty as they come and he wasn't doing anything to help his case. Instead of showing contrition in court as she had asked him to do, he sat there with a smug, superior expression on his face. He made no attempt to hide his contempt for the court that held his fate in its hands.

No matter what fancy double talk she used to make this man out to be a hero, she knew deep down that he was a monster. In one of their private chats he leaned in close and in a creepy whisper told her, "if you fuck this up I will ruin you." There was no humor in his voice. He was serious.

Still, she was a professional and did her job. She put her all into the case, passionately pleading for the life of Darrin Morehouse. Her arguments told of a man who loved his community and had devoted his life to the betterment of mankind. With the skill of a master artisan, Laura painted a portrait of a devoted family man with deep seeded roots in the community.

But as good as her arguments were, the District Attorney's were better.

On January 24, 2003, a cold Friday in Atlanta, Georgia, the twelve members of the jury, five men and seven women, in the State of Georgia v. Darrin Morehouse unanimously declared that her client was exactly what she knew him to be. Guilty.

Guilty.

Guilty.

Guilty.

The word rang over and over in her head long after the judge's gavel banged for the last time, calling a close to the proceedings and signaling both Darrin Morehouse and Laura Sellars' fates.

It had been the trial of the year and it could have made her career had she won. With her client on his way to prison, she had lost everything. It was not long afterward that she was summarily *"let go"* by Johnson, Murdoch, and Lower. They had given her reason for termination as one of lack of work within the firm, a politically correct way of saying *"downsizing."* She knew it was utter bullshit, but in a work-for-hire state like Georgia, there was little or nothing she could do about it.

Her former client had told her he would ruin her and as good as his word he had. When Laura fell from grace she fell hard. Although she had hit rock bottom *-through no fault of her own-* it was a long, hard climb back up. To her credit, she handled the situation with professionalism and decorum. She walked out of Johnson, Murdoch, and Lower with her head held high. She refused to give them the satisfaction of seeing her angry, or worse, seeing her cry. There was a better chance of hell freezing over before that happened. Whatever else she had lost, Laura Sellars still had her pride and her self-respect.

It took a good deal of work, but she clawed her way from the bottom of the barrel back toward the top. She took on cases for little to no money, but that really didn't matter to her. At least that's what she told everyone while she secretly clipped coupons, scraped, and scrounged just to get by.

In truth, she had a lot of difficulty adjusting to her new position in life, but her pride would not allow her to admit it publicly. Money was tight and there were weeks when she couldn't afford to buy groceries. It would have been so easy to give in, but she swallowed her pride and forced herself onward, pushed herself harder than ever before. She discovered more strength of will than she had once thought possible.

It was a long hard struggle uphill, but she eventually made it back to a similar position as the one she held before she'd ever heard the name Darrin Morehouse. It was finally all behind her, the whole trial, everything. She had moved on.

She had hoped to never hear the name of Darrin Morehouse again.

Opening her morning mail, all of those old threats welled back to the surface again. For no reason she could fathom, with the exception of sheer terror, Laura Sellars began to shake uncontrollably as she sat on the kitchen floor of her modest apartment, her back pressed against the cabinets. She would sit there for three hours before she could force her body under control. It would take far longer to push away the nagging feeling that was creeping up in her gut.

It was starting all over again.

He had threatened revenge.

It had taken six years, but he was finally coming after her.

And she knew from experience that Darrin Morehouse was a man of his word.

CHAPTER 12

Attorney Philip Jason Hall sat alone in his office.

He had been there for several hours, though everyone else was long gone for the day. As far as he knew, there were no other people in the building, which suited him just fine. He liked the privacy and he found the quiet of an empty office conducive to productive work. Plus, he wasn't what you would call a real *people person*.

Usually he felt that way, but not tonight. He had a strange feeling tonight. Not something he could place a name to, but a nagging tightness in his gut that told him a storm was brewing. He easily dismissed the notion as nonsense. Hall was not one prone to superstitions. He was a lawyer. He dealt in facts, in absolutes. Nothing else mattered.

Which went a long way toward explaining his solitary life. He had no girlfriend, no wife, no kids, no friends, no life outside of his cramped depressed little Midtown office. The closest thing he had to a relationship was the law. He was married to his work. Not that he minded being alone. For the most part he enjoyed the solitude, but there were exceptions. He hated to sit in a restaurant and eat alone. He always believed that people were staring at him, which was probably not the case, but he was never able to shake that feeling no matter how silly it seemed. He also hated going to the movies alone. As a result, he couldn't recall the last time he had stepped foot inside a movie theater. He usually waited for the DVD or On Demand if he even bothered to watch at all.

Hall could count on one hand the number of people with which he had ever been able to spend any lengthy amount of time so being on his own was no big deal. He enjoyed the peace and quiet that came from being on his own.

Still, when the phone rang, disturbing the solitude of his thoughts, he jerked reflexively, startled by the shrill intrusion.

"Hello," he answered quickly. He hoped that the person on the other end of the line wouldn't detect the nervous catch in his voice. "Philip Jason Hall. How can I help you?"

"Mr. Hall," a deep baritone voice growled on the other end of the phone line. He recognized it as belonging to his client's proxy. Hall had only met the man in person once, which was enough for him. The proxy had an air of menace about him that scared Hall. He had stopped by the office the same morning that the envelopes were delivered to him along with the personal items belonging to his client.

The client's associate identified himself as Nick Wilson. From his size and bearing, he reminded Hall of a wrestler playing a military man in a movie. His bearing was coiled as if he were always waiting for trouble to strike. Wilson had waited at the office for the delivery from Westmore Prison and watched as Hall logged the belongings and went over the client's revised instructions. He had made a few last minute notes before the end and had included those in a sealed envelope with his lawyer's name scrawled on it.

Wilson had not said much during that time, but he watched everything. Once he was satisfied that Hall had everything in hand, he left the office.

That was the last time Hall had spoken with the man. The phone call tonight was a surprise.

"Have you completed your task, Mr. Hall?" Wilson asked.

Yes, sir" Hall answered. "All of the envelopes have been delivered as per your employers instructions."

"Good."

"Is there anything else I can do for you, Mr. Wilson?"

"No."

"Very well then. I will meet you in the morning to verify the seating arrangements."

"Of course, Mr. Hall. We will see you at the reading tomorrow. Pleasant dreams."

A click, followed by a buzzing sound and the call was disconnected. Hall slumped back in his chair and exhaled deeply. He was surprised to find himself relieved that the call had ended. Something about Tom Wilson set him on edge. There wasn't one particular thing he could put his finger on, but there was an edge to the man that made him uncomfortable. He was thankful that after tomorrow their business would be concluded and he would not have to deal with the man ever again.

It was late and seeing no reason to remain at the office, the attorney grabbed his briefcase and made his way to the front door of his firm's midtown Atlanta office. He was glad to be leaving before the clean up crews came in for the evening. He found it very difficult to work on his briefs with a vacuum cleaner whining in the outer office or the two of them, a husband and wife team, chattering away in a language he didn't understand. He often wondered if they were talking about him, but dismissed it as a silly notion.

He yawned as he reached his car, a cherry red Mustang convertible. The car he had wanted since he was a teenager and could finally afford. He went out and bought it the day he landed his first whale, what lawyers called wealthy clients when they weren't listening. This particular whale's retainer more than covered the down payment on his midlife crisis mobile.

Tomorrow would be a big day for his firm and for him as an attorney. He decided to pick up some take out food on his way home instead of relaxing at the restaurant. A creature of habit, there were only a few places where he stopped to eat before heading home each evening.

It was a long drive to the estate in Sommersville where the will would be read. He would have to head out early in the morning to get there before the people he had delivered the letters to. He had to have everything prepared before the reading of the will.

Philip Jason Hall hurried home; unaware of the plain brown sedan that followed him every step of the way.

CHAPTER 13

The alarm clock sounded promptly at five a.m.

Benjamin West reflexively tapped the snooze button, returning the apartment once again to blessed silence. The last thing he wanted to do was wake Sarah this early, especially since she usually stayed up until the wee hours working in her studio. She was a great many things, but a morning person was not one of them.

Slowly, Benjamin unfolded Sarah's left arm from across his chest. She grumbled something unintelligible before rolling over and falling quickly back to sleep with her head buried in a pillow. Benjamin slid out of the King Size bed as quietly as he was able, which wasn't nearly quiet enough. He stubbed his toe against the stair railing as he moved from the elevated bedroom loft to the expanse of the apartment below and tried to silence the cursing that followed. The metal stairs were mighty chilly this morning.

It would take time for him to get used to where everything was located. Especially since he didn't have a hand in the decorating. Given a little time he knew he would get comfortable in these sur-roundings, then he would stop bumping into things, provided Sarah could resist the urge to redecorate without telling him. It wouldn't have been the first time she had gotten a wild hair and moved the furniture around while he was out. Once, while he had been on an assignment that kept him out until the wee hours, he came home to their old apartment and fell over the love seat because he wasn't expecting it to be where it was. Thankfully, he hadn't been hurt and they shared a good laugh at his expense. It remained one of Sarah's favorite stories to tell at parties.

He hoped she could control her impulses and not rearrange the furniture again without giving him some kind of heads up, but she could be rather impulsive. That was just one of the many charms he has grown to love about her. Without her impulsiveness they might not have met.

It took Ben nearly ten minutes to find a decent pair of pants out of the boxes yet to be unpacked. Finding a clean shirt proved to be an even tougher challenge, but after much rummaging, he found adequate clothing for his day in the sticks. Then, still trying to be as quiet as possible, Ben moved across his new apartment to the shower.

On his way there he noticed the unfinished painting that Sarah had started the night before. Although her usual taste tended more toward landscapes and fantasy pieces, Sarah had begun a beautiful portrait of herself and Benjamin that she told him she planned to hang over the fireplace in the living room. She had only gotten the heads painted before he finally convinced her to come to bed. Knowing Sarah, she probably would have stayed in her studio all night if he had not intruded on her and reminded her that she was mortal and had to sleep. Reluctantly she agreed and he led her upstairs to the bedroom.

The portrait was beautiful. Sarah was an extremely gifted artist. She could do things with a paintbrush that amazed him no end. Considering his drawing ability peaked at stick figures, Benjamin marveled at the amount of talent his wonderful girlfriend possessed. He made a mental note to tell her how much he liked it after he got back from the reading of the will, but that would be later on tonight. It could wait. He saw no reason to wake her just for that. She needed her rest because she would probably still be hard at work when he arrived home.

He smiled, not fully realizing until that moment how completely happy she made him. Even when she was asleep in another part of the apartment he just felt happy.

It must be love, he told himself.

Or something really, really close.

#

Benjamin West was ready to leave an hour after rolling out of bed.

He mentally patted himself on the back for somehow managing to not wake Sarah from her slumber. Once outside he could make all the noise he wanted.

He had decided to take his motorcycle out of storage and drive it to Morehouse's estate just north of Sommersville, Georgia, which was roughly sixty-five miles away. Benjamin figured it would take at least an hour or so to reach his destination. Plus, he would give himself an extra half an hour for those *"just in case"* moments that happen all too often in this city. Add to that, the fact that Atlanta traffic was well known to be horrendous, especially during the weekday rush hour so he factored in an extra hour. He hated to be late.

West had the Atlanta transportation situation down to a science.

Most times he was even right.

Zipping his windbreaker up as he stepped outside into the brisk morning air, he immediately noticed the black limousine parked across the street from his apartment. The driver was leaning against the front fender smoking a cigarette. From the number of butts lying on the ground near his feet the reporter assumed he had been waiting there a while.

"Mr. West?" the driver asked upon seeing him walk down the steps.

West noted that this man was very well built. He looked more like a bodyguard than a chauffeur. The man was definitely a bodybuilder from the look of him.

"Benjamin West?" the limo driver asked again, adding the first name for clarification.

"Yeah, I'm Ben West," the reporter said carefully. He felt an odd sensation knowing that this man had been waiting for him. The hairs on the back of his neck rose, curious about the man waiting outside his new home. He had not even given his new address to his friends at work yet. How did this guy know where to find him?

"And you are?" West asked.

"Your driver."

"I... don't have a... driver," he said, clearly surprised.

The man shrugged. "You do now, I guess. I'm supposed to drop you and another passenger off at the reading of a will or something."

"Uh huh," West snorted. Suddenly it all made sense. This was another one of Morehouse's games. It had to be. Even dead, that bastard was still pulling their strings. "Who sent you?"

"The attorney handling the will," the driver said as if he were used to being questioned. "I guess it was part of the arrangements, I really don't know. They just pay me to drive. They say go here and pick this guy up, I go there and pick that guy up."

"This attorney you work for, he have a name?"

"I'm sure he does, sir."

Smartass, West thought. Aloud he said, "And that would be...?"

"I'm only paid to drive you and the other person to the estate in Sommersville, sir. I don't know anything beyond that. I wish I could tell you more, but I can't so knock off the twenty questions, okay?"

"Right."

"What if I prefer to take my own car?"

The driver shrugged.

"I guess that's your choice, sir."

"Uh huh." West wasn't convinced.

"I just drive the car," the driver said again as he opened the door, ushering the befuddled reporter into the car. "I do have another guest to pick up, Mr. West. Are you coming or not?"

Reluctantly, the reporter slid in the back seat. He was more curious than worried, but he decided it best not to let his guard down. Unconsciously, he thanked the driver once inside and the door closed even as he said it. The driver quite possibly didn't even hear it.

"Just sit back and enjoy the ride, sir," the driver said as he took his place behind the steering wheel in the front seat.

"Who is the other passenger you have to pick up?" West asked, remembering that the driver had mentioned it before.

"Another person named in the will. A cop, I believe.."

"A cop?" West asked, trying to keep the groan from his voice.

"That's what they tell me, sir."

"Great," the reporter said. "Just great.

The driver smiled thinly, enjoying the younger man's discomfort.

Benjamin West let out a stressed breath.

"It's going to be a long day."

#

Twenty-three minutes later the limousine stopped next to the curb on the side of a small two lane road in a Marietta subdivision.

The driver parked the limo in front of what the reporter guessed was the home of John Bartlett. It was an older house with a carport off to the side and a walk up to the front door. He assumed, based on other houses he had seen that from the front door you could either go upstairs or down. The house was nice, but it was past due for a fresh coat of paint.

Benjamin West had never actually visited the police officer's house before. That probably had something to do with the fact that the two men weren't exactly friends. Truth be told, half the time it was all the two men could do not to slug one another.

Once upon a time, at Sarah's urging he had made a concerted effort to make nice with John Bartlett, but the officer was, well let's just say he was less than receptive to the idea. He chalked it up to the man having something against reporters and moved on.

Now that he was looking at it, the exterior of Bartlett's home seemed to fit its owner's rough exterior. West knew that Bartlett had been married once upon a time. Elizabeth, he thought was her name, but he wasn't certain. He was also aware that their split had not been a pleasant one. Rumor had it that she had left him without a word and that they had not spoken a word to one another since. Her leaving had messed him up pretty bad, West remembered. Bartlett fell apart for a time and he started drinking heavily, which had a negative impact on his job. The reporter remembered hearing stories about how Bartlett came within a hair's breadth of losing his job. Thankfully, with the help of a friend of his named Mac Sperling, he had been able to pull himself back from the brink.

This was early during the Morehouse case and Bartlett and West were nothing more than passing acquaintances at the time. Not that they were exactly close friends now, but there was definitely more familiarity. West thought Bartlett was a pain in the ass, but that didn't mean he didn't like him.

"We're here, sir," the driver said as he killed the ignition.

"You don't say," West quipped.

The driver shot him a nasty look.

Although he rather enjoyed rattling people's cages, especially people with *attitudes --and brother, did this guy have an attitude--* West decided not to press his luck any further than he already had. It was going to be a long enough day as it was and the last thing he needed was more hassles. He didn't relish the idea of spending the majority of the day with Morehouse's people. That was bad enough, but he sure as hell hadn't planned on having to put up with John Bartlett all day either. Although, he had to admit it was nice to have back up just in case things went sideways. And when Morehouse was involved, dead or alive, things had a habit of going sideways very quickly."I'll be right back, sir."

"I'm not going anywhere," West said as he watched the driver step out of the car. He followed the man's lumbering path up the driveway to the front door. There were four concrete steps up to a small porch with an old wooden box full of plants that were long dead. The driver took the steps in two strides. West found something off putting about the driver, but choked it up to his nervousness about the day.

But it wouldn't hurt to keep an eye on the man just in case.

The driver knocked twice and waited at the front door for a few moments. He was about to knock again when the door opened and a bleary-eyed John Bartlett peered out at the man on his porch. Clearly, he had awakened the officer from a deep sleep.

They exchanged a few words and Bartlett waved the driver away. Soon, the driver was standing beside the limo much as he had been when West saw him outside his own apartment. He pulled a pack of cheap cigarettes from his inside pocket and lit one.

"He'll be along in a minute, sir," the driver told the reporter, who had not asked.

"Of course he will," West muttered as he stretched and leaned his head back against the seat. He closed his eyes for a moment, deciding it best to get a little rest before the police officer arrived. On a good day, Barlett was an irritable lout. He could only imagine how grumpy the man could be first thing in the morning.

He closed his eyes, certain it would be the last rest he would get until the business with Darrin Morehouse's will was far behind him, a distant memory best forgotten.

Yes. It would be better when this was over. At least that's what he told himself.

It had to be.

He did not see how it could get any worse.

#

Benjamin West awoke with a start, gasping for air.

"Welcome back to the land of the living," he heard John Bartlett's voice say from somewhere nearby. "I was beginning to think you were going to sleep the whole way."

"Where..." he coughed. "Where are we?" the reporter asked groggily.

Bartlett looked out his window and shrugged.

West could see trees moving past the window in a blur.

"We're roughly ten miles from a small town called Sommersville," the driver said plainly. "We should be at the estate in about twenty minutes or so."

"Great," West said. "Maybe I can get a nap in before we get there."

Bartlett leaned in close to the reporter. "Try to stay awake, huh?" he whispered. "I want you to be alert when we get there."

"Is that concern I hear in your voice, Detective Bartlett?"

"Not likely," Bartlett muttered instead of ignoring the sarcasm. "Look, West, I know we aren't best buddies or anything like that, but we are walking into what could be one hell of a trap."

"Or an ambush."

"Or an ambush," Bartlett agreed. "I would like to go into it awake and alert. Backup wouldn't hurt, but since I don't have any backup you'll have to do."

West rolled his eyes. "You're all heart, John."

"I do what I can."

It's going to be a long day, West thought for the second time that morning.

And the day was only just beginning.

CHAPTER 14

The Channel Ten News Building was a permanent fixture in the Atlanta skyline.

It has been an Atlanta landmark since the early 1960's when Bernard H. Mastin founded the station. Mastin was a self-made millionaire who wanted to be in show business. Mastin bought the facilities for a news division, contracted rights as a local network affiliate, purchased a tower, and began hiring what he hoped would become the best news team in the city.

It took Bernard H. Mastin ten years to achieve that final goal.

After fighting against established news professionals, he was able to give his little news division a fighting chance when he convinced Carter Seagraves to sign on as lead anchor after his contract with CBS ended in 1968. Seagraves' announcement of the move shocked the television news division at CBS. It even garnered a story on the national news. Quite a coup for Mr. Mastin's fledgling little station.

Under Carter Seagraves the news division took flight. An experienced newsman, Seagraves brought twenty years of contacts, experience, tricks of the trade, and simple know how to Channel Ten. The ratings increased exponentially.

There seemed to be no end to the heights that Carter Seagraves would be able to push the eager reporters that served under his tutelage. There was no where to go but up.

Carter Seagraves died on August 28, 1978 at the age of 62 after a long battle with lung cancer. To his credit, Carter Seagraves continued to work until his doctors admitted him to Grady Memorial Hospital. Once that happened, Seagraves friends, relatives, and doctors knew that he did not have much time left.

Three days before his death, Carter Seagraves got the chance to speak one final time on the air to the people of Atlanta and her surrounding communities. This was his chance to say good bye to the city he loved.

Carter Seagraves died content in the knowledge that Channel Ten would continue onward as he had instructed them. They would put the story first. Nothing else mattered. The story was the important aspect to the news.

"Get the fact and get them right," he had said on numerous occasions. That was his legacy to Atlanta's television news.

Today, Carter Seagraves would not recognize the news division. Nor would Bernard H. Mastin, who passed away in 1985 after suffering a fatal heart attack. The news was no longer about just the facts. Today, the reporters had to entertain as well as inform. The anchors were viewed as if they were celebrities. Suddenly, the reporter was more important than the report.

Carter Seagraves would not have approved.

Fabian Alexander, lead anchor for the *Channel Ten Noonday News* was not around in those days. He had never met Mr. Seagraves or Mr. Mastin. He only recognized the names from the large plague in the lobby that paid tribute to these two men. Fabian Alexander was one of the new breed of reporters. He preferred to be called a journalist as opposed to reporter.

Journalist had such a nice flair to it. It made him sound more important than he actually was.

Fabian had rose through the ranks very quickly, partly due to his skills as a journalist, but it was the Darrin Morehouse case that had put him on the map and made him a household name in the Atlanta market. Alexander had been a beat reporter at the time that prominent Atlanta businessman Darrin Morehouse had originally been arrested by Officer John Bartlett. He prided himself on being the first reporter on the scene after receiving an anonymous tip that the police were closing in on their quarry. He never discovered the identity of the tipster although he assumed it was someone on the police department payroll. Having such a high profile arrest captured on film was a big check mark in the win column for the Atlanta PD.It was also a major victory for the Channel Ten News and the start of Fabian Alexander's amazing journey that would elevate him quickly through the rank and file of the televised news division to a place of power and respect in the bureaucracy that was Channel Ten.

Fabian was proud of the job he had done in covering the Morehouse case. It was the first in a series of stepping stones that he would climb on his way to his dream job of lead anchor. The Morehouse case thrust him into that position far sooner than if another reporter had arrived first on the scene.

Fabian Alexander was respected in the community, more or less. More often than not his reports were not as well researched as his producers would like, but Fabian did not worry about it too much. He had a contract. That was the bottom line. He had a stable job.

At least for the next two years.

Then it would be time to renegotiate.

He liked to renegotiate. After all, the people of Atlanta loved him. The General Manager would be a fool to fire a strong presence like Fabian Alexander. At least that's what Fabian told himself on numerous occasions.

No, what Fabian needed was a news story that would remind his viewers and his bosses that he was still the top dog of the televised news division. Something that would remind them that he was still one of the preeminent journalists of his day.

A real journalist.

Research was clearly needed.

Fabian tapped the button on his desk. He heard the faint buzz emanate from the outer office.

"Yes, Mr. Alexander," came the voice of Fabian's assistant, Mrs. Janice Kilpatrick. Janice was a lovely young woman, fresh out of journalism school. She had come to work for Mr. Alexander with such high hopes. She wanted to be an anchor. Boy, was she surprised when the only work she could get with the station was as a secretary. Still, one foot in the door was a good step. A first step. She was a very determined young woman. At least that is what her husband kept telling her.

"Could you come in here for a moment, please?"

She didn't answer, of course. In less than the amount of time it would have taken to speak the words, Janice Kilpatrick was standing in her boss' office, notepad in hand and ready to write.

"Take a seat," he told her. She did so.

"What can I do for you, Mr. Alexander?" she asked.

"I need you to do some research for me."

"Okay," she started.

His gaze stopped her in mid sentence.

"I want to do a big story for the weekend expanded edition. This weekend's show looks a little..." he paused, searching for the right word. "...thin," he finished. "I need a good story to jumpstart the show. Something big."

"Do you have a specific topic in mind?"

"No," he answered. Clearly, the anchor had no desire to do any of the legwork himself. That's what he had an assistant for after all. "I want something with some punch. We need to make sure the people are watching."

"Yes, sir. I'll see what I can dig up." Janice started to stand.

"Thank you, Janice. Do me proud."

"Absolutely," she told him as she walked out of his office. She was the image of perfect professionalism. Until she reached her desk. Then the feeling of dread descended on her as it did every time her boss requested her to "find" a story for him. She would search for hours, sometimes even days, to find a story with the kind of "punch" that Fabian Alexander's reports were known for.

She felt bad at about it at first. He gave her no credit for the stories. The general public probably assumed that he did all the research himself. Her husband told her that she was getting excellent experience in dealing with interviews, article set up, research, and making contacts. He convinced her that this would only help her career down the road. She hoped so, because it seemed more and more like she was doing most of the work while Fabian Alexander simply read her transcript and took all the credit.

Janice slid into her lumpy office chair. Grabbing the mouse with her right hand, Janice Kilpatrick started her research. "Where to begin?" she asked the computer console. She clicked on to the Internet and typed in the subject of her search.

"Let's start simple," she said as she typed out a name.

F-A-B-I-A-N A-L-E-X-A-N-D-E-R

The possibility of revisiting an old segment with an update was always a good place to start. With so many shows under his belt, surely there would be some follow ups that he might consider *big* news. The computer began cycling through a list of web sights that mentioned the reporter's name. Sadly, it was a short list as there were not many.

He had his own web site which featured excerpts from a great American novel that he was trying to complete. It was a five-year work in progress about an ace journalist who uncovers and ultimately stops a government conspiracy. Clearly, the lead character was based on an idealized version of Alexander himself.

From what Janice had read, the writing was *so-so* at best and the story totally unbelievable. Not that she would risk her career by telling him any of that, of course. Considering how infrequently he worked on the novel, she doubted it would ever be finished. The man had no drive to work on the story so it languished. She half expected him to ask her to do research for it as well.

She quickly scanned the site. Nothing of interest peered back at her. With no information on that site, Janice clicked on the Channel Ten site.

There was little information of note on the companies' official site. There were lists of the shows that the station's network affiliates would be airing this week, transcripts of previous broadcasts, biographies of the anchors, field reporters, producers, directors, camera crews, etc. There was also a detailed history of the station. Janice knew there would be little or no new information there.

She clicked over to the Channel Ten secondary site. This one was titled TIP SHEET. She scrolled through a morass of e-mails sent in by various viewers who thought they had a good idea for a segment of the broadcast. The Tip Sheet was always good for a laugh or two. She decided that it couldn't hurt for her to give it a glance.

Most of the bits found on the Tip Sheet tended to be useless as far as the reporting pool was concerned, but the occasional gem somehow always managed to slip between the gossip and rumors that usually filled the site. The Tip Sheet let the viewers feel as if they were a part of the process. Janice guessed it made people feel good to help out.

The amount of information, not to mention misinformation, she discovered would have shocked her if this had been her first time working with the Tip Sheet.

She blew out an exasperated breath. "Damn," she muttered as her left hand reached out for the telephone. Without looking she hit the speed dial for her husband's work number. She would probably have to stay late to work on this research project.

"Atlanta Journal and Constitution," a pleasant computer generated female voice answered. "If you know your party's extension, please enter it now."

She entered extension twenty-one twenty-three.

"Thank you. Please hold as we transfer your call."

A click and the phone went silent as the call transferred. Janice was happy that they got rid of the classical music that used to play whenever she had been put on hold. The silence was less relaxing, but she could concentrate on her computer search while holding.

"This is Brian Kilpatrick," her husband's cheery voice sounded over the phone.

"Hi, sexy," she said.

"Shh..." Brain pleaded. "I've told you repeatedly that my wife would not approve of such language."

"Good answer."

"What's up, baby?" Brian asked. "Anything the matter?"

"No. No, I just got stuck with yet another research project for Mr. You-Know-Who. I may be here for a while. Looks like you get take out again tonight. Sorry."

"Hey, I like take out food."

Yeah, right." She snickered quietly. "Seriously, though, I have to find something for the weekend show."

"Any ideas?"

"No. I'm drawing a complete blank at the moment."

"You try the Tip Sheet?" her husband asked.

"Even as we speak, my love."

"Nothing of interest?"

"Nada. I may have to try this the old fashioned way."

"You mean, you're going to act like a real reporter? That's great."

"It's been known to happen, mister."

"Perhaps you could teach your boss how to do it. I think he's been behind that anchor desk so long that he forgot what it is like to be a real reporter."

"I won't argue that point," she told him.

"You'd lose anyway."

"You wouldn't happen to have any tid-bits you'd like to throw my way, would you, Mr. Kilpatrick?"

"None that I can think of at the moment, Mrs. Kilpatrick."

"I guess there's just nothing exciting going on in the world, huh?"

"Guess not," he agreed.

"What about your buddy, West. He always has a good angle. You think he'd be willing to share?"

"With you, maybe. I'm not so sure he'd be willing to do much for your boss though. There's no love lost there."

"Believe me, I've heard."

"Besides, Ben's not here today. Took a personal day."

"I didn't think you newspaper boys got to take time off. He's not on a story?"

"Not sure, Jan. I don't think so. He went to the reading of a will or something. I think he was named in it or something like that. I didn't think he had any family around here. He was uncharacteristically tight lipped about it, which makes me wonder. You know Ben. It's not like him to stay quiet unless there's a good reason."

"Hmm. There may be something there."

"I doubt it. What could be newsworthy about the reading of a will?" he asked.

"I guess that would depend on whose will it was," she answered.

"I guess it would at that. Of course, if that were the case I'm sure he would have already turned in a budget report for it and I don't remember it being mentioned in the meeting earlier."

"You're probably right. I'm just grasping at straws. I'll keep digging."

"Whoops, I've got to go. Neil just came in. I'll see you at home," he said over the line. She knew that Neil was the city editor and a friend of the family. Since they were on deadline Neil wouldn't have time to chat.

"Bye, Brian. Say hi to Neil for me. Love you."

"Will do. Bye, honey." Janice Kilpatrick hung up the phone as her husband said he loved her too. She was no closer to solving her particular dilemma than she had been moments ago. Still, she couldn't get this strange feeling out of her mind that she had overlooked something. She could feel it gnawing at the corners of her brain, fighting to come to the surface.

"Oh well. It'll come to me sooner or later," she said. "It always does."

She pulled up the Tip Sheet once again and started reading again from the top of the list. Somewhere in that massive mess of half-truths and unsubstantiated rumors had to be a story that would make her boss happy.

All she had to do was find it.

How hard could that be?

CHAPTER 15

The limousine pulled off of Highway 316 onto State Highway 11.

Benjamin West thought he read on a rusted green street sign that Sommersville was two miles away. He was considerably out of his arena. The tiny town of Sommersville, Georgia was small enough to fit inside Atlanta at least twenty times over, if not more. There was a cozy feel to it, he knew, even though he did not share the sentiment. It reminded him of something straight out of a Norman Rockwell painting, but with a few modern additions. He had seen a coffeehouse, although not one of those nationwide chains that seemed to be on every corner near his house, and a Wal-Mart after all so he knew that some form of civilization had taken root in this sleepy little town.

He regretted that they were just passing through, however.

His former writing partner had relocated to Sommersville a few years earlier when he bought the local newspaper and decided to make a go of it. It had been a long time since he had seen Franklin Palmer. It would have been nice to stop in and see how his old buddy was surviving out here in the sticks. Palmer had invited him up for a visit, but West always seemed to find a reason to not make the trip. Had he brought his bike as planned he could have actually popped in and said hello before heading back home after this will nonsense was over.

The fact that he made the trip at the request of a murdering bastard that had tried to kill him instead of his friend's polite invitation was not lost on him. It was enough to give him pause. He vowed to make a return trip in the very near future to see his friend.

"How much further?" the reporter asked the driver.

"Maybe another ten or fifteen miles, sir," he answered in a tone that told the reporter he was getting tired of him asking. "It shouldn't be long now."

"That's what you said half an hour ago," Benjamin West murmured as he slouched back in his seat like an angry child who wasn't getting his way. He crossed his arms on his chest and grimaced.

"Will you relax just a little bit," his companion said, trying not to laugh at the man's childish behavior. "Are you in some kind of hurry or something? We'll get there when we get there."

"Easy for you to say, John."

"Well, I guess I'm just not in as big of a hurry to get there as you are?" Bartlett said, his patience with the younger man almost at its breaking point.

"I don't exactly want to be here," West declared. "I just want to get this over with so I can get on with my life."

"Yeah," Bartlett agreed. "Hassling me for an exclusive story, right?"

"Possibly."

"Look around you, West. You are smack dab in the middle of an exclusive story right now."

"Yeah. So?"

"Do you see any other reporters around here? Do you see Fabian Alexander here?"

West seemed confused by the question.

"Well, do you?"

"What's your point? He's dead. That's not news, John, a reason for joyous celebration maybe, but not news. Now, when we arrested him, that was news."

Bartlett turned, giving the reporter a curious glance, eyebrows raised. "When *we* arrested him?"

"Okay," he conceded. "When *you* arrested him."

"Bullshit."

"What bullshit?"

"No matter how much we wished he wasn't, Morehouse is news.

If someone in your office found out about this don't you think they would be all over it?"

West seemed to be thinking it over.

"You know I'm right."

"Maybe."

"No. Not maybe," Bartlett said. "You're the only reporter here because you're the only reporter with a personal connection to Morehouse. That's the reason you're here. It's the same reason I'm here and you know it."

"That seems a little far fetched, don't you think?"

John Bartlett shook his head and blew out an exasperated breath. "You are an idiot, you know that, West?"

"Sticks and stones, John. Sticks and stones."

"Think about this," the police officer insisted. "Have you seen or heard anything about Morehouse's death aside from the letters we received from the will probate? Anything at all? I haven't heard word one from the TV, radio, or the newspaper. My captain didn't even know about it. Think about it. Aside from the letter that was put in my mailbox by someone other than the Post Office, have you heard so much as a whisper?"

The reporter seemed to think about it for a second. "Now that you mention it, I haven't. I really hadn't paid much attention, but things have been moving rather fast since I got the letter yesterday. I didn't even stop to check the news or the paper to see what the deal was."

"Neither did I, but now that I've had time to think about it, I can't recall seeing anything about it on the news. Now that I think about it, no one called to see if I'd heard the news. The only person I was able to talk to was Francis Chalmers and that was so he could tell me that the Medical Examiner misplaced the body."

"They lost the body?" West asked, unable to hide the surprise in his voice.

"It seems that way," Bartlett admitted with a shrug. "That's sensitive material and off the record, by the way. You keep that to yourself, okay?"

"Are you kidding me?"

"No, but that's beside the point. No reporters have attempted to call me or the station for a reaction to the news or a quote, and you know as well as I do you people would be camped out in front of my house."

"You people?"

"Reporters."

West groaned. "Are you saying it's being kept quiet? I find that hard to believe, John. Do you know how hard it is to keep a secret these days? One little comment on Facebook or Twitter and suddenly the world knows."

"I find it hard to wrap my brain around too. When Morehouse went before the parole board last year the press was all over me for my take on it both before and after the board's decision. Yet, he's been dead for four days and no one's asked any questions. Not. One. Question. Don't you find that just a little bit odd?"

"Well, when you put it like that, yeah, I guess I do," West agreed. "How does something like this stay quiet? I don't think Morehouse is big news anymore, but his croaking is worth a mention, if not on the front page, on the second at the very least. The fact that the body is MIA would've definitely been front page news."

"And don't you find that just a might bit strange, West?"

"A bit, yeah."

"Now I'm no expert but I'd bet it takes quite a bit of doing to pull off a media blackout on this scale, wouldn't you say?"

"If such a thing were possible, and I'm not one hundred percent sure it is, it would take someone with a whole mess of power to pull the right strings to keep this quiet. That adds a few interesting wrinkles to this story. You're right," West said, rubbing his hands together. "Now I'm intrigued."

"So, if you look at it from that perspective, this might be one of those exclusives you reporters like so much."

Benjamin West smiled. "It might be at that."

Bartlett waved his hand as if to make the annoying reporter vanish from the backseat of the car by magic. It didn't work.

"Nice try, Mandrake," West said as he shot his companion an annoyed look.

Bartlett had a feeling it would not be the last of those he received today. "Good," he said. "Maybe this story will be enough to make you people leave me the hell alone."

"Gee, thanks, John," the reporter offered. "But not a chance. You've become too much of a celebrity. It's your own fault for being so damned good at your job."

"Yeah, whatever. Just try to pester someone else with your questions, okay?"

"No promises," the reporter said with a grin. "But I'll see what I can do."

"You do that, West. You do that."

Before the younger man could respond, the limousine turned off of the main road onto a narrow lane road. The small green sign with white letters announced that this was Miller's Chapel Road. After another few minutes on the empty street the car turned again. This time neither man saw a street sign.

They had gone a quarter of a mile down the road before the two men discovered that this was in fact a driveway, not a road. Thick clutches of trees and brush ran along the sides of the curve-filled narrow drive.

"I've seen fewer curves on a ride at Six Flags," West commented.

Despite himself, Bartlett laughed. He doubted that two cars could pass one another on the driveway, which effectively created a bottleneck, especially since cars had to constantly apply the brakes before each curve. Morehouse was always thinking three moves ahead. That was one of the reasons he had been so difficult to catch. Even the design of the estate's driveway was planned out to serve a purpose.

In several sections the trees reached across to the other side, effectively blocking out the sun for long distances. Images of old horror movies crept into John Bartlett's mind. He had hated those old scary movies as a kid. Eventually the limousine cleared the dense foliage and the morning sunlight once more bathed them in its precious warmth. They could see the estate now.

There were trees all around them as well as areas that would have made for good pastures, but neither West nor Bartlett noticed any animals grazing.

"Where's the house?" Bartlett asked.

"Over the next rise, sir." The driver navigated a slight turn and started up a small incline. "There it is, sirs," he said when the house came into view.

"Wow," West said.

His companion couldn't help but agree. "Yeah. That is some house."

"I don't think the word "*house*" does it justice."

The Morehouse estate was situated smack dab in the middle of a nine hundred acre tract of land. Far larger than John had suspected.

John Bartlett and his partners had tried to find this place on several occasions when they had belief that Darrin Morehouse or one of his scumbag cronies was doing something shady at the estate. That was the only name they had for it. In several wiretaps they had heard mention of the estate. They couldn't put a location with it. John soon suspected that there was no such place. Perhaps it was code for some safe house they had in the city.

From the looks of things it had not been a code after all.

The estate house was technically a mansion and was undoubtedly not listed in Morehouse's name or in the name of one of the many dummy corporations Bartlett and his team had uncovered. He had always suspected they had missed one or two dummy businesses, but once Morehouse had been sentenced he had been ordered to move on to the next open case. *Let it go*, he had been told by his superiors through Captain Miller. *There are always more open cases to focus on.*

From the car, John Bartlett was able to count four stories, not even taking into account the basement or the attic. The mansion was made of brick and featured elaborate ironwork as well as detailed carpentry on the roofline and banisters. The place was a fortress, but an immaculate one. He also noticed a guesthouse, boat storage, garage, and greenhouse. All of which were separate from the main house.

The sight of the mansion made John Bartlett hate Darrin Morehouse even more than he already had, if such a thing were even remotely possible. Although he had been taught at an early age not to think ill of the dead, he couldn't help but feel happiness knowing that after today he wouldn't have to deal with Darrin Morehouse's bullshit again.

After today, his game playing days would truly be over.

Or so he thought.

CHAPTER 16

Tom Myers was not a morning person.

He never had been and somehow he suspected he never would be. As far back as his earliest memories, there was a battle every morning when his mother tried to rouse him from sleep. Then, as he got older he took night work while going to school, then college, during the day. By the time he was on his own his disdain for morning was fully ingrained. And now, after years of getting up early, he knew it wouldn't take much to slip back into the routine of sleeping late.

Of course, having a wife who liked to rise with the chickens made sleeping in a rarity, even on his days off. It was a rule of the house. When Mildred was up, everyone was up.

Despite his night owl tendencies, the morning had started out fairly normal with him moving through shaving and showering with his eyes half closed, then breakfast, brushing his teeth, then out the door. Even with the healthy breakfast his wife had cooked for him he was still hungry this morning. Mildred had been on a health and diet kick of late and the first casualty was the normal large breakfast that she had been making for him every morning in the twenty-two years they had been married. Gone were the greasy fried eggs with the edges so crisp they crunched when he bit into them or the bacon that made a similar crunching sound. Toast with butter and jelly were also *verbotten* these days as well. And he knew better than to ask for pancakes again after the lecture he'd gotten a couple weeks before about his blood sugar levels and maple syrup and why he and Mrs. Butterworth were no longer allowed at the same table.

The only morning vice that survived this new health kick was the pot of strong black coffee that greeted him each morning. Cutting out the greasy foods and the fat was one thing, but Tom drew the line at his coffee. He had been ready for all out war on the subject, but thankfully, his wife had not argued the point since neither of them was willing to give up their morning caffeine jolt.

Although he was still hungry after the bran cereal and fruit slices Mildred had called a meal, Tom resisted the urge to stop by *The Kettle* for a little something extra. Though tempting, he knew that, thanks to Amy, word would get back to Mildred and that would just lead to another confrontation he didn't have a snowballs chance in hell of winning.

Besides, I quit smoking, he reasoned. *After that, this should be a piece of cake.*

Amy Doster was the head waitress at The Kettle, Sommerville's locally owned and operated greasy spoon diner. Amy and Mildred had been friends for years. They were in the same book club and had recently started taking Pilate's classes together at the Sommersville Community Center twice a week. Tom knew that they talked often and that it would get back to her if he cheated on his diet. It wasn't that Amy was so much a tattletale than a gossip. She would get word to Mildred that he had gone off his diet, not out of malice, but just to have something to talk about.

In a town as small as Sommersville, a place where everyone knew almost everyone else, gossip has a tendency to spread like wildfire. People who referred to the Internet as *the information super highway* had obviously never ate at The Kettle or met Amy Doster. Not that she was the only one there who liked to gossip. The other ladies who worked the counter were just as bad, if not worse. If you wanted to know anything about whatever was happening in town, The Kettle was the place to go to hear all about it.

As sheriff of the small Northeast Georgia town of Sommersville, Tom Myers headed up a staff of deputies that patrolled the county as well as the town proper. No one that lived there would ever classify

Sommersville as a sleepy little town, but it was more laid back than larger cities like Lawrenceville, Alpharetta, and especially Atlanta. And it was growing. Developers had already broken ground on a shopping plaza at the edge of town and there were rumors of a movie theater coming down the pike. All of these would benefit Sommersville with jobs and tax revenues.

There wasn't much in the way of major crimes in a town like Sommersville, with only two major exceptions.

A case the year before involved a lunatic who went on a killing spree and started knocking off his former schoolmates who were all in town for their ten-year high school reunion. The after incident report read like the plot to a direct to DVD slasher flick, complete with twists and turns that no one involved could have seen coming. With a lot of luck and a little help from an FBI agent who just happened to be in town for personal reasons, the killers were both killed in a showdown at Potter's Ravine, neither willing to be taken alive. During the confrontation, Tom had taken a bullet to the left arm.

He had been lucky.

The bullet was what the doctors referred to as a *through and through*, which basically meant that the bullet went through the skin into his arm and exited through the other side of his arm without tearing any vital organs or muscle. The prognosis was that there would be no permanent damage from the wound and that he would make a full recovery. Physical therapy had been a big help, but the arm still stiffened up from time to time, most often at night while he slept. Doc McNally assured him that this was normal for this type of injury and that it would subside, but probably not completely considering the sheriff's age. The doctor had a habit of working in the phrase "*at your age*" when they talked. It made Tom feel old.

Tom found himself unconsciously massaging the arm with his right hand from time to time out of habit. No one said anything, but Tom was taking great pains to stop himself from this nervous tick. So far he hadn't been as successful at kicking it as he had hoped.

Now that some time had passed several of his deputies, mostly the ones that weren't actually involved, jokingly referred to the incident as the *Showdown at Potter's Ravine*. Tom told them it sounded more like the title of a western than what he and the others went through. With his fondness for movies, Tom thought the title was funny. If he had any writing ability at all, he might have considered writing the story and, like the old TV series said, change the names to protect the guilty as well as the innocent. He had mentioned the story idea to Franklin Palmer, who owned and operated the local newspaper office. Not only was a he a reporter, but he had been working on a novel of his own for a couple years, trying to get it "*just right.*"

Like Myers, Franklin Palmer and his FBI agent brother, Harold, had been involved with the incident at the ravine as well. When Tom had mentioned the book or movie idea to him, he simply said it was a good idea and he would think about it, although he didn't seem overly enthusiastic about revisiting the incident.

Tom knew better than to press so he let the matter drop.

The only other time Sommersville had made the news in such a big way was when the mansion belonging to the suspected killer, Darrin Morehouse, had been raided by the GBI six years earlier. The Georgia Bureau of Investigations had been working in concert with detectives from Atlanta in building a case against the suspected criminal and had searched the mansion. Tom and his deputies had assisted them with the initial serving of the warrant, but afterward the GBI handled everything on their own and Myers and his team were relegated to the role of spectator. Like everyone else in the area, he got his news on what was happening there from the TV.

It was a sunny Tuesday so Tom's rounds were far more enjoyable than normal. Since he lived outside of town, the sheriff's morning commute included a drive through the community and outer areas. He often stopped and talked to some of his neighbors and made sure everything was going well for them. One of his goals was to make the sheriff's department easily accessible to all and to do that he had to get out there and talk to the people. His daily route took him around to various parts of the outlying county.

This included driving past the Morehouse Estate on Miller's Chapel Road.

As suspected, all was more or less quiet.

This morning he noticed that several cars arriving at the Morehouse place, but there was no reason to suspect anything was amiss. As a precaution he called Chris Jackson, one of his deputies, and set up several drive-bys throughout the day just to keep an eye on things. Chris had only returned to duty a month earlier and Tom was trying to ease him back into the day to day activities and thought this would be the perfect assignment for him.

Every hour or so one of the deputies would drive down Miller's Chapel Road in front of the property. They had no cause to go onto the actual property, but showing their presence was never a bad idea, especially considering the kind of people Morehouse had been in business with, if you believed what the TV news had reported.

So far there had been nothing out of the ordinary. If he hadn't noticed the string of limousines pulling into the drive, he wouldn't have known anyone was out at the old Morehouse place since the actual house sat so deep inside the property that you couldn't see it from the road.

Tom would take the same route back home each evening as a capper to his workday. Of course, as sheriff he was on call twenty-four hours a day if he was needed.

None of his deputies had reported anything since the cars had arrived earlier, but he couldn't shake the feeling that something was happening. Call it intuition or a Spidey Sense or just the experience of over twenty years on the job, but something was gnawing at him about the whole thing.

Despite an uneasy feeling, he headed to the office.

CHAPTER 17

"I wonder if this is where all the bodies are buried?" West asked. Bartlett *harrumphed*.

Though said in jest, the reporter was only half joking. Morehouse had a list of enemies - alleged or otherwise - longer than his arm. Not all of them had been as fortunate as both he and Detective Bartlett had been. There was a long list of men and women that had crossed the man and vanished without a trace. The man was responsible for a great many open/unsolved cases.

The limo driver followed the driveway in a loop around the front of the house. He came to a stop at the steps leading up to the front door. Bartlett noticed several other limousines already parked just off the loop. *Probably the other lucky recipients of Darrin Morehouse's unbridled generosity.* He nearly choked on the thought.

The driver opened the door and John stepped out, squinting in the morning sunlight.

Benjamin West didn't wait for the driver. He opened the door himself and stepped out of the limo. He stretched and yawned once he was free of the car's confines.

"You got a signal?" Bartlett asked, holding up the cell for the reporter to see.

He looked at his cell phone and noticed there was no signal. He assumed that was all part of the plan. *The signal is probably being jammed*, he thought. *No way would Morehouse have spent time in this place without a cell phone*. West shook his head.

"Convenient."

"You thinking set up?"

Bartlett looked at him across the roof of the car. "You aren't?"

Now it was West's turn to grunt a response.

A man in a deep gray Armani suit stood at the top of the stairs. He looked more like a bouncer than a door greeter and West immediately didn't trust him. The man waited for the two guests to reach him before welcoming them. "Ah, gentlemen. So glad you could make it," he said. "You are John Bartlett and Benjamin West, I take it?" He asked it like a question, but something told them the man knew exactly who they were.

"I'm John Bartlett," the officer said as he stepped forward. He did not offer his hand. "He's West."

"Howdy."

"You are the last ones to arrive," Armani told them. "The others are waiting in the stateroom." The man opened the front door and escorted the two men inside. "If you'll follow me please."

A look of mock surprise passed between them. They mouthed the word "*Stateroom?*" to one another without uttering a sound.

The man in the Armani walked quickly across the massive open area just inside the front door, obviously uninterested in the dawdling sightseers he was escorting. The two men picked up the pace to keep in step behind him. Bartlett noticed the bulge of a shoulder holster and gun beneath the suit jacket. He wondered if West had noticed as well.

"One hell of a foyer you've got here," West joked.

His attempt at humor fell on deaf ears.

The reporter and the police officer followed their silent guide up a flight of stairs that curved up the wall off to their left. They could not help but be impressed by the immaculate furnishings of the house. Statues and paintings worth more than either man made the year before occupied places of importance on each wall. It was very well decorated for a house whose owner has been in prison for the past five years. West knew that Sarah would love to get her hands on some of the art he was seeing.

"And very clean," Bartlett noticed. "Morehouse sure knew how to live didn't he?" he said aloud.

"You kidding," West answered. "My apartment could fit in the foyer."

"Just imagine," Bartlett continued as if the younger man had not even spoken. "I would guess that all of this…" he gestured to his surroundings. "This stuff is worth a small fortune. That sound about right to you?"

"Sounds reasonable."

The officer sensed that their guide was about to say something, but then decided against it. He continued as if he hadn't noticed. "I figure Morehouse probably killed… oh I don't know, maybe ten people for every piece of garbage in this place. That sound about right to you?"

"Again, reasonable."

"So glad you approve, Mr. West."

The reporter shrugged.

"What can I say? Morehouse might have been a walking, talking piece of shit, but he sure knew how to live." He paused, a smile tugged at the corner of his lips. "At least until last weekend."

Bartlett thought their guide was going to explode. Benjamin West had that kind of effect on people. Bartlett found himself enjoying watching the reporter in action when he wasn't on the receiving end of it. For the first time since they met, he appreciated West's skill. He was a talker and a damned good one.

Still, the man he had come to think of as *Armani* kept his composure and said nothing. He kept a professional air about him for the duration of West's monologue. Their host's attitude put Bartlett more on guard, if such a thing were possible. This was not a man accustomed to playing tour guide for a rich criminal.

When they reached a doorway just left of the top of the stairs their guide spoke. "In here," he said as he pushed open the heavy oak door.

John Bartlett stepped into the room.

Benjamin West followed three steps behind.

Once inside both men seemed to relax a bit. They were no longer alone with strangers. The room was filled with faces they recognized. Some where friends, while some others were not so friendly. Others were a complete surprise.

The man in the Armani suit closed the door behind them and Bartlett immediately noticed that their guide had not followed them inside the plush stateroom. He started to ask after the man when another stranger stood from his seat and walked to the head of the room. This man's bearing was more composed than the Armani wearing bodyguard. He guessed this one was a lawyer.

"Welcome gentlemen. Please have a seat and we can get started," the man said.

"And you are?" West asked even though he also presumed him to be a lawyer.

The man stopped in front of the ornate, hand carved fireplace. There was a full size television set mounted to the wall where the man had just passed. *A fifty-two inch plasma from the looks of it*, West thought enviously. *One of those would great in the new loft*. He made a mental note to take Sarah shopping when this was all over.

The man ignored the reporter. He draped his hands behind his back and introduced himself. "My name is Philip Jason Hall. I am the attorney for the estate of the late Darrin Morehouse," he said, his voice was a dull monotone that did not change tempo. West took an instant dislike to him.

"Oh," the reporter said as he took a seat where a placard with his name was located.

"On behalf of my client, thank you all for coming," Hall continued as if the reporter hadn't spoken.

To West's left was Laura Sellars. On his right, at the end of the rectangular table was John Bartlett. Bartlett and Sellars, who most often found themselves on opposite sides in court, nodded a polite greeting. On the other side of Bartlett, across from Ben, sat Warden Francis Chalmers. John and the warden shook hands and whispered a hushed greeting, which seemed to annoy the deceased's attorney, no end. He looked as if he would rather have been anywhere but inside the Morehouse mansion and West had a mental image of his pinched face cracking.

Next to the warden sat Vivian Morehouse, the grieving widow. Well, maybe in some alternate reality she would be grieving, but Benjamin doubted that anyone in this room was sorry that the man was no longer around to cause trouble.

Judge Nathan Hughes sat at the far corner next to the former Mrs. Morehouse. He looked tired. West wondered if the man had gotten any sleep at all. Or was it his health? The Judge wasn't getting any younger. It was probably difficult for a man his age to continue smoking two packs of cigarettes a day. He was glad that Sarah had been able to convince him to stop smoking. Those things were killers.

West finally noticed the District Attorney, Michael Coombes seated on Laura Sellars' left. They filled in the seats around the table. The head of the table was reserved for the will lawyer, Philip Jason Hall.

He knew that everyone in the room was connected in some way with Darrin Morehouse's fall from grace, as it were. He was rather surprised that Fabian Alexander had not been invited to the reading. Fabian had built his career from Morehouse's trial. Maybe that was enough of a reward for the man. Far more than he deserved in West's mind. The Channel Ten Anchorman was not of his favorite people in the world.

"I would like to thank you all for coming," the lawyer began. "I understand that many of you were surprised to find yourselves included in my client's will. I have heard from a few of you enough to know that many of you were shocked at that particular revelation."

"That's putting it mildly," West muttered. Laura Sellars turned to give the reporter a threatening glance. For a change, he took the hint and fell silent. *Great. Now I'm getting it from both sides.*

First time for everything, Bartlett thought at the sight of their exchange. The police officer kept his opinion to himself, lest Miss Sellars turn her scorn his way.

"Uh, yes," the attorney said. "If the gentleman is quite through we can begin."

"He's through," Judge Hughes said, also giving West a hardened look.

The others around the table nodded their agreement. None of them really wanted to be there and the reporter's comments were only slowing things down. They all wanted to get it over with and get back to their lives as quickly as possible.

West let out a soft groan that reminded Bartlett of the sound his young nephew used to make when he was in trouble. Reluctantly, he kept that particular comment to himself as he saw no need to further disrupt the proceedings by getting West riled up. Once he started on a rant there was no slowing him down. It was best to keep things moving so they could get this over with and get the hell out of there.

The lawyer stood at the head of the table. "As I stated earlier, my name is Philip Jason Hall. I have been assigned the duty of carrying out the final wishes of my client, Mr. Darrin Morehouse. I believe that all of you here are familiar with him."

Simultaneously, Laura Sellars and John Bartlett turned to give West a stern look.

Surprisingly, the reporter said nothing.

What do you know, Bartlett thought. *He's trainable.* Again, he kept this thought to himself. Best not to stir up any more trouble than they already had.

The lawyer continued, oblivious to those seated around the large, ornate wood table. "My client, the late Mr. Morehouse left strict instructions pertaining to the disposition of his last will and testament. The seven of you are the sole recipients named in the will."

"Why?" Judge Hughes asked. His voice was laced with a certain spark that had sent many an attorney cowering from the bench, but Mr. Hall did not flinch. Perhaps he had never had the privilege to stand before the honorable Judges Nathan Hughes in the courtroom. Or he just refused to let himself be intimidated by the judge's reputation.

Whichever the case may have been, Philip Jason Hall was in charge of the room and he knew it. "Mr. Morehouse's reasons were his own, I assure you, Mr... uh… Hughes, is it?"

"That's *Judge Hughes* to you, Mr. Hall. Or Your Honor." The Judge's smile was sinister and seemed out of place on his face. To those who had never stood before him in court, Nathan Hughes looked like a kindly old man. Those who knew the man were painfully aware of just how ornery the man could be, especially if you crossed him the wrong way. "I'm flexible," he said in a tone that dared the lawyer to push his luck further.

Hall moved on without acknowledging the Judge's comments, but a good deal of color had drained from his face. The Judge's point had been made.

"As you are aware, a person can name anyone in his will that he sees fit," the lawyer offered by way of explanation. "For reasons that I have not been privy to, Darrin Morehouse named all of you as heirs to his estate, save for some long standing charitable contributions. My client was a well respected pillar of the community, after all."

There were selective coughs and gurgled noises from around the table.

Judge Hughes was not convinced, but he let the matter drop. "Whatever," he finally decided. They could debate things later. At the moment everyone was interested in just getting it over with.

The attorney started. "I have a list of Mr. Morehouse's belongings. It is a very selective list, but he has been more than fair to each and every one of you if I may say so."

There were exchanged stares all around the table.

"And what if I don't want anything from that bastard?"

"Mr. West, I assure you that you do not have to accept any of Mr. Morehouse's charity. Anyone that wishes to pass on their inheritance can sign any particular items over to me and I will them dispense them to one of Mr. Morehouse's favorite charities as stipulated in his will."

"Toys for killers," West quipped. No one moved to stop him this time.

"I assure you that is not the case, Mr. West. You may feel free to supervise the transfer of funds to whichever charity I choose to forward them to from the approved list to verify everything is on the up and up if you wish. I promise you that everything here today has been handled diligently and within the letter of the law."

"Oh, well I guess that's a different story then, huh?"

"It is nothing less than fair, Mr. West. For each and every one of you."

"If you say so," Michael Coombes added, but remained unconvinced.

"Why don't we just get on with it?" Vivian Morehouse insisted. "I just want to get this over with and behind me once and for all."

"I second that motion," Bartlett added. "If we can allow Mr. Hall to finish..."

Before the officer concluded his thought, the attorney lifted a small remote control box from beside the television set. "Thank you, Mr. Bartlett," he said with a nod.

The attorney held up the box for everyone to see, giving it a light shake in his hand. There was a rattle from inside that sounded like a broken piece of plastic was bouncing around inside. "Anyway," he continued. "We can go into all of the details in a few moments."

The lights dimmed.

"But first, Mr. Morehouse would like to have a few words with you."

CHAPTER 18

The phone rang.

Sarah Park huffed at the interruption. "It never fails," she muttered as she reached for the cell phone that lay on the rolling microwave cart that held her painting supplies. "Never rings until I'm in the middle of something," she groused.

Her first reaction was to let it go straight to voice mail, but it might be Ben calling. He had not seemed overly pleased to be going on his little trip to the country with his cop friend and she was expecting him to call in sooner or later. They had decided not to set up a landline in the new apartment since they were both constantly on the go and both had cell phones with them all the time. So far she hadn't regretted the decision although it felt strange not having a phone hanging in the kitchen like had been hanging in her parent's house when she was a child.

She picked up her iphone and pressed the TALK button without checking the caller ID screen and placed it in the crook of her shoulder so she could keep working while she talked. "Hello?"

"Hi, Sarah. This is Janice Kilpatrick."

"Hi, Janice," Sarah said pleasantly. Janice and Brian had been friends with Ben long before Sarah had met him. They were a warm and friendly couple and the four of them often went on double dates together.

"Is Ben around? Can I speak with him please?"

"I'm sorry, but Ben's out for the day."

"Darn. Do you know when he'll be back?"

"I'm afraid not. He had to go out of town. Did you try him on his cell?"

"I did, but it went straight to voicemail. I thought maybe I'd get lucky and catch him at home."

"I wish," Sarah said with a laugh. "It would be nice to have him hear to help unpack some of this stuff."

"Men," Janice said sympathetically. "Brian's the same way. He has this uncanny ability to get home five minutes after I finish cleaning. Sometimes I wonder if he's got the house bugged or something so he knows when I'm done."

Sarah laughed. "Ben too. Maybe they're in cahoots. Look, I don't expect him back until late tonight at the earliest. He does have his cell with him, but said he'll probably have it turned off for the next few hours. Is there a message you would like me to leave for him if he calls to check in?"

"Not really. I was just doing some research on an old case of his and I needed a little more information. You know... deadlines. Nothing major. I guess I can get it from him later."

Sarah sat down her paintbrush on her workbench and turned her full attention to the telephone and Janice Kilpatrick. "What case?" she asked.

"Oh," Janice said as if caught off guard. "I'm looking into an old case. Something he and John Bartlett were working on."

"The Morehouse case?"

"Yes. I believe that was it," Janice said. She was surprised that Sarah had figured it out. Morehouse might have been the most high profile thing Ben West and John Bartlett had been involved with, but it wasn't the only time their paths crossed. "I needed a follow up on Morehouse for one of those *A Look Back* segments my boss loves to trot out."

"You may be a little late, Janice."

"Late?" Janice drew in a deep breath and felt her heart stop in her throat. "What's happened? Where exactly is Ben anyway?"

Sarah sighed. If it had been someone other than Janice, who had been a friend of Ben's for years, Sarah would have played dumb. But she was aware that Ben had trusted Janice with details from his cases from time to time and she had done the same with him. Ben had said several time that if the newspaper business wasn't in such dire straits these days he would have tried to get her a job at the paper with him. Sarah had no doubt that he would undoubtedly fill her in on the details when he got back from the reading of the will.

"Sarah?"

"Oh. Sorry," Sarah said as she realized that her thoughts had drifted from Janice Kilpatrick and their telephone conversation. "Sorry. My mind wandered there for a minute."

"That's okay. You were telling me where Ben went," she prodded.

"I'm not sure exactly where he went. To some estate out in the country, I think he said. He went to the reading of a will. He didn't want me along from some reason so I can't give you any specifics. Sorry."

"And John Bartlett went there with him?"

"I think so," Sarah said. "They both worked on the Morehouse case a few years back. Maybe you can find out from the police if Bartlett went. Maybe they will have a location."

"Maybe," Janice agreed although she had already made the call to the Atlanta Police Department. Bartlett's boss, Captain Miller would not comment on Bartlett's current location or assignment. Miller had stonewalled every question she had asked. He probably wouldn't have confirmed or denied that an officer named John Bartlett worked for the Atlanta Police Department at the rate he was going. He wouldn't even confirm that Morehouse was indeed the one that died. Her *fishing expedition* with Sarah all but convinced her though.

Darrin Morehouse was dead and Bartlett and Benjamin West had gone to the reading of their greatest enemy's will. If she couldn't find a compelling story in that then it might be time to consider a career change.

"Sorry I couldn't be of more help, Janice."

"That's okay, Sarah. You've been a great help," she said. "I'll keep trying his cell."

"I'll let him know you called when I talk to him in case you don't connect before then."

"Sounds like a plan," Janice said. "I'll talk to you guys later.

Brian and I want to come by and see how you guys have your new place set up. Maybe we can grab dinner one night this week?"

"Sure," Sarah agreed. I'd like that. This place is great." She smiled and took in the open space around her. "And the room. Oh man, I love it."

"Now all you have to do is get the big idiot to marry you," Janice added.

"Oh, that's all I have to do," Sarah said with a chuckle. "I've been working on that for a couple of years now, but you know how stubborn that boy can be."

"He's a tough cookie to break," Janice agreed with a laugh.

"But he'll crumble. I hope."

"Me too. Look, I have to go. I'll talk to you later, Sarah. Tell Ben I'll call him sometime later and we'll figure out what night's a good one to stop by for a visit."

"Sounds like a plan. Take care of yourself, Janice. I'll talk to you in a couple days."

"I will. Bye."

"Be seeing you. Bye."

Sarah clicked off the telephone and dropped it back onto the supply table. She had allowed Ben to convince her that there was nothing to worry about with this Morehouse business. She wanted desperately to believe him, but there had been a lingering doubt in the recesses of her mind. It wouldn't be the first time he had left out details about his job because he didn't want her to worry.

Janice's inquiry had sparked those fears again. Sarah could not place what her exact fear was, but she could not discount those feelings either. All she could do was wait. Ben would be home tonight and everything would be all right with the world, as it should be.

She nearly had herself convinced.

Almost.

Sarah sat and stared at her half-finished painting for an hour before she felt secure enough to pick up the paintbrush again. She just couldn't get that bad feeling out of her mind and she knew that it would not go away anytime soon. No, this bad feeling would haunt her until Ben returned home.

Then everything would be all right.

CHAPTER 19

Philip Jason Hall motioned to the television set mounted to the wall.

Immediately all eyes focused on it and the little black box the attorney held in his right hand.

"A DVD?" Laura Sellars asked. She did not seem as surprised by the fact as some of the others at the table, which made sense. Once upon a time she had been Morehouse's lawyer so she had a unique perspective on the man and his methods.

"If this turns out to be a porn flick-- or worse yet, a Will Ferrell movie-- I'm going to have to hurt someone," Benjamin West joked, trying to lighten the mood of the room. The tension was so thick he felt like he could have cut it with a plastic butter knife.

"West!" John Bartlett said sternly. As usual, the detective's sense of humor was missing in action. "Quiet."

West shrugged. "I mean, that is Morehouse's style isn't it? Dragging us all the way out here to the middle of nowhere just to screw with us is exactly the kind of trick I'd expect from that bastard. This is probably his idea of a sick joke."

"I assure you that this is no joking matter, Mr. West," Mr. Hall, the attorney for the deceased, said as he popped the disc into the DVD mounted on a shelf below the television set. "Before we begin there are certain ground rules that were laid down by my client. This DVD is to be viewed once and only once, then it is to be destroyed. We will not rewind for any reason whatsoever. It is his request that this be viewed only this one time and I plan to see that my client's wishes are observed. Is that understood?" He waited, not saying another word until they were certain that they understood his client's position.

"Are you serious?" Vivian Morehouse asked.

"Those are my client's wishes, Mrs. Morehouse," the attorney said. "It is my duty to see that those wishes are carried out to the letter."

"I just bet you're a hit at parties," West remarked.

Ignoring the comments of the reporter, the attorney removed the remote control from his jacket pocket and pointed it to the DVD player. He pressed the play button. "As we shall now see."

The screen flickered as it found focus. On the screen sat an exquisite desk, framed with untarnished wood and antique lamps. It looked like the office of a dignitary or a lavish entrepreneur. A large bay window featured a beautiful view of a wooded area. It seemed peaceful and serene.

"That's here," West said. "This was filmed in this house."

"Yes," Vivian Morehouse agreed. "That looks like Darrin's study on the third floor."

The camera shook as it was adjusted by unseen hands. Seconds later a man moved in front of the camera as he slowly walked around the desk from the front to the rear. The man took a seat at the desk. He was sitting in a very plush leather executive's chair with a high back.

"Morehouse," Bartlett whispered between gritted teeth as the man came into view on the screen.

The man on the television screen acted as though he did not notice the camera at first. He opened a hand cared wooden box on the desk and selected a nice cigar for himself. Slowly he clipped the end and lit the cigar, exhaling a thick plume of smoke, but never once looking in the direction of the camera.

"What is this?" Warden Chalmers asked. He had been silent long enough and his frustration was starting to show.

Suddenly, the man on the screen turned to look at them, or rather at the camera that had recorded these events. To those seated around the massive table it looked and felt as if man were looking directly at them, as if he were only now noticing their presence for the first time. He cocked his head from one side to the other as if trying to figure out what it was he was looking at.

The image of Darrin Morehouse puffed on the offensive cigar and let a small smile play across his lips after a few seconds of pretending he didn't know the camera was there recording him. He was enjoying himself as he addressed his captive audience.

Just another game.

"Greetings," Morehouse said pleasantly.

John Bartlett was on his feet in a shot. "When was this made?" he demanded of the lawyer. "When was this tape made, Mr. Hall?"

Hall pressed a button and the image froze in mid puff for an instant until the screen returned to the full blue screen image with the word **STOP** in white letters in the upper left corner. "I have no knowledge of the exact date that my client recorded his will, Mr. Bartlett."

"That's awfully convenient."

"How so?"

"Your client has been in prison for the past six years. He died in prison." He pointed at the television set. "Are you telling me that this was made six or more years ago? I don't buy it."

"Neither do I," Francis Chalmers added.

"I do not know what answers you seek," the attorney said. "My job has been to deliver my client's final thoughts to you in the manner he dictated. I was not present when Mr. Morehouse recorded his will and I have not yet seen it myself as per my client's express written condition. I do not know any more about the contents of this DVD than you do."

"How long have you had this disc in your possession?"

"It was delivered to me two days ago, Mr. Hughes."

"Delivered by whom?" Laura Sellars piped in.

"By messenger."

"I see," Bartlett said as he rubbed his chin. He was beginning to like this less and less with every word the attorney uttered. Because this involved Morehouse, his guard was already raised, but he wasn't about to let anything slip by him.

"You know, it is possible he recorded this before he was sentenced," Michael Coombes said. "John, you know better than anyone that this guy was always thinking four or five moves ahead. You told me as much yourself."

"True," Bartlett admitted. "Still, this is a bit much, even for More-house.

"You think so?" West said skeptically. "I think this sounds just like him. Before he was arrested he hadn't had any connection with the judge or the warden. And since they're here…" his voice trailed off, letting the meaning behind his words sink in."

Bartlett opened his mouth to respond, but the lawyer interrupted before he could say anything. "If we could please continue," he said. Hall was beginning to allow these people to annoy him. They all had questions that he had no answers for, but he would be damned if he was going to let any of them disrupt his client's final wishes.

Reluctantly, Bartlett returned to his seat.

When there were no objections to the attorney's suggestion, he pressed the play button on the remote before returning it to his jacket pocket.

"As I was saying," the deceased's image said as if he had been expecting the delay. Morehouse had been a planner so it was entirely possible that he anticipated the interruption from the group. Certainly, he knew the players. He had gone up against them all at one time or another.

"Greetings one and all," Morehouse said with gusto. He had control of the room and he relished it. The man liked to be in control. "I assume that there has been a rigorous little debate over when and how I had time to make this little video from my home here."

He made a swirling gesture with his hands to take in the expanse of the study. It was a beautiful room, very extravagant. Morehouse's image looked over to the side of the room where Warden Chalmers and Judge Hughes sat.

"I assume that this revelation might have a profound effect on Warden Chalmers," he said with a sneer and a puff on his cigar. "Wouldn't you say so, Frankie?"

Bartlett noticed Chalmers flinch, but he kept his composure. At least now he understood the seating arrangement. They were like pieces on a chessboard. He suspected that Morehouse's little video was going to single each one of them out one by one. All part of the game.

"You are probably wondering right about now whether or not I managed to escape from the hospitality of your quaint little prison to record these, my final thoughts. Are these questions filling your mind right about now, Francis? Oh come now, you and I both know that they are. You are as inept as ever..."

Francis Chalmers got to his feet quickly, his composure gone. "Damn you!" he screamed at the television screen. The image of Darrin Morehouse leaned back in his seat and puffed on his cigar. It almost looked as if he was watching the warden's sudden outburst. Or expecting it. He knew each of them so well that predicting thir responses wouldn't be all that difficult. Score one for the villain.

Bartlett put a reassuring hand on the older man's shoulder. "Easy, Francis," he said. "Easy. He is just trying to rattle you. Come on. Sit down. It's all part of his game. Don't take the bait."

Before the warden was completely back in his seat Darrin Morehouse leaned forward to face the camera again. Thick smoke clung around his head from the cigar.

"Hit a nerve did I, Frankie boy?"

Once again, Bartlett placed a hand in front of the warden, keeping him in his seat.

"Of course I did," the image of Darrin Morehouse began again seconds later. "We both know that I have..." his voice trailed off. "Excuse me, *had* more power in your prison than you ever did. Now that I'm dead, I suppose you can start running the place again. I'm sure your chief of security won't like it since I paid him more than you did, but these things happen. We can't all live forever, right Judge?"

The image of Darrin Morehouse turned to stare down Judge Nathan Hughes. The older man did not flinch under the gaze of the deceased lunatic.

"What does that mean?" he said as he looked at the others to see their reactions to the man's comments.

The image of Darrin Morehouse did not respond. He simply stared at the judge's assigned seat.

Everyone around the table let out a single burst of laughter at the judge's blank expression. Score one for the judge. He hadn't taken the bait. Apparently, Morehouse had not anticipated the responses of everyone as well as he might have thought.

Or had he.

"It wasn't that funny," Morehouse said on the television screen before the laughter died down.

Then, as soon as the words left his mouth, there was silence in the room, save from a small giggle that rang from the television monitor.

Darrin Morehouse was playing them all like a well-oiled machine. He was in his element. Plus, he had six years worth of preparation before arriving at this moment. John Bartlett, Benjamin West, and the others were now on his playing field and playing by his rules. The only thing that worried Bartlett was that they did not know what the rules were or whether or not Morehouse would change them in the middle of the game.

With a maniac like Darrin Morehouse making up the rules as he went along, there was no way he could even hazard a guess as to what might happen next.

"Now," the image of Morehouse said. "I have called you all here today to my lovely home away from prison to bestow upon you the collected sum of my wisdom, generosity, and kindness."

West let out a half cough half laugh. The others just gave him a look.

"I, the honorable Darrin Morehouse, being of sound mind and body do hereby bequeath the following...."

"Here we go," Bartlett muttered as he straightened in his seat. *Be ready for anything,* he told to himself.

The image of Darrin Morehouse scratched at his chin. "On second thought," he said. "Why don't we just come back to that later. Since I have all of you here in one room... a captive audience, so to speak. God, I love irony. Anyway, I would like to take a moment and say a few things to each and every one of you before I bestow my good fortunes upon you. Kind of like my parting thoughts."

Gasps of astonishment escaped from a few of the people seated around the table.

"Let us start with my lovely wife. *Hmmm...* I guess you are technically my ex-wife now, but why split hairs. My darling, Vivian, we spent so many years together and I loved you more than..."

He paused as if to choose his next words carefully.

"Well, lets not go into all that just yet," he said with a villainous smirk. "I just want you to know how much it hurt me when you decided to testify against me at my trial. You have no idea how it felt to have a knife twisted in your heart like that. Especially to have it twisted by the one person in the world that you would never have suspected. I was, shall we say less than happy that you would do that to me, Vivian."

Bartlett looked at the former Mrs. Morehouse. She had begun to physically shake and a single tear rolled down her cheek. He had always wondered if she was in any way complicit in her husband's illegal activities. As part of the investigation he dug into her life, but couldn't find anything that tied her to her husband's dealings. He had trouble buying it because there was always something a little off about her, but there was no evidence to back up his gut feeling.

Vivian looked as if she wanted to speak, to cry out, but no words formed. Perhaps he had been wrong. The detective no longer suspected her and seeing her reaction to the video only compounded that belief. Vivian Morehouse didn't strike him as being that good of an actor that she could fake the nervous breakdown she seemed on the verge of having.

Bartlett could only guess what turmoil was happening inside her mind, but there was nothing he could do for her. He turned his attention once again to the monitor and the image of his most hated enemy.

"However, dear Vivian," her ex-husband continued. "I do not hold a grudge--"

"Yeah, right," West said. He made no attempt to hide his contempt.

"--against you anymore. In fact, there are days when I almost forget that you even existed." He shifted in his chair and took a long draw off of his cigar. He let the smoke billow forth and cloud around his face. "But you were a large part of my life at one time," he continued. "I cannot forget about you now like you did about me. I will not have secrets from you as you did from me. I sincerely hope that you are as prosperous in life as you have always wanted to be. To help you with your goal to be wealthy beyond your means I leave you a substantial sum of money for your very own use."

"Wha...?" she managed to stutter.

"Of course, this money is for use however you see fit, Vivian," Morehouse said as he puffed again on the offensive cigar.

"For me?" she squeaked.

"Provided," he continued. "That you always remember from where this money came. You must always remember that it came from me. You'll have to live with how I came about earning this money. Can you live with yourself day in and day out knowing that the very money that sustains you came from me? You once told me that you could not abide by how I did my business. A business you wanted no part of, if I recall your testimony correctly. Does that still apply,

Vivian. Or are you willing to cleanse yourself of your newfound conscience and take what I have offered you?"

All eyes in the room were on Vivian Morehouse, those of her former husband's on the television screen as well. There was an internal struggle within her and the signs were evident on her tortured face. Morehouse was playing her conscience against her lifestyle. It would be a toss up to see which side would win out in the end.

"If you can live with my conditions Vivian, my attorney will discuss the sum with you shortly and it will be wired to your private account. You know the one I'm talking about."

A pause as Darrin Morehouse smiled a toothy smile for the camera.

"He will also detail the conditions I mentioned."

Bartlett thought Vivian was going to explode. She finally broke down and cried. She could no longer stand the verbal abuse of her late husband. He started to stand and tell the attorney that enough was enough when the image of Darrin Morehouse turned toward another at the table.

"Ah, Mr. District Attorney Coombes. How nice it is to have you with us here today. I understand that you are probably a very busy man. There are all of those nasty criminals to put away and the like. Just like me," he said as he tapped himself on the chest. The man was obviously very proud of himself.

Michael Coombes said nothing. He stared point blank at the smiling visage, but tried to act calm. John knew it was an act. He could tell these things. It was probably obvious to the others around the table as well. The police officer wondered what type of game Morehouse had planned for the district attorney that prosecuted him.

"Do you like your job, Mr. Coombes?"

"Of course I..." Michael caught himself before he could finish. He had no intention of playing into Morehouse's game, whatever it might be.

Morehouse continued, "Of course you do. It must be very satisfying to be a protector of the innocent and punisher of the wicked. Your mother must be very proud of you. I know I would be if you were my son."

The DA still said nothing. He was resisting the urge to yell at the image as was probably what Morehouse had intended. The man had obviously studied each of them very closely. He was using clinical psychology against them and one by one the pawns were falling into place exactly where and how Darrin Morehouse wanted them to. The only question was *why?*

"I have afforded my attorney a check to help fund your political aspirations. I know that you have held an interest in running for a higher political office for some time, maybe even becoming Governor one day. I want to help you make those dreams a reality. I am willing to furnish you with a campaign staff and all the materials you could ever possibly need to run a successful campaign and crush your opposition."

Michael Coombes coughed once, then adjusted his tie. That was his tell. In court, he tended to fidget with his tie when things were not going his way. It was an unconscious tick he was trying hard to stop. He let out a breath.

"As with Vivian's inheritance, there is a catch. You too would have to know that I funded your political career. You would owe everything to me, if only in part. And of course, you would always have to wonder whether or not someone working under my orders would be buying your election for you. You see, Michael..."

Morehouse's image leaned in close to the camera.

"May I call you Michael?" he asked, but continued without waiting for the man's reply. "Anyway, Michael, it's like this, my influence reaches far and wide. Some of the people that work for me probably don't even know it. No matter what you accomplish, whether on your own or with aid from others, that small sliver of doubt will always be there. Did I do it? Did you do it on your own? Who can you trust? Those are the questions that will haunt your dreams nightly. You will never know when or where or how someone under my instructions will knock at your door."

The DA allowed his head to drop. Just like Morehouse's ex, he too was now dealing with a question that had no simple answer.

"You just never know," Morehouse reiterated.

Underneath his calm demeanor, Michael Coombes was seething. How dare this... this... man do this to him-- to him of all people. He knew that the man on the recording was only trying to taunt him, to make him suffer. Wanted to make all of them suffer, but Coombes refused to become a pawn in the madman's game.

"But we shall wait a little longer for your answer, Mister District Attorney," the image that was Darrin Morehouse said as he sat back comfortably in his chair. "Let's see. Who's next on the list. Ah, yes, the honorable Judge Nathan Hughes. Who would ever have suspected that you, of all people, would outlive me? Ha! Now isn't that a laugh riot, you old coot?"

The room stayed silent.

"Ah, come now," Morehouse continued. "Can't you see the humor in that? You people are pathetic. Why so dour? You've all won. I'm the one that's dead. Remember? You win. I'm gone. Can any of you honestly admit that you have not thought of my death some time in the years since my imprisonment? This should be like a party to you people. *Sheesh!*"

No one dared speak. Benjamin West opened his mouth, but a gesture from Laura Sellars at his left convinced him to keep quiet.

"Oh well. As I was saying, Judge. I know that you cannot be bought. I tried that during the trial. Hell, I even had my -*ahem*- associates try to convince you to swing things in my favor."

"The bastard tried to threaten me off. Threatened my family!" the Judge exclaimed. Morehouse kept talking even as the judge did, their voices overlapping.

"But did you?" the man on the screen continued uninterrupted. "Noooooooo!" He drew out the word. "You were too high and mighty to do that. I remember what you told me right before the trial started. You told me that I was going to hang for what I had done. You had pronounced me guilty before the first witness had even been called."

Laura Sellars let out an audible gasp, a seed of doubt and distrust successfully planted. If she had been informed of any threat made by a sitting judge to her client before him she would have made a motion to have the judge recuse himself from the case. She wondered why this piece of important information had not been shared with her.

"You wanted me gone as much as any of these other vultures in the room with you now. You just hid behind the law. That and that big black robe you were wearing."

"You..."

"Judge..." Warden Chalmers warned as he got a firm grip on the man's shoulder. The judge calmed slightly and stayed in his seat.

"Well, since I know that you are above bribes I'm not even going to try. I guess I'll simply have you killed."

"What?"

That protest came from several different people around the table.

The judge's face went ashen and he seemed in shock.

"This has gone on long enough," Coombes shouted.

Morehouse's image said nothing more.

John Bartlett got to his feet and pointed a finger toward the attorney. "Alright," he demanded. "That's enough! How much more of this do you expect us to sit through?"

"Mr. Bartlett," the attorney spoke quietly. "The views of the deceased are his own. I am only required to deliver my client's final comments. No matter how despicable I may or may not find them. I will see my duty through to the end."

"Your client just threatened a man!"

"I understand that, Detective," Hall said in the same monotone voice. "However, I think we can both agree that it is an empty threat at best since my client is, in fact, deceased."

"Obviously, you don't know your client as well as you think," Bartlett said, the muscle in his jaw tightening.

Mr. Hall was unfazed. "As I said before, Detective, none of you have to stay here. You are free to leave as soon as you're ready." He motioned toward the door. "However, if you intend to stay I would ask that you return to your seat."

Bartlett opened his mouth to retort, but thought better of it and silently sat back down.

"If you will all take your seats we can continue," Mr. Hall said calmly.

Slowly, the other guests returned to their seats as well. Somehow, Darrin Morehouse had managed to unhinge three of the people around the table already with nothing but words. Mere words that had cut to the quick far more severely than any knife could. It was a not-so-subtle reminder that they were playing in his arena now and just like the lawyers in the room, he knew how to make words work for him.

Bartlett's internal alert went up a notch. He knew that his turn would soon come. He began to prepare himself mentally for the challenge.

In the commotion, Mr. Hall had switched off the VCR and the familiar blue screen was prominent again. Something about that made John think, but he had no time to further ponder the outrageous thought that had just filtered through his brain like a rogue bolt of lightning.

The cop spared a glance toward Benjamin West and his suspicions were confirmed as the two men locked their gazes upon one another. The reporter had his suspicions as well and he was fairly certain that the younger man had noticed the same clues that he had. Still, he could not make himself believe the ridiculous thought that kept running through his mind.

Why does he keep cutting it off? Why not just pause it?

He closed off the rest of the room from his thoughts and he focused on the attorney at the far end of the room. He stood stiff as a rail at the head of the table, his body framed by the ornate brick fireplace where a portrait of the deceased hung proudly. The television sat next to Phillip Jason Hall.

The blue from the screen stared back at Bartlett.

It's crazy, he thought to himself. He was fairly certain that West was having similar thoughts and he also wondered if any of the others had picked up on it.

Maybe, he thought. *Maybe, just maybe Darrin Morehouse isn't dead after all.*

What if he's somewhere in this house right now?

Toying with us.

Is this all a game?

CHAPTER 20

"Darrin Morehouse is dead?"

"Yes, sir," Janice Kilpatrick confirmed for a third time since she had told her boss what she had discovered. He was not acclimating well to the news.

"Dead?"

"Dead," she echoed.

"Dead, dead?"

"As a doornail, yes, sir."

"Dead." He blew out a breath. "Well I'll be damned."

"Yes, sir," she agreed again, trying to hide a smile.

"You're sure?"

"Fairly certain."

"Now what does *'fairly certain'* mean?" He blew out another breath. "Come on, Janice. If you want to work in this business you have to lead with facts, not supposition. Guesswork can launch a story, but you need facts to back it up."

"Let's just say it's all but one hundred percent confirmed."

"Okay," Fabian Alexander said as he tried to catch his breath, ignoring the sarcasm. Or simply not recognizing it for what it was. "Tell me what you know. I need details. Where? When? How? Why? Why

136

is important. I need to know why."

"Mr. Alexander," she pleaded. "You need to calm down, sir, or you're going to give yourself a coronary. All of the details that I could dig up are in the file I just handed you."

"This file here?"

"Yes, sir." She leaned across the desk and tapped it with her polished fingernail. "This file here."

She ignored the annoyed look he shot her.

"Who else did you tell about this?"

"No one," she said. "I tried confirming it through the cops, but for a change our friend, Captain Miller, doesn't feel like talking to the press, which only leads me to believe that it is all true. Confirmation by denial."

Fabian's mouth fell open. "Well that's practically news in and of itself," he said. "If Miller isn't talking then he's trying to protect one of his men. That's the only thing that makes sense. Otherwise he'd trip over himself trying to get on camera. Any ideas on which one?"

"My first thought was John Bartlett," Janice said. "Who else on the force is more associated with Morehouse than him?"

"That makes sense. If Benjamin West is involved then it is a good bet that Bartlett is in on this too. Those two were on the top of Morehouse's shit list," Fabian said. "I should know. I was on it too."

Janice seemed to consider that. "Then I wonder why you weren't invited to the reading of the will."

She regretted it the second she said it. The look on his face told her that her comment, though innocent, had stung.

The anchor stood up from his desk and picked up the phone, angrily tapping buttons with his finger. He wasn't going to let the comment go. He dialed a ten-digit telephone number and waited impatiently. When the person on the other end answered, he told them he needed to speak with Katherine DePlana and that it was an emergency.

While he waited for the producer to pick up the line, he turned his attention back to his assistant. "Well, I'm invited now," he told her definitively. "Find out where they are, Janice. Go. I'll get us a cameraman and we'll head out as soon as we have a location. They aren't leaving me out of this. Not this."

"I'm on it," Janice said as she headed out the door to her cubicle.

"Oh," Fabian Alexander said before she could close the door. "Good job on this, Janice. Damn good job."

Janice Kilpatrick smiled as she gently pulled the door closed. This was the part of her job that she loved, especially since her boss was not one to heap praise on others. Anytime she could get an *attagirl* out of Fabian Alexander was a golden moment because they happened so rarely.

"You're welcome, sir," she said once she was alone in the hall. "You are more than welcome."

Janice was smiling all the way back to her desk.

# # #

Fabian Alexander was in a hurry.

If not for protecting his reputation, he would have run toward his producer's office. Such a thing might work for TV shows and movies about reporters, but he lived in the real world. Such unseemly behavior was not his style and was not something a man of his position would do.

The story that his assistant uncovered was so hot that it might catapult the anchor to a network position and get him out of the local scene. The man wanted to advance so badly that he couldn't wait to tell his producer about the information his assistant had found.

Of course, Janice Kilpatrick's name would be conveniently left out of their conversation except where absolutely necessary. Fabian had made a career out of climbing over the work of others and he made no apologies for it. The new game was a brutal one and in the dog-eat-dog world he lived in, Fabian wanted to be the top dog. Years earlier, he had used Benjamin West to get from a beat reporter to co-anchor. West was hip deep in the Morehouse case and Fabian Alexander smelled a chance to move up so he took it. Never did he give any thought to the repercussions of his actions.

His interference nearly cost Benjamin West and John Bartlett their lives, but it had the desired effect. Not only did the Morehouse case catapult Fabian into a co-anchor spot on the evening news, it also made him a local celebrity in his own right. He eventually made it to lead anchor of the midday news as well as the six o'clock news spot. There was nowhere else for him to go in the local circuit as far as he was concerned.

That left the national networks.

And he had already started dreaming nation wide.

Fabian pushed his way past his producer's assistant and rushed into the office. His producer was engrossed in an intense telephone conversation with someone from the art department. She was asking about a piece for a story for that evening's special assignment report that was apparently overdue. Katherine was a very busy woman and didn't take kindly to unexpected interruptions from the on air talent.

Upon noticing Fabian's abrupt intrusion, Katherine Deplana ended the phone conversation with a curt, but polite word and a promise to call back if that art wasn't on her desk in an hour. Once finished with her business, the producer turned to her star anchor.

"What can I do for you, Mr. Alexander?" she asked, offering him a practiced smile. This was not the first time the spoiled news anchor had burst into her office unannounced and it was growing tiresome. She almost hated to see him come into her office, but part of her job was to keep the talent happy so she would paste on a smile and listen to whatever rant or rave they needed to get off their chest.

Fabian Alexander was the worst of the lot.

The meetings with him generally ended with needing either migraine medicine or a stiff belt. A few years back, when Fabian was selected as co-anchor, Katherine found Mr. Alexander's rude behavior in concern to office politics somewhat amusing. Now she simply felt annoyed that he had yet to learn any self-restraint. It no longer won him points with her, despite how good his approval rating was. Still, she resisted the urge to tell him to get the hell out of her office.

"I've got a story here, Katherine," he started without so much as a hello. "I'm going to run it as the top story."

"Oh really?" Katherine asked, her face a mixture of shock and mild annoyance. The fake plastered on smile was gone. "I thought I decided who ran what story and where we aired it. Isn't that what a producer does? Or did I misread my employee handbook again?"

Fabian *huffed* at her remark. "Come on, Katherine. I have a story that beats anything we've got on the plate right now. This is big and it is now!"

The last part of his pitch captured Katherine's attention. Alexander was a pain in the ass, but he did have a nose for news. He had sniffed out several good stories over the years. As much as she hated these unscheduled one-on-ones with the reporter, she also couldn't really ignore him. She leaned back in her high top, cushioned executive's chair.

"Well now," she said. "I'll admit that you've piqued my interest, Mr. Alexander. Please, tell me more. And you'd better *wow* me."

"Oh, you are going to love this."

"We'll see," she said with a smirk. "Now get on with it."

"Okay. I have incontrovertible proof that Darrin Morehouse committed suicide while in prison." A large smile had spread across the anchor's face as if that was enough to convince her. He was expecting her to jump at the chance to sing his praises on just that tidbit alone. Fabian loved it when others stroked his ego.

"So what?" Katherine asked, quickly deflating Fabian's ego.

"So what," he repeated. "I can't believe you said that."

"Morehouse is old news, Fabian. He certainly isn't *now*! We need something fresh for lead story. Morehouse is little more than a filler piece or a sound bite hidden somewhere in the second half hour. You of all people should know that. He was news six years ago. Now he's old hat. People just don't care about that case anymore. Nobody cares about that case anymore."   "Except me."

"Except you," she echoed as if he were making her point for her.

"But Katherine..."

She held up a hand, silencing him in mid sentence. "I'll tell you what," she started. "I'll give you one chance to convince me. Let me know what you have and we'll see if I can salvage anything from it."

The anchor glowered at her, but said nothing. He did not like having to defend his position.

"It's a one time deal, Mr. Alexander. I'm a very busy woman. Take it or get out."

"Okay," he conceded.

"Start from the beginning," she said. "How do you know that Morehouse has died? Why has there been no word from the prison or the DA's office? Have you spoken with any of the individuals involved with the original case? What are their thoughts? Do you have any actual facts to back up your claim?"

Fabian twitched nervously. "Well, I suppose that Morehouse's death was not reported as a means of keeping the contents of his will a secret."

"His will?"

"Yes. Our... my best estimate is that Morehouse named those responsible for his fall from grace in the will. It appears that there is a reading today, possibly as we speak. Other than that, I have no particulars."

"No confirmation from the DA's office?"

"They won't take our calls."

"Morehouse's lawyers?"

"No comment at this time."

"How about the prison?"

"Nope."

"The cops?"

"Ditto."

"Yeah, but not getting a comment from them is encouraging. It usually means you're onto something."

"I was just explaining that to my assistant."

"How about his ex-wife?"

"Unreachable. She's disappeared down a rabbit hole somewhere and hasn't been seen."

She sat back in her chair. "How does something like this get covered up, Mr. Alexander?"

Fabian shrugged and smiled.

That was not the answer Katherine Deplana wanted to hear, but she did like exposing cover-ups and she was starting to think her spoiled anchor might have stumbled onto something newsworthy after all. "Have you tried to contact any of the individuals involved?" she asked "John Bartlett? Ben West? The judge? Can anyone corroborate this?"

"All of them are apparently unreachable. I've tried every number I can find and have even reached out to known associates, but not a one of them can be found for a comment at the moment. It's my belief, based on what I've been able to piece together from what tidbits I've picked up, is that they have all been named in Morehouse's will, possibly as beneficiaries of some sort or another."

"You're kidding." Katherine could scarcely believe her ears. "Why on earth would he do that? That doesn't exactly make a whole lot of sense. I think you're reaching."

"Oh, please, you know as well as I do that this screams of one of those stupid games Morehouse was so fond of playing. Remember when he lured both Bartlett and West to the same warehouse separately with the intention of having them shoot one another?"

DePlana blew out a breath. "I've heard that one before," she said with derision. "And while it makes for a great episode of Leverage there's not a scrap of evidence to prove that it really happened."

"Oh yeah? How about the time he planted the bomb in my car?"

"Occupational hazard."

Alexander grunted.

"If they aren't trying to kill you then you're not getting all the news, Fabian."

"Uh huh."

Katherine leaned forward in her chair and rested her elbows on the desk. She often did this maneuver when trying to make a point.

"And just in case you've forgotten, Mr. Alexander," she said, her voice dropping to a smoky octave. "We're in the news business. That means we rely on facts, not hearsay or urban legend."

"But I---"

She cut him off. "Do you have any actual proof about anything you've told me?"

"Not yet, but I will."

"Spoken like a true reporter."

"Look, Katherine, I told you this was hot," Fabian said, pumping his ego up another notch. "Let me prove it. What have you got to lose by letting me ride out there and take a look? If I'm right it'll be one hell of a story. It'll be ratings gold, Katherine. Ratings gold."

"Reign it in, Mr. Alexander," Katherine said. She had no intention of letting him get anymore full of himself than he already was. "I will admit that this peaks my journalistic imagination, but there isn't enough here to be a lead story. Please tell me you have something more to go on."

"Not much," Fabian admitted. "I have my assistant running down some leads even as we speak. We're hoping to find where the reading of the will is taking place. I have an idea of where, but we're tracking down the facts to support my theory. Once it's confirmed, I'll go in there and find out just what the hell's going on and you'll get the scoop of the century."

Deplana rolled her eyes at her reporter's hyperbole.

"Think about it, Katherine," he pleaded.

His producer nodded. "Alright. I'll pull you from the evening report. I'll get Bill Pruitt to fill in. I'm sure he won't mind the extra screen time. We'll say you're on special assignment or some bullshit like that. You have until tomorrow morning to get me the story. If it's not on my desk by eight a.m. then you drop it and walk away."

"But I--"

"I'm not kidding. Eight a.m."

"Come on, Katherine."

She wasn't hearing it. "This is not a negotiation."

"Katherine…"

"Take it or leave it."

He blew out a breath. "I'll take it."

"Am I understood?"

"Absolutely," he said.

"No bullshit on this one, Fabian. I mean it. Eight a.m."

"I read you," the reporter said with a hint of irritation. "Thanks, Katherine."

"Now get out of here and bring me that story."

"Ratings gold, Katherine," he promised with a smile as he stood.

"We'll see," she said, waving him away with a flip of the wrist.

Fabian Alexander ran from the office, no longer worried about appearances. He was on a hot story. Nothing was as energizing as the jazz you felt when you were working a hot tip. He was even more excited than he had been before talking to Katherine. "Ratings gold," he repeated as he closed the door behind him.

Once he was out of earshot, Katherine allowed herself to snicker at the man's bumbling ways. Fabian Alexander's desire to get to the root of a story had been one of the things that had impressed her back when he was first hired, but he sometimes took it just a bit too far for his own good. He hadn't yet learned to reign himself in, a self-preservation instinct that many other reporters had figured out by the time that they reached his level in the business.

Still, she was impressed by his hunger for a story. So few "professional" anchors would have left all the work to their assistants. Fabian Alexander was an obnoxious pain in the ass, but he was a popular obnoxious pain in the ass. And he belonged to her. She could excuse the man a few indiscretions like manners and egotism.

As long as he got the story.

Plus, as much as would never say it in front of him, but he was right. If his theory was true then it had the potential to be a rating's gold mine. Ratings made the broadcast world go round and they had taken a dip in recent months. If Fabian's story had any legs it might just catapult the ratings back to where they belonged.

Katherine Deplana tapped a button on her intercom and called her assistant. "Monica. Put in a call to Bill Pruitt right away."

"Yes, ma'am."

"Tell him I need a big favor."

CHAPTER 21

"This is bullshit!"

"Benjamin!" It was Laura Sellars who spoke and she had reached her limit with the reporter's interruptions.

"Please, Mr. West, restrain yourself," the attorney for Darrin Morehouse said softly.

"This is bullshit!" Benjamin West declared for the fourth time since he sat down.

Philip Jason Hall stood patiently at the head of the table, waiting for those around him to settle down again. After a few moments of arguing amongst themselves, he got his wish as order was restored. Laura Sellars convinced the others to take their seats. When everyone was back where they belonged, sitting behind the name placards with their individual names inscribed on them. Seated right where Darrin Morehouse wanted them. Even from beyond the grave, he was running the game under his own rules.

And no one knew those rules save the deceased. And he sure as hell wasn't going to tell them before he was good and damned ready.

Without preamble, Mr. Hall activated the tape player once again and Darrin Morehouse's image returned to the screen. The face of their hated enemy smiled at them all as they sat around the large conference table.

"My dear Francis," Morehouse said as he turned to face the warden. "I understand that things have been tense for you the past few years. I know all about your little drinking problem. Fortunate for you that I don't pass judgement on the way others live their lives. For you, Francis, I offer something that will put to rest fears that you have had since my arrival at your lovely little prison."

"And that would be...?" Warden Chalmers started to ask, forgetting momentarily that he was watching a previously recorded tape.

"Just between you and me, Francis," Morehouse said. "We both know that you have a very large problem at your prison. There is a large leak. How else could I have gotten away long enough to make this recording, eh?"

Francis Chalmers tensed.

"I can give you the names of those individuals at your prison who are... shall we say, less than appropriate to the tasks you have charged them with."

"Gee, Warden, I wonder how much that'll cost you?" West whispered.

"There is a catch to this, of course," Morehouse's image continued.

"Told ya so."

Morehouse's image seemed to be thinking it over.

"Why doesn't he just get on with it?" Warden Chalmers said. Morehouse's mind games were starting to have an adverse effect on those around the table, as was obviously the point of all of this. It was just another one of Morehouse's sick little games.

"Easy, Francis," John Bartlett whispered. "Take it easy."

"What I want is simple. I want you to name the prison after me."

"What?"

Shouts came from around the table as Darrin Morehouse began laughing hysterically on the television screen. Luckily, everyone managed to regain composure relatively quickly. "Oh, come on," he said. "The Darrin Morehouse Memorial Prison. Has a nice ring to it, don't you think?"

"He's insane," Vivian Morehouse said as if she could scarcely believe it.

"You're just now figuring that out, lady?" Ben questioned.

Vivian gave the reporter a stern, hate filled look.

146

"Okay. Okay. Okay. I guess you haven't the power to change the name of the penitentiary. Maybe you could just name a wing after me. Ha. Ha. Ha. Seriously though, I do have some information for you, Warden. My attorney will pass this information to you at the conclusion of this meeting. Assuming, of course, you'll believe the information I'm giving you to be accurate."

Silence filled the room.

Chalmers sagged visibly. Even if the information were on the money, what could the warden realistically do with it? He could not simply fire everyone on the list flat out, primarily because Morehouse would love nothing better than to punish an innocent man. And Morehouse was a sneaky bastard. He was not above tampering with a person's official records. Chalmers seethed.

"I would offer you a monetary settlement. You know, help pay off those debts you've been racking up, but that might look like a bribe. Can't have that, now can we? No, didn't think so."

A pause.

"No. We wouldn't want to sully your good name and all that, eh?"

Darrin's image turned away from the warden and he fixated his gaze in the direction of Laura Sellars. The lawyer stiffened under the man's gaze. Benjamin West placed a reassuring hand on her arm, calming her slightly. Even after she had shouted at him, he was trying to help her deal with whatever was coming her way. Not for the first time since she arrived, Laura found it telling that no one from her former law firm had been invited to attend this... farce was the best word she could think of to describe it. *Once a sacrificial lamd, always a sacrificial lamb*, she supposed. Apparently, her former client held her, and her alone, responsible for losing the case.

The only thing she knew was that whatever Morehouse had in mind for her it probably wasn't going to be pleasant.

"My dear, dear, Laura." Morehouse said with a condescending air as he let out repeated *tsk's*. "I had such high hopes for you, my dear. You were a brilliant lawyer when you first entered my employee. I had faith in your abilities and I put all my trust in you completely. And what did you do with it, huh?"

"Mr. Hall..." John Bartlett started, but a curt look from Sellars silenced the police officer's objections.

"You failed completely, didn't you? Failed me, failed your firm, failed in every sense of the word. You should have emerged victorious. You had every means at your disposal to bury that weasel, Coombes -no offense, Mike- and win that case. You could have won!" he screamed. "You should have won," he said, now more calm than before. "You know what your downfall was, Laura?"

"Yes," Laura Sellar's whispered. She no longer faced the television screen.

"Your conscience got in the way of your job. That was it, wasn't it?"

"Yes."

"You let your feelings get in the way of doing what you knew you had to do, what you were being paid to do. And paid well I might add. Just like a woman," Morehouse spit out as if Laura Sellars were nothing but dirt in his eyes.

West kept his hand on her arm. "Laura?" he asked.

She did not respond.

"A weak, pitiful woman. You were not worthy of my trust or the trust of those you worked for."

Bartlett started to stand. He wanted, needed, to do something. The whole situation had gotten out of hand and it was time to put a stop to it.

Morehouse continued. "You have spent a long time working your way up the ladder since your miserable defeat in two thousand three. You've worked hard to put your life back together, haven't you?"

"Yes," Laura muttered. West did not know how much more the poor woman could take before she crumbled completely.

"Of course you have," Morehouse continued. "I have been keeping a close, personal eye on your progress. I like to check in on you from time to time. And I must say that you have preformed remarkably well for yourself over the last couple of years. I'm rather impressed by what you have accomplished, my dear. I dare say that you are twice the lawyer now than during my trial. I would almost wager that if my trial were to take place today," he chucked a thumb toward the opposite side of the table. "You could probably wipe the floor with Deputy Dawg over there."

Michael Coombes looked up at the monitor. Hatred burned behind his eyes.

"Would you not agree, Mike?"

Coombes bristled, but remained silent.

148

"Anyway, I digress. You'll pardon me my ramblings. I'm a dying man. Oops! Dead man, I'd guess at this point. I want to bequeath you the one thing that I took from you in your career. I'm offering you a full partnership in the law firm that dropped you after your failure during my trial. They weren't happy when I suggested it, but I do have a few items on each of the partners in the firm. They fear blackmail more than they fear you, Laura dear. I hope you'll be happy there."

Silence. Apparently, Morehouse had expected her to say something. Laura was fighting an urge to throw something through the television monitor.

"My new attorney will forward all of the dirt I have on your new partners to you. It is yours, Laura, to do with as you see fit. I know you'll make the right decision. A decision worthy of me."

"Bastard," she said between gritted teeth.

"And that, at last, brings us to everyone's favorite photojournalist," Morehouse began again. "Benjamin West." The image pointed toward the seat reserved for the reporter.

"Thank you. Thank you very much," West joked. "I'm here all day." He was doing his best to make a mockery of the proceedings.

Usually, John Bartlett would have tried to silence the younger man, but not at that moment. West was fighting his battle with the best weapon in his arsenal, his mouth. Not to mention the wit contained within.

"Benjamin West," Morehouse repeated. "You are one giant pain in the ass, boy. I hope you understand that."

"It's a hobby," West remarked.

A flurry of laughter echoed around the table, temporarily breaking the tension.

"I could have you killed. Hell, I might even enjoy seeing it, but..." He let his voice trail off and shrugged as if he wasn't worth the effort to keep reminding everyone again that he was no longer among the living.

"Take your best shot, buster," West muttered. He was ready for whatever the maniac on the television monitor threw his way.

Or so he thought.

Morehouse tossed his hands in the air as if surrendering that last thought. "Hey! I can let bygones be bygones, and rot like that. Hell, son, I might even had liked you if you hadn't been trying to destroy me and mine. You remind me a lot of... well, of me. I was just like you once."

"Now that's a depressing thought."

"So full of life. I know what it's like to be driven to do the best damn job you can and not giving a damn about who you might hurt in the process. Tell me, Benjamin, how many backs have you stepped on to get where you are today? Not counting our boy John over there, just how many enemies do you have out there just waiting to plant a bigger knife in your back than the one you used on theirs? How many?"

"Probably a lot less than you do," West sneered.

Bartlett was impressed. He had not expected the reporter to remain this calm. For the first time in a long time, he suspected that West would be able to handle himself.

"Probably too many to count," Morehouse said as he took another drag off of his cigar. He blew smoke rings in front of his face. "Just like me," he said at last.

"Not a chance," West said. "No way."

Morehouse leaned casually against the back of his cushioned chair. He looked comfortable, but no one at the table lowered their guard. Dead or not, Darrin Morehouse was in charge of the proceedings. Anyone that did not understand that would doubtless leave the room unscathed.

"Oh well, "Morehouse started. "Enough with the psychoanalytical bullshit, already, right? I mean, we're both pretty straightforward men, Benjamin. We always have been, even when we were enemies. I want to be straightforward with you now. We see something that needs to be done and we do it. Simple. Efficient. I like that about you."

"*Feh!*" West let out a breath.

"You take the same approach to life that I do, or used to do as the case may be. That ability is a rare commodity in today's society, Benjamin. In a time when people spend a majority of their time wasting away in front of a television or a computer, people like you and me are out there taking what we deserve. People are not even trying to stop us from taking their rights from them. People just don't care. And we care even less about them. Isn't that right, Benjamin?"

"Not bloody likely."

"Of course it is. You may try to deny it, but the truth is there, buried deep down in the recesses of your soul. Inside you is the core of the man that I became. The only difference is that I use a gun while you use a camera and a computer."

"What does this have to do with anything?" Bartlett asked the attorney. "How long to you expect us to sit and listen to this shit?"

"Hey!" West snapped. "Sit down, John!" The command was forceful and the officer took his seat, albeit reluctantly.

If West thought he could handle it, then Bartlett was going to let things play out.

During Bartlett's outburst, the recorded image of Darrin Morehouse had continued to speak. He hadn't said anything of importance. Simply more of the same rhetoric spilled out.

"--but I'm sure what you really want to know is what you get. Isn't that right? You wonder what I could possibly give you."

"I am rather curious," Ben said, addressing those around the table, not the TV screen. *Two could play these mind games*, he decided.

"So am I," Bartlett echoed.

"I'm giving you my criminal empire."

The words hung there as those around the table stared slackjawed at the screen. No one was more surprised than Benjamin West.

"That's right," Morehouse said with a smile. "No tricks. It's yours to do with as you please."

West felt his jaw drop.

"You win, Benjamin."

CHAPTER 22

"His what?"

"I've thought long and hard over this one, Benjamin," the taped image of Darrin Morehouse continued on the television screen. "I narrowed it down to two things. The first choice was for you to take my place as head of..." his words trail off. "Oops," he said as he put a hand over his mouth. "Have to be careful what I say here, huh? Wouldn't want to rat out my comrades, now would I?"

With casual grace, he let his hand fall from his face. "Oh well, fuck them. I'm dead. What're they going to do, kill me again? Take it out on my family?" He glanced toward Vivian's spot at the table and laughed. It was a scary sound.

West leaned over toward Bartlett. "I'd say he's enjoying this just a little too much, wouldn't you?"

"Oh yeah. Although, he did just admit to running a criminal organization so that's something."

"Not much."

Morehouse's image stopped laughing abruptly. "Does no one understand my humor?" he asked. "You people make me sick."

"Feelings mutual." Surprisingly, that comment came from Laura Sellars, who had managed to remain quiet until that point during her former client's diatribe.

"As I was saying," Morehouse continued. "Benjamin, I mentioned two choices for you, didn't I? I have this sneaking suspicion that you won't accept my offer to replace me in the organization. Just in case I'm wrong, my attorney will stop the tape and ask you a few questions now."

Morehouse's image looked over toward the wall where his attorney was standing with the remote. "Stop the tape," he ordered.

The tape stopped at the command of attorney, Philip Jason Hall. He looked at Benjamin West, waiting for the young reporter's answer. All he received were astonished stares from those seated around the table.

"Mr. West?" he asked after a moment of silence.

"*Heh*," West hissed. He rubbed a hand over his forehead, which had suddenly become drenched in nervous sweat. "Of all the things I expected to happen," he laughed. "This one takes the cake."

The judge smacked the table with his open hand. "What, are you thinking it over?" he asked. No doubt his question reflected the thoughts of everyone in the room, including Benjamin West himself.

"Uh, no," West answered. "Not really. I mean, this is a lot to take in, but... No!" He looked up to the attorney. "No," he reiterated, more forcefully for effect. For some reason, he felt the need to convince the others.

Philip Hall walked to the head of the table, standing directly before the television monitor. "Is that your final answer Mr. West? I have been instructed to reiterate to you that this offer has a time limit. I will only ask for your answer one more time."

Benjamin West made no effort to hide his annoyance with the attorney. "Yes. Of course that's my final answer. I--" he considered his words a second. He motioned to the group of people sitting around the table. "We spent more time than I care to think about trying to bring that... that... *man* there to justice. How can you even think that I would even consider his offer for even a second?"

"Very well, Mr. West."

"Shove your boss' deal!"

"Very well, Mr. West," Mr. Hall repeated as he took three steps back to the side of the television monitor. He pressed the remote control and Darrin Morehouse's image was once more staring at them as if eager to continue.

"Back so soon?" he asked with a laugh. "So tell me, Benjamin. Did you accept my gracious offer? Of course you didn't. I expected no less from you. I must admit that I am somewhat disappointed, though."

West grimaced. "Great. Now I'm predictable."

"Like a clock," Bartlett commented.

The reporter said nothing, but passed a *'bite me'* look in Bartlett's direction.

"I did say that I had a second choice for you, though. Before I tell you what it is, let me just say that you should have taken my first offer. Things would have gone much easier if you had."

"What the hell's that supposed to mean?" Michael Coombes asked.

"Sounded like a threat to me, Counselor," Bartlett said.

"Me too," Judge Hughes agreed.

West waved away their comments. He wanted to hear what was being said on the DVD.

"Since you will not share in my hospitality I will give you a gift in keeping with our past relationship."

"This should be good."

Darrin Morehouse leaned forward, taking on a powerful posture. It looked as if he were trying to intimidate the reporter. Fat chance of that happening. "My gift to you, Benjamin is this: I'm going to kill you last."

There were astonished gasps from around the table. Even Philip Jason Hall was startled by the remark, but he quickly recovered his composure.

"Is that so?"

"You will live long enough to see everyone in this room dead in my name before you die. Still glad you turned down my generous offer?"

"Immensely."

"You should have taken me up on that offer, Benjamin. Too late now, though. This was a limited time offer. Guess I'll see you in hell, son."

"That bastard!"

"Easy, West," Bartlett said. "Easy." He placed a reassuring hand on the younger man's forearm.

West jerked his arm away from the officer's grasp. "Let go of me!" he said loudly.

The tension in the room was palpable. The situation was becoming explosive, volatile. Probably as it was meant to by their tormentor.

The late Darrin Morehouse's voice cut through the noise of the room. "And now," he said. "Last, but certainly by no means least. We come to the man who has been the biggest pain in my rear since before we even met. John Bartlett."

Bartlett stood. He stared at the image of his greatest enemy on the television monitor. Morehouse spoke. "Your turn, John. Ready to play?"

"You bet," he whispered. "I'm ready for you this time, you bastard. Take your best shot."

"Good," Morehouse said, almost cutting Bartlett's comment short. "I have a special treat for you, John. Trust me, you're going to love it. Actually, it's really something for all of you. You see, John, since I can only assume that your friend, Mr. West has chosen to turn down my offer to replace me, I make an offer to you..."

"Fat chance."

"Not to take my place as I did dear Benjamin. No. No. No. I would not even consider wasting my breath with you, John. What would be the point, right? After all, are you not the stalwart and true hero of our little tale? Of course you are. Despite the accusations made against you by my defense during the trial, I know you to be a man of impeccable morals. If not, don't you think I would have tried to buy you off when you were after me?"

"You did," Bartlett grumbled.

"Oh, that's right, I did," Morehouse said, snapping his fingers as if it was something he had just remembered. "You probably won't believe this, John, but I've always admired you. Hell, I'm proud to have known you for the short time I have."

"You're right. I don't believe it."

"To prove my sincerity, I want to show my gratitude to you as a worthy adversary by giving you something you have been looking for a long time. I offer you, John Bartlett, all the proof you will ever need to rip my former organization apart. It's all right there in that briefcase my attorney should be showing you right about now."

Sure enough, Mr. Hall held up a briefcase. He paused the recording then walked across the room with it in hand. "As per my client's wishes, this briefcase belongs to you, Detective Bartlett." He handed the case over to Bartlett, who simply stared at it.

"It's locked."

"Also per the deceased's wishes. He said you would know how to open it."

"Another fucking game," West said. "Ain't that just peachy?"

Bartlett was calmer than the reporter expected. He said nothing, just stood there looking at the briefcase as if he were waiting on it to do something.

"Well?"

"Well what, West?"

"Aren't you going to open it?"

"No. Not yet. Not here." He pointed toward the screen. "What say we get this over with?" he asked Hall.

"Very well," Hall said and resumed the playback.

Morehouse was all smiles as he finished. He made no mention of the pause this time. "As I said before," he continued. "I'm dead so... fuck 'em! They can't do a thing to me for turning on them like this. My former associates will hound your every waking moment to retrieve that information. The information you've sought so badly over the years is yours, John. So is the target that comes with it. Can you live with that, John? What am I saying? Of course you can. You're John Bartlett and we all know that John Bartlett is a bad-ass motherfucker, don't we? I mean, we're talking *Shaft* here."

Morehouse laughed.

"Of course we do. You people need to liven up."

Bartlett's clenched jaw twitched, but he said nothing.

Morehouse paused and looked about the room.

For a moment Bartlett wondered if this was another pause in anticipation of an interruption. If so, maybe the bastard didn't know him as well as he thought he did. It was a small victory, but one he savored.

"You're probably wondering why I'm doing this," Morehouse asked. "It's quite simple, really. This world is divided into two kinds of people: the hunter and the hunted. Luckily I'm the hunter. Nothing can change that. By the time you see this I'll be dead so there's really not much any of you pathetic assholes can do to me. I simply cannot lose in this matter. The only thing that bothers me is that I won't be there in person to see you die, John. But don't worry. When the time comes, I'll be there in spirit. You can count on it."

156

"What's the catch?" Bartlett asked, but his attention was focused on the attorney, not Morehouse's image. "With Morehouse there is always a catch."

"There is, of course, a catch," Morehouse's image said as if on cue.

"See?"

"I want to play one final game with you, John. With you and West and all of your friends."

"Uh oh," Bartlett muttered.

"I do so miss our little games, John. Truly I do and I'm sure you do too, although I understand that for the sake of appearances you certainly can't admit it in public. But that's okay." He tapped his chest. "I know the truth in here. You might have fooled all of your co-workers, your boss, and those jackasses in the press... uh, no offence, Benjamin, but you can't fool me, John. I know you better than anyone else in that room."

"This ought to be good."

"You see I've studied you, John Bartlett," the image on the screen said. "Oh yes. I've seen you at your lowest and I've watched you spiral out of control. I simply cannot believe that in this day and age you would let a woman mind fuck you like that. I mean, seriously, John. She was way out of your league and you knew it. Or you should have. You were lucky she put up with you as long as she did. I watched her too, you know."

Bartlett's face went ashen.

"Yeah, I know, I know," Morehouse's image said. "It really wasn't any of my business, but you were my friend, John, my partner. Or at least I always thought of us that way. That woman made your life hell. I mean, really, what did you ever see in such a selfish bitch. Okay, now granted, my taste in women leaves a little something to be desired... and yes, the offence was intended on that one, Viv, but that bitch you married was something else, John. I honestly don't think you could have done anything that would have actually made her happy, but kudos for trying."

Bartlett stood silent, his teeth clenched tight.

"She had you off your game, John. Even you have to admit that. If you won't take my word for it ask Benjamin. I'm sure he noticed. She had you so twisted up inside that you weren't thinking clearly. You weren't fully invested in the game and that troubled me. It's no fun playing against an opponent that's not putting everything into it so I had to intervene on your behalf."

"What the hell did you do, you bastard?" Bartlett exploded, his anger threatening to overwhelm him. "What did he do?" he shouted toward the attorney, who simply shook his head. He'd had no idea what he was getting himself into when he took on this particular client. Like the rest of them, he was just a pawn on a mad man's chessboard.

On the screen, Morehouse continued without pause. "She would have left you eventually. I think we both know that.

Bartlett heard a gasp and muttered curses from the room, but ignored them.

The man on the video continued without pause. "But the longer she stuck around the more messed up you became until... well, let's face it... you weren't any fun anymore." He leaned in closer to the camera. "So I took care of it for you."

"What?" The color drained from Bartlett's face as the realization of Morehouse's words sank in.

"I took care of her," he said solemnly.

"No."

"I did it for you, John."

"Elisabeth," Bartlett whispered, his voice beginning to crack

"And I was right," Morehouse said, perking up. "Once the little woman was out of the picture you got your shit back together-- you got your mind right-- and most importantly, you got back in the game." He over-enunciated the last five words, giving them added punch.

"You son of a bitch."

"I don't expect you to thank me, John. I mean, even I'm not that delusional. What I can offer you is peace of mind, maybe even some closure. It's the least I can do. I have a letter all set to be messengered to your office via courier tomorrow morning provided you accept my terms for one last little game. It should be waiting for you on your desk when you get back. Inside you'll find everything you need to locate your missing bride. It's the least I can do, partner."

"Well this is fucked up," West muttered.

Morehouse leaned back in his comfortable chair and smiled. "And all it will cost you is a game. Just one more game, John. Come on, what do you say, pal? You game?"

Bartlett stared at the screen, but said nothing.

"I'll assume that's a *yes*. Not that you have much of a choice at this point. This one's for all the marbles as it were. If you win, I turn over everything to you, John Bartlett for use any way that you see fit. And when I say everything, you better believe I mean everything. If you lose... well, let's just say that my organization will be as safe as if I were still there, shepherding it into the future. Unless I totally misjudged our Mister West and he actually accepted my earlier proposal, then I figure it's fucked either way."

"So what do you say, John? Want to play one more game for old time's sake?"

"What kind of game?" It was West who asked, but they were all thinking the same thing.

"Since you have no choice but to participate my little game, I may as well define the parameters for you. After all, what is a game without rules? Anarchy, that's what. And I cannot abide a game that has no rules. It somehow makes it less sporting. Wouldn't you agree, John?"

Bartlett seethed, but still said nothing.

"Have I ever told any of you what my favorite movie of all time is?" Morehouse asked the room. "Vivian might know this. Maybe. Who knows when she was actually listening to me? I know Detective Bartlett knows this one. The Most Dangerous Game. Any of you seen it? Oh, it's great. Came out in 1932. Leslie Banks plays Count Zaroff. He's a man of culture and breeding, but he's also something of a skilled huntsman. He stalks and kills the most dangerous prey. That would be *man* for the confused among you. Anyway, Zaroff chases Joel McCrea and Fay Wray through the jungles of his island home. You really should at least rent it. Terrific movie. You really should watch it if you ever get the chance. It'll change your life. It did mine. I remember seeing the original when I was a kid. Something about it spoke to me. I've always wanted to reenact that movie and I've come close a time or two, but none of my previous work ever felt like it quite measured up, you know. I've spent a lot of time working on a way to really do it justice and now's my chance. I'm sure you all know the premise of the movie. Well, one of the more educated among you will have to explain it to my darling Vivian."

"What's he...?

"It's quite simple really," the image on the monitor continued. "All you have to do is get off of my property before my hunters track you down and kill you. Once you step off the property you are safe."

"What?"

"As we speak, there is a small group of talented gentlemen, each hand-picked for this assignment. Anyway, these gentlemen are even now preparing themselves within this very house. I won't tell you where they are, of course, but I will tell you that they are highly trained in their respective jobs. I assume I don't have to tell you what these men do for a living, do I, John?"

Bartlett shook his head.

"What does that mean?" Vivian asked, her voice cracking.

"They're hired guns, Mrs. Morehouse," the detective told her. "Killers."

"And highly motivated too, I might add," Morehouse said. "You see, I paid them very well to do one last job for me. You might not think much of money, John, but take it from me, it buys a great deal of loyalty. Even from beyond the grave."

Bartlett noticed that the attorney no longer held his calm reserve. The rules of the game were startling to him. Apparently he had not been let in on his client's plans as completely as he had believed. Suddenly, he saw the man for the monster the rest of them knew him to be.

"I did not set a time limit on this little adventure as some of you aren't as fleet of foot as you used to be." He turned to stare toward his former wife, who was still at her assigned spot. "Some of you never were."

Morehouse's image took in the group again, moving from person to person at random. "There are roughly one hundred acres here," he explained with a broad hand gesture. "The house is located almost, and you'll excuse the pun, dead center of nine hundred acres. That's..." he appeared to be doing the math in his head, the started counting off on his fingers. "Well, hell, let's just say it's a lots of ground between you and sweet, sweet freedom." He leaned back in his chair and propped his feet on the desk. "So, pick a direction, any direction and get the fuck out of my house."

"Sounds easy enough," West quipped. "I wonder, what's the catch?"

As if on cue, Morehouse smiled over his stippled fingers and spoke. "There is, of course, a catch."

"Why am I not surprised?"

"Ben," Laura Sellars said between grit teeth. She was growing tired of his sarcasm. "Quiet!"

"Despite what you may have heard, I am a fair man," Morehouse continued. "So, in the spirit of fair play, and as a man of my word, I feel it only sporting to tell you that my security detail has orders to keep the riffraff off of my lawn. In other words…"

"Here it comes."

"Anyone caught trespassing on my property will be considered an intruder with hostile intent and will be shot on sight. And just so there is no misunderstanding, you should know that all of you in this room will be considered trespassers. I've already seen to that."

Silence descended on the room for several seconds until Morehouse laughed like a madman in one of those old movies he liked so much.

"Oh God," Vivian Morehouse cried. "He's serious. He's going to kill me."

"Dammit. I knew it," Bartlett swore. "I fucking knew it."

Darrin Morehouse's image held up a finger to get their attention. "Before I sign off, I have one last thing to say. Kind of my parting words of wisdom, if you will since we shall never speak again, unless we all end up swapping stories around the same bar in heaven."

"Somehow I suspect heaven's not his destination," West whispered.

"In the off chance that you do not take my threat seriously," Morehouse continued. "I have orchestrated a little demonstration for you. A show of good faith, if you will so you understand that like all games, this one carries stiff penalties should you lose."

The man on the video screen motioned toward the room's only entrance from inside the house.

"If you will observe…"

CHAPTER 23

On the TV screen, Morehouse's image motioned toward the room's double doors.

John Bartlett stiffened, his hand instinctively reaching for his service weapon.

The door that he and Benjamin West had walked into earlier flew open abruptly. A man stood in the doorway. A very large, well-built man wearing military style fatigues. Detective Bartlett recognized him immediately. He was dressed like an extra in a Rambo movie, no longer wearing the expensive Armani suit that had not looked right on him to begin with as he had ushered them through the mansion and into the room. Now the man he thought of as "*Armani*" was decked out with serious hardware. Although most of the equipment appeared used, Bartlett had no doubt it was all in working order. If these men were what he thought they were, then they knew their way around weapons.

The man's demeanor screamed that he was a professional soldier, probably a mercenary for hire. Bartlett had run into the type before. None of those encounters had ended well. From his position in the open doorway, *Armani* could have wiped out everyone in the room before Bartlett could even pull his hidden gun.

Everyone in the room got to their feet and started to back away once they noticed the firepower in the newcomer's possession.

Bartlett pulled his Smith and Wesson from its holster and pointed it toward the intruder.

Vivian Morehouse screamed.

"Mr. Hall," Morehouse's image said solemnly from the television screen. "I'm afraid your services are no longer required."

"What are you…?"

With one fluid motion, a single shot was fired toward the attorney, who jerked backward on impact.

The double doors slammed shut without being touched as if by remote control.

Bartlett did not have time to fire before the doors were closed. He heard the lock ratchet into place as the room was sealed faster than it took the attorney's body to hit the floor.

Obviously, the entire house is wired, Bartlett speculated. Somewhere in the mansion there was a person, *or more likely persons*, with his, her, or their finger on the controls that ran the house. Whether or not it was actually Darrin Morehouse was a thought that they would have to worry about later. Whether he was alive or not, Morehouse had set events into motion that had resulted in a man's murder.

Knowing the man who planned this little escapade, he suspected that Mr. Hall would be but the first to fall unless they got out of there quickly. Bartlett holstered his weapon and leapt over the table and came to a stop next to the first victim of Darrin Morehouse's deadly game.

He felt for a pulse. It was faint, but growing fainter by the second. Philip Jason Hall lay bleeding on the expensive carpet of the study as Detective Bartlett ripped a strip from the lawyer's jacket and tried in vain to plug the wound. He had only minutes left, but he tried to speak. Unfortunately, the most he could manage was a gurgled cry. The wound was fatal and he was dying. The attorney knew there was no chance for him and that he had only a few minutes of life remaining to him.

There was nothing that any of them could do to save him.

John Bartlett tried to comfort the man as he tried to staunch the bleeding by telling him not to move, to try not to speak, and that it would all be okay. It was a lie, of course, but not one anyone would condemn him for speaking. He felt the man's pulse slow, then stop.

He contemplated attempting CPR, even though he knew it would be a futile attempt at best. There was nothing he could do to save the man's life. A similar incident had occurred years earlier while trying to collar Morehouse the first time.

A fellow police officer died that time.

"Bastard probably planned to kill him from the beginning," Bartlett said as he closed the dead man's eyes.

"What are you saying?" Laura Sellars asked.

"The attorney was expendable," Bartlett said as he got to his feet.

"Expendable?"

"Yes, Your Honor," Bartlett said, his voice just above a whisper. "He was expendable. I doubt he was ever meant to be a part of the game because he didn't have the connection to Morehouse that we do. He was an example for us, proof of Morehouse's threat that those... men out there won't think twice about pulling the trigger. Mr. Hall was an innocent bystander doing his job. Just another pawn to be used and tossed away when he was through with him." He had seen this type of casual disregard for human life while on Morehouse's trail six years before. It sickened him now as much as it had then.

He felt his anger begin to boil.

Morehouse's image was still on the monitor, smiling silently at them as though he were some malicious Cheshire Cat. He smiled like that for a few moments before he began to speak again. "As a rather famous writer whose name escapes me once, Bill... something, made a statement that I've always appreciated. It went something like, '*kill all the lawyers*' or something like that."

He laughed again.

"I still count three lawyers in the room. I wonder which of you is next? My men have been instructed to give you a head start of about ten minutes, give or take. I would make damn good use of that time, if I were you, John."

He laughed again as he checked the expensive gold Swiss watch on his wrist.

The detective used a towel from a nearby shelf to wipe the attorney's blood off his hands.

"I would wish you all good luck, but none of you have a chance in hell of getting out of here alive," Morehouse boasted. "You never *really* had a chance. You were doomed from the moment you stepped foot in this house, but I couldn't let you out of here without playing just one more game. I just couldn't let such a golden opportunity pass by. I'm sure you understand."

"Bartlett tossed the bloody towel near the lawyer's body. He started toward the balcony exit.

"Just answer me one question before you go, John," Morehouse said, stopping the detective in his tracks. Bartlett turned his attention back to the TV screen. "Would you change places with the tiger?"

"Well," Bartlett said, drawing out the word. He couldn't help but laugh at the question. "Not now."

"What the hell does that mean?" West demanded.

"It's from that damned movie," Bartlett said.

"And you just happen to know it?"

"What? I own a DVD player."

"Uh huh. This is more of that *know your enemy* bullshit, isn't it?"

"Something like that."

"This is going to be fun," Morehouse's image said from the screen. "Adios, John. It's been a blast."

"Let's go," West said as he moved across the room to stand behind Bartlett.

"Have a nice day," Morehouse's image said before it froze into a still image of the man smiling at them. The television monitor was obviously being controlled from elsewhere within the house, just like the doors had been, just as the lawyer had been until they didn't need him anymore, and just like Armani and his men. There was an army of hired killers hiding God only knew where waiting for the order to hunt them down and take them out. Whoever was controlling the doors would be controlling the grounds as well.

Bartlett had to get the people out of there.

Enraged, Bartlett screamed as he jerked the television monitor off of the wall. The monitor exploded in a rain of sparks and shards of razor thin glass as it shattered on impact with the hard wood floor.

"All right," Bartlett said, taking charge of the situation. "What say we get the hell out of here?"

"I'm with you," West said.

"Good," the detective said, ignoring the nagging voice telling him to stay far, far away from Benjamin West. West might be an asshole, but he knew how to take care of himself and could be trusted to help keep these people safe. In a fight, having the reporter on his side was a good idea.

A double panned, glass door provided them with an exit to the grounds surrounding the mansion. There was also the door they had originally used to enter the study, though he was reluctant to move deeper into the mansion. Two avenues of escape had been conveniently provided for them.

To John Bartlett, that meant a fifty-fifty chance of success and success meant survival.

Throw in the Morehouse factor and the odds changed dramatically. Darrin Morehouse hated to lose more than anything else. Even in death, he would have found a way to tip the odds in his favor.

Then again, John Bartlett didn't like losing any more than his adversary, which evened the odds considerably.

"Who's armed?" he asked the crowd inside the room.

"I am," Warden Chalmers said as he pulled open his sport coat to show a .45 millimeter in a shoulder holster.

"I have a pocket knife," Judge Hughes said. "Ain't got much call for guns these days. At my age, I don't think I could handle one anyway."

"Mike?"

The DA shook his head. "Sorry."

"All I have is my spray bottle of mace," Laura Sellars added when the police officer turned to her.

"And I simply abhor firearms," the former Mrs. Morehouse exclaimed in a shaky voice. Bartlett was surprised she hadn't hyperventilated yet.

"West?"

Benjamin West looked at the man asking the questions. "Oh yeah," the reporter said as he pulled a gun from a holster strapped to his ankle. "You didn't think I was going to come to this party unarmed did you?"

"Good. That gives us a few weapons, but not much to work with. Knowing Morehouse, this place is probably crawling with mercenaries and I bet they've all got plenty of guns."

"That tracks,' West added. "And no doubt they're going to be armed to the teeth."

"Count on it," Francis Chalmers said.

"So what's the plan, boss?" West asked Bartlett.

Bartlett looked at the reporter before turning toward the faces around the room. They were all looking to him for answers. They probably suspected he had a cop secret to get them out of the predicament they were in, some plan that police officers were trained with in cases such as these. Bartlett was starting to wish he had one.

"I'm working on it," he said as he moved to the door that led outside. He started feeling around the edges. The door did not appear to be wired, but that in no way meant he should take any chances. "Everyone move over to that far wall," he told them.

The small group did as they were told.

"Do you think that's a good idea?" Vivian asked as she complied. "What if…"

"Would you please shut up?" Laura asked her, menace dripping off every word.

Vivian fell into silence and chewed on her lower lip.

The police officer jiggled the doorknob. To his surprise, the door was not locked. Slowly, he opened the door a crack and ran his fingers along the edge of the frame. There were no wires. The door was not rigged.

Surprised by how easily it opened, Bartlett turned back to face the group. "Okay. I'm ready to get out of here. Our best option is to get outside. Maybe we can overpower a driver and steal one of the cars and hightail it out of here."

The six people looked at him for leadership. Even Benjamin West, who normally argued every point, stood by quietly. He would follow whatever plan John Bartlett laid out for them.

"Sounds like a plan to me," Judge Hughes said.

"Works for me, too," Michael Coombes agreed.

"Vivian Morehouse nervously shook her head in agreement. With the added stress, her nerves were touchy at best. Bartlett wondered if she would be able to handle the trip out of the mansion in one piece. If not, he would have to carry her. He hoped it didn't have to come to that. He was afraid he would need both of his hands free to counter any opposition they would face.

"Agreed," Laura Sellars said. "Let's go."

"I'm with you," Francis Chalmers said as he pulled his gun from its holster and checked the safety.

Bartlett looked at West and shrugged. Without words, the officer posed the question. They had been in similar situations in the past.

West knew what was at stake. He shrugged. "What say we blow this Popsicle stand?" he said as he headed toward the open door.

Bartlett smiled. "Good. Let's get out of here," he said as he began herding the small group toward the exit.

"I've had about all the fun I can stand at this funeral."

CHAPTER 24

John Bartlett ran across the balcony.

Made of concrete and steel, the balcony ran four feet to both sides of the double doors that led from the study. Suspecting a trap, he leaned over the railing and looked down. It was a long way down to the ground, possibly as much as ten to fifteen feet. John doubted that some of those trapped with him could make the jump. Certainly not all of them would be able to make the jump without injury.

He motioned for the others to hold their position as he ran along the outer edge of the balcony. It stretched around a corner of the house. There was a small wall rising up to mark the end of the balcony on the left. It was a dead end, but there was enough of a rise in the lawn on the other side of the wall that made it less of a drop. He decided it was their best shot for getting away from the house.

He leaned around the corner of the mansion and motioned for the others to follow. As quickly as the slowest among them, they ran toward Bartlett. Francis Chalmers took up position in the rear and Benjamin West positioned himself in the middle of the pack. Those two had guns and both knew how to use them and would do so if they had to. He hoped they could protect those unarmed by sticking close.

Bartlett quickly announced his intentions to go over the wall.

There were a few minor protests, mostly from Vivian Morehouse, as to the plausibility of the plan. He couldn't think of any other way to get out of the mansion without fighting their way through a bunch of gun-totting mercenaries, and told her as much. As he suspected, none of them relished the idea of going that route either.

Not that his words convinced Vivian.

"Look," he finally declared. "Morehouse gave us a ten minute head start, which I doubt he's going to honor. We don't have much time left so get your asses over that wall or stay here and wait for the man's firing squad to show up. The choice is yours, but for me personally, I'm getting out of here." It was a bluff. Had she not agreed to go over the wall, he would have knocked her out and carried her like a sack of potatoes.

Thankfully, it did not come to that as there were nods of agreement from all around. Bartlett helped West over the wall first. Once on the ground, the reporter checked the area. It was secure.

Once they were certain there was no one waiting for them on the ground, Bartlett and Warden Chalmers began helping the others over the wall. Judge Hughes went first, followed closely behind by Vivian Morehouse, Laura Sellars, and Michael Coombes. Bartlett helped each one of them to the ground safely. Thankfully, no one fell and they each appeared none the worse for wear. Once they were on the ground, the warden made his way clumsily down the rugged wall to the moist grass.

John Bartlett was the last one over the wall. He contemplated taking the briefcase with him, but decided against it. With his luck, it was probably wired with a GPS tracker. The last thing he planned to do was make the bad guys' job easier for them than it already was. Besides, if there was any information in there that could help him dismantle Morehouse's operations then he would get it when he came back.

And he would be coming back just as soon as he got the others to safety.

"Now what?" Michael asked as the officer landed in the grass.

"Now we go," West said as he pointed toward a nearby clump of trees. "That way!" he ordered. The group acknowledged quietly and ran full out toward the trees. Bartlett covered them from his position next to the wall.

They reached safety at the trees without incident.

"That was almost too easy," Francis Chalmers said between gulps of air. The warden was wheezing, terribly out of shape. West sympathized with him as he tried to slow his breathing. When this was all over, he decided that he would do something about getting in better shape himself. *If we survive, that is.*

Bartlett joined them seconds later. He knelt next to West and Chalmers. "I'm going to check on getting us a ride. West, I need you to cover me."

"No problem," the reporter answered. "Just say the word."

"Let's go."

The officer turned to the others. "Wait here," he told them. "We're going to go see about our rides out of here."

Bartlett sprinted across the open lawn toward the far corner of the mansion, near the front where they came in. He stopped, pressed flat against the brick exterior.

"Be right back," Ben West told the others right before he made his move. He ran across the grass toward Bartlett, stopping only a few feet shy of the other man's position. Both of them had their guns drawn and ready.

Bartlett eased his way to the corner of the mansion. He stole a quick glance toward the parking area, then jerked his head back quickly. West waited less than patiently as John eased around the corner. "Well?" the reporter asked.

Bartlett came around the corner. The look on his face told West all he needed to know. It wasn't good news. "The cars are gone," he whispered. "Damn it, I should have known."

"No time to worry about that now," West said as the two men sprinted across the lawn to meet with the others. "Let's just get these folks out of here. Then we can come back and deal with Morehouse."

"What?" Bartlett asked, startled by the suddenness with which he said it.

"You heard me," West said. "I think that son of a bitch is still alive and he's somewhere in that mansion laughing at us."

"West, are you out of your fucking mind?" Bartlett couldn't believe the words the reporter was saying.

"Sometimes, but not about this," the reporter declared.

Bartlett motioned the others to follow him through the thick growth of bushes toward the woods. Although he had other plans, Benjamin West followed closely behind. He understood the need to stay together.

"The cars are gone so we're not getting out the same way we came in," Bartlett told the group. "That means we move to plan B."

"And what, pray tell, is that?"

"Oh, you're going to love plan B, Miss Sellars. Since we can't drive out of here the way we came in, then we're hoofing it out of here on foot. And we can't trust the driveway because we'd be too exposed out there. Easy pickings. So our only other alternative is to take it cross country."

"Cross country?"

"Through the woods."

"Great. That's just peachy, boys."

"Over the river time, Your Honor," West added playfully.

"As much as it pains me to admit, it's been a long time since I was considered nimble, gentlemen," Judge Hughes reminded them. He was less than appreciative of the reporter's attempts to lighten their mood. "I was about your age the last time I had to trudge through dense foliage and speed wasn't really an issue back then."

"I appreciate that, your honor, I really do, but I don't see any too many other alternatives, do you?" Bartlett said. "But if you've got a better suggestion I'm all ears."

"I wish I did," the judge said. "But nothing springs to mind. Lead on. I'll keep up."

"I appreciate that, sir." He faced the collected group. "Look, none of us were expecting this and I know it's not going to be easy, but this is our only way out of here. You see that tree line over there?" he asked, pointing toward their first stop on this little exodus.

There were nods from the assembled players.

"That's our target. I'll go first to make sure there are no surprises waiting for us. Once I'm sure it's clear I'll signal you." He kept his tone even, no inflection. Bartlett had to keep them calm, especially Vivian, who looked like she was on the verge of breaking down completely.

"Once I signal the all clear I need each of you to make a beeline for the tree line. Keep your eyes focused on where you're going. Don't look around or behind you. Try to stay in a single line if possible, but don't bunch up. We need to keep some distance between us so we don't make for a tempting target. Once you get to the trees I want you to find a spot behind a tree or in a ditch over the hill and stay there until I tell you."

"We have to assume Morehouse was telling the truth and he's got men out there," Chalmers added.

"It's a distinct possibility," Bartlett agreed. "But I'd rather take my chances on the move than sitting on my hands waiting around for them to find us. This is the best plan."

"I'm sold," Coombes said. "We go."

There were nods from almost everyone.

"Good. Everybody ready?"

"Does it matter?"

"Not really, West. Watch my back."

"I got ya."

"Get ready."

John Bartlett sprinted across the open lawn toward the woods.

Despite the possibility of a sniper waiting somewhere nearby to pick him off, the officer kept his gaze fixed on the tree line like he had instructed the others. He had learned the important lesson of lead by example after rejoining civilian life. His stint in the Army had taught him many things, but in the military you did as you were told. *Do as I say, don't do as I do* was very much the rule of law there.

When he joined the police department, Mac Sperling taught him the importance of leading by example. As a training officer, Mac taught him a lot. As a partner and mentor, Mac shaped his experience into knowledge. His training made John both a better cop and a better human being.

With this group, Bartlett realized that Mac's method's worked best. He knew that West, Mike, Francis, and the Judge all had military experience, but with the exception of the journalist who spent time in war zones at least once a year, it had been some years since the others had served. He couldn't treat them as combatants anymore.

He made it to the tree line without incident, which surprised him. He had expected those mercenaries to be waiting to pick them off one bay one. If they were half as competent as he expected them to be, they would be aware that this was the only way they could have gone. If they were actually adhering to Morehouse's ten minute head start, then they had a chance, albeit a small one.

He leaned against a thick tree to catch his breath and waited, giving himself a mental ten count. When he didn't hear anything he chanced a quick peek back in the direction of the house. Everything looked fairly normal. He didn't see any people scurrying about on the roof or the balcony. He also didn't see any movement through any windows, but most of those had the curtains drawn.

If there was anyone out there watching him, and he was fairly certain someone was watching, then they weren't doing anything except watching. He checked his watch. There was still eight minutes and twenty seconds left on their head start.

Having the group make a break for it was risky, but there really weren't any alternatives. There was no choice but to chance it.

"Now or never, John" he whispered.

Bartlett stepped out from behind the tree he had been using as cover and motioned for the others to make a run for it.

Vivian Morehouse was the first in line, with Laura Sellars hot on her heels. Michael Coombes stayed close to Judge Hughes and helped him along. With their weapons drawn and at the ready, Chalmers and West brought up the rear, each scanning the area around them just in case.

Once they reached the tree line there was only seven minutes remaining on their head start.

"No time to rest, folks," Bartlett said once the group was back together. "We're on a clock and we need to put as much distance between us and the mansion as we can in the next seven minutes. West, bring up the rear."

"This is as far as I go."

"I beg your pardon?" For a second, Bartlett thought he had heard Benjamin West incorrectly.

"You heard me. I'm not going."

At least he had waited until they made the tree line before dropping his little bomb.

"For God's sake man, why?"

"You know why."

"This is no time for one of your wild theories, West. He's not in there."

"You can't know that for certain."

"Yes I can. Francis was there. He confirmed it. Morehouse is dead. He's not hiding out inside the mansion."

"I've got to know for sure, the reporter said. "Not just for my own personal satisfaction, even though that would be all the reason I need, but it'll make a hell of a story. What kind of reporter would I be if I walked away from a scoop like this one?"

"Well, you'd be alive for starters," Michael Coombes interjected. "I shouldn't have to remind you just how dangerous that man is."

"See, that's just it. Even you said '*is*' instead of '*was*.' You know I'm right."

"No! You're not!"

"I'm telling you, Bartlett, the rat bastard is alive and I'm going to prove it."

"Why? Why? What makes you think he's still alive? Do you have anything even remotely resembling proof to back it up?"

"I've got that damned video tape we just watched. Do you think he really anticipated our responses that accurately? Come on!"

"I didn't think so. There isn't enough on that tape to prove he's alive. He knows us better than we probably know ourselves. He could have made that stupid tape as far back as two months ago. It is ludicrous to think he's alive based on that. It's flimsy at best and you know it."

"Oh, yeah?" the younger man snorted. "It's not like he's ever, oh, I don't know, tried to play us before or anything," West said passionately, sarcasm dripping off every word.

Bartlett threw up his hands in front of himself, partly to calm himself and partly to make West stop talking. One out of two wasn't bad. "Come on, West," he said. " I need more than that to buy into your conspiracy theory nonsense."

"Look man. I'm telling you..."

Bartlett spun around to face him.

"And I'm telling you to lay off it until we get these folks to safety, godammit! Then, we'll come back here and I will personally help you tear this goddamn place a part brick by brick if you want." He pointed in the direction of the mansion. "But for now...."

West conceded the argument, albeit reluctantly. "Okay. Okay. For now, we leave. Got it."

"Good," Bartlett said. "Let's get these people moving."

"But I don't have to like it."

"No you don't."

Once the group got going, they moved with relative ease through the trees, deeper into the woods. They stayed together; moving only as fast as the slowest member of the group did, which in this case was Judge Hughes. At age eighty, he had trouble maneuvering over the rough terrain with any kind of speed or agility, much as he had predicted. Michael Coombes had opted to stay by the judge's side to help him if he needed it.

This suited Bartlett well. That way, he, West, and Warden Chalmers could be on guard for the hunters. Although things were running smoothly at the moment, he knew better than to think of Morehouse's threats as hollow.

The hunters would come soon enough.

Morehouse liked to drag his games out to their greatest possible length. He had received a sick sense of pleasure from watching his targets frantically trying to stay a step ahead. Or so he had when he was alive. Despite Benjamin West's assurances to the contrary, Bartlett was certain that the death had not been faked.

Although, he had to reluctantly admit that if anyone could convincingly fake his own death and orchestrate the current predicament, it would be Darrin Morehouse.

Suddenly, West's notion that their enemy might still be among the living seemed less far fetched than it had before.

And that thought worried John Bartlett.

It worried him greatly.

To his amazement, they managed to travel for quite a while without any distractions or attacks upon them. Ever alert, Bartlett expected attack at every turn. Surprisingly, nothing had happened so far and he was happy to be disappointed, but he knew it wouldn't stay this easy. Whatever Morehouse had planned was going to happen eventually. Of that he was certain.

The question was how.

And when?

CHAPTER 25

Nick Wilson snickered.

A massive man, Wilson towered above most at roughly six foot four. Although he was rather husky, a majority of that was pure muscle. A true professional, he was very focused on his job and indulged himself in the rigorous training that went along with said job. His daily routine consisted of a ten-mile run followed by a mile long cool down walk, thirty minutes of cardiovascular, pull ups, crunches, weight lifting, etc. etc. etc.

As a result, Nick Wilson was a perfect specimen.

Well, perfect for a professional mercenary.

And he was damned good at his job. Even if modesty prevented him from admitting as much aloud, his resume spoke volumes. Before going into the 'consulting business,' Wilson had proudly served his country as a Ranger. After his honorable discharge, he discovered that the quote/unquote 'real world' wasn't near exciting enough to suit him. An adrenaline junkie, Nick went out and found the first war he could and signed up. The rest was history. There were very few places on God's green earth he had not crawled or bled. Were he still in the service, his record could have made him a general by now. Not that he had any interest in doing so. He wanted to be the man on the ground.

That's where the action was and that's where he would be.

One prospective employer had commented that Wilson's exploits would make a wonderfully entertaining novel or movie. Nick liked the idea, but had no intention of pursuing it. Especially since he would have to kill anyone who read it or saw it. Most of the activities he had been involved with over the last ten years, while exciting, were less than legal.

Besides, he had other, more pressing, business to attend to. Specifically, killing those people that had been branded as targets by his employer. He snickered again as he watched through his binoculars as the targets scampered away like frightened animals. For a moment it actually looked like they were going to make it, which made Nick laugh. He couldn't help it. There was no way that one cop, an uncooperative reporter, a pudgy old warden, some washed up old politicians, an elderly judge, and a fat debutante could escape the team he had hand picked for this little operation.

Training operation is more like it, he had thought that several times. It was just too easy. They were being paid extremely well to stalk and kill some people who could have just as easily been snuffed by an amateur. Not that he wouldn't take the man's money and do the job, but he preferred a challenge. But a gig was a gig and paying work was always welcome. Still, he wished the job presented more of a challenge.

Perhaps the only exception was the cop, Lieutenant Jonathan Bartlett. The file Wilson had read on him was impressive. Bartlett had also spent some time in the military, doing a tour in the Army during the first Gulf War. Wilson found himself reminded of those cops or private detectives you'd see on the TV and in movies. They always got their man. Never gave up. Shit like that. Well no matter if this guy thought he was *Magnum P.I.*, *Hunter*, or *Lethal Weapon* all rolled into one, Nick Wilson was better, stronger, and faster.

And he knew it.

And he had given his men standard instruction to save the cop for last, to save him for him. Tom would do him up close and personal. Just like the man wanted.

It had been too long since he had a challenge worthy of himself. Maybe the cop would prove to be one, but he doubted it. If past experience were any indication then John Bartlett would prove to be a disappointing adversary. Still, one could hope every now and again, couldn't he?

And then there was that loudmouthed reporter.

He didn't consider Benjamin West to be much of a threat, but he was definitely an irritating little prick. Wilson would be happy to pull the trigger on that one as well, but he needed to allow his men a chance to bag their own prey. That was okay. He was content to watch the smart ass die. Wilson hated reporters almost as much as he hated lawyers. And this one thought he was a comedian to boot. And he hated comedians almost as much as he hated reporters. Oh yeah, he'd have to die painfully. Perhaps if they cut out his tongue first. He made a mental note to pass that directive along to his people.

The communication headset he wore clicked once in his ear. They were using static bursts as a signal. No one who might be listening in would understand just what a squelch indicated unless they had been invited to the briefing. The squelch of static told him that his men were closing on their first ambush. He squelched three times in quick succession. This signal told them to stand by.

On your mark.

He turned up the sound to a more audible level and listened.

Another click of static filled his ear as one of his team answered in the affirmative.

It was a go.

Wilson couldn't help but snicker again as he squelched two times. *Get set.*

He loved his job. No denying it. He was professional, but there were moments, like now, that he felt an almost euphoric joy from his work. The thrill of the hunt exhilarated him, filling him with happiness that he found to be often lacking from his life. But to taste the hunt on the wind, to feel the tension and the fear in the air as the prey hurried to get away. To know that the great hunter was following them, stalking them, and be able to do nothing about it. Plus, it wasn't often he got to play with his targets before pulling the trigger. He found himself enjoying it far more than he expected to when he accepted the assignment.

As he said, exhilarating.

He wished he could stay and watch, but he had other matters to attend to. Turning away from the window in the study, the same window his prey had passed in their escape, Wilson made his way to the door. At his feet, he noticed the unmoving form of Phillip Jason Hall, the scumbag lawyer he had shot earlier.

His first victim.

He had no idea why this man was targeted. Truthfully, he could care less. At ten thousand bucks a head, he would start knocking off his own team if he were asked to. However, since his benefactor was dead, he doubted the option to renegotiate was available. Still, he knew that if the word came down from on high that the ghost of Darrin Morehouse wanted more folks dead, then Tom Wilson would happily kill them. Providing that the money was real. It was kind of hard to spend spectral money.

He pushed the lifeless body of Philip Jason Hall aside as he passed. "Fucking lawyers," he muttered with obvious disdain. "Ought to kill them all." He snickered again, giddily. "Hell, I'd almost do it for free."

Exiting the study, he turned left and made his way to the room he had set up as his command center. Two other mercenaries, hand picked by Wilson himself, fell silently into step behind him. They were well trained. They did what they were told and did not ask a lot of questions.

Perfect soldiers.

Wilson toggled the talk switch again. *Go*!

"Light the fuse," he said, thumbing down the volume before he even heard the static-filled reply. He knew the other's abilities and he even trusted them, but only to a certain extent. At least as much as he trusted anyone. He knew that those men out there were already in the process of taking out the first target.

Everything was proceeding exactly as his employer had wished and according to the plan they had laid out together. All of which made Nick Wilson happy.

And when Nick Wilson was happy, then the world could breath a little easier.

Now all that was left was to pull the trigger. He chambered a round from the gun he plucked from its holster under his arm. This was his favorite gun. This small piece of steel had taken more lives than he could count.

He pointed the gun toward the woods where last he had seen his prey and smiled.

"*Bang!*" he said.

"You're dead."

CHAPTER 26

"I don't like this!"

"I'm not crazy about it either, Ben," Warden Chalmers said. Like Bartlett, he was growing tired of the reporter's constant complaining about their predicament. Clearly chagrined, Benjamin West said nothing further, which was as welcome as it was surprising.

John Bartlett fought down a cheap shot that any other time would have sprung forth unbidden. West was not known for being a team player. It had to be his way or else everyone would be miserable. Occasionally, the reporter had to be taken down a peg, usually by Bartlett himself. He felt that the warden had achieved a victory, albeit a minor one, and there would be nothing gained by pissing West off any more than he already was.

The group had been taking the path of least resistance as a courtesy to Judge Hughes and Mrs. Morehouse, but they couldn't keep it up forever. Just because the bad guys had not come after them in full force yet, Bartlett knew they weren't too far away. He had no doubt they were coming and would be on them soon. They needed to be evasive and do the opposite of what their pursuers expected. That meant taking a path that would be more difficult to follow.

"We've got to get off this path," he told them. "We're going to have to make it so we're harder to find."

"And just how are we going to do that?"

"By taking the road less traveled." He motioned toward an incline that led into deeper growth. "I know this is going to slow us down, but if we stay on these marked paths they will find us."

There were a few groans of protest, but no real argument. They all knew the danger they were in and differed to the officer's wisdom and experience. Surprisingly, West had not argued with his plan.

"Which way?" Laura asked. It was the first time she had spoken since they entered the woods.

"Up the hill," Bartlett said, pointing out the intended destination.

Michael Coombes, still assisting Judge Hughes, asked the older man if could make it.

"Don't worry about me, boy," he answered. "I may be old, but I'm far from helpless. Point the way, John."

"Just what I wanted to hear, Your Honor. This way." Bartlett broke from the marked trail up a fairly steep incline. There were leaves of varying shapes, sizes, and color scattered across the ground. As a result, he slipped once, but remained standing. On his second attempt, he made it to the top of the small rise and looked over the crest to the other side.

"It's clear," he called down. "Everybody up and over. Let's go."

They proceeded in order as called for by Bartlett. First up was Laura. She eased herself up with little incident. She was halfway up the incline when he signaled for Mrs. Morehouse to start her climb.

That's where things got tricky.

Vivian Morehouse was a healthy woman, but her lifestyle favored lavish parties and huge dinners. Those years of one hundred dollar a plate dinners had started to take their toll on her figure a few years back. As a result, she was less than graceful in her climbing skills. Fortunately, Laura reached down and offered her left hand to the woman even as she held tight to a small tree with her right. Benjamin West followed her up the hill, helping keep her steady so she did not fall.

Laura helped the former Mrs. Morehouse up the incline and Bartlett eased her over the top. Gravity did the rest and Vivian slid softly, if not quietly, down the opposite side. The selfsame leaves that had hindered the climb served as an excellent cushion for the slide down to the flatter area below.

Once she was safe, West went back to help the others.

It only took a few more minutes to get everyone else onto the other side. DA Coombes and Judge Hughes followed Vivian and Laura. West eased himself slowly to the top and waited there to cover Warden Chalmers as he scrambled up behind. The climb was rather tough on the warden as it had for Mrs. Morehouse.

After reaching ground level again, Bartlett led the others through some rather dense trees. It didn't take long until they reached a small clearing in the midst of the trees. "We'll stop here for a minute to rest," he said as those in his care eased themselves into a seated position on the cool, hard ground. He walked a perimeter as the others rested.

All save Benjamin West. "What are you thinking, John?" he asked.

Bartlett looked tired. "I don't know," he said. "I don't even know if we're going the right direction. We could be headed toward anything from a pasture to a country road. I think we're headed toward the main road, but it wouldn't take much to get lost in this mess."

"You're telling me. I wish I had been paying more attention when we drove in."

"Yeah. Me too. I should have been on guard. I knew he had to be up to something, but I never expected this." Then Bartlett's voice dropped to a whisper. "And we aren't making good time either."

"I know," West whispered in return. "The Judge and the princess over there are slowing us down big time."

"I know. I'm open to suggestion. What do you propose we do with them? We can't leave them behind. I damn sure won't desert them."

"And I wouldn't expect you to." West took a small step back. "Nor would I even suggest it," he added angrily.

"Sorry."

"You should be. I'm not as heartless as you might think, you son..."

West never got the words out as the crack of a gunshot filled the air, echoing off the trees that surrounded them.

The sound was followed quickly by a scream.

# # #

A crack split the air.

The sound echoed through the forest. Bouncing off the trees, there was no way to pinpoint from where the sound had originated. It was all around them. At first it seemed like something a million miles away that was of little concern to anyone.

Until Michael Coombes' blood splattered across Vivian Morehouse's dress and arms. Her scream shattered the reverie of the others, to whom everything seemed to be moving in slow motion until that second. Coombes hit the ground immediately, his eyes wide with shock, blood pooling beneath him in the dirt. Suddenly, the reality of their situation was very real to all of them.

Judge Hughes grabbed for the hysterical ex-wife of their tormentor and tried to pull her a safe distance so Detective Bartlett could get closer to the wounded DA. It was not an easy task as Vivian was easily twice the judge's weight. She thrashed about wildly as panic set in. She had been a ticking emotional time bomb since this whole thing started. It wouldn't take much to push her completely over the edge.

"Michael!" Bartlett shouted as he fell to his knees beside the DA. They had never been what one would call close, these two crime fighters, but they shared a level of respect that was evident in their association with one another. John considered the man a friend.

To see a friend lying on the cold, damp ground, bleeding was almost more than he was willing to take. "Hold tight, pal," he said as calmly as possible as he began ripping away shred from his blue button up shirt. He tied the strips tightly around Michael's arm as a tourniquet. Rule number one: stop the bleeding.

"Ben?"

"Stand by! Warden?"

"Nothing," Chalmers said as he checked the area.

"West?" Bartlett called again.

"We're clear," the reporter shouted back as he and Warden Chalmers stood at the ready should their pursuers come over the ridge like the villains in some B movie western. "For now."

"Any idea where that shot came from?" Chalmers asked West.

"No idea. Could be anywhere, but if I had to guess, we've got guys bird dogging us."

"Great. That's all we need."

"Well, we can't say he didn't warn us," West added.

"That's hardly comforting."

West simply smiled.

"How bad is it?" Laura Sellars asked as she knelt down to help Bartlett with their wounded associate. He was ripping strips from both his own and Coombes' shirts and using them to pack the wound. Blood poured between his fingers despite the pressure he was applying so she started tearing strips for him so he could use both hands on the injured attorney.

"It could have been worse," he finally told her. "The bullet went clean though his shoulder, but he's bleeding pretty badly. If we can pack enough material in there it'll slow it down until we can get him to a hospital."

"And you really think we're going to get out of here?" she asked softly, echoing the sentiment she suspected they were all sharing.

"Yes," Bartlett said matter of fact. "Yes I do. And you'd better start believing it too."

"Okay," she said, clearly chastised.

"Look, I…" Bartlett started.

"It's okay," she said. "I get it. No worries."

"You sure?"

She ignored the question. "Moving him is going to be tough, isn't it?" she asked instead.

"Damned near impossible, but I think that was the point." Bartlett slipped an arm beneath the injured man's back. "Help me with him."

Together, they lifted Coombes up and moved him out of the clearing. He grunted in pain and Bartlett whispered apologetically. "Sorry about this, pal. Just a second or two more, okay?"

Coombes grunted out a pained agreement as they leaned him against a large rock.

"No sense making you an easier target than necessary, right?" he said with a reassuring smile. When Coombes didn't respond, Bartlett nudged him. "Talk to me, Mike," Bartlett prodded the wounded man. He tapped him lightly on the cheek. "Come on, pal. Stay awake. Come on."

Suddenly, Benjamin West was at their side. "We've got to move. Chalmers thinks we've got a shadow tailing us through the woods. The last thing we need is for them to catch up. We need to go. And soon."

"I know," Bartlett whispered. A nod told Laura told her to watch their wounded companion while West and Bartlett spoke privately out of earshot. Her return nod was all the answer the police officer needed.

"Where are they, West?"

"I've got no idea. Can't get a visual on the shooter, but if the warden's right, they're following our path."

"That makes sense. All they have to do is track us so they know where we are at all times and then pick us off one by one. It's a smart plan."

"You know they're just playing with us, right?"

"Yeah. They could have easily killed Mike, but instead they wounded him to slow us down."

"Or to see if we'd leave him."

"Well, that's not happening."

"How bad is it?"

"Bad enough. Moving him is going to be tricky. They knew just where to hit him to seriously wound him, but keep him alive so he can slow us down."

"And Mrs. Howell over there isn't going to help matters," West said, indicating the whimpering Vivian Morehouse. Judge Hughes was still at her side, trying to keep her calm. Bartlett was surprised the stress of the day had not sent her into a catatonic state yet. She did not appear to handle stress well.

"I know." Bartlett took a deep, cleansing breath. "Let's see if we can get Mike moving. Then we'll worry about our next move."

"Is he going to be okay?"

"Honestly? I don't know." Bartlett returned to his friend's side with West in tow. "But staying put is not an option."

"You'll get no argument from me," West agreed as he helped Ms. Morehouse and Judge Hughes to their feet. "You okay, Your Honor?"

"I'll live," the older man replied. "I assume you have some sort of crazy plan?"

West looked shocked, a moment of levity in a dire situation. "Not me, sir," he said with a grin. He pointed toward John Bartlett. "He's the brains around here. Any crazy plans are all his."

"You always have to be a goddamned comedian," the judge grumbled, which only made West's grin widen.

"It's a gift, Your Honor."

Hughes *harumphed* as he dusted dirt from his trousers.

Bartlett was helping the wounded Michael Coombes to his feet. "Okay," he told him. "I'm not going to lie to you, Mike. This is bad, but it could be a lot worse."

"Worse?"

"Yes, Laura," he said, shooting her a look that told her to keep her mouth shut. "Worse." He looked at the others, each one of them scared or angry, and in some cases both. "Look, whoever fired that shot could have easily killed Michael with it. The fact that they didn't tells us something."

"And that would be?" Laura asked.

"It tells us that it's not just about killing us. Think about who it was that orchestrated this entire thing. That bastard got his jollies making us jump through hoops before. What makes you think he wouldn't do it again just for kicks? I think these guys mean to play with us a bit first."

"Play?"

"Oh, yes, Mrs. Morehouse. Your husband liked to play the most dangerous of games. Something tells me that hasn't changed simply because he's dead."

"Oh, God," Vivian whimpered.

"And you call this good news?" Judge Hughes asked, ignoring her.

"It gives us a chance."

"Why are they doing this to us, Mr. Bartlett?"

"Because that's what your ex husband paid them to do. I don't know why I keep having to remind you of this, but he was an evil man. This was the kind of stuff he did. A lot." He instantly regretted his harsh tone. This was not Vivian Morehouse's fault any more than it was his own. They had both been used and abused by the same man. Everything that was happening to them was Darrin Morehouse's fault. Taking it out on her was not fair.

"I'm sorry, Vivian," he said. "Look, we need to get moving. You're going to have to trust me. I need you to hold it together long enough for us to get out of here. Can you do that?"

"Yes. Okay." She looked on the verge of a breakdown.

"Good. Let's go. West, can you help Michael?"

"I got him," said West as he slipped the DA's uninjured arm over his shoulder, freeing Bartlett to take charge of the group. West kept his gun, tucking it into his belt.

Bartlett slipped the gun from his belt so it would be in his hand if he needed it. "Alright, we're going to take this slow and easy. I'll take point. The rest of you follow me. Francis, can you take the rear?"

"No problem," Warden Chalmers said. Like West and Bartlett, he two came to the party armed.

As a group, they moved further down the gently sloping hill toward the thicker trees that made up the woods surrounding the mansion. As before, Francis Chalmers took up the rear, making sure no one was following.

What the good warden did not know was that the man who had shot Michael Coombes was staring at him through the cross hairs of a very powerful rifle.

His finger slowly squeezed the trigger.

CHAPTER 27

Fabian Alexander exited Interstate 85 North.

Exit 41 put them on Rural Highway 316 heading northeast toward Athens, away from Atlanta. He had been driving for roughly forty minutes and had spent the entire trip in relative silence. Save for the occasional off color remark about Atlanta's shitty traffic situation. Thankfully, it improved once they were outside the city, not that it kept him from complaining about "lost time" before lapsing back into silence.

Uneasily, Janice Kilpatrick sat in the passenger seat. She said nothing, just like her boss. She wasn't entirely sure why she was there. It wasn't like he needed her to do the reporting. No, he was very good at that part. Of course, he was also very good at delegating authority, which she knew well as she was the one usually delegated to.

She had protested at first. Her husband and baby boy were both waiting for her at home and she really wanted to spend some time with them. With her and Brian both working such long hours, the weekends were supposed to be a time for them to spend time together.

Then along comes her boss to throws things out of whack.

Brian had understood. He even encouraged her to take the trip. It wouldn't take long and it could possibly help her career. He didn't want to deny her that so he convinced her to go without complaint.

And Janice was glad of it. This was a good opportunity for her. She doubted Mr. Alexander would impart much credit to her, if any. The latter was more likely, she suspected. That was usually the case in these situations. Fabien Alexander was not much for sharing credit. Still, upper management had to be aware of what she contributed to this team. Ms. DePlana had to see it, Janice told herself.

"How far?"

At first she thought she had imagined it.

"How far, Janice?"

"Oh," she said, startled from her reverie. She unfolded the atlas to the appropriate page and ran her index finger along the brightly colored line that indicated the highway they were traveling. "At least forty miles," she announced.

"Who knew there was this much country land outside the city," Fabian remarked.

"I know. It's beautiful isn't it?"

Fabian gave her a stern look that said he disagreed.

"It's underdeveloped," he said. "Look at all the wasted space."

"I think it's lovely," Janice added. She was entitled to her own opinion. Even if the great Fabian Alexander did not think so.

"Of course you do," he said.

They didn't speak again until they reached Sommersville.

# # #

Fabian Alexander hated the country.

A proud "*city boy*," he was more accustomed to walking on concrete and asphalt than grass and gravel. As such he shied away from stories that involved his visiting places like the small city that sat just ahead of him.

Sommersville, Georgia was a small pit stop on the road from Atlanta to Athens. Before the state had constructed State Highway 316, which ran from Duluth to Athens, there were only two direct paths to the city that housed the University of Georgia from Atlanta. The most direct route was traveling up rural highway 29, a rustic two lane that passed through several small towns with many stoplights and low speed limits. The other was State Highway 78, which made fewer stops and boasted a faster speed.

If not for the Morehouse connection that he had reported on during the trial and a story a few years earlier about a string of murders that had happened here, it was doubtful that he would have ever heard of the place. Which would have suited him just fine.

After stopping for gas his assistant offered to drive since she had the directions and had confirmed them with the middle-aged man working the cash register. Since she knew where they were going he let her take the wheel. He also loved the idea of having someone driving him places, although he never admitted such a thing publicly.

"Do you believe this place?" he asked, not really expecting an answer.

"I kind of like it," Janice Kilpatrick answered regardless.

"Of course you do."

"What?"

"Are you serious? Would you ever consider moving out here to the middle of nowhere? I mean, they don't even have a Starbucks or a Barnes and Noble. I wonder if they get wi-fi out here in the sticks? I wonder if they've even heard of wi-fi."

"Don't be ridiculous. Just because it's not got the same hustle and bustle you're used to does not make it any less civilized than where we live. There are plenty of towers and our cells have a clear signal and I would bet you can get wi-fi at any--" she pointed to a restaurant and coffee shop that sat on the corner just ahead of them. "See? That sign advertises free wi-fi."

He mumbled something under his breath.

"I can't believe you're this intolerant."

"Yeah, well, what I am or am not isn't important right now. We're here for one reason and one reason only and that's the story. Let's just find this place and get what we came for so we can get out of here and back to civilization."

"Whatever you say," Janice sighed. "According to the guy at the gas station, we'll make a left turn at the third red light on this street, just past the newspaper building."

The reporter grumbled again about the lack of a GPS in the car he had signed out. Unlike the rest of the world at large, Fabian Alexander seemed to be ignorant of the recent cutbacks in the news divisions across the country. With newspapers going bankrupt and closing right and left, journalists were left having to make due with fewer resources. Gone were the days of unlimited expense accounts and open-ended budget reports.

Everyone in the news business had to tighten their budgets. With her husband working for a newspaper this was a constant source of discussion. With both of them working in a dwindling industry, they had to prepare for the worst. Thankfully, Brian had survived the lay-offs that had happened earlier in the year. He told her that there would probably be more to come and they had started making plans to insulate themselves should the worst happen.

Janice looked out the window and took in the scenery. There was a quietness to Sommersville that was inviting. Despite that, she could not see she and Brian moving so far away from their respective careers. But in thinking about the future, the place held a certain appeal. She made a mental note to talk to her husband about it tonight over dinner.

"Here's the turn," she said, pointing at the stoplight ahead. It was green and there was no oncoming traffic so she took the left quickly, tires squawking against the pavement.

"So that's what passes for a newspaper in these parts?" Alexander pointed to the small building that housed the local newspaper, *The Sommersville Gazette*. A small sign out in front of the building was the only indication that it was the newspaper office.

Janice thought it was quaint, but knew better than to get into a debate with him on the subject. It was best to just let the comment slide without response. Instead she looked back at the directions. "We stay on this road for about five miles, then make a right," she said, reading from her notes while keeping an eye on the road. "We're not far away now."

"Good," he said without looking at her.

Janice sighed and watched the trees pass as they moved out of the city.

She hoped something good came out of this trip.

CHAPTER 28

One little squeeze.

That's all it would take. One little squeeze and the pudgy little warden's head would no longer be attached to his neck, such as it was. Somewhere under all that flab had to be a neck, didn't it?

So easy, he thought. But such was not the plan.

No. That was not the plan at all.

"What the hell are you doing, Mr. Ryan?"

"Why are we doing this, Top?" the man identified as Mr. Ryan asked, his focus never wavering from the gun site.

"Because we were paid quite a bit of money, as I'm sure you remember," Nick Wilson answered. He noticed that the man had not actually answered his question, but he decided to let it go. "Isn't that a good enough reason?"

Ryan shrugged. "It used to be."

Slowly, Wilson's hand inched toward the holster under his left arm. He and Ryan went way back. They had been in the service together, fought in some of the world's most hellish conflicts together, bled in the same mud, and sweated in the same desert together. For years they were part of the same unit before each left the service, one with honor and the other dishonorably. Despite their many differences, they had stayed in touch after returning to civilian life. Neither of them acclimated to that life very well and it was only a short time before they started looking for new wars to fight.

When Wilson began putting his own team together Ryan was on the short list. They had probably saved one another's life at least three or four times each. Not that either of them was counting. There was a bond forged during war. These two men shared such a bond.

Still, if Ryan was slipping, Wilson would not hesitate to put him down.

Nick Wilson was a professional soldier. While he hated to see death and destruction, he had no fear of it. If Ryan slipped then Nick would take him out. He would feel bad about it for a minute or two, but he would pull the trigger without hesitation if it came to that. He had done so with people whom he concerned better friends than Ryan. During his career he had committed many an atrocious deed in the name of God and Country. He wasn't proud of all of those acts, but he was damned proud to have carried them out as per his orders, even when his heart just wasn't in it.

As long as there were enemies to fight, Nick Wilson knew that he would be needed. As long as his country needed a protector, he would be active. But, once his beloved United States decided they no longer needed him, Nick Wilson found himself a soldier without a war. Such was hardly a pleasant situation for a warrior to find himself in.

So, he, and a few like him, sought out the nearest war they could find.

The bloodier the better.

There were still wars to fight and enemies to round up. The face of that enemy, however, had changed. Nick Wilson would remain a patriot until the day he inhaled his last breathe. He hoped that moment would come while fighting. He would protect his country.

Whether she wanted it or not.

But waging a war was anything but cheap. Ammunition, guns, explosives, rations, and other essentials cost money. That's when he hit upon a grand idea.

"Mercenary is such a dirty word," Nick told those men he recruited into his new venture. A dirty word, perhaps, but an accurate one. Tom and his associates went freelance, working for anyone who could afford the lucrative protection and/or services they offered. At first, they would only work for a select few, trying to remain true to their principles.

Sadly, those reputable people in trouble rarely had the right amount of money to finance anything more than a weekend hunt. He knew that if they were going to get weapons and the equipment they needed other arrangements would have to be made.

Some of their earliest clients were truly the scum of the earth. In many ways, the patriots had become the enemy they had meant to defend the country against. The thought nearly drove Nick Wilson to madness.

Then he hit upon a plan.

He would work for the corrupt. He would do whatever dirty work was required of him. And then he would happily take the money they offered and put it to good use. But he would also work in secret against them. It was a beautiful plan, a plan worthy of a patriot.

The symmetry was not lost on Nick or his men either. The slimy, spineless villains were bankrolling the very people who were hurting their business interests. Then, when they criminals were on the brink, Nick and his associates would offer to take care of the problem for a nominal fee. In essence, they were getting paid to do nothing but stop what they were already doing.

It was a brilliant scheme and had become quite a fruitful business venture.

That's how Darrin Morehouse found him.

He had contacted Nick Wilson from prison. Even in a place like that, the man was treated like royalty. He had several guards on his payroll and it appeared that he had more power than the inept warden who jokingly ran the place, which Wilson found hilarious.

Morehouse intrigued Nick. He was a gambler, a man who liked to play the odds. He had paid big bucks for Nick Wilson and associates to go on a little hunt and he agreed to pay a heavy up front fee. "A sign of trust," he had called it.

At first, the thought sickened Nick and he refused. However, upon further debate he realized that the mission would serve as an excellent training exercise for his men. Not much of one to be sure, but you could never train enough. Or so his former commanding officers had drummed into his head. How hard could it be to chase down an old man, a fat socialite, two lawyers, a chubby warden, a loudmouthed reporter, and a cop?

Nick probably could have handled the operation alone, but the client had other plans. Their employer had left explicit instructions. And since he paid handsomely Nick was willing to follow said instructions to the letter.

For now.

Morehouse was a gamester of the highest order. As part of his research for this Op, Nick had read Benjamin West's book, *Deadly Games!* He had hoped to get some insight on the players involved by reading up on their past exploits. While the book was entertaining, there seemed to be very few detailed facts. West was a capable reporter, but it was clear that fiction was his forte.

The book had made a few points perfectly clear. Morehouse put Benjamin West and John Bartlett through hell all in the name of fun prior to his 2002 arrest and subsequent conviction. This little *Most Dangerous Game* scenario made more sense once he understood the relationship. It was all about fear and power. Morehouse wanted to prove that he had power over these people, even after his death.

What rational human being wouldn't be scared by something like that?

"It's time," a familiar voice said from nearby.

If Ryan had startled him, Nick gave no indication. His years of training had taught him to be aware of his surroundings. Even daydreaming as he had been, Nick Wilson had heard the mercenary approaching long before he was in range.

"Where are they?"

"Right where we expected, boss." Ryan points out toward a dense section of trees. "Just on the other side of those trees. Should hit the lake in about ten to fifteen minutes."

Nick checked his watch.

"Right on time," he said. "I'm impressed. Our Detective Bartlett is proving every bit as good as his reputation."

"Shall I proceed with the next stage?"

"By all means," Nick said. "Send the men to their phase two positions and have them wait for my signal."

"Yes sir," Ryan said, snapping off an official salute. Nick gave an informal tap of three fingers against his forehead. He found himself becoming less and less rigid the farther away he moved from the United States Military life.

"Ah'm huntin' wabbits," he joked as he stared through the rifle's scope at the trees that encircled the estate and the lake that lay just beyond. Through the thinning leaves he could just make out the movement of their quarry.

"Bang," he whispered.

CHAPTER 29

The going wasn't easy.

John Bartlett leaned against an oak tree as he waited for his charges to catch up with him. Between the wounded district attorney, the arthritic judge, and the whiny socialite, they were making less than stellar time. The others were doing well, especially Laura Sellars, whom Bartlett had not been so sure of at first. She seemed to be handling the climb well and was alternating turns with Benjamin West helping the injured Michael Coombes. The warden wasn't doing badly either, though he was breathing quite heavily.

"Why don't we take a minute to catch our breathes," he told the group when they reached his location. "I'm going to scout ahead and make sure we're clear up ahead."

"Are you sure that's a good idea?"

Teeth grit behind a tight smile, he once again told Vivian Morehouse that, good idea or not, it had to be done. She had posed the same question each time they had stopped and had second-guessed every decision he had made. Not that she had any better suggestions to offer. She had done nothing but complain since they had made their escape. It was beginning to grate on his nerves.

"How's Mike doing?" Bartlett asked West, turning his back on

Morehouse before she could protest further.

"*He's* doing just fine," Coombes said weakly. "I'm not dead yet, John."

Bartlett smiled. "Let's see what we can do to keep it that way, okay?"

"Will co, boss," Coombes answered with a pained grimace. Bartlett remembered that he had been in the military before turning his attention to politics. One night not long after the Morehouse verdict they had gone out for beers to celebrate the win. Bartlett wasn't a big fan of lawyers, but after spending time off the clock talking with the DA, he came to respect the man. They had been friends ever since. No way was he going to let him die like this.

"You guys just hang tough a bit. I'll be right back," Bartlett said.

"Be careful," Laura Sellars said, her hand touching his arm.

He gave her a playful wink before scrambling up the next rise. Without looking back he knew that Benjamin West would have already slid into a defensive position near the top of the rise. He and Francis were armed so they would keep the others between them at all times.

It was inevitable that Morehouse's goons would be coming after them. It was only a matter of time. Time. The one thing they did not have in abundance. There was only one reason the men from the house had not descended on them in force. Morehouse had a plan, which was not really all that surprising considering the man's track record. The man was a brilliant strategist. Even Bartlett had to admit as much. If only the madman's plans had not revolved around murdering him in the most violent ways imaginable.

In one of those rare moments during the hunt for Morehouse when they were not at one another's throats, Bartlett had once confided in Ben West that the constant games and schemes that their suspect put them through sometimes felt like one long episode of *MacGyver* after another. They had both laughed at that. So naturally, as he had with so many other things Bartlett wished he hadn't, West put the quote in that damned book of his. It led to a seemingly endless string of jokes that got old very quickly. Although he had found some good uses for all the rolls of duct tape that the guys in the precinct had left on his desk. Most notably when he had covered West's car with the sticky gray material.

It was an empowering moment that he felt bad about almost immediately after. If the reporter had ever discovered who had vandalized his car he wisely kept the information to himself. Bartlett suspected that he knew and was holding that information close to the chest. No doubt he would one day drop the hammer on Bartlett and call in that marker.

And he would honor it.

The woods were quiet, save for the usual sounds one expected to hear. Birds flew from tree to tree, chirping loudly as they did so. Although it had been some time since he had gone, John loved to hike. Back when he had been a kid he had been a *Boy Scout*. He hadn't enjoyed the pomp and ceremony that went with membership, but he loved the monthly hiking and camping trips his troop took. There was nothing quite as free as being out in the middle of nature, far from the prying eyes of civilization and listening to the constant bickering of his parents. In the woods, no one argued, no one threatened, and more importantly, no one made wild accusations or screamed threats.

As a child he had often fantasized about running away to live in the mountains like *Daniel Boone* or *Grizzly Adams* did on TV. It seemed like the perfect life.

Then he grew up and life, as it so often did, put the lie to the fantasy. Sometimes even now he wondered what it would be like to just pack it in and head for the hills. He had not gone hiking in years. He had once dated a woman, a high school teacher, who loved to hike. When they were together they had gone out to the trails of several state parks across the Southeastern United States. He had not been back out since their split.

Until now.

He could not help but notice that a small part - a very small part - of him was enjoying being out in the woods again. Perhaps, when this was all over, he would get back out on the trails.

There were no clear-cut paths in front of him. That worked in their favor almost as much as it worked against them. No path meant rough terrain, but it also meant they would be harder to follow.

He blew out a breath. There were no good options, which is probably what Darrin Morehouse had planned.

Not for the first time, John Bartlett regretted that he had ever heard the man's name.

#

"Well, I've got good news and bad news."

"I don't like this already."

"Welcome to my world, West," Bartlett said. "The coast is clear, but I'm afraid the going is only going to get rougher."

"Is there no other way we can go?" Laura Sellars asked. "I'm not sure the DA can handle too many bumps."

"You don't worry about me," Coombes said, his voice strained, but firm. "If you have to, you leave me here and get these people the fuck out of here."

"Not gonna happen," Bartlett said.

"Dammit, John, listen to me," Coombes started.

"No way, Mike!" Bartlett shouted before the DA could continue. He leaned over his injured friend. He noticed that the bleeding had slowed, thanks to their first aid, but it had not stopped. He had lost so much blood he was beginning to pale.

"Look, find a place to stash me then get them to safety," Coombes said, his eyes pleading. "Then you can come back here and rescue me."

Bartlett shook his head.

"You know I'm right, John. There's no way you and West can get them all out and still take care of me. Don't be stupid, pal. You can't get me out of here, but you can save them and you know it. Now get moving."

"I can't," Bartlett whispered.

"Sure you can," Coombes said, managing a pained smile.

"Are you sure?"

"Go!"

"Okay, let's find a hidey hole for you."

"Now you're talking."

With the help of the others, Bartlett built a small lean-to, another skill he had picked up during those Scouting days. It would shield the man from the elements, but should also effectively hide him from the men who would undoubtedly be heading their way soon.

"Just don't get too comfortable in there," he told Coombes. "I'll be back to rescue your sorry ass."

"You'd better," Coombes laughed.

Bartlett turned back to the others. "Okay, you heard the man. The clock's ticking. Let's go."

The group began their trudge up the incline in silence. Even Vivan Morehouse, who had complained every step of the way, said nothing as she climbed.

For a moment, John Bartlett wondered if that was a blessing or not.

CHAPTER 30

John Bartlett felt his breath catch.

They had been walking for quite some time, not that he knew exactly how long. He had given up hope of finding a cell signal. Whoever the men chasing them were, they had undoubtedly found a way to either block the cell reception or disabled the appropriate tower. The group was tired and thirsty. He wasn't sure how much longer some of them could hold out. Clearly, this was more exertion than either Vivian Morehouse or Francis Chalmers was accustomed to. Poor Francis was huffing and puffing so hard he was afraid the man was going to have a heart attack. The one who really surprised him was Judge Hughes. Considering the judge's age, Bartlett had expected him to be the weak link. He was happy to be wrong.

Finally, they caught their first break.

Looking both ways to make sure no one was waiting to ambush him, he stepped out of the woods into the long private drive he had been driven on earlier that morning. He wasn't sure how far it was to the main road because he had been focused on ignoring West on the way in than he had been on scooping out the scenery.

It was a mistake.

He chastised himself for not suspecting that all of this, from the suicide to the summons, to the reading of the will all the way out in the middle of nowhere was just another one of that madman's schemes.

Dead or not, Morehouse was still a pain in the ass.

He walked out into the middle of the drive, keeping a wary eye for any sign of movement that would alert him that the hunters were nearby. He heard nothing but the sounds of nature all around him combined with the thudding of his heart. Everything seemed clear, but something told him not to accept it so easily. Dealing with Morehouse had made him paranoid, almost to the point of lunacy. His partner on the force referred to Bartlett's feelings of danger as his *Spidey Sense*. While not wholly original, it had garnered a laugh at the time.

Now, he wasn't so sure he partner had been far from the truth.

Everything looked clear in both directions, but the feeling that someone was watching, lurking just around the corner, remained. He was tempted to whistle a little tune just to annoy whomever it was that had eyes on him.

He knew the driveway had been long and windy. The ride in had taken several minutes, but he had not timed it. Since he could not see the house he knew that the distance was considerably shorter than walking the drive from the house to the highway.

He might not know where he was exactly, but he had a better idea of where he was than he had a few moments ago. And he knew which way would lead them to the highway.

That thought was enough to give him hope.

Once he was certain that no one was going to come crashing out of the tree line at him, he ran back across the street and returned to the woods the way he came. Once under the cover provided by the trees and tall grass that had not seen a mower in months, he stopped again and waited. Chest flat against the cold ground he held his breath, listening and watching for the slightest sign that their pursuers knew where they were.

For long moments nothing moved.

The men that killed the lawyer and shot Coombes were professionals. Of that he was certain. That meant that in a combat situation they had a distinct advantage over his out of date training. Throw those in his care into the mix and there was no way they were getting away in a fair fight. Not that he really expected his enemies to play fair, but that was okay. He didn't plan on playing fair either.

The question of why they had not come for them yet still gnawed at him. He had expected something to happen after Michael had been shot. He could think of no reason why they had not come for them yet.

It just didn't make sense.

At least not to Bartlett.

To Morehouse and his men he was certain it made some kind of sense. Despite the often times ludicrous nature of Morehouse's games, there was always some logic to them. There had always been a way out. On the video, Morehouse told them that they would be safe if they made it off the property. Dead or not, he knew Morehouse's code of ethics, skewed as they may have been, would remain true. Once he got the judge and the others to safety he would come back with force and take care of the man's mercenaries.

But first things first. He had to get the others out of there.

He watched the drive a little longer, but nothing changed.

"No way we got this lucky," he whispered.

He waited another couple of minutes before heading back to the others.

# # #

"What do you mean the coast looks clear?"

"What part of that statement confuses you, Mrs. Morehouse?"

The socialite turned in a huff and stomped toward a nearby tree. While a small part of him felt compelled to go after the woman and try to allay her fears, another part of John Bartlett was just as glad to be rid of her for the moment. He tried to be understanding of her situation, truly he had, but she was starting to tug on his last nerve. With everything Vivian Morehouse had been through the past few days, her nerves were frayed to their breaking point. He would never say it aloud to her, but he was surprised she had lasted this long without breaking down completely.

"So what's the plan?" Francis Chalmers asked.

"The driveway gives us at least an idea of where we are, kind of."

"Kind of?"

"I have no idea how far the walk from here to the main road is. If we follow the road we'll definitely be on the right track."

"But?" This time it was Laura Sellers who spoke up. She had tied her hair into a ponytail and Bartlett noticed the dried blood on her hands and smeared on her neck and blouse. Helping with Michael Coombe's injuries had covered her suit jacket as well, but she had left it behind as a blanket to cover him.

"But, we'll be out in the open," Bartlett said with a grimace. "If one of the jackasses that are after us decide to take a drive they'll cut us down before we could get back under cover. It's a risk I'm not so sure we can afford to take."

Judge Hughes got to his feet with a grunt. The trek through the woods had taken a toll on the man, but he did not complain. A decorated war hero in his youth, the judge would be the last one to admit there was something he couldn't do if he put his mind to it. But he was exhausted and John had noticed that he was starting to limp.

"How much longer do you think we'll last out here in the rough?" the judge asked. "I'm game, John, but not to put too fine a point on it, not all of us are built for this shit."

"I'm open to suggestions, Your Honor."

"Wish I had something for you, son. Sadly, I don't. So what's your plan?"

Bartlett's brow creased. "Well, I…" he started, but a sound made him stop. He raised a hand to silence the others.

"Is that…?" Hughes whispered.

"Yes," Bartlett said.

"What's going on?" West asked.

"There's a car coming."

# # #

Janice Kilpatrick saw the men before her boss did.

One moment the long driveway was clear and the next a man stepped out of the woods and onto the pavement in front of her and held up a hand commanding her to stop. His tattered shirt was covered in what looked like blood, but she couldn't be sure of that at this distance. In his other hand was a gun, which she had no trouble seeing plainly. A second armed man stood off to the side of the road.

She tapped the brakes at the same moment Fabian Alexander noticed the man standing in the pavement, blocking their way.

"What the fuck?" the reporter shouted. He instinctively placed a steadying hand on the dashboard in front of him as the car decelerated.

The brakes caught and the car stopped in the center of the drive with a screech.

Janice was so intently focused on the gun pointed in her direction that she did not recognize the man wielding it at first. But she did recognize the man standing at the side of the road. He too was armed.

Benjamin West lowered the gun and walked toward the car from the passenger side. "Janice?" he said skeptically. Apparently, it had taken him a few seconds to recognize her as well through the windshield. "What are you doing here?"

"Ben!"

"Stand down," West told the man standing in the middle of the road. Janice now recognized the man as John Bartlett. Her boss obviously recognized him as well.

"Bartlett?" the reporter shouted angrily.

John Bartlett lowered the gun to his side and let out a breath. Janice could see him mouth the words, "Alexander? Shit!" as he walked toward the car. "What the fuck are you doing here?"

Both men stopped next to the car as Janice and her boss stepped out.

"What the hell is going on here? How dare you point weapons at me?"

"Nice to see you too, Fabian," West said. "Janice, you okay?"

She smiled and nodded.

"Sorry we startled you, ma'am," Bartlett told her. He had yet to speak to her boss.

"You're sorry you startled her? Alexander shouted. "What about me?"

"You I'm less sorry about," West said before turning his attention back to Janice. "What are you doing here?"

"Looking for you, believe it or not," she said.

"Me? How did you know we were in trouble?"

"I didn't. I got a tip about Morehouse's will reading so here we are." She pointed toward the guns they carried and the blood on the officer's shirt and arms. "I'm guessing things didn't go so well, huh?"

"Whatever gave you that idea?"

"We don't have time for joke, West," Bartlett said. "Get the others out here. We have to move quickly. This position isn't secure."

"What do you mean it isn't secure? What's going on here?"

The police officer ignored Alexander and kept talking. "I've got some tired, scared folks just out of sight over that rise. I need you to get them out of here and notify the sheriff -I believe his name is Myers- and have him come out here with as much backup as he can muster. Tell him to call in the FBI if he has to."

The reporter started to protest, but then they saw Benjamin West lead a small group from the woods toward the car. Both he and Janice recognized many of them. "Is that Judge Hughes?" Alexander asked.

"I'm afraid so. Morehouse's goons are all over the place. They shot Michael Coombes and the lawyer handling the will."

"Coombes is dead?"

"Not yet, but he will be if we don't get some help out here. He's still in the woods."

Alexander started to speak, but the officer didn't give him an opening.

"I don't have time to debate this with you, Fabian," he said pointedly. "We need an ambulance, but he's lost a lot of blood so an airlift would be even better. And we need it fast."

The reporter stared at him like he was speaking a alien language.

"Fabian, do you understand me?"

Alexander nodded.

"We'll get them out of here and call in the cavalry," Janice said.

"Thank you," Bartlett said politely. Thankfully, the police officer's animosity toward Janice's boss did not extend to her as well. She understood his reasons for not liking Mr. Alexander. The man had built his career by attacking the officer's credibility.

Judge Hughes and Vivian Morehouse slid into the backseat as Laura Sellers and Francis Chalmers waited their turn. It would be a tight fit.

"No way we all fit in here," Chalmers said.

"I'm not going," Bartlett said. "I have to get Mike out of there."

"Neither am I," West chimed in.

"I'll stay too," Chalmers added. "You could use another gun."

"I appreciate it, Frank, but I need someone who can handle himself to take care of the Judge and the ladies. I need that to be you."

"But I can…"

"Please," Bartlett said. "You know the tactical situation. I'm counting on you to rally the troops and come back in here and get us. Go. Please."

Reluctantly, the warden agreed and squeezed himself into the back seat. Laura Sellars shifted around until she was almost sitting on top of Judge Hughes. The old man seemed to enjoy it. Bartlett could-n't help but smile as he closed the door. It was a tight squeeze, but they managed to fit, albeit uncomfortably.

"I'm going after Morehouse," West told him once they were once again near the front of the car. "That bastard's alive and I'm going to prove it."

"This isn't the time, West. We have to get these people to safety before…"

Before he could finish the thought something smashed into the windshield just inches from them. They heard the impact before any of them even registered that a shot had been fired.

Bartlett spun, dropped to one knee, and fired three quick shots. All three found their mark and the lone gunman dropped to the asphalt further down the driveway.

"Time to go, folks," West said as he started herding the reporters inside the car while the officer ran toward the fallen attacker to make sure he was really down for the count.

West slammed the door and slapped his hand on the top.

"Go, Janice!" he shouted.

She did not need to be told twice. Janice backed the car up and with a squeal of tires leaving rubber on the driveway, barreled off in the direction they had come.

Once they were out of sight, Benjamin West blew out a breath.

CHAPTER 31

Benjamin West breathed a sigh of relief.

He stood and watched Janice Kilpatrick and the others drive away until the curve of the driveway took them out of sight. He hoped there were no more surprises waiting for them. It was a gamble, but he figured they would be okay since Janice and Fabian Alexander had somehow managed to drive onto the property without running into any of Morehouse's goons. Hopefully, the way out would prove to be just as easy.

Once the car was out of sight he ran over to where John Bartlett was knelt over the man he shot. "They gone?" the officer asked as he checked on the condition of the wounded man. He felt for a pulse at the man's neck and found none.

"Yeah."

"Good. One less thing to worry about."

"What now?"

"Now we take care of business."

"About time," West said.

Bartlett blew out a breath. "Damn."

"He dead?" West asked.

"Yep."

"So not much chance of questioning him, huh?"

"I'm afraid not."

"Did it ever occur you to not to kill him?"

Bartlett shrugged as he picked up the dead man's rifle and slung it over his shoulder. "I guess I could have put one in his leg so he'd still have a chance to shoot everyone in the car or call for help before I got to him. Would that have worked better for you, West?"

West held up his hands in surrender. The last thing they needed to do was fight. "I see your point. I'm just saying, it would have been nice to find out what they're up to is all."

"I'll try not to kill the next one we run into, okay?"

West gave him an irritated look, but kept the comment that came to mind to himself.

Bartlett pulled the man's Sig Sauer from its holster and checked the clip before tucking it into his waistband before retrieving the dead mercenary's backpack which had some essentials they might find useful. He slung the pack over his shoulder as well.

"Now come on, let's get this guy off the road."

Together, they dragged the body off to the side and rolled him into the ditch.

"You recognize this guy?" West asked.

"No. He's not one of Morehouse's regulars and I'm pretty sure we ID'ed them all. I don't know. I guess it's possible we missed one or two."

"I doubt it. I figure he's a hired merc."

"Yeah. Gun for hire would be my guess too. Probably ex-military the way he moved," Bartlett said as he tossed some branches over the body. "Anybody you know?"

West snorted. "I was about to ask you the same thing."

"Not my kind of crowd anymore."

Once the body was covered, they moved back toward the cover of the tree line.

"Well, it's a good bet this guy's got buddies out there so I'd recommend we make tracks."

"That might be the smartest thing I've ever heard you say," Bartlett said as he headed back into the woods they had been so desperate to escape not ten minutes earlier. "I know you want to go back to the house," he told the reporter once they were safely out of view of the driveway. "But I need you to stay focused. Our priority has to be getting Mike out of here, not chasing ghosts."

"You know I'm right, don't you?"

"I don't know."

"Come on, John. This is classic Morehouse," West said as he stepped over a fallen tree as they made their way back to where they had left Mike Coombes. "That son of a bitch is sitting up there in his big old mansion laughing his fucking ass off at us just like before. You know it as well as I do. He's alive."

"Maybe."

"Maybe? Oh, come on! That bastard faked his own death and set this all up from the beginning. Think about it, John. What other possible way could he get all of us in the same spot at the same time? Can you think of another good reason any of us would even think about stepping foot in this place except if he was dead. You know it as well as I do."

"No," Bartlett said angrily. "No, I don't know it! And neither do you! I mean, you might be right. Hell, I don't know. I certainly can't dismiss the possibility. If anybody could successfully pull off faking his own death it would be him, but it just seems so outrageous. I'm having trouble wrapping my brain around it."

"Just remember who it is we're dealing with here," West reminded him. "Morehouse was always a sick fuck, but he was smart sick fuck. He was the man with the plan. Remember how he covered every contingency."

"Not every contingency, obviously, since we nailed his ass the first time," Bartlett argued.

They came to the ravine that had given the others troubles climbing on the way out. They stopped at the top for a moment. Bartlett knew that going down the steep sloping grade would be easier for him and West than climbing up it earlier with their group in tow had been. He also realized that getting the injured Coombes out the same was not going to be easy in his weakened condition.

"You think he didn't plan for this?"

"I tell you what," Bartlett said. "We get Mike out of here and then me and you will go up to the house and kick down the goddamn door if we have to and see what's what. Okay?"

"Fair enough."

"Good."

"And if he's alive?"

"I guess we'll jump off that bridge when we get to it," Bartlett said.

"You know, technically he is dead already. We could always make sure he stayed..."

Before Benjamin West could finish the sentence the sound of gunfire echoed through the woods and the tree off to his left exploded.

# # #

The last thing Benjamin West remembered was John Bartlett slamming into him.

End over end they toppled down the embankment, kicking up leaves and twigs in their wake. He lost his grip on his gun and felt it tumble away from him. They slid to a stop at the bottom of the grade, each man gasping for breath and covered in sticky wet leaves.

"What the hell did you do that for?" West shouted at the man that tackled him as he crawled over to retrieve his gun.

Before Bartlett could answer several bullets struck the ground near them, sending plumes of dirt into the air.

"Never mind," West shouted as they scrambled for cover around the bend in the shallow riverbed. Crouched behind a tree and boulder, respectively, Bartlett and West steadied their weapons and waited.

"What do you think?"

"I don't know," Bartlett answered. "I didn't get a count, but it's a good bet we can't stay here. We're too exposed."

"I'm open to suggestion."

"As best I can tell, we've got two options, neither of them good."

"And those would be?"

"Run or fight."

West weighed the options. His natural instinct was to fight, much as he knew it would be Bartlett's as well, but the enemy had the high ground, a batter strategic position, and more firepower. All he and Bartlett had were a handgun each and the rifle and pistol the officer had taken from the man on the drive as well as a few extra clips in the backpack. They might put up one hell of a fight, but it wouldn't take much for the bad guys to get the drop on them. As much as he hated to admit it, running was the only logical choice.

"Running sounds good right about now," he told Bartlett.

"Yeah. To me too."

"Climbing up the other side isn't an option. You got any ideas?"

Bartlett thought it over for a moment. "I seem to recall that the ravine gets more shallow back toward the drive. We crossed that small bridge on the way in."

"Really? I don't remember a bridge."

"Not all of us slept the whole way here," Bartlett said with a smile as he started rummaging through the backpack while West kept an eye out for their friends with the automatic weapons.

"Anything helpful in there?"

Bartlett's eyes grew wide as did his boyish grin as he pulled two of the four grenades from the pack. It was the closest to joyful excitement West had ever seen from the normally agitated police officer.

"Oh yeah," he said.

West glanced back and saw the new toys in his erstwhile partner's hands and understood the normally stoic cop's excitement. "Cool," he said.

"You know how to use one of these?" he asked the reporter.

"What do you think? I spent time with the guerillas in Guatemala, remember? And I was entrenched with the troops in Afghanistan a couple years ago. Those guys had all kinds of cool toys."

"I'll bet. Just one question."

"What's that?"

"How's your throwing arm?" he asked, his eyes pointing toward the ridge above.

West smiled.

Bartlett handed him one of the grenades and kept one for himself. "Make sure you clear the ledge. There's nowhere to go if it drops back down. Toss it and run like hell toward the bridge."

"Just try to keep up, grandpa."

Bartlett grimaced.

"Ready?"

"Yep."

"I'll take the right side, you take the left. Give it a two count them let her rip."

"Call it," West said.

"Now."

They each pulled the pin on the grenade they held and after a mental one… two… count both men tossed them with all his might. As soon as the grenades were out of site over the ravine's top edge they ran as quickly as they could, splashing in the shallow creek bed.

A commotion overhead told Bartlett the good news. The enemy saw the grenades and beat a hasty retreat. There was a slim chance that one of the mercenaries, which is what he believed them to be, could grab and toss one of the grenades back down into the ravine. It was a long shot, but it was possible. Certainly, the few professional mercenaries he had met were crazy enough to attempt such a thing. He hoped these guys weren't quite so nuts and would run instead.

Regardless, as soon as the grenades blew there would be a lot of dirt, rock, and possibly trees crashing down into the ravine. Getting as far away as possible before that happened was the only thing on his mind after throwing the explosive.

The first grenade detonated with a loud pop followed by a second explosion that seemed louder. What followed sounded like rain as earth and rock fell into the shallow creek bed, churning the water before damming the flow from upstream.

"WOO!" West shouted as he ran a few steps ahead of Bartlett. As he ran he could see the bridge in the distance. Luck was with them because he did not see anyone guarding the bridge. *We're going to make it*, he thought.

The sound of gunfire echoed all around them.

Bullets smacked into trees and the mud, sounding like angry bees as they whizzed through the air.

Remarkably, nether of them were hit as they ducked beneath the concrete bridge.

"They're firing blind," West said.

Bartlett leaned against the bridge support column, trying to catch his breath. "Maybe they heard some dumb ass shout and give away his position," the cop said without humor.

West grimaced. "My bad," he whispered.

"Uh huh."

Before Bartlett could say anything else, they heard the sound of an approaching vehicle on the driveway. It had not reached the bridge yet.

"Car?"

"Bigger," Bartlett said. "Truck or SUV from the sound of it."

"What now?"

"Just hang tight, West. Let's see what they do."

CHAPTER 32

"Are they back there?" Janice Kilpatrick shouted.

She had heard the gunfire in the distance, but dared not turn to look. Instead, she kept her eyes on the narrow winding road that served as the private driveway for the mansion. She was concerned with keeping the car on the pavement at the moment and couldn't chance a look behind her. The spider-webbed crack in the windshield was a constant reminder of the danger.

Janice was frightened, but she held back the emotions fighting to get out. She knew that the last thing that would get her out of this mess was breaking down. Besides, the last things she would ever do was let Fabian Alexander see her cry. She gripped the wheel so tight that her knuckles turned white, but at least that kept them from shaking.

The others in the car also heard and several of them did turn to make sure they were not being followed. Janice knew most of them from her research into the trial, although she had not met them personally. The trial was before she came to work for the station. She had read about what they had all been through six years earlier.

"Well?" she asked when no one answered.

"Coast is clear," Francis Chalmers answered, grunting as he

twisted himself at an odd angle to glance out the back window despite being packed into the backseat with very little in the way of wiggle room.

"You sure?"

"I don't see anybody following us."

"But I heard--"

"We all did," the Judge said calmly. "Nothing we can do about it. Just stay calm and you'll be okay."

"Stay calm? That's all you've got to say?" Vivian screeched. "My husband's trying to kill us and all you can say is stay calm? Are you insane?"

"Don't make me slap you, young lady."

Janice, unfortunately, did not hear the judge's remark as she took a curve a bit too fast and the tires slipped off the pavement and chewed up grass and dirt before she jerked the car back on to the pavement.

Vivian Morehouse screamed.

"Watch where you're going," Janice's boss shouted from the front passenger seat. "Keep your eyes on the damn road!"

She'd had about all she could take of her boss' condescending attitude and she'd be damned if she were going to let him curse at her. If not for her, he wouldn't even know about this meeting and wouldn't be at the heart of this story. Although, now that people were shooting at them she really wished she had found another story for them to follow. She gave him a look that told him to back off.

Oddly enough, he got the message.

"Keep your eyes open back there," Mr. Alexander told the people in the back. "The last thing we need is for them to sneak up on us."

Chalmers opened his mouth to protest the reporter suddenly barking orders like he was in charge, but Laura Sellars cut him off.

"Not now, Warden," she said, holding up a hand to tell him to remain calm.

"Thank you," Alexander said from the front.

"Don't think me just yet. Why don't you take your own advice and keep an eye out ahead so she doesn't have to, okay?"

"Now look her, lady," the reporter shouted just as Vivan Morehouse screamed again.

Janice saw it at the same instant.

"Oh, shit," she muttered.

"What now?" the judge asked.

"Trouble!"

Near the end of the driveway sat a burgundy SUV. Her first instinct told her it was a Chevrolet, but it was still too far away to tell exactly what make and model. But Janice wasn't worried about those details. Instead she was focused on the two men carrying semi-automatic weapons. Those she saw clearly.

"We've got company!" she shouted

Instinctively she lifted her foot from the gas pedal.

"No!" Chalmers shouted, leaning forward so that his head was in the front next to hers, his arm stretched between her and Mr. Alexander as he pointed straight ahead. "Don't stop!" he told her. "Speed up! Head straight for them!"

"Are you insane?" Alexander shouted.

"Are you nuts?" Janice asked, talking over her boss' shouted concern.

"Trust me! Punch it!"

Janice did as requested and the car sped up. Since defensive driving was not one of her specialties, she had a hard time keeping the car moving in a straight line, which she assumed was a good thing. A moving target would be harder to hit. Or so she hoped.

Chalmers dropped back into his seat as best he could in the cramped space. "Everybody keep your heads down!" he said.

"Are you crazy?" Vivian shouted.

"Shut up," Judge Hughes told her without raising his voice.

Surprisingly, she complied.

The warden fumbled around for the window controls, but the back window's child safety system was activated and the window wouldn't lower. "Put down my window," Chalmers said.

With Janice fighting the wheel, Alexander flipped the switch that lowered the window. It slid down, but stopped at the halfway point because of the shape of the car's door. There was no way a big guy like Warden Chalmers would be able to squeeze through such a tiny opening.

"Watch your eyes!"

He slammed his palm into the window repeatedly. Finally, after the fifth hit, the window shattered into tiny fragments that blew into the car like tiny missiles. Then, the warden leaned through the window, his gun arm first. He winced as glass fragments tore into his skin.

"Get ready to turn hard to the left then back to the right," he told Janice. "But try and keep it on the pavement, okay?"

"O--okay."

The guards ahead must have noticed because they lifted their weapons. Janice saw the muzzle flash before she heard the loud bark as the guns fired. The first salvo of bullets peppered the hood and the already cracked windshield. The fact that no one in the car was hit was a minor miracle.

"Cover your ears," Chalmers warned the group.

Janice took a deep breath and held it.

"Now!" the warden shouted.

Janice jerked the wheel hard to the left, exposing the passenger side of the car, where the warden was hanging out the window, to the gunmen as the tires screamed in protest at the wild maneuver.

Chalmers squeezed off two shots, one immediately following the other.

A split second later one of the gunmen twisted around, grabbing at his chest before landing face first on the pavement.

Janice fought for control and spun the wheel to the right, but she wasn't fast enough to keep the front driver's side tire from going off the pavement at an angle. The tire bit into the grass along the side, cleaving a deep muddy blemish in its wake.

When she brought the car back to the right the wheel bucked in her hands as if the car had a mind of it's own and wanted to go in a different direction than she wanted it to go. Janice held firm and the car fishtailed uncontrollably back onto the drive.

The remaining gunman had nowhere to go.

He tried to run for cover on the side of the road. It was a valiant attempt, but at the speed the car was coming at him there was no way he would make it. There was no time for him to leap out of the way. With nowhere to run, the expression of fear and surprise that registered on his face an instant before impact announced to the world that he knew he was about to die.

The driver's side of the Channel Ten News car slammed sideways into the startled mercenary at sixty-eight miles per hour. Blood splattered across the side windows and the roof as his body exploded on contact. Out of control, the car continued on after the lethal impact, leaving a bloody trail that had once been a person in its wake.

Janice turned the wheel in an effort to straighten the car, but it was no use.

The car slid off the side of the pavement into a ditch that ran along the length of the driveway, pinning what little remained of the gunman's lifeless body between the steel and fiberglass frame and the packed earth of the ditch.

Smoke poured from the wounded car's hood as the engine gasped, choked, then died.

Inside there was only silence.

CHAPTER 33

Tom Myers parked his new department pick up out in front of the station.

After a busy morning buried beneath a ton of administrative paperwork, he finally worked his way to a stopping point. Even though he had brought a tuna sandwich from home, Tom was feeling confined and needed to get out of the office for awhile. He decided to grab a bite to eat elsewhere. Although he knew he'd probably regret it once he got home, Tom stopped for lunch at The Kettle. It was a delicious lunch and he enjoyed some pleasant conversation with some of the retired locals who liked to hang out and play cards, checkers, and sometimes chess during the day. Like everyone else in town, he referred to the group as *The Old Men* even though several of them were not much older than he was.

After lunch he took a walk around the square at the center of town. Not only did the walk help burn some of the extra calories from lunch, it gave the sheriff a chance to check in on some of the local downtown businesses. Tom was very hands on and liked to meet those he served. Plus, he would be up for reelection next year and it never hurt to make the public aware of you early.

An hour later he parked once again in front of the Sheriff's Department office. The town council had offered to paint a reserved spot for him, but he passed on the invitation. He didn't think walking a few extra steps would hurt him.

Coffee in hand, Myers stepped inside the busy police station. Once the door closed he removed his sunglasses and dropped them in his shirt pocket.

"Good afternoon, Sheriff," Madison Fuller said when she saw him enter. Madison was new in the office. She worked afternoons behind the main desk and handled the files, the phones, and the mail. She was a college student at the nearby Gainesville Junior College in the mornings and worked in the office to help pay for her tuition. She had been a Godsend for the sheriff and his deputies, who seemed to misfile more often than not. She had not yet arrived when he had left for lunch.

"Afternoon, Madison," he said as he headed toward his office.

Madison grabbed a small stack of paper and followed a couple steps behind and stopped at the door.

"Anything pressing for me to look at?" he asked once he was behind his desk.

"Nothing serious." She held up a stack of small scraps of paper. "Mostly phone calls to return."

"Anybody I need to call right away?"

"I don't think so. There is a detective from the Atlanta PD that has called a couple times. Didn't leave a message other than he would call back again later."

"Okay, thanks," he said as she laid the papers on his desk. "Unless it's important, keep taking messages and I'll get back to them later. I really need to finish this stuff today."

Once he was alone in his office, Tom dove back into the file he had been working before lunch. He was a few days behind on paperwork, plus it was time for the annual performance reviews for his staff, and he was behind. He wanted to get it under control before going home tonight, but the only way that was going to happen was if he could work undisturbed. His deputies should be able to handle any issues that might crop up. If something came up they couldn't handle on their own they would let him know. Otherwise, he planned to devote the rest of the day to playing catch up.

Once he got started all thoughts of phone messages were forgotten.

Including the two from Shan Lomax.

# # #

When the phone rang, Tom Myers was surprised to learn that two hours had passed.

The sad part was that he was not as far along as he had hoped to be. Paperwork was the least favorite part of his job. Although it was a necessary evil, he would have been just as happy to never sign his name to another form again. The people who droned on and on about the paperless society we had become obviously did not work in law enforcement.

He tapped the speaker button on the phone.

"Yes, Madison?"

"Sorry to bother you, but that detective from Atlanta is on the phone again. "He says it's urgent."

"That's okay. I'll take it. What's his name?"

"Detective Lomax. He's holding on line three."

"Thanks. I've got it."

After disconnecting the speaker and picking up the phone he leaned back in the chair and propped his booted feet up on the corner of his desk. It was the most comfortable he'd been all day. "Detective Lomax? How ya doing? This is Sheriff Tom Myers," he said. "How may I help you?"

"Thank you for taking my call, Sheriff," the man on the other end of the line said politely. "I really hate to bother you with this, but I think we may have a situation happening in your town and I thought you should be made aware of it."

That got Myers attention. "Oh," he said, sitting up straight in the chair, his feet hitting the floor. "What kind of situation?"

Detective Lomax laid it all out for him. He told him about the Morehouse suicide, his partner's previous dealings with the deceased, the reading of the will in Sommersville, and his concern that the whole thing was a setup of some kind although he had absolutely no proof of any of it. The detective's story helped explain the traffic around the old Morehouse estate that morning. He also told Myers that he had lost contact with his partner, who was at the reading of the will along with a few other prominent law enforcement officials, including a sitting superior court judge. "He's not answering his cell phone and he missed a prearranged check in time we had set up."

"How overdue is he?"

"A couple of hours. Not quite long enough for me to sound the red alert here, but it's enough to make me nervous."

"I can understand that," Myers said. "Well, we do have a few intermittent dead zones once you get out into the county," he explained. "There aren't that many cell towers out in farm country and I'm not sure how much you know about Sommersville, but the Morehouse estate is pretty well in the middle of nowhere way outside the town limits."

"Maybe, but considering who is involved, I'd rather be safe than sorry on this one."

"I can understand that. If it were my partner I'd probably be worried too. So what is it you need from me?"

"I was wondering if you might consider sending someone out to take a look just to make sure everything's on the up and up?"

"I don't have any probably cause to actually head out to the property. The estate sits well back from the road. You can't even see the house from the road because of all the trees. Before I send people in there I need to have something more to go on than a missed check in."

"Look, I know my partner. The only reason he'd miss a call in is if he's in trouble. If I'm wrong, I'll apologize, but this whole thing makes my neck hairs stand up on end. I can't help thinking that there's something rotten in your jurisdiction, Sheriff."

"I can understand that," Myers said. "I'm not too keen on there being anything rotten in my town part any more than you are." He chuckled. "I recall reading about the Morehouse case back when it happened. Pretty nasty stuff. I'm surprised there's been nothing on the news about his death. You'd think somebody would have found out and reported it by now."

"That's part of what makes me nervous. No one knows what's going on. I'm actually on the road now and heading your way. I should be there shortly, but I'm way out of my jurisdiction. Can you maybe have someone swing by and check on things? If for no other reason than to set my mind at ease?"

The sheriff chuckled. "I noticed the increased traffic this morning and I've actually got a car driving by every hour or so, but we've not gone onto the property. I guess it can't hurt to swing by myself and convey my condolences, maybe take a look around while I'm there."

Detective Lomax let out a breath. "Thank you," he said. "I'll call when I get into town."

"I'll see you when you get here," the sheriff said before hanging up the phone. He sat there for a moment, pondering everything the detective had told him. If Morehouse's reputation was to be believed, he could understand Lomax's concern for his partner, especially given their history. If something funky was going on out there he needed to find out sooner rather than later.

Myers stood, stretched out the kinks in his back and moaned softly as he felt muscles contract and tighten. He hadn't noticed how uncomfortable his desk chair was until he started the performance reviews. It was murder on his back and after a couple hours sitting behind the desk, he needed to get up and move around. Being chained to a desk was his least favorite part of the job. He did not enjoy it at all.

He grabbed his hat and jacket from the old coat rack in the corner and tapped a finger against the framed JAWS poster hanging in his office as he headed for the door. Even though it had scared the shit out of him at the time, JAWS had been his favorite movie since he first saw it as a kid. For that reason alone, the poster would have been the highlight of his collection of classic movie posters even if it were not autographed by the movie's star, Roy Scheider. He got the autograph when he ran into the actor several years earlier while on vacation at Universal Studios in Florida where he was filming the TV series seaQuest DSV. It was perfect timing as he had just bought the poster at one of the theme park stores just moments earlier. It was the best ten dollars he'd ever spent.

The JAWS poster was, sadly, only a reproduction of the original, but he hadn't found a good copy of the real thing he could afford so the reproduction had to do and since it was signed, it would never come out of its frame. The collection was his pride and joy. Not only did he have three posters in his office, two of which he cycled out every few months. JAWS had remained in its location since he brought it home and it he had no plans to relocate it anytime soon. In addition to his office at the sheriff's station, the room that doubled as his study at home was covered with them as well. He would have decorated the entire house with them if Mildred would let him. Unfortunately, she wasn't quite the movie fan he was and put her foot down on the matter.

The three he had hanging in the office at the moment were JAWS,

The Maltese Falcon, and the George Clooney version of Ocean's Eleven. In another week he would change them out again. He had a sharp Tombstone poster hanging up at home that he wanted to bring in and show off to the deputies. It was one of the movies everyone in the station agreed on when they talked about their top five picks.

Sadly, the collection had not grown much these past months. The unexpected side effect of Mildred's healthy eating kick was that they were now spending almost twice as much on food than they had been before the diet. Eating healthy was oddly expensive, which boggled his mind no end. He assumed more people would eat a healthier diet if the food weren't so damned expensive. After buying groceries, there wasn't much left over for non-essentials like buying and framing movie posters. At least that's what she kept telling him.

"Madison?" Myers called as he stepped out into the squad room.

"Yes, Sheriff?"

"I've got to take a ride out toward Miller's Chapel for a bit. If that detective from Atlanta calls back, patch him through to my cell. Oh, and have Dooley and Chris meet me out there by the old Morehouse place, would you?"

"Sure. You expecting trouble?"

"I doubt it. It's probably nothing, but better safe than sorry, right?"

"Sounds logical to me."

"Yeah. If nothing else it gets me out of the office for awhile."

"Right."

". It'll be nice to take a relaxing ride in the country," he joked as he stepped out into the sunlight.

# # #

For all of its size, the town proper of Sommersville was relatively small.

If there was no traffic through town, Tom Myers could drive from one end to the other in a matter of minutes. Most of Sommersville was made up of farmland that bordered the town proper, but a few housing developments had begun clearing off land for new subdivisions recently. One of the downsides to having farms in the family for generations was that many of the children and grandchildren of the farmers had not gone into the family business. When the farmers passed on, their heirs often did not want to keep the land so they would put it up for sale and the developers would line up with enticing offers. Not long after a new subdivision, strip mall, or Tom's favorite, a car wash would be announced as coming soon. Sommersville had so many car washes that he had lost count. Since most of the farms used well water as opposed to city water, they weren't subject to water restrictions after the past few summer droughts, they washed their vehicles at home.

The town council was currently deep in negotiations with a clothing manufacturer about building a new manufacturing and warehouse facility just outside of the city limits. They were always reaching out to charm businesses into moving into the county.

Change was in the air.

Or, as Dooley had put it, "*civilization was finally coming to Sommersville.*"

Tom wasn't against growth in the area. New homes meant new money and new faces. His only hope was that new crime did not also come with the expansion, although he suspected he would be disappointed on that score.

Speaking of crime, the Morehouse mansion was located on Miller's Chapel Road, one of those off the beaten path areas out in the middle of nowhere. The mansion sat smack dab in the center of 900 acres and was surrounded by dense wooded areas on all sides. There was only one driveway that lead to the house, though Myers knew of one dirt road that exited the rear of the property. He wouldn't have been surprised if there were more, especially after hearing stories about the mansion's owner.

Miller's Chapel Road was just ahead. A car passed him going the opposite direction. Ordinarily this wasn't something he would have paid much attention to, but today had been far from ordinary so far. He kept one eye on the unfamiliar vehicle in the rearview mirror when he noticed the car's break lights flare into existence.

The driver pulled to the edge of the road and made a quick U-Turn just as the sheriff turned left onto Miller's Chapel Road.

Myers sped up and took the first curve on Miller's Chapel at speeds he would have given someone else a ticket for had he seen them attempt it. Once he was around the curve and out of sight he pulled over and stepped out of his vehicle, unsnapped his holster flap, and waited.

The car came around the curve just a couple of seconds later.

The driver swerved when he saw the sheriff's truck sitting at a dead stop across the middle of the road, blocking both lanes. A screech of tires and the smell of burnt rubber filled the air as the car left a black skid mark on the asphalt.

The driver opened the door and stepped out.

Myers released the snap on his holster. His hand rested on the gun, but he did not pull it..

"Sheriff Myers?" the driver asked carefully, staying in the crook of the open door.

"That's me. Is there something I can help you with, sir?"

"I certainly hope so. I'm Shan Lomax," he said as he held up his police ID and badge. "We spoke on the phone earlier. I was just on my way to your office when I saw you on the road."

"Oh. Right." The sheriff slid his hand off his service weapon and snapped the clip onthe holster holster. "Nice to meet you, Detective," Myers said. "I wasn't expecting you quite so soon. I'm afraid I haven't located your partner yet."

"Oh."

"The Morehouse place is about two miles down the road, that way," Myers said as he hitched a thumb over his shoulder. "I've got a couple of my deputies sitting on the place. I'm heading that way now if you'd like to follow me."

"Sure."

"Try to keep up," the sheriff said as he slid behind the wheel.

Shan Lomax couldn't help but smile as he pulled out onto the road behind the truck.

CHAPTER 34

John Bartlett didn't know how much longer he could control the situation.

Benjamin West was growing impatient and in his fervor to prove that Darrin Morehouse, the man responsible for their current predicament was still among the living threatened to overwhelm any good judgement on his part. Bartlett was surprised he had been able to restrain his new *"partner"* from running off half-cocked to the mansion. It was a tactic that would surely get him killed, but West wasn't thinking about anything other than getting his hands on Morehouse. This was one of the biggest problems he had with the reporter. He had good instincts, but he tended to leap before he looked.

His tendency to act before thinking had almost gotten him killed on a couple of occasions. And those were only the ones that Bartlett knew about. He wouldn't have been surprised to find out there were other instances where West's recklessness nearly did him in as well. Although he hardly considered the man a friend, Bartlett was a bit concerned for the man's survival. Perhaps when this was behind them, should they make it out in one piece, they would have a long talk.

Yeah, that'll go over real well, he thought. *Like a lead balloon.*

But first they had to get out of this situation alive.

While he did not necessarily buy the journalist's assertions that Morehouse was still alive and pulling all of their strings like some insane puppet master, Bartlett certainly couldn't dismiss the notion out of hand either. He knew from firsthand experience that their common enemy was certainly capable of such deception and manipulation. He had clearly demonstrated that even prison couldn't stop him from playing his sick little games.

West was under the impression that Morehouse had faked his own death in an attempt to lure all of his enemies, of which there were many, to the mansion so he could corral them in one central location so that he could kill them all.

Even with their history dealing with the man's twisted schemes, Bartlett couldn't help but think that everything that had happened to them today seemed just a little too out there, like something out of a pulp novel or a Hollywood action movie.

However, despite the evidence before him, he couldn't shake the feeling that perhaps, just maybe, Benjamin West was right. It was possible that he might be on to something. If anyone had the wherewithal and the means to fake their own death, lure each of them out here to the middle of nowhere, and pull the strings that kick started this sick *Most Dangerous Game* scenario into motion, it would be Darrin Morehouse. Surely, none of them would have come out here to this secluded mansion otherwise. He doubted that any of them would have voluntarily stepped foot in Morehouse's mansion under normal circumstances. But yet, there they all were. Each of them had come of their own free will, if only out of curiosity of seeing what was in the will. Or just to make sure the bastard was dead.

Although he wasn't ready to believe Benjamin West's wild theory that he had faked his own death and was hiding somewhere in the mansion laughing his ass off as they jumped through his hoops, but he couldn't help but wonder what Morehouse's endgame was in all of this. The man was many things, but in all the time he had spent pursuing him Bartlett had never seen him do anything without a specific purpose. Sometimes that purpose wasn't readily apparent, but eventually the pieces came together. Whether he was dead or not, Morehouse obviously had a plan for all of them. He always had a plan. It could have been as simple as the recorded image said and his ultimate goal was to gun them all down, but that wasn't really Morehouse's style.

He might want them all dead, but he wouldn't just have them

killed.

No. He would want to play with them first.

The kill would come later, after he'd had his fun.

He heard West say his name, which broke his train of thought. "What?"

"I said, what now?" the reporter asked as they listened to the approaching rumble of a very large vehicle. He was growing impatient with the waiting and Bartlett could understand the feeling. The last thing he wanted to do was hide under the bridge while the men with guns looked for them.

"Car."

"Sounds like a big one-- powerful engine."

They listened carefully from their hiding place crouched beneath the narrow bridge that crossed the ravine and the shallow creek that ran through the middle of it. The bridge above them was part of the driveway that snaked through the nine hundred acre estate from the road to the mansion at its center.

West adjusted his position because his legs were burning from squatting for such a long time, but kept his gun aimed toward the lip of the bridge in case anyone bothered to lean over and take a look. In the unlikely event that happened, he and Bartlett would be sitting ducks.

Bartlett knew he wouldn't be able to keep West in place for much longer. The reporter was getting edgy, fidgeting as he kept shifting from one leg to the other. He was like a pit bull. Once he grabbed on to something he wouldn't let go until he proved his point. An admirable trait in a journalist, but in a situation like the one they found themselves in at the moment, not so much. Bartlett knew this from experience with the man that if he hadn't been here to reign him in West would have already made a run straight toward the mansion without any regard for the mercenaries that were tracking them and in the process get himself killed.

"Just hang tight, West," he whispered as the vehicle drew closer. "Let's see what they do first, okay? Just hold steady."

"You know what they're going to do," West whispered between grit teeth. "They're going to shoot as soon as they see us."

"Then let's make sure they don't see us, okay?"

West grumbled something unintelligible, but Bartlett was already on the move and wasn't listening to him anymore. He walked in a crouch to the far end of the bridge, which was only six or seven steps away. Wild brush and thick weeds provided sufficient cover that he was able to rise up from beneath the bridge and take a quick peek in the direction of the vehicle. As he had guessed, it was an SUV. He could make out multiple shapes inside, but with the reflection of the sun on the windshield he couldn't make an accurate count.

The rest of the bridge was empty, although he suspected that would change soon enough once the men who had been chasing them in the woods a few minutes before came out to join with their rein-forcements. He wished he knew how many mercenaries Morehouse had hired for this job. There seemed to be an almost inexhaustible supply of them. Some on foot chasing them through the woods, others in the SUV, and probably even more back at the mansion. He hoped they were all too busy chasing after him and west to worry about going after the others in the car. With any luck, they would have made it to safety by now.

"We need to get out of here before they get here and one of them gets the bright idea to check under the bridge," West said.

"I know," Bartlett said as he walked back toward the reporter. "I'm thinking."

"Think faster."

Bartlett slid into position next to West. "Okay, here's our options. Number one: we blow the bridge as they cross overhead."

"That's a crappy idea."

"Agreed. Number two: we head out into the underbrush and try to make our way around them and head back to the house."

West blew out a breath. "That's not much better. I hope you've got a third option."

Bartlett smiled. "Third option is to toss the grenades before they get here, split up and run for cover back in the woods. If one of us gets caught the other one keeps hauling ass. That way at least one of us gets back to the house."

"All of those options suck, John."

"I never said they were good options, but they are the only ones we've got. If you have a better idea I'm all ears."

West was silent for a moment.

"I didn't think so."

"If we run, these guys are going to cut us down before we get to cover."

232

"I know," Bartlett said. "But it's a damned sure bet they're going to find us if we stay here. Personally, I'd vote for option three. That way at least one of us stands a chance of getting out of here."

West blew out a breath in surrender. "Fine. What do we do?"

"How's your throwing arm?"

#

John Bartlett gave a silent countdown from three seconds using his fingers.

When he reached one, he gave his partner the go ahead sign by pointing toward the target.

Not liking the plan, but resigned to do his part, Benjamin West stepped out from under the protection of the bridge while simultaneously pulling the pin on the grenade he carried. A mental *one... two...* count followed before he tossed the pineapple with all his strength in the direction of the approaching SUV. Without waiting to see if he hit his mark, the reporter beat feet away from the safety of the bridge, heading back in the direction he had come earlier, splashing in the shallow creek bed as he ran as fast and as far as he could away from the bridge.

The grenade bounced once then twice before it rolled under the approaching vehicle.

Having obviously noticed the incoming explosive device, the driver swerved hard to the left, too hard as it turned out for such a narrow drive. The tire slipped off the road into the grass. Instinctively, he jerked the wheel back in the opposite direction, which sent the SUV into a slide as the tire failed to find purchase in the slick glass. Instead of gripping pavement, the rubber tore a gouge through the unkempt grass as the vehicle threatened to careen out of control.

Once he realized he couldn't move around it the driver slammed on the brakes. The squeal of tires was quickly followed by shouts of alarm and the unmistakable sounds of car doors opening as the mercenaries inside leapt from the car to the safety of the ditches on either side of the winding drive.

The grenade detonated with a loud pop underneath the SUV, instantly disabling the mercenaries' mode of transportation. This put all of them on somewhat equal footing. They were all hoofing it now, but the bad guys were still better armed and outnumbered Bartlett and

West by a pretty wide margin. West hoped that this made the odds a bit more even. At least that had been the plan.

A second after West's grenade detonated, John Bartlett stepped from beneath cover, pulled the pin on their last remaining explosive, and tossed it in the opposite direction. They knew that there were men coming at them from that direction as well since they had shot at them from the top of the ravine. The grenade would hopefully keep those men under cover and off the road long enough for Bartlett and West to get a decent head start.

The second the grenade left his hand, Bartlett took off in the same direction as West. The chaos on the drive behind him drowned out the sounds of his splashing as he bolted along the edge of the creek, slipping in the loose dirt and water as he ran.

West was up and over the embankment ahead of Bartlett, which was all part of the plan. As they had worked it out, West would head back the way they had originally planned before the guys with guns had started shooting at them. Bartlett, on the other hand, would run further down stream and take a different route. That way, if the bad guys followed one of them, then the other still had a shot at getting back to the main house.

If all went as planned, they would both be up their selected embankments before the bad guys noticed which way they went.

Sadly, such was not the case.

Bartlett heard shouts from behind, but he dared not turn to look. Adrenaline surged and he picked up the pace despite being exhausted from spending hours on the run through the woods already. There was little doubt that they would be after him, which is what he expected. That's why he had insisted the reporter go first.

He just hoped it bought West enough time to get to safety. If West followed the plan, and John had to admit that it was a big *if*, then he would have a big head start while the men with guns chased him. Or, as he had put it to the reporter when the hatched the plan, "I can play fox to their hounds." The blank stare on West's face told him that the reference was lost on him. It made Bartlett feel old.

Out of the corner of his vision, something caught his eye.

Unfortunately, he had little time to react before one of the men who had shot and he and West earlier came over the edge of the embankment toward him. Halfway down the slope he launched himself at Bartlett. With no time to get out of the way, John braced for impact.

The mercenary tackled him about the waist, knocking him off his feet. Both men fell into the icy water tangled together in a knot of flailing arms and legs.

The mercenary had the advantage not only in surprise, but he was also younger and faster than Bartlett, who had absorbed most of the impact when they hit the rocky bottom of the creek bed. The mercenary was obviously well trained, but Bartlett was a scrappy street fighter who had been in more than his fair share of dust ups over the years. He knew how to fight, but more importantly, he knew how to win. John Bartlett was not above fighting dirty.

He twisted, rolling himself into position on top of his attacker. The mercenary held tight with one arm around the cop's neck while the other crossed his chest and squeezed. Under the pressure on his chest, Bartlett exhaled loudly until there was nothing left.

He couldn't breathe.

Bartlett brought his elbow down hard and slammed it into the man's face. He repeated the move four times before he heard bone crunch and the man's grip on him lessened. Bartlett rolled free into a crouch and gasped for breath now that his chest was free of the big man's vice-like grip. He wanted to roll over and lay there, gasping in one beautiful lung full of air after another, but there was no time for that. He knew it would be only a matter of seconds before the man was on him again or until his friends arrived. He grabbed a smooth stone about the size of a tennis ball from the creek bed and cupped it tightly in his fist. Before the man could get back to his feet, Bartlett planted a punch across the dazed mercenary's face with the stone, taking him out of the fight in an instant. The man dropped to the water, blood pouring from his freshly broken nose.

Bartlett coughed and tried to suck in air, which resulted in another wracking series of coughs. He knew that the others would be on him soon and that he did not have time to catch is breath. He had to move and willed his legs to start running again even though they felt like lead weights and did not want to cooperate.

He heard the sound of splashing behind him and knew it was too late.

"Just hold it right there, pal," an unknown voice said.

Still crouching, Bartlett pivoted and pointed the Sig Sauer toward the voice and pulled the trigger. There was no hesitation. He didn't even take time to aim.

The mercenary had a surprised look on his face as he dropped to the creek bed in a heap next to his friend with the broken nose. He was dead before he hit the water.

Bartlett got to his feet, the gun still pointed toward the approaching men who now moved toward him a lot more cautiously than before. He needed to take advantage of their hesitation. Surprise had worked for him once, but he couldn't count on it again. If these men were half as professional as they seemed, they were already making a plan to catch him. He knew it wouldn't be long before they caught him, but he'd be damned if he was going to make it easy for them. If they wanted him they were going to have to work for it.

Ignoring every muscle in his body that was screaming for him to stop, he started moving slowly up the embankment behind him, his gun still pointed at the approaching mercs.

"Hey."

It was instinct that made him turn at the sound of someone speaking to him from behind and he realized his error as soon as he made it. The last thing John Bartlett saw was the butt of a rifle flying toward his face.

Pain quickly followed.

And then there was nothing.

CHAPTER 35

Shan Lomax wanted to say something.

He didn't know Sheriff Myers, but what he had seen of the man and his deputies so far he had liked. The sheriff and his men seemed capable enough and knew their jobs. They had mobilized on nothing more than his word that there *might* be a problem at the Morehouse Estate. Previous experience with others in similar situations had shown him that such professional courtesy was not the norm when it came to police jurisdiction. Local cops were notoriously territorial when it came to their little piece of the landscape. Most did not tolerate intrusions well. Tom Myers had proved an exception.

After meeting up with him on the road, Lomax followed the sheriff's pick up truck to the entrance of the Morehouse estate. Two of his deputies were already on site, each one standing next to one of the police cars, talking casually. The sheriff pulled his pick up off on the side of the road and Lomax followed suit and parked behind him.

A quick round of handshakes followed as Sheriff Myers introduced Detective Lomax to Deputy Benjamin Dooley and Deputy Chris Jackson. Like their boss, neither of the deputies seemed put out by the inclusion of an outsider. Shan found it refreshing to work with such welcoming people. It certainly wasn't the usual reception a police officer from another jurisdiction expected when he came calling. Cops tended to be rather territorial. He understood it all too well. He doubted he would be very happy if an out of town officer popped into Atlanta the way he had dropped in on Sheriff Myers.

"So what's the word, Ben?" the sheriff asked one of his deputies.

"Not much, Tom," Deputy Dooley said as he scratched at the stubble on his chin that Shan guessed was only a couple days old. "No one's gone in or out since this morning," he paused and spit tobacco juice onto the side of the road. "At least not through here." He pointed off to the left. "The property is bordered by two other roads. There aren't any driveways cut in those roads officially, but it wouldn't be hard to make one on the fly."

"We did hear the faint echo of some gunfire a few minutes ago," Jackson added. "But since it's hunting season there's really nothing unusual about that this far outside town."

"Gunshots," Myers said softly.

"Well, the echo of them anyway," Jackson said. "We've no way of knowing if they came from the estate or across the road. You know how the sound carries out here. They could have come from anywhere."

Myers pushed back his hat and scratched his forehead.

"What you need is an anonymous complaint from a concerned citizen."

"Oh? And just where do you expect us to find this *anonymous complaint*, Detective Lomax?" Myers asked through a big smile.

Lomax rolled his eyes, but decided to play his part. "Help. Police," he said quietly. "I heard gun shots and I'm scared that someone might be hurt. Please send someone to check it out."

Dooley and Jackson exchanged an amused glance.

"How's that?" Lomax asked.

Both men shrugged simultaneously.

"Works for me," Myers said with a laugh. "Let's go check it out." He turned to Lomax. "You got a vest?"

Shan nodded.

"Put it on. Last thing I need is to get an out-of-towner shot."

Lomax popped the trunk and pulled out his deep indigo kevlar vest with POLICE etched on it in large white box letters. He pulled out a leg holster and strapped it on as well and slid in his back up weapon. His primary weapon was tucked securely in the shoulder holster he wore beneath his blazer. Before slamming the trunk he pulled a shotgun and a box of shells. He carried them back toward the sheriff's truck.

"I see you came prepared."

"My partner's something of a Boy Scout. It rubs off on you, what can I say?" Lomax laughed. "Besides, I hear it's hunting season." He shrugged. "When in Rome..."

Myers laughed as he pulled on his own vest, which was black and did not have the giant POLICE written on it. He had a belt holster with a .45 Magnum cradled in it. He didn't carry a back up weapon as far as Shan could see, but the truck had a gun rack that held two shotguns and a rifle.

"Looks like I'm not the only one," he said, motioning toward the rack of guns.

"Never know when you might run into a bear out here," Myers said matter of fact.

"Right." The detective couldn't tell if he was kidding or not.

"Your partner isn't the only one who used to be a Boy Scout."

"I'm starting to realize that."

"Chris, call in some back up and wait for them here," Myers told Deputy Jackson. "I want this entrance blocked. That means no one in or out. And let's get some cruisers out there to check the perimeter and make sure there are no more ways on to or off of the property."

"Will do."

"Oh, and call Jimmy Griffith over at the Forestry Service and see if we can borrow his chopper. Some air support couldn't hurt."

"You got it, Sheriff." Jackson walked toward the road as he used the walkie clipped to this chest to call it in.

Myers pointed at Lomax and motioned toward the truck. "You're with me, Detective."

Shan nodded. He knew he was lucky that the sheriff was letting him tag along as a courtesy so he didn't protest leaving his car parked on the side of the road.

"Dooley, you follow us in. Stay close."

"Got it, boss," Dooley said as he opened the driver's side door and slid a rifle into the seat beside him.

"And watch your back," Myers told his deputy as he followed suit.

Dooley grunted a laugh.

Detective Lomax slid into the passenger seat of the pick up and rested the shotgun against his leg, open so it couldn't accidentally discharge in the vehicle.

"You ready?" the sheriff asked.

"You bet."

"Then let's go find your partner."

# # #

Shan wanted to thank Sheriff Myers for helping, but knew it wasn't the time.

The sheriff drove as they took the sharp curves of the long winding driveway that led to the mansion at the center of the estate. Myers took the curves as if he were driving a stock car at the Indy 500 instead of a battered pick up truck. The squeal of tired on the pavement accompanied each turn.

Not surprisingly, Myers' deputy had no trouble keeping up with them. He was barely a car length behind them in his cruiser and made the curves with ease. Neither the sheriff's truck or Deputy Dooley's car was running lights or sirens. If there really was something going on at the mansion they didn't want to ruin the element of surprise by coming in with sirens screaming.

If they were wrong and everything was okay, then he could simply state they were responding to a curious call into the station, which wasn't so much a lie as a broad stretching of the truth. Still, Lomax had witnessed his partner do some incredible tap dancing with suspects and witnesses to get them to cooperate. It was an acquired skill that he was quickly learning.

"How long is this road?" he asked as they took the next curve.

"Not sure," Myers said without looking at him. "It goes back quite a ways. The mansion sits smack dab in the middle of the estate, which is somewhere south of a thousand or so acres, I think."

Lomax whistled.

"Yeah. It's a big one," the sheriff said. "I've only been out here once, but I remember it took us quite awhile to get all the way out to the mansion. Don't know why they couldn't make this damned driveway a little straighter, though."

"I'm guessing that's intentional," Lomax said as he gripped the handle above the door tighter. He now understood exactly why they were often called *"Oh My God Handles"* because the sheriff's break-neck turns made him want to scream, "OhmiGod!" more than once.

"Why's that?"

"What?"

"You said it was probably intentional," Myers said as he sped up along a small straightway. "What makes you think that?"

"Oh. I assume the curvy drive was designed this way to slow down anyone coming in, especially anyone unannounced. You know," he smiled. "People like us."

"Well, doesn't that make me feel special."

Despite the seriousness of the situation, Lomax couldn't help but laugh as the sheriff sped into the next curve, tires squealing the entire way.

CHAPTER 36

Janice Kilpatrick felt something tapping on her temple.

She woke feeling strange. She ached all over in a way that re-minded her of when she got on a health kick the year before and started going to the gym every day. She had never hurt so much as she had after the third day of working with the personal trainer from Hell. This felt a lot like that, except for the pounding headache she was sporting this time.

She realized that no one was actually tapping her on the temple as she had originally thought. She felt another tap as something dripped on her. She touched a hand gingerly to her sore head and felt some-thing warm and wet there. Whatever was dripping on her was warm, but she couldn't make her eyes open to see what it was.

Janice sat up and felt the seatbelt dig into her neck. The car was tilted on an angle, with gravity pulling her down toward the driver's side door on her left. She tried to shake away the flashbulbs going off behind her eyes and focus.

She regretted it instantly.

The irritating flashes exploded into a dizzying wave of vertigo and suddenly everything around her spun out of control as if she were trapped in some crazy carnival's whirl-a-gig. She felt the bile rise in her throat as her nauseated stomach threatened to erupt. She closed her eyes tight, which did nothing to dim the brilliant flash of colors, but it did help her resist the urge to vomit. There was a familiar burning metallic smell in the car that was not helping the situation, but Janice couldn't place it. All she knew for certain was that she needed to get out of this car and she needed to do so now.

Miraculously, she had somehow managed to keep her breakfast down, but it wasn't easy. She was suddenly very glad her companion had been in too big a hurry to stop for lunch.

She pushed against the door, but it groaned in protest and refused to budge. That was when she noticed that the window was covered by something thick and wet that was keeping out the sunlight. She opened her eyes just a squint. The last thing she recalled sliding out of control as those men were shooting at them. And she also remembered feeling the impact as the car slammed into... what? Was it one of the gunmen? She had hit something, that much was certain. Whether she had hit the man with the gun or something else, she was afraid she knew exactly what the sickly smell was that made her stomach twist into knots.

The blood was thick as it rolled down the glass and began to seep in through the cracks in the passenger side window. Little chunks of... something... were caught in the flow that rolled down the front window. Janice could only assume that was all that remained of the man she had hit. Her only solace, such as it was, was that he had tried to kill them first. Dumb luck had simply allowed her to get there first.

Janice fought back the urge to scream.

"Everyone okay?" she asked, trying to focus on something other than the dead man dripping from her window.

Judge Hughes groaned so she knew he was alive, but he might have been injured. At first glance he appeared to be in one piece. The last thing she needed was for him to have broken something. All of the information she had on the judge came from his public record. The Nathan Hughes she was familiar with was a strong man who ruled his court with an iron fist. The frail man in the back seat was a far cry from the mental image she had painted of the man. She hoped he was all right.

The fact that the former Mrs. Morehouse wasn't screaming bloody murder meant that she was probably out cold. Had she been injured or awake, Janice had little doubt she would be as quiet as she was at the moment.

The same was true for her boss. Fabian Alexander's head was propped against the passenger side window, which was surprising considering the way the car was tilting. He wasn't moving and she was afraid he might be dead. If he had not been wearing his seatbelt he would have probably fallen atop her when they hit the ditch.

Laura Sellars was also out, having been sitting by the driver's side door. Her head was lying against the cracked glass with dirt and grass just on the other side. Janice couldn't tell from her angle if the glass was cracked as a result of the car hitting the ditch or Laura's head hitting the glass. She didn't see any blood so she hoped for the former option.

Janice reached over toward her boss to check for a pulse, but her seatbelt had locked in place so she couldn't get to him. After struggling with the lock, it finally released and she was able to free herself from the restraint. Holding onto the headrest and planting her feet on the driver's side door, she pulled herself over to him. A quick check of the carotid artery told her that he still had a pulse and breathed a sigh of relief when she found one.

He moaned softly when she touched him.

"Mr. Alexander?" she shouted happily. "Are you okay?"

"Is shouting really necessary, Miss Kilpatrick?" he asked after a moment. His voice was weak and shaky, but he was alive.

"Oh, thank God," she breathed loudly. As big a pain in the neck as her boss could be, Janice didn't want him to get hurt. "I thought you were…"

"Well I'm not," he said as he sat up as straight as possible in the leaning seat. "What happened?"

"We ran off the road."

"Nice driving," he said with a pained laugh.

Janice grimaced. "Next time you drive," she told him, assuming that would make him offer a rebuttal. She needed to keep him awake and talking just in case he had a concussion. She wasn't sure if there was any truth in it or if it was simply one of those things she had always heard on TV and in the movies so it felt like common knowledge.

A trail of blood ran from his nose down over his lips and onto his chin, but it appeared to have stopped, or at least slowed. A large stain covered his chest from where it had dripped onto his shirt made it look like his injuries were more severe. Janice tried to check to make sure, but he waved her away and assured her that he was okay.

"Just leave me alone," he mumbled and pushed her hand away.

"We need to get out of here," she told him.

"You'll get no argument from me," Warden Chalmers said with a grunt from the back seat. It was the first indication that any of her passengers were still conscious. "What happened?" he asked.

"That seems to be the question of the day," Janice said. "Honestly, I'm not sure what--"

"We slid into a ditch," the judge interrupted weakly. "Now get off of me!"

"I'm trying, Judge," the warden grunted as he pulled himself closer to the door that was now pointing skyward at an odd angle.

"Any chance we can drive out of here?" Laura Sellars asked with a strained voice that told Janice she was in pain.

"I can try," Janice said as she slid back into her seat. The car's engine was no longer running so she tried the ignition switch. It coughed and choked with each try, but finally on the third try it roared to life. Putting the gear in reverse, Janice tried to back out, but nothing happened. She could feel the car trying to move, but the tires in the ditch were only digging them deeper into the wet grass and mud. The tires on the driveway were angled in such a way that they couldn't grab enough traction to pull them free.

"Okay, if you can't go forward," Janice said with annoyance as she tried putting the car in drive. The tires spun rapidly, but did not catch. Although she tried several more times she knew they were stuck but good. "We're not going anywhere," she told them as she turned off the engine.

"Well, one thing's for sure. We can't stay in here," Warden Chalmers said.

"What if there are more of them out there?" Janice asked.

"If they're out there then it won't be long before they come over here," Chalmers said as he tucked his gun back in its holster. He needed both hands free to try and open the door.

"I'm pretty sure you hit them," Janice reassured the warden as she watched him wiggle upward as he pushed against the door. "Nice shooting."

"Not a bad bit of driving on your part either, ma'am," the warden said as he pushed against the door again. "But, personally, if there are more of them out there - and I'm pretty sure there are - I'd rather not be stuck in here when they get here with their automatic weapons, if you know what I mean?"

Janice gave him a grim smile.

He returned it before resuming his work on the bullet-riddled door.

On the third shove the door opened, but gravity worked against Chalmers and it closed again, but he somehow managed to keep it open a crack. The warden braced the door with his shoe to keep it from closing back against him since the car was tilted at an odd angle in the ditch. He pushed it open again with his foot and scooted out.

"Be careful," Janice said.

"Don't worry," Chalmers said with a smile. "We got them, re-member?" Then he dropped over the edge and out of view.

That's when someone opened fire on the car again.

And Vivian Morehouse screamed.

#

Francis Chalmers hit the pavement hard and felt a jolt of pain run up his right leg.

An instant later he heard the first impact as a bullet smacked into the metal frame just inches above his head. A second later the car door slammed as gravity tugged at it, leaving him out in the open all alone and exposed.

Before the gunman could fire again, Chalmers crawled around the rear or the car and rolled into the ditch. It was cover, but it was far from ideal. Based on the events of the day, he doubted that these men, whoever they were, would have the least little qualm about shooting up the car or the people inside so he had to move fast. He was all that stood between the people in the car and certain death. He could hear a scream from inside the car and wondered if anyone had been hit or if the former Mrs. Morehouse was screaming just because that's what she did. A lot.

He checked the clip on his gun. Three shots left. Plus, he had one spare clip in his jacket pocket. He hoped it was enough, but even if he was only facing off against one opponent, the mercenary's automatic machine gun carried a lot more bullets than his Glock. And he could fire them a lot faster.

A quick glance under the car showed only one pair of legs walking toward him, but he had a sneaking suspicion that the man wasn't alone. Chalmers exhaled slowly, trying to calm his labored breathing even as he once again mentally scolded himself for not losing weight, which he did every time he started wheezing from any type of exertion. He always meant it. Until he passed a vending machine and his sweet tooth demanded candy. His heart thundered in his chest. Despite the fact that he dealt with vicious criminals daily, Francis Chalmers did not routinely find himself in situations such as this one. He'd faced prison riots and the occasional skirmish, but this was his first shoot out and he was scared.

But the others were counting on him so he pushed the fear aside and made it work for him instead of against him. He felt the adrenaline flow, his breathing slowing as he focused on the task at hand.

Focus, Francis, he told himself. *One thing at a time.*

He lurched forward, throwing himself from the safety of cover, such as it was, and into the middle of the driveway. He landed on his right side. Jarred by the impact, it took him a fraction of a second to recover.

The gunman saw him and swiveled, changing targets from the car to the warden.

Chalmers raised his gun, aimed quickly, and fired the final three shots in the clip.

The gunman took one in the shoulder and spun around, his finger instinctively tightening on the trigger as he lost balance. Bullets sparked against the pavement as they ricocheted wildly. The warden released the spent clip and quickly slapped in a replacement, his last.

The gunman stopped firing once he hit the ground. Chalmers pulled himself back to his feet, bracing against the tilted car with his left hand while never taking the gun off the man who had shot at him with the other. The man was injured, but still alive. He could see his chest rise and fall with each breath.

"Everyone all right?" the warden asked, chancing a look inside the car through the broken window. He noticed that Judge Hughes had a hand firmly clamped over Vivian Morehouse's mouth in an effort to keep her quiet. He wasn't going to complain. Her screaming fits and general whining had gotten old real fast. There was blood on the older man's shirt.

"We're alive," Laura Sellars said with just a hint of apprehension.

"The Judge took a hit in the arm off those last shots. Looks like glass from the window."

"Is he alright?"

"I'll live," Judge Hughes said, his voice tinged with pain. "Just get us the fuck out of here, will ya?"

"Yes, sir. Just hang tight a moment."

"Is it safe to come out?" Fabian Alexander called from the front seat.

Chalmers held up a hand. "Probably, but hang on just a minute," he cautioned. "Let me check it out first, okay? Just to make sure we're alone out here. No sense giving them more targets if we can avoid it."

Surprisingly, no one argued the point.

He stepped slowly around the front of the car, gun still held in front of him and pointed at the wounded mercenary, who was not moving. He was about to tell the others that it was clear when he heard a shot ring out.

It would be the last sound he ever heard.

CHAPTER 37

Benjamin West watched the tackle that took down his ersatz partner.

His first instinct had been to turn back and help, but they had made a deal that if one of them was captured or injured then the other one kept going. The police officer had been adamant that they both agree to follow through if one or the other were captured. He had made West promise to stick with the plan if something went awry. John Bartlett was many things, but stupid was not among them. The chances of both of them making it to safety were minimal and getting to the truth was the priority.

Even if it cost one of them their life.

He was beginning to wonder is Bartlett had purposefully gotten caught so he could get away, but West quickly dismissed that idea. Getting caught wasn't the smart play. Plus, there was no way of knowing if the men with the guns would try to take him alive. They were under orders to shoot first, weren't they? Morehouse had told them as much during the reading of the will. Prisoners weren't part of the plan.

Of course, with Morehouse, West knew that the plan could change in a heartbeat.

It went against every instinct he had, but West knew that there was nothing he could do to help Bartlett so he did the only thing he could.

He ran.

When he heard the gunshot a few moments later, he wondered if the mercenaries had shot their prisoner. As big a pain in the ass as Bartlett was, West didn't wish the man dead. He couldn't say the same for Morehouse's hired goons, however. Especially not after losing their ride and Bartlett thinning their ranks by a few hands. It made sense to kill him because as long as they kept him alive there was the chance that he might just cause more problems. Putting a bullet between Bartlett's eyes might have been the smartest thing they could do, but a nagging thought kept tugging at West's brain that made him think that they couldn't kill him because the boss wouldn't allow it. He hoped he was wrong, but now more than ever he knew his suspicions were true.

Morehouse is alive!

And for once in his life, Benjamin West hated being right.

The mercenaries had demonstrated quite effectively that they had no problem with killing any of them. They proved that when they took out the lawyer, Philip Hall, back in the study. And that was before they shot Mike Coombes and attacked the rest of them. There was no reason to expect they would keep Bartlett alive unless he was right and Morehouse was alive. If that were the case then he would probably want to pull the trigger himself. The perfect cap to this, his greatest game. It made sense in that same twisted way that Morehouse's other schemes had played out. There was a form of logic at work there, but only the madman's warped brain could make sense of it.

If Morehouse is still alive, West thought. *Then he would want to be the one to pull the trigger. He all but gloated about it during the taped reading of his will, hadn't he? He's said that he would kill John last. Wasn't that how he phrased it?*

West knew that the only person who was a bigger thorn in Morehouse's side than John Bartlett was himself.

It had taken them almost two hours to make it from the house to the road where they met Janice. Since he didn't have to worry about waiting on Vivian, Francis, or the judge this time around, he made it back to the tree line across from the mansion in half that time. Nothing appeared out of place. He didn't see any guards walking the perimeter or stationed on the roof as they had been before.

His only stop was a quick detour to the spot where they had stashed Michael Coombes. West wanted to check on him and make sure he was okay. As he approached, he called out Coombes name, but no reply came from underneath the brush they had used to camouflage the wounded DA's hiding place. Worried, West moved in closer. He had to wonder if Morehouses's men had found Coombes or had the wound been more serious than they thought? The last thing he wanted to do was find Coombes' body, but he couldn't decide which scenario was worse, finding the DA dead or not finding him at all?

Thankfully, he didn't have to worry. Michael Coombes was right where they had left him. He was asleep-- or unconscious. West couldn't tell which, but he was relieved when he felt for a pulse and found one. It was weak, but steady. He decided not to wake him because it might be better for Coombes to simply sleep through the rest of his ordeal. If Chalmers and Janice couldn't bring back help then they were all just as good as dead anyway.

Once he was satisfied that Coombes was stable and that no one had followed him to their wounded man, West resumed his path through the woods toward the main house. For his plan to work he needed to reach the house before the mercenaries did.

Once he made it to the tree line at the edge of the mansion's manicured lawn, West allowed himself to catch his breath. Since he and Bartlett had taken out their vehicle the odds were slightly closer to even since the men with the big guns would be on foot as well. Plus, they would have to carry Bartlett's unconscious body as well, provided his guess was right and they hadn't killed him on the spot. There was also the possibility that another car had been dispatched to collect them. That seemed a more reasonable scenario, so he was not surprised to see one of the limousines that had been parked out front pull up to the front steps.

Two men carrying automatic weapons stepped out and took a quick scan of the perimeter. Once they were certain the coast was clear, they reached in and pulled the limp form of John Bartlett from the vehicle, which surprised the reporter. It also made him wonder why they hadn't simply killed him and gotten it out of the way. Two more armed men got out behind them. Hefting him by the arms and legs, the four men carried the unconscious police officer inside the mansion, his head slumped forward.

At least he's alive, West thought as he breathed a sigh of relief.

I've been doing that a lot since I came to the country, he realized.

He had to move quickly since only four of the mercenaries had returned. That meant there were at least four, maybe five that didn't return with them. He had to believe that some of them had probably been sent after Janice and the others. That still left one or two highly trained killers with automatic weapons tracking him through the woods. He assumed that with their training they would make better time than he did.

Time to move, West!

As soon as the door closed behind the four men carrying Bartlett and the limo pulled away, West broke from the cover of the tree line and sprinted across the freshly mowed lawn toward the mansion.

He knelt beside the outer wall with his gun leaning steady against the red brick. He was beneath the same balcony they had used to make their escape from the mansion a couple hours earlier. It was a small drop from the balcony to the ground below. That meant it should be a fairly easy climb to get back inside provided no one saw him scampering up the wall. All he had to do was find some leverage and he was in.

Once he was certain he hadn't been spotted, West tucked the gun in his waistband at his back instead of the holster on his ankle. Once he was on the balcony he needed quick access to the weapon and the ankle holster was good for concealing a weapon, not for the quick draw. He reached out and ran his fingers across the bricks. They were rough and jagged, not good on his hands, but his shoes would be able to grip easily enough.

He leapt straight up and grabbed for the balcony. His fingers brushed against the concrete base, but did not find purchase so West fell back to the grass. He landed in a crouch and remained in that position as he waited to make sure his failed Six Million Dollar Man impersonation had gone unnoticed. When it was evident no one was rushing toward him he tried again.

On his fourth attempt he managed to grab a decent hold on the concrete base and pulled himself up using the soles of his shoes on the brick was to help keep his balance. He shimmied up and onto the balcony's ledge while using the railing as camouflage.

There were no sounds coming from inside the room so he lifted one leg, then another over the railing. Once he was on solid footing, he slid the gun from his waistband. With his back to the wall, listened at the door. As before he did not hear anything from inside. His mind ran through two possible scenarios. Either no one had seen him and he was extremely lucky or it was a trap and a room full of sharpshooters with guns and itchy trigger fingers were waiting for him just on the other side of the door.

Preferring to remain hopeful, he decided to opt for the first scenario.

The door was still open a few inches from before so he pushed it open with the tip of his shoe and entered the study gun first. The room was dark, but pretty much the way they had left it. The body of Phillip Jason Hall had not been moved. Morehouse's men had left him to rot where he fell. It had only been a couple of hours so there had not been enough time for rigor to fully set in, but the smell of dry blood warming up in the heat of the room was less than pleasant. A couple of flies had discovered the body and were hovering around the open wound. He felt bad about the lawyer's death, even though he did not know the man and hadn't particularly liked him based on first impressions. Philip Jason Hall was just another in a long line of bodies Morehouse had left in his wake. Another pawn in a never-ending game.

West glanced at the TV and DVD player. They were still right where they had been before. West did notice that the briefcase the lawyer had given to Bartlett, the one the officer had left on the table when they fled, was still on the table right where he'd dropped it. West was still curious about its contents, but this was not the time to try and open it and find out what was inside. With his luck there would be a bomb inside just waiting for some poor sap to open it before it detonated.

It looked as if Morehouse's people hadn't even come back into this room after killing Hall and locking the rest of them inside. After he pushed the OPEN button on the DVD player to eject the disc he wasn't so sure. He was not surprised to find that the player was empty. There was no disc. That was further proof that Morehouse was alive and had faked his death.

"I knew it," he whispered when he saw the empty player. He was now more certain than ever that the bastard was alive and well and hiding somewhere inside the mansion.

All he had to do now was find him before he killed John Bartlett.

###

John Bartlett didn't want to open his eyes.

His entire body ached and he felt lightheaded. He was reminded of something his father liked to say, "I hurt all over more than anyplace else," which was a fairly true statement. John had been in more than his fair share of fights over the years, but never had he felt so utterly and completely beaten as he did at that moment. Not even that dust up he got into with that loudmouthed Army Lieutenant named Bowers when he was stationed in Kuwait and that scrap had ended with a trip to the infirmary to have a cast put on his broken hand. The hand had never quite healed one hundred percent and sometimes it ached when it rained, but it had been worth the discomfort to put that sorry bastard in his place. That had been the first time John had ever broken another man's nose.

It was not, however, the last.

He didn't like to think of himself as a violent man by nature, but sometimes his profession required him to apply a little pressure to get the job done. He could play rough when he had to and he had long ago come to terms with the fact that sometimes circumstances dictated that a man had to do awful things to accomplish good. Sometimes that meant roughing up a suspect and other times it meant breaking a superior officer's nose.

It had been a long time since he had been knocked out and as he slowly regained consciousness he remembered just how painful waking up after a knock down drag out knuckle-buster felt.

He was lying face down on a small sofa, his legs hanging off one end. He had been there awhile, he guessed, because one of his legs had fallen asleep from dangling off the edge at such an odd angle. The sofa was red and comfortable and he thought he recognized it as the one in Morehouse's mansion so he assumed that's where he had been taken. Otherwise, he was going to have to have a word with his priest because neither Heaven nor Hell, whichever this place was intended to be, did not live up to the hype. Lying on a red sofa was not how he envisioned spending Eternity.

At least he hoped the sofa was red and not another color simply covered in his blood. He felt the wet, sticky stream on his face and tasted the metallic twang that accompanied a bloody nose. Thankfully, the flow of blood had stanched itself while he had been out. His instinct was to reach up and touch his nose just to make sure, but he didn't want to alert his captors to the fact that he was awake until he had a chance to get his bearings and try to figure out exactly what was going on. Hopefully, the room would stop spinning by that time.

One thing he did know, jokes about Heaven and Hell aside, was that he was alive. He hurt too much to be dead. That in and of itself raised a few interesting questions. *Why didn't they just kill me and get it over with?* Being the first of those on his mind. The Morehouse video plainly stated that the hunters had been instructed to shoot on sight, which obviously didn't happen. The question was why? And for that, he had no answers.

He could hear the men talking, but their words were muffled and muted. It was like listening through cotton that had been stuffed in his ears. That and the slight constant ringing sound drowned out a lot of it. He wondered if he had a concussion from the blow to the head that he had received earlier from the butt of G. I. Joe's rifle. He hoped not, but there was nothing he could do about it if he did. Regardless of whether or not he was concussed, Bartlett knew that he had to stay awake. If he could play possum for a while longer he might just find a way out of this mess.

There was also Benjamin West to consider. West was no doubt on his way back to the mansion, if he wasn't there already. West was smart and capable, but he was also impulsive, which often got him in over his head. Bartlett had no doubt that West would get into trouble and need back up. Unfortunately for them John was it. As much as he wanted to, he couldn't count on Francis and the others getting help from the local sheriff there in time. Two against a small army were far better odds than West trying to do it alone.

John needed to bide his time and regain his bearings.

His mouth was also dry and felt like he had swallowed some of that cotton that had been shoved in his ears. Hoping that the men who had brought him in weren't paying close attention, Bartlett took a chance on wetting his lips. Even if they saw it such an action might be perceived as involuntary.

He stuck out his tongue just enough to moisten his cracked lips.

When no one responded he sighed inwardly. He would play possum a little longer and hopefully figure out what they were up to while he was at it. If West's harebrained theory about Darrin Morehouse faking his own death was true, which he still doubted, then this was the best way to find out. If West was right then there was no way Morehouse would let anything happen to him without gloating over his victory first. The man played his games not only to win, but he liked to lord his victory over his opponents as well. Not only was a he sore loser, but a bad winner as well.

If Darrin Morehouse was alive then he would know it soon enough.

And if it was true, John Bartlett swore he wouldn't stay that way for long.

CHAPTER 38

A few minutes earlier...

Mr. Ryan watched as the warden stepped away from the cover of the car.

Not smart, tubby, he thought as he lined up the scope on the warden. *Not smart at all.* He noticed the slight limp, but wasn't really surprised. With all that they had put them all through, he was surprised the man hadn't keeled over from a heart attack by now. He had probably been more physically active today than he had been in years, from the look of him. Mr. Ryan had taken an instant dislike to the warden, although they had never met. Still, he knew the type. His sister, brother, and mother had been much the same way. They loved to eat and eat and eat, but never did any exercise. Unlike Ryan and his father, who both kept in shape and got plenty of exercise.

The slovenly lifestyle of his mother and siblings had been more than his father could take so he left. Much to Ryan's disappointment, he didn't take him with him. Instead he left him there with the pigs he called family.

Ryan hated all of them and couldn't get out of that house fast enough.

The day he turned eighteen he enlisted in the Army and volunteered for every dangerous assignment he could get his hands on. He wondered if his family had even known he was gone. He had not spoken to any of them in years, even though he had heard about his brother's premature heart attack at age thirty. He considered going to the funeral for a minute or two until he remembered how much he hated his family.

He volunteered for a dangerous CIA black bag operation with questionable intel instead. His superiors did not deny him the assignment. He had become something of a favorite among the command staff. He got things done.

The mission did not go well, but he made it home alive, if not in one piece. Several surgeries and moving from one rehabilitation center to another had kept him out of action for almost two years. It was only his dogged determination and fierce stubborn attitude that helped him fully recover.

The Army offered him a medal.

Had he not killed the CIA agent that had provided the sloppy intelligence, he might have received the medal. Instead, what he got was a dishonorable discharge and a criminal record. Had it not been for the intervention of a few well-placed words by some higher ups for whom he had done some less than legal operations for, he may well have gone to prison. Thankfully, there were still those who felt that his talents were still in demand.

There was still need of his services.

As a freelance soldier for hire, Mr. Ryan had traveled the world. He had seen more than most people could even dream about. Some of it was quite beautiful, but most of it was horrific. If he was prone to dreaming, some of those images might cause nightmares. But such things didn't burden him. He slept the sleep of the just and the righteous.

When Nick Wilson approached him for this assignment he almost turned it down. Terrorizing a bunch of civilians seemed almost beneath him, but the more he heard of the plan the more excited he became at the prospect. He had hoped for better opponents to face off against. Sadly, in the group they were targeting only two seemed to provide any type of challenge. And out of those two only one of them seemed worthy.

The cop had experience and a military background. The reporter was plucky, but at the end of the day he had no training. Mr. Ryan did not see him as much of a threat.

Warden Chalmers reminded him of his brother. He couldn't help but imagine that this is what his brother would have looked like had he not died at such a young age. The only difference being that the warden knew how to handle a weapon. Ryan doubted his pansy-ass brother would have known how to hold a gun, much less fire one.

"Say goodnight, Gracie," he whispered from his sniper's nest in a tree at the curve in the driveway. With only the slightest repositioning he had coverage on both sides of the driveway from the curve. It was a perfect place to pick off his targets.

"Bye bye, Warden," he whispered as his finger squeezed the trigger.

A loud crack split the air.

The warden dropped right in the middle of the driveway.

Ryan smiled. There was nothing quite so satisfying as a fresh kill. Even if there wasn't any challenge in it, a kill was a kill and on this job, there was a bonus for every one of the targets a shooter put down. With incentive like that he planned to cash in. Especially since there was a carload of bonus checks just sitting in the damaged car down there waiting for him to pick them off.

He laughed. One well-placed grenade could have taken care of the lot of them in a single shot, but no, such a thing wasn't permitted. It still confounded him all of the rules that had been placed on this game. If the money wasn't as good as it was he would have packed it up and headed home.

He did not like playing games.

Ryan slung the sniper rifle over his shoulder and started to climb down from his post when he heard something that caught his attention.

He froze.

Slowly turning toward the sound he saw two vehicles approaching from the opposite side of the curve. And they were approaching fast. Had he not picked such a perfect spot for his nest he might have missed their approach and been on the ground, a less than ideal position, when they arrived.

He repositioned himself in the branches, effectively camouflaging himself as he had been trained to do. He would take care of the uninvited guests first, then he'd take care of the people in the car. After all, they weren't going anywhere.

He looked through the small magnifier and saw a pick up truck speeding toward him far faster than was safe on such a narrow, curved piece of pavement. Behind the pick up he spotted a second vehicle. Both had police markings belonging to the local sheriff's department. They must have heard shots or someone got sloppy and they found out what was going on.

Great, he thought. *Fuckin' cops*!

The only thing Mr. Ryan hated more than fat people were cops.

He smiled. It had been a long time since he'd killed a law enforcement officer. He wondered what the bonus would be for capping a couple of local LEOs who stumbled upon the game. He planned to find out.

He raised the rifle and took aim.

# # #

"There!"

They heard the gunshot before they saw anything.

Shan Lomax saw them the instant Sheriff Myers came out of the curve. He pointed at the SUV parked off the side of the road in a small clearing. The vehicle appeared to be empty. It didn't take him long to realize why. Just ahead he saw a man lying in the center of the driveway and just a few feet beyond a car was partially in the ditch, steam rising from the crumpled hood. A thick brownish red substance that he quickly deduced was blood was splattered across the windshield and hood.

Another body lay next to the car.

"I see 'em," Myers said.

"There are people in that car!"

"I see that too."

"Where's the shooter?"

"Him I don't see."

Before either of them could say another word the window in the passenger door exploded as it spider-webbed next to Lomax's head. He shouted and instinctively raised his hands to cover his face as small shards of glass flew into the cab.

Myers jerked the wheel hard and hit the brakes, throwing the pick up into a slide to one side of the road. Dooley, in the police car following them, mirrored the maneuver and pulled to the opposite side of the driveway.

The sheriff kicked open his door and dropped to the grass, pulling Shan Lomax into the floorboard as he did.

"You okay," Myers shouted as he pulled his Magnum.

Lomax shook his head. "What the hell was that?" he asked. Small cuts peppered the right side of his face, but they looked superficial. He pulled hi service revolver from its holster.

"Stay down," Myers told him.

"You see him?"

"I think so." He clicked his walkie. "Dooley?"

"I got him."

"Take the shot if you've got it."

"Roger that."

Myers crouched next to the open door. "You hit?" he asked Lomax.

The detective touched the side of his face where small red dots were starting to run from the glass cuts. "No," he answered hesitantly.

The sheriff's look of disbelief told him he didn't believe him.

"No," he repeated with more authority. "I'm good."

"Just stay down and let Dooley take care of this guy."

"I'm assuming your deputy is a good shot."

Sheriff Myers only answer was a smile.

#

"Dooley?"

Ben Dooley heard Sheriff Myers voice softly next to his ear. "I got him," he answered.

"Take the shot if you've got it."

"Roger that," Dooley whispered.

He stared through the scope attached to the high-powered rifle he kept in the trunk of his cruiser. He had moved it to the front seat when the sheriff had told him they were going in he had a feeling he might need it.

The rifle had a few years and even more miles on it. Dooley had carried the rifle during his tour of duty as a sniper in Afghanistan during the first Gulf War where his commanding officer had referred to him as "one of the best goddamned natural shots I've ever seen in my entire life."

Although he hadn't had to use this particular skill on the job as deputy, Dooley liked to keep his skills sharp. He often spent time at the range with his Kate, a name snipers often called this particular style of weapon. He had shown the sheriff the weapon on one of their trips to the range, which was really just the field behind Tom Myers' house. Myers had been equally impressed with Dooley's skill with a rifle, although he had hoped never to have to call upon this particular talent in the line of duty.

Until today.

Dooley saw the sniper hiding amongst the trees. He had taken the shot at the sheriff's truck from an elevated position. The man was good, whoever he was. Dooley only caught quick glimpses, but then lost them in the tree cover. He knew where the man was. He just needed to draw him out.

"Boss," he whispered into his walkie.

"Yeah," Myers replied.

"I'm going to need a favor."

# # #

"I need you to draw this guy out just a bit," Dooley said over the radio.

"Okay. Hold on a sec," the sheriff replied as he slid into position next to the front driver's side tire. He clicked off the safety on his gun.

"What's the plan, Sheriff?" Lomax asked from inside the truck.

"Dooley needs us to draw him out."

"Okay." Lomax had his gun in hand as he lay in the truck's floor-board. "What do you need me to do?"

"Put three bullets into those woods at your two o'clock."

"No problem. Say when."

"Give me a three count and then you go."

"On your mark," Lomax said.

Tom Myers took a deep breath and exhaled loudly. This wouldn't be the first time he had stepped in front of a killer with a gun, but no amount of experience made the idea of doing what he was about to do any easier.

He clicked his walkie.

"Get ready, Ben."

Myers popped up and draped his arms over the hood of the truck and squeezed off three rounds into the trees across the drive. As soon as the third bullet left the chamber he ducked back behind the tire, which offered limited protection, should the sniper open fire on him again.

"Go!" Myers shouted.

In the cab of the pick up, Shan Lomax kicked open the passenger door of the truck. As soon as it opened he sat up from the floorboard and fired three shots through the opening between the door and the frame. After the third shot he too dropped back down and out of sight.

"You think that got his attention?" Lomax asked.

A crack filled the air, followed by something hitting the open door hard enough to slam it shut. A shower of glass from the spider-webbed passenger door window rained down on Detective Lomax. He covered his head instinctively for protection.

"Never mind," Lomax said as he buried his head in the truck's floorboard.

"Any time now, Dooley," Myers whispered.

#

Ben Dooley heard three shots ring out.

From the sound of it, he knew those shots came from the sheriff's .45 Magnum, which had a very distinctive sound. The three initial shots were followed quickly by another three quick shots, which he assumed came from Detective Lomax.

The shots had the desired effect. The sniper leaned out from behind his cover to get a decent shot. He fired a round into the open door of the truck, slamming it closed and throwing tiny splinters of glass from the shattered window across the seat.

The sniper pulled back behind his cover.

Dooley watched through the scope, his finger hovering a hair's breadth above the trigger. All he had to do was wait for his moment and take the shot.

Patience.

For a sniper, patience is everything.

"Wait for it," Dooley whispered.

The sniper leaned out for a second shot.

Wait for it.

The sniper took aim.

Wait...

"Gotcha, you son of a bitch" Dooley whispered as the sniper leaned out just a bit too far.

He pulled the trigger.

#

Mr. Ryan pulled the trigger.

He smiled with satisfaction as the passenger door window exploded into a spider-webbed pattern of cracked glass. The driver swerved and pulled off to the side of the road, just as he had expected him to do. The car brining up the rear pulled tot he other side and the driver dove from the car looking for cover.

This is too easy, Ryan thought. All he had to do was wait until one of them poked his head out to see if the coast was clear and then he'd have them.

Sure enough, a minute later it happened. Only instead of peeking out the driver of the pick up truck squeezed off three shots in his general direction. The shots missed by a couple feet, smacking harmlessly off the next tree over. No doubt they were trying to draw him out, but he was smarter than that. He wasn't going to take the bait.

Then the door opened and another three shots rang out. These passed a little closer, but were still off the mark. Mr. Ryan was surprised. He thought he had hit the passenger. It wasn't often he missed a target. *No worries*, he thought as he shifted against the tree, crouched on a thick limb. He took aim on the open door. *I'll pick up the spare.*

He fired once and hit the mark, closing the door and raining tiny glass missiles down on whoever was lying in the seat.

He stood, balancing himself against the tree as he gained enough altitude to see the person lying in the truck. Never taking his eye from the rifle scope he took aim and--

He heard the crack of a rifle firing a split second before he realized what had happened. He felt a sharp sting and suddenly he was unable to hold onto his rifle. It fell from his hand and clattered among the branches as gravity pulled it back toward earth.

Mr. Ryan looked down and saw the blood pouring off his shirt.

He tried to speak, but couldn't find his voice.

Well ain't that some shit? he thought as the world spun around him and he lost his grip. The last thing he felt was his face smashing into a tree limb.

He was dead before he hit the ground.

CHAPTER 39

Without looking, Shan Lomax slapped a new clip into his weapon as he ran.

He had watched from the relative safety of the sheriff's truck as the deputy's first shot knocked the sniper from his perch. The suspect dropped like a stone, a good twenty-five feet, to the ground below. He landed with a sickly wet thump.

Lomax was a few years younger and even more pounds lighter than Sheriff Tom Myers so he ran a bit faster. He reached the suspect first. He had little doubt that the would-be assassin was dead, that Deputy Dooley's shot had hit the mark, but the smart move was to verify the fatality. The last thing he wanted was to assume the danger was past and carelessly walk in front of a bullet.

It had happened before. One of the uniformed officers in his first precinct, Robert Edwards, had come under fire from a drug dealer. After pulling the man over on a traffic violation, the drug dealer and his companion in the passenger seat, opened fire, winging one of the officers. They ran and the officers gave chase. In the ensuing shoot out one of the drug dealers was dropped in an alley. Shan and his partner had arrived just in time to see the shot. The other suspect tried to get away, but tripped, lost his balance, and fell. Officer Edwards ran with all his might toward the suspect to catch him before he could get back to his feet. Unfortunately, he didn't check the man he had shot, who was still very much alive and playing possum. He shot Robert in the back as he ran past. The suspect he thought was out of play have enough life left to get off one more shot.

Officer Edwards lost the use of his legs that day and Shan Lomax learned a very valuable lesson.

Pointing his weapon at the immobile sniper, Detective Lomax kicked the rifle away and the suspect didn't move. He knelt next to the sniper and felt for a pulse. As he suspected, there was none.

Breathing heavily, but not completely out of breath, Tom Myers slowed as he approached. Like Lomax, his weapon was also drawn. "Is he…" Tom started.

Lomax shook his head no.

Neither of them shed a tear.

Myers approached the car, gun pointed ahead of him. Lomax and Dooley were a few steps behind him. "Sommerville Sheriff's Department!" he shouted. "You! In the car! Let's see your hands!"

"We're here," someone shouted from inside the car. A pair of hands shot out the passenger side window but had trouble staying there. From the angle the car was tilted, it was understandable.

"Hold tight," Myers said. "We'll have you out in a second."

The sheriff pointed toward the car and Dooley nodded. He took up position at the edge of the car and waited. If there were hostiles in the car, he was ready for them.

Lomax knelt in the center of the pavement next to the body.

"Detective?"

"He's dead."

"You know him?" Myers asked.

"Yeah. Francis Chalmers. He's the warden at Valdosta State."

"Valdosta State? He's a long way from home."

"Yeah."

"So what's he doing here?"

"Darrin Morehouse was being held in his prison."

"Morehouse? You mean--"

Lomax twirled a finger in the air. "Yep. The guy who owned all this."

"You think he was tied up in all this?"

Lomax blew out a breath. "Francis was a good guy. If he's here, it's for the same reason my partner is."

Myers tapped him on the shoulder. "Come on. Let's get these people out of the car."

Shan nodded and cast a last look at Francis Chalmers before following the sheriff to the car.

"We're opening the door. No funny moves or my deputy will shoot you. Understood?"

A chorus of agreement poured from the car.

"You ready?"

Dooley and Lomax both nodded.

Myers pulled the rear door open. Small shards of glass sprinkled to the pavement below, tinkling like ice in a glass as it bounced around his feet. As soon as the door was open, Detective Lomax stepped over and pointed his gun inside the damaged car as he looked inside.

"Don't worry," he said. "We're going to get you out of here."

After a few quick introductions and showing the people in the car their badges to prove they were who they said they were, Ben Dooley called in Deputy Jackson from the road just as back up arrived. The deputy couldn't rightly blame them for being a little skittish after he heard them recount what had happened to them. From the sound of things, they were lucky to be alive.

Jackson and another officer came up the serpentine driveway a few minutes later. Like the sheriff and Dooley had done before, they did not have their sirens on.

"Let's get these people out of here," Sheriff Myers whispered to Chris Jackson once he reported in. "Take them back to the station and keep them there. No calls until I talk to them."

"You got it, Tom."

The deputy corralled the others toward the car. He helped the hysterical Vivian Morehouse into the back seat and then made room for Judge Hughes, who was having trouble walking. He was favoring his leg and walked with a limp as he held onto the deputy for support. The car crash had banged them all up pretty good, but the judge and that reporter from Atlanta seemed to have taken the worst of it.

"What can you tell us about the estate?" the sheriff asked Laura

268

Sellars, who seemed to be in the best shape of the survivors. She, along with Fabian Alexander and Janice Kilpatrick stood with the sheriff and Detective Lomax.

"That place is a maze," she said. "When we arrived we were escorted inside. I think they purposefully took us the long way around just to get us mixed up."

"How many men does Morehouse have?"

"Beats me," she started.

"Morehouse?" Fabian Alexander interrupted. "Are you telling me he's not dead?"

"Easy, Fabian," Lomax said, holding out a hand in case the reporter decided to advance on the lawyer.

"Don't you tell me to take it easy," he shouted. "Do you have any idea what that man's capable of?"

"Yes. I do. Now," Lomax said, trying to draw the conversation back on target. "How do we get in?"

"That's easy," Laura said. "The driveway takes you right to the front door. I have no idea how many men there are in the mansion, but there were quite a few of them chasing us."

"Where's John Bartlett?"

"He and Ben West went back to the house once we were in the car."

"Why would he do that?" Myers asked.

"Because we were in the car and he thought we were safe."

"I don't think that's what he meant," Alexander said with just a hint of condescension.

"John and West were the ones who caught Morehouse the first time," Lomax explained after seeing the Sheriff's odd look. "If they thought these guys were out of harms way they would have gone after Morehouse."

"And if he's really dead?"

"Then at least they'll know that," Lomax said. "Right now all they have is hearsay and rumor. The last time I talked to John he wasn't one hundred percent sure that he was dead."

"What do you mean he wasn't sure?"

"Exactly what I said, Mr. Alexander," Lomax said plainly, a sharp contrast to the anchorman's snarky demeanor. Fabian Alexander was not his favorite person in the world, mostly because of the way the reporter had treated his partner, but the man was a weasel and Shan din't like him. "The only reason John came out here today was to put his mind at ease by making sure Morehouse was really gone. If I had to guess, the rest of them are here for pretty much the same reason."

"That's why I came," Laura said, nodding in agreement.

Shan shrugged. It took all of his willpower not to say, "See? I told you so."

"You're going after him, aren't you?" Laura said. It wasn't really a question.

"Yes I am, Miss Sellars. He's my partner and my friend. I intend to back him up so any information you have on the house will be of great help."

"I'll come with you," she offered.

"No you won't," Lomax and Myers said at the same time.

"Look," Laura said, her demeanor as stern as it had been at the height of her trial lawyer days. "This isn't open to debate. We left Mike Coombes out there and he needs medical attention. Do either of you know where he is?" Off their blank expressions she added, "I didn't think so." Her cheeks flushed an angry red.

"It's too dangerous," Shan started.

"More dangerous than being locked inside a house with armed men under orders to kill me?" she said, cutting him off before he could continue. "More dangerous than trudging through the woods while sharpshooters take potshots at me? More dangerous than that, Detective?"

"Well, I... I guess not," Lomax said.

"Then let's stop arguing and get a move on," she said, the redness fading from her cheeks as her anger subsided a bit.

Shan pulled his backup weapon, a .38 caliber from an ankle holster and held it out toward her. "You know how to handle one of these?"

Laura took the offered gun and checked it like a pro before sliding it into her waistband. She almost laughed at the identical expressions on both Detective Lomax and Sheriff Myers' faces. "Don't look so surprised," she said. "I was a defense attorney working for a firm with... questionable clients, as you may know. My first week on the job I was sent to mandatory weapons testing."

Myers whistled appreciatively.

"I can drop a target at twenty feet," she added with just a hint of pride.

"There's a big difference between shooting at the gun range," Myers said. "Those targets don't shoot back."

"We don't have time to argue about this, Sheriff. My friend is out there - and so is your partner - and they need some help." She opened the passenger door on the pick up and used a towel from the floorboard to wipe the shards of glass off of the seat.

Myers and Lomax exchanged a look.

"Lady has a point," Lomax said as Myers walked around to the driver's side.

"According to my wife, they usually do," Myers said as he slid behind the wheel.

"If she's going, then I'm going!" Fabian Alexander shouted as he followed them to the truck. He grabbed the open passenger door before Detective Lomax was in his seat.

"Oh, I don't think so," Lomax said around a crooked grin. "Your kind of help I don't need."

"Now just a damned minute," the reporter said defensively. "This is my story and I've got just as much invested in this than anyone. I should be there!"

"Then why weren't you invited?" the detective asked as he wrenched the door from the reporter's grasp and slammed it closed.

"You ready?" Myers asked.

Shan didn't look his way. "Let's go," he said.

Sheriff Myers put the truck into gear and pulled away, leaving a fuming Fabian Alexander in the rearview mirror watching as they drove off without him. The reporter glared at them until they rounded the next curve in the driveway and disappeared from sight.

"I hate that guy," Shan Lomax muttered to no one in particular as he checked the clip on his gun.

CHAPTER 40

"You can stop pretending now, Detective. I know you're awake."

John Bartlett ignored the advice and didn't move. He lay on the comfortable red couch with his eyes closed. With an incessant headache pounding in his brain, lying there in this position was extremely comfortable. He suspected that opening his eyes or even moving would only make his head hurt worse, a sensation he was not looking forward to experiencing. He'd had hangovers that hurt a lot less than what he was feeling at that moment.

He had actually been awake for some time, only occasionally nodding off for the briefest of moments only to snap back to wakefulness just as quickly. Sleep sounded great right about then, but it wasn't really good idea. No matter how much he wanted to drift off, John knew he had to stay awake. And not just for the obvious reason. For starters, it was possible that he might have a concussion from the beating he had endured out in the woods. The butt end of a shotgun to the face could certainly work a number on a guy and he was worried about passing out.

Secondly, he wanted to hear what the men who had dragged him inside were saying. He would have a better chance of throwing a monkey wrench in their plans if he knew what they were and as cliché as it

272

sounded, movies and TV shows had one thing right, the bad guys usually liked to talk. Many a case had been broken based on what Bartlett referred to as *the stupid criminal philosophy*. If you could get even the smartest criminal talking, you would be amazed to find that most people would tell you everything you need to know about them. Those that were overly excited about their scheme did it out of pride, but most did it just to show the cops that they were smarter than they were.

The phrase, *"Pride goeth before a fall"* could have been coined by a cop.

This bunch was well trained, Bartlett decided. So far they hadn't said much of consequence, when they bothered to speak at all in his presence. He was convinced that most, if not all, of them were just hired guns, former soldiers that were looking for new wars to fight. They were all too happy to do someone else's dirty work, but in his experience, mercenaries were rarely the instigators of elaborate plans like the one that had lured him and the others to a mansion in the middle of nowhere. That meant that someone in this house was pulling the strings.

Not for the first time he wondered if West's theory that Darrin Morehouse had faked his own death had some merit. When the reporter had first said it aloud, Bartlett easily dismissed the notion as ridiculous. Even with all of the things Morehouse had done, John couldn't accept West's wild theory. But now it didn't seem quite as farfetched as it had then.

And if it wasn't Morehouse, then who else had the foresight to pull off such an elaborate stunt?

Moreshouse's cronies were the obvious choice, but John's experience dealing with them told him that they were not the sharpest knives in the drawer. In his heyday, Darrin Morehouse had surrounded himself with people he could manipulate and control. Independent thinkers need not apply.

"Enough fooling, Detective," the man said again, this time nudging him with the tip of his hiking boot.

And now, apparently, the jig was up.

They knew he was awake so there wasn't much to gain from ignoring him any longer. The last thing he needed was for them to use their fists again. He was still reeling from his last encounter with them. Bartlett lifted his head slowly, still feeling the invisible drummer doing a solo there.

He tried not to wince at the pain.

He was not successful.

Bartlett had hoped to buy more time to recover by playing possum, but that hadn't worked out quite as planned. "Who are you?" he asked weakly, wanting to portray the illusion of weakness. Unfortunately, it wasn't much of an act. They had really done a number on him.

"That's right. We haven't been properly introduced," the man he had come to think of as *Armani*, the same man who had escorted he and West into the mansion just a few hours earlier said. "Where are my manners? My name's Nick Wilson." He did not offer his hand.

"Is that supposed to mean something to me?" Bartlett asked as he pulled himself into a sitting position on the bright red couch.

"I would be surprised if it did," he said. "In my line of work anonymity is a sign of success and I'm rather good at my what I do, Detective."

"And what you do isn't pretty, right?"

The mercenary looked confused.

Before he could ask, Bartlett waved it off. "Inside joke," he said. "I'm guessing you don't read many comic books."

Wilson chuckled. "Not since I was a kid. All of that Bif! Bam! Pow! Stuff always struck me as a little silly."

"Your loss," Bartlett said.

"I assume you know what type of work it is I do," Wilson said, getting back to the matter at hand. He smiled like the predator the police officer knew him to be.

"I have an idea," Bartlett said. As long as he kept them talking he had time to come up with a plan that would get him out of there in one piece. At least in theory.

The mercenary smiled.

"So, since your goons didn't just put a bullet in my head out in the woods I assume you wish to have a chat," Bartlett said as he motioned to the four other men in the room. "So let's chat."

"Very astute."

"I've been told I have my moments."

"I'm sure you have."

Bartlett sat back and crossed his arms as if his life weren't in danger. "What's on your mind, Nick?" he asked as if they were old friends.

Nick Wilson sat in a plush chair across from him. The chair sported the same bright red fabric as the couch inside an ornate wooden frame that was obviously part of a set. The mercenary sat on the edge of the chair and leaned forward with his elbows resting on his knees. To the untrained eye his demeanor was casual, but Bartlett knew the man could launch himself forward easily from that position and be on him in a second.

"I thought we might talk about your future, Detective."

Bartlett barked a laugh. "You mean I still have one?" he asked as if they were two old friends sharing a laugh, trying to keep the mood casual and light. He leaned forward and mimicked the mercenary's posture. "That's good news."

"For the moment," Wilson said with a smile that was anything but pleasant.

John returned the gesture, trying to appear casual. "I'm all ears, Nick," he said.

"Good. Then I've got a proposition for you."

# # #

Benjamin West couldn't get over the size of the Morehouse Estate.

The place was huge, with many locked rooms. After leaving the room where Philip Jason Hall had been murdered, West began looking for the nearest stairwell. He remembered seeing an elevator when he first arrived, but decided against using it because the noise would probably alert the angry men with the guns that he was inside the house. And he was hoping to avoid them as long as possible.

Vivian's admission that the video her former husband had supposedly made was recorded in an upstairs office. He still wasn't convinced that Morehouse was dead and if he was right then there was a good bet that he would find him in that same office.

It was a thin plan, but a plan nonetheless.

West checked every door he came across, opening the few that were unlocked and pushing them open slowly just in case anyone was hiding out inside. So far all of them had been empty and none looked like the office he had seen on the plasma.

On doors that were locked, he listened for any movement within.

So far he had heard nothing and was beginning to wonder if there was anyone in the house except him. He kept searching. If Morehouse was in the mansion he would find him. If not… well, he would jump off that bridge when he came to it.

After several minutes of searching, he hit pay dirt. When he finally found the office where Morehouse's will had been recorded, West entered cautiously. Gun in hand, he swept the room. It was empty, but the smell of cigar smoke lingered. The smell was much too fresh to be a holdover from six years earlier. He flashed back to earlier and remembered seeing a lit cigar on the TV screen.

"I knew it," West whispered.

He rifled through the desk drawers, but there was nothing of use in any of them. He cursed as he slammed the last drawer. He wasn't sure what he had been hoping to find in the desk, but he figured there would be something, some clue to help him. He was disappointed when there wasn't.

"What now, West?" he muttered to himself as he often did when frustrated. Sitting in the soft leather desk chair, West leaned against Morehouse's desk, drumming the fingers of his left hand on the hard wood finish while matching the beat with a finger tapping against his right cheek. He felt like there was something there he should have seen, something he missed. But what? Whatever it was that nagged at him, he couldn't quite put his finger on it and it bothered him.

"Nowhere left to go but down," he said before pushing himself off the desk and toward the door.

Heading down the stairs was considerably faster than up had been, but West was still out of breath by the time he reached the first floor. He took a moment to slow his breathing before continuing on. He couldn't believe that he hadn't seen anyone else since he started searching the place. He knew for a fact that there were people here as he had watched them drag John Bartlett inside. Finding them in a place as large as Morehouse's scary mansion was not proving to be as easy as he had hoped.

"Where are you, John?" he whispered.

That's when he heard voices.

He crept forward, suddenly self conscious of his own footsteps, afraid that they might hear. The gun he carried eased his apprehension somewhat, but he suspected there were still more of *them* out there than he had bullets. Not that West was against taking a risk, but he didn't like the odds. He decided to keep looking for Bartlett first then together they could come back and take care of these guys.

Then he heard John Bartlett laugh.

West froze and listened while trying to block out every other sound around him. Hearing Bartlett laugh was rather disconcerting. It wasn't something he had heard the man do very often. He made out most of the words. If he didn't know better, West might have thought they were two old friends having a polite conversation. Then again, most buddies didn't go around kidnapping one another just to have a friendly chat. Well, at least his friends didn't go to such extremes. Who knew what kind of silliness guys like John Bartlett and his friends did when they got together.

West inched forward and stopped next to an opening in the wall that separated the hallway from a sitting room that was slightly lower than the main floor by four steps. He couldn't see John Bartlett, but he could hear him, which gave him some hope. At least he was still alive. Up until now West hadn't been sure of the detective's fate. He had looked to be in pretty bad shape when those four heavily armed muscle-bound jackasses had carried him inside.

""I'm all ears, Nick," Bartlett said from somewhere in the sitting room

"Good. Then I've got a proposition for you," someone else said. West thought it was the same man that had escorted them inside that morning. He shook his head. It was so hard to believe it was still the same day as all this began. It felt like he'd been running around Morehouse's estate for weeks.

"Oh?" Bartlett asked, sounding genuinely curious. "This seems to be a day of them."

"I can imagine."

"Why don't we just get to the point, Nick," Bartlett said. West had heard that tone before. It was a combination of irritation and impatience that the police officer had mastered. Sometimes he wondered if the man got along with anyone very long. He really needed to work on his people skills.

"Fine," the man named Nick said. From his perch, West could see him sitting in an ugly red chair. Nick leaned forward, presumably, West believed, to talk to Bartlett, who he still couldn't see. "In the event that you came back to the mansion and made it back inside I have been instructed to make you one last offer," he said. "Mister

Morehouse has a proposition for you."

I knew it! West wanted to shout, but he held his tongue.

"And just what does he propose?" Bartlett asked.

"Same as was mentioned on the video," Nick said. He dropped his voice lower as he leaned forward. Even from where he was standing, West recognized the inherent threat. "It's all yours for the taking, Detective. All you have to do is agree to a few certain terms."

"And those would be?"

"Same as before.

The man Bartlett called Nick held out a hand and one of the other men in the room placed a gun in it. He chambered a round and pointed it at Bartlett. "And I assure you, Detective," he said. "This is the last time this offer will be repeated."

West cursed under his breath. He knew there was no way John Bartlett was going to play ball with these bastards. The man was incapable of bluffing and despite the way Fabian Alexander had tried to portray him on the news, he was an honest man. West's mind whirled as he tried to come up with a plan. As soon as Bartlett told Nick to "*go to hell*" it would all be over. He decided to chance it and go in shooting and hope for the best. Hopefully, he would be able to take out a few of them to make the odds a bit more even before they killed the policeman.

"What do you say, Detective?"

West was about to make his move when he heard Bartlett say something.

It was the last thing he had ever expected to hear.

"I'll take it," Bartlett said.

CHAPTER 41

John Bartlett was overjoyed by the astonished look on Nick Wilson's face.

He had obviously been expecting a completely different answer so John took a page from Benjamin West's play book and threw him a curveball. The confused look on the mercenary's face told him that it had worked. He didn't seem to know what to say next.

"Problem?" Bartlett asked, seeing just how far he could press his luck. He was curious to see the look on the faces of the other four mercenaries in the room, but he dared not take his eyes off of Nick Wilson. Wilson was obviously in charge, and no matter how dangerous the others might be, they took their cue from him.

After a moment's hesitation, the mercenary smiled. "Nah," he said, trying to sound as nonchalant as possible.

It was a valiant effort to hide his surprise, but Bartlett wasn't buying it. It was written all over his face. The mercenary hadn't counted on the possibility that he would actually accept the offer. Considering that they had probably been briefed by men who knew Morehouse, or by the man himself before his death, unless, of course, he were somehow still alive and pulling the strings. Regardless of who briefed them, Nick Wilson and his men had a picture of John Bartlett in their minds.

He could use that preconception against them.

"Then let's hear it. I don't have all day."

Nick grunted a laugh. "Okay," he said as he snapped his fingers and called over one of his lieutenants. John watched as the mercenary brought a familiar briefcase over to him and set it in the center of the glass-topped coffee table near the police officer.

"I take it you recognize this?"

"It does look familiar," Bartlett said as if he were not surprised to see it, which was nowhere near the truth. In all of the excitement of the day he hadn't given the briefcase a second thought since they left the study where the reading of the will had taken place.

"I've been led to understand that you know how to open this," Nick said.

"I heard that too," John said as he leaned the case on its side and looked at the locks. There were two locks, one on each side of the handle, three digits on each. He smiled and entered a combination. It was the same for each side. He lips twitched into a cautious grin as he tried the briefcase's latches.

Both snapped open with a click.

"Impressive," Nick Wilson said.

"Not really," Bartlett said as he sat the case back flat on the edge of the table instead of opening it. Morehouse knew me pretty well. I figured it would be something I would easily know. I figure it was one of two numbers. I got lucky and guessed right."

"What was it?"

Bartlett clucked a short laugh. "My badge number."

"Crafty old bastard, wasn't he?"

That he was." Bartlett laughed again, noticing that they had both used past tense in reference to Darrin Morehouse. It was the first time any of them had done so. *Why are they suddenly dropping the pretense*? John wondered. *Or was it just a slip of the tongue*? "You really planning to let me keep this?" he asked as he nodded toward the still unopened briefcase.

"You don't trust me?"

"Well, to be fair you have been trying to kill me for the better part of the day," Bartlett said matter-of-fact. "It's not something that's easily forgotten."

"I can understand your reluctance, Detective. I would love nothing more than to let you keep everything inside this case, but I can't.

I'm sure you understand."

Bartlett leaned back on the couch, resting comfortably in the center with his arms draped across the back rest. "Aren't you afraid of pissing off the boss by not following through with your instructions?" he asked.

"Which boss would that be?" Nick asked with a smile. "Oh, you think he's still alive, don't you?"

"Let's just say I've not ruled it out completely," Bartlett said as he crossed one leg over the other and made himself comfortable on the couch. "It's like in a horror movie. Never believe the bad guy is dead unless you see a body. And the last time I saw your boss was when he was being carted off to prison."

"That long, huh?"

Now it was John's turn to smile. "He tried to get me out to the prison for a visit, several times in fact, but I wouldn't do it. Our business was concluded. I moved on to other things. Apparently, the same can't be said for Darrin if after all these years he's still thinking about me. I'm not sure if I should feel flattered or creeped out."

"I wouldn't know," Nick said. "I've never met the man. I was told he was dead and his check cleared. That was good enough for me."

"So you don't really know if he's dead or not, do you?"

"Not really," the mercenary said after thinking it over.

"And you don't have a problem playing this game of his?" Bartlett asked. "I admit, I'm surprised. You strike me as a man who likes to make his own way. You don't strike me as some rich criminal's puppet."

"I do what I have to do to make my living, Detective. Usually that means trouncing around some backwater country I can't spell looking for bad men that think they can hide from me," he said. "And sometimes that means I have to hurt good people."

"Sounds like you're ready for a career change," Bartlett offered.

"Hardly. I sleep just fine at night so you can lay off the quarter-bin psychobabble. Better men than you have tried that trick and it doesn't work. Trust me."

Okay, then." The detective shifted in his seat. "So, what happens now, huh? I assume you've got a plan of some kind."

"Something like that."

"Well, don't keep me in suspense, Nick. I love a good plan. Thrill me."

The mercenary leaned forward across the coffee table as if about to impart a great secret. "Morehouse had partners, and if I'm not mistaken, what he wanted to give you would not be good for them." He reached across and tapped a thick callused finger against the closed briefcase. "I'm betting they would each pay handsomely for the information inside this case. Wouldn't you agree?"

Bartlett nodded.

"So, you can see why I can't just… give this away, don't you?"

"Of course. Perhaps you and I can make a deal that will let all of us walk out of here alive?"

"What do you have in mind, Detective?"

"Let me take a look at the evidence."

"Why?"

"I probably know most of the names on the list. I could let you know which ones are most likely to go along with you little blackmail scheme and which ones would probably kill you and dump your body out in Lake Lanier."

Nick seemed to be thinking it over, but wasn't quite ready to go along with the officer's proposal.

"You don't trust me?" Bartlett said, echoing the mercenary's earlier comment.

Nick Wilson laughed. "Well, to be fair you've not given me a lot of reason to trust you, now have you?"

"Well, you were just trying to kill me so I'd say I've earned about as much trust as you have."

"It's a tempting offer, Detective," Nick said, still keeping things friendly. "But I think I'll take my chances."

Bartlett shrugged. "It's your funeral."

Nick stood and pulled a nickel-plated .45 from the holster at his side. The gun was gorgeous, polished to a shine. It could have been a show piece. He pulled back the hammer then pointed it at John Bartlett.

"Actually," I'm afraid it's going to be your funeral, Detective."

"Nick," one of the other men said from across the room. He was next to the window that faced the front of the mansion. From the window he could see the drive and part of the turnaround in front of the mansion. He had drawn lookout duty.

Nick *harumphed* at the interruption.

"Hard to find good help, ain't it?" Bartlett joked at Nick's irritation.

Wilson ignored him. "Kind of busy here," he told his lieutenant in a tone much less friendly than he was using with the police officer.

"Well you'd better get unbusy," the man said. Bartlett recognized him as the man who had hit him in the face with the butt of a rifle back at the stream. The man had damn near broke his nose.

"Why?" Nick asked, never taking his eyes off of Bartlett, who was still sitting comfortably on the couch, his arms dangling comfortably on the back as if his life were not about to end. The detective made a play of stifling a yawn.

"Because we got company," the mercenary said from the window.

CHAPTER 42

"Does this look right to you?" Shan Lomax asked.

"Not even a little bit," Sheriff Tom Myers answered as he put the pickup truck in Park and killed the engine. "I would have expected guards or something."

"Yeah," Shan agreed as he opened the passenger side door and eased out of the truck, but never taking his eyes off the front of the Morehouse mansion. He felt an incredible urge to say, *I've got a bad feeling about this*, but refrained. He had been told by more than one person that his habit of quoting movies was a bit annoying. Especially when on the job so he said, "So would I" instead.

With weapons drawn, the two men sprinted up the steps and took up position on either side of the front door. After a hand signal from Shan, Laura Sellars stayed back near the truck, but also had a gun in her hand. She seemed comfortable with it, but he was still a bit nervous about having allowed her to come along.

Myers pointed his gun at the door as Shan tried the handle. "Locked?" the sheriff mouthed.

Shan shook his head as he tried it. They were both surprised to find it unlocked. Shan opened the door slowly at first then with a shove pushed it open the rest of the way. Sheriff Myers went through the open door quickly, his gun pointing ahead of him. Once he passed, Lomax also brought his weapon into a similar position and stepped inside.

"Clear," Myers said softly.

Lomax motioned for Laura Sellars to approach and she came up the steps more cautiously than the men had done. She took the spot next to the open door's hinges where Myers had been earlier.

"Stay here," Lomax told her.

"But--"

"Just stay here," he insisted.

She nodded in agreement, but was clearly unhappy with the decision. Regardless, she would wait for them to clear the hallway before she entered.

The sheriff moved deeper into the foyer and peeked around the corner. He held up a hand that told them to wait. After a second, he motioned Lomax forward. Like a chain, as one link in the chain moved farther ahead, the next in line did the same. Shan kept Laura Sellars at the rear of the chain, but made sure he kept her in sight. He wanted to make sure she stayed out of harm's way. *If you wanted her safe you shouldn't have brought her along*, he thought. It was a risk, but he still thought bringing her along made tactical sense. That didn't mean he had to like it.

"Any ideas?" he asked her softly as she slid in behind him at the end of the foyer.

She shrugged. "We were taken upstairs to a study on the second floor. Stairs are that

way," she said, pointing.

"You think they would head back there?" Myers asked.

"Doubtful."

"Why?"

"Probably because of the dead guy."

"What dead guy?" Shan asked.

"The probate attorney, Phillip Hall," she said with a calm voice. "These guys burst in and shot him. We didn't stick around long after that."

"I imagine not."

"When we left the room he was still laying where he fell. Your partner checked for a pulse, but he was gone," she told Lomax. "After that our focus was on getting everyone out in one piece. As busy as they were chasing us, I can only assume they haven't moved the body."

"One problem at a time," Myers said. "Let's find your partner and make sure he's okay. We can tear this place apart after we put the cuffs on these hired guns you mentioned."

"Okay."

Lomax also nodded his agreement.

"I hear something," Myers continued. "Sounds like it's coming from this way." He craned his head in the direction he wanted to go. A quick look told them that it was a hallway that led to another wing of the house.

"I've got point," the sheriff said.

"After you," Shan agreed, motioning him on.

Myers moved carefully into the open room. If there was going to be an ambush waiting for them then this was the place where the trap would be sprung. The room was an open floor plan with its high-vaulted ceilings and long curved staircases running along opposite walls to the second floor landing where there were ideal hiding spots behind the three foot tall safety railing. Also set into the wall were several alcoves where plants, statues, and other expensive looking trinkets rested.

Myers moved quickly toward the hallways, scanning the room as he did so just in case. He made it without incident so Lomax sent Laura Sellars next. As she crossed the room both police officers covered the room.

Once she was safely behind Myers, Shan stepped out and sprinted across the open room to meet them.

"That was--" she started once he was in the hallway.

"Too easy," he finished. "Yeah. I noticed that."

"This way," Myers said and once again took the lead. He stopped at the end of the hallway where it intersected with another hallway. He held position and listened, a hand held high and open palmed letting them know to stop.

Myers turned toward Lomax and held up a single finger.

There was someone coming and they were alone.

Backs pressed against the wall, they waited until the person stepped into view. Myers grabbed him and jerked the man into the hallway and slammed him against the wall. Lomax had his gun pointed at the man's face before he could utter a warning to his partners.

And then Shan recognized the newcomer.

"What the hell are you doing?" he asked a stunned Benjamin West.

# # #

"What do you mean, *we've got company?*"

"Cops," the lookout said from his place next to the window at the far end of the room. There were only two windows in the room and the mercenary leader had smartly placed one of his men at each of them to keep an eye on things. The other two were positioned on opposite sides of the small set of stairs that led from the hallways down into the room. Very defensible positions and each man smartly placed.

"How many?"

"Can't tell. I saw at least one, but there's probably more."

"You see anything?" Nick asked the guard at the other window.

"No," he said sharply. "But he's right. They wouldn't come alone."

"Agreed. Keep your eyes open."

"So what's the plan now, Nick?" John Bartlett asked without any attempt to hide the snark from his voice as he uncrossed his legs, but stayed reclined. He appeared comfortable.

Under normal circumstances, he would be the first to admit that purposefully trying to annoy the man holding him hostage probably wasn't the smartest of moves. *West's bad habits are starting to rub off on me*, he decided. But no matter how much he hated to admit it, the tactic was having the desired effect. On the surface, Nick Wilson was the epitome of calm. He hadn't shouted or screamed. Nor had he lost control.

At least on the outside.

But John could see his eyes and in them he witnessed a tumultuous storm brewing. Despite all of the planning and set up, the plan had started to unravel around the edges. He hadn't expected anyone to show up before he was finished, but that was exactly what had happened. He would have to improvise and that meant John had a slim chance to get out of this in one piece.

"There's only one way in or out of this room," Nick shouted and pointed toward the opening at the top of the short stack of steps. "You two," he told the guards, suddenly not remembering either of their names. Like he himself had been, the men in his company had been hand picked by his employer. As a result, he had not seen any of them in action until today. So far all of them had performed pretty much to his expectations, but suddenly he wasn't so certain that was good enough. "Anyone comes down those steps you take them out."

The two guards moved silently and took up positions where they would not catch one another in the crossfire, their weapons drawn and at the ready. Like Wilson, this was not their first mission.

Bartlett just had to time things just right and hope Sommersville's Sheriff, for that's who he assumed it to be, had plenty of backup with him. Inwardly he felt a sense of relief. If the sheriff's department was here then that meant Janice Kilpatrick had gotten the others to safety and called in the cavalry.

"Not to pressure you or anything, Nick," Bartlett said. "But if you surrender now I'll make sure you and your men all walk out of here in one piece."

The mercenary glared at him.

"Think about it, Nick. It's a good deal."

"Why don't you shut the hell up before I blow your fucking brains out?" Wilson shouted at the officer as his cool exterior began to crack. He took a step forward, his leg just a couple of inches from the coffee table.

It was the opening John Bartlett had been waiting for. There was no longer any time to waste waiting on the sheriff and his men. He had to act fast or lose the moment. Despite being outnumbered five to one, he didn't see any other alternative.

That's when John Bartlett made his move.

CHAPTER 43

John Bartlett made his move.

He lifted his leg as if he were going to cross it over the other one, a move he had mimicked several times since the conversation with the mercenary began. What had appeared to Nick Wilson as nervous fidgeting on the part of his hostage was actually Bartlett testing his escape plan.

The plan was simple and John wasn't even certain it would actually work. As his leg came up he kicked the part of the briefcase that was hanging over the edge of the table. He kicked it with enough force to flip it over and toward the man pointing the gun at him.

Instinctively, Nick Wilson flinched and broke eye contact, his gaze following the case. It was an involuntary reaction and the mercenary realized his mistake as soon as he made it.

Too bad for him he realized it too late.

Bartlett planted both feet on the coffee table and pushed it forward, slamming it directly into Wilson's legs, hitting the tender shin area between his knees and ankles. The mercenary shouted in pain and tipped forward--

Right into John Bartlett's fist.

Fueled by adrenaline, the detective was on his feet in a shot. He landed an uppercut to Nick Wilson's jaw as the mercenary fell forward. Then, before he could regain his balance, a second punch to the head sent him face first into the coffee table.

Nick dropped his nickel-plated weapon. It bounced off the coffee table and came to rest in the plush white carpet.

The entire encounter took less than two seconds. By the time the others realized what had happened, Bartlett had already dove over the coffee table, landed in a roll, and scooped up the fallen weapon. He didn't know how many bullets were in the clip and didn't have time to check. Weapons training 101 drummed the rule into rookie's heads that it was never a good idea to pull the trigger on an unknown gun without checking it first. However, since the owner of the gun had been ready to pull the trigger he figured he could risk it just this once.

The four other mercenaries moved in response to the attack, but Bartlett had the element of surprise on his side. Everything seemed to be moving in slow motion. They had all been focused on defending the room from outside attacks. None of them had been expecting an opposition from inside the room.

Bartlett squeezed the trigger and the guard closest to him at the window pitched backward, slamming against the wall before dropping to the carpet, leaving a blood smear on the wall to mark his passage.

And as quickly as it began the element of surprise went away. The guard from the other window had his weapon up, the same rifle he had clobbered the cop with earlier, and opened fire.

Bartlett dove behind the ugly red couch as bullets tore into the couch, sending plums of fluffy white material into the air. Under different circumstances it might have looked pretty, but the bullets were a real threat.

Bartlett hit the floor and stayed as flat as he could make himself as the furniture that was his cover was quickly destroyed. He squeezed off two shots blindly in the direction of his attacker in a desperate attempt to get lucky.

The return fire told him he had missed the mark completely.

He quickly ejected the clip and did a quick count. Four shots remained. He was not optimistic about his chances unless those deputies hurried up and got there. He was wondering just what was taking them so long when he heard someone shout.

"Police! Drop your weapons and step out into the center of the room!"

Bartlett didn't know the voice, but he was happy to hear it all the same. Although he

didn't expect Morehouse's hired goons to surrender, the arrival of the police officers gave Bartlett a little breather and allowed him time to think.

He balanced himself on one knee and chanced a peek from behind the damaged sofa, resting the gun on the armrest and keeping it steady. There was no way he would miss from this angle. The two guards near the stairs had kept their position. If anyone tried coming down the stairs they would be easy targets. The rifle wielding guard from the window was closer than he had been when John dove for cover, but he had stopped as well.

"I'd listen to them if I were you," Bartlett said, hoping they wouldn't turn and shoot him first. It was also a warning to whoever was out in the hall. He didn't want them walking into an ambush.

"There's only one way in or out of this room," he added when no one made a move to say anything. He raised his voice in the hope that whoever was out in the hallway was listening. He wanted to feed them as much information as he could. "You three can still walk out of here if you play this cool. Step away from the stairs and this ends here."

Nobody moved.

"Come on, fellas," he tried again, gun still aimed directly at the closest man. "What's it gonna be?"

The answer came from the guard who had hit him with the rifle earlier. He ratcheted his weapon around and opened fire on Bartlett's position. He was fast, but not fast enough. And he hadn't had time to aim. He fired blindly and Bartlett's luck held out. The red fabric of the couch exploded and added more white fluff to the air.

Bartlett squeezed off two shots, putting them squarely in the man's chest, center mass. The force of the hit threw him backward a couple of feet before he dropped to the floor. He was dead before he hit the carpet.

The two men near the steps turned and sprayed bullets in Bartlett's direction. He had nowhere to go but down so once again he kissed the floor as the mercenary's weapons disintegrated the ugly red couch. He wasn't as lucky this time as he felt a sting in his right shoulder as a bullet bit through skin. A second sting told him it was a through-and-through, not that the knowledge made it any less painful. His right arm all but useless now, he could barely hold the gun so he used both hands. He would wait, play possum, and be ready for them if they were stupid enough to run toward him. Only four bullets in the clip meant two bullets for each of them. He hoped there weren't more of Morehouse's men in the house or he was sunk.

As suddenly as it had begun, the shooting stopped.

Bartlett rolled away from the couch and came to a stop with the gun pointed in the direction of the shooters, but he didn't pull the trigger. His mind quickly focused on the gun men as a man Bartlett didn't recognize slammed one of them against the wall, but from his uniform, he assumed this was either the sheriff or one of Sommersville's deputies. Either way, he was damned glad to see him.

The second shooter had been knocked to the floor by another newcomer, this one he did recognize. At first he was startled to see his partner, Shan Lomax, there, but he quickly realized that he shouldn't have been surprised at all. "What took you so long?" he wanted to say, but stayed quiet until the room was cleared. Once he was sure the threat had been neutralized he'd talk to his partner.

"Clear," Lomax shouted.

"Clear," another voice said, but Bartlett couldn't see the owner of the voice. *He sure does sound familiar though*, he thought.

"All clear," the sheriff echoed. Then he cuffed the hands of the man he had pushed face first into the wall. Once he maneuvered the man to a sitting position against the wall, he clicked his shoulder-mounted walkie. "Dooley, we've secured Detective Bartlett and the first floor is clear," he said. "Move in, but be cautious. There might be some stragglers."

"Roger that," a tiny voice said from the talk box.

"You okay?" Shan shouted across the room at his partner even as he slapped cuffs on the perp at his feet. "John, you okay? John?"

Bartlett didn't answer. The adrenaline that had fueled his Hail Mary attack on Nick Wilson and his men left him as soon as his brain realized that the danger was past. Bartlett dropped the gun and his body slumped to the carpeted floor.

"Check him," Shan told someone, but Bartlett couldn't guess who it was. When Laura Sellars came running toward him brandishing a firearm he thought he might be dreaming. Of all the people to ride to his rescue, she wasn't one he expected, but in his condition he really didn't care. With the concussion, he was probably imagining her anyway.

He was spent.

Laura Dropped to her knees at his side, sitting her gun on the carpet next to him. "Are you hurt?" she asked, her tone even, much as it had throughout the entire ordeal. "Are you all right, Detective?" she asked again with more urgency.

John remembered being rather impressed with how well she had handled herself in the face of danger. He tried to tell her as much, but he couldn't make his mouth form the words correctly. Everything was slurred.

"John?" she shouted.

Through blurred vision, he was his partner lean in behind her. He also asked if he was okay, but the words still wouldn't come. "Stay with us, John," he said. "We'll get you out of her, buddy."

"Ambulance is on the way," Benjamin West said from somewhere nearby. Bartlett hadn't even known the pain in the ass reporter had come back for him. The only downside to all of this would be living with the knowledge that West had helped save his life. Again. If he thought the reporter had been insufferable before, he could only imagine how bad things were going to get.

Bartlett sighed and rolled over onto his back.

He had won the game.

He had earned a rest.

Exhausted, John Bartlett closed his eyes and let the darkness take him.

Before he passed out, he could swear he heard Darrin Morehouse laughing.

CHAPTER 44

Once again Fabian Alexander sat behind the anchor's desk.

"Welcome back to the Channel Ten News at Eleven," the reporter said with a polished smile as the director led him back from the commercial break. Despite the wonders that Mira in makeup could do in covering any blemish, the reporter sat behind the desk with visible cuts and bruises on his face. His left arm was in a sling as well, which clashed with his freshly pressed suit.

In the three days since the takedown of the hired muscle at the Morehouse estate, Channel

Ten's spin machine had been working overtime to make Fabian Alexander into the hero of the hour. There was little doubt by anyone in the industry that he was a shoe in for an Emmy after all of the publicity he was getting in the wake of the Morehouse debacle. Alexander's stock in the Channel Ten News Corporation had skyrocketed in the past three days. There was very little Channel Ten wouldn't offer him to keep the reporter happy because the national news outlets had come sniffing around. For the first time since the original Morehouse case, Fabian Alexander held all the cards.

"Join us this weekend as I sit down for a one on one intimate interview with Nick Wilson, the man behind the attacks at the mansion in Sommersville, Georgia where Darrin Morehouse's final revenge was executed," Alexander said as he closed out the segment. "Our coverage of this incredible drama continues throughout the week, culminating in an hour long special report this weekend where I sit down with all of the principle players, including hero cop, John Bartlett."

The camera moved in on the reporter as he ended the evening broadcast. His smile looked painful with the bruising around his broken nose and the split on his lip. "Good night, Atlanta," he said. "And God bless."

"And we're clear."

As soon as the camera turned off Fabian Alexander slipped his left arm free of the sling and with his right hand tossed it onto the desk. The arm was sore, but that was to mainly because of the bruise on his left side that had happened when his assistant tried to kill them by driving the getaway car into the ditch. He didn't need the sling, but he appreciated the sympathy it garnered.

"Beautiful show," Catherine DePlana said as she walked on to set to basically kiss his ass. She had been doing a lot of that since word spread that the Networks were looking at Fabian for possible recruitment. He had no intention of telling her that he was the one who had set those wheels in motion. Channel Ten and Catherine DePlana had been taking him for granted for years, he decided, so he figured it couldn't hurt to let them twist in the wind a little bit.

"Why didn't you tell me?" she asked.

"Why didn't I tell you what?" he said with a dismissive wave.

"How did you talk John Bartlett into coming on the show Sunday?" she asked. "I've been trying to get him on the phone since you broke the story and his people are telling us he's incommunicado and that he will not be giving any interviews." To avoid a scene with the reporter she left off the *"Especially with you"* part.

"Maybe I've got a little more pull than you, Catherine."

"Okay, that's enough," she said, clearly fed up with his arrogance. "Despite the fact that we're all treating you like you're hot shit around here, the fact remains that I'm still your boss so when I ask you how you managed to book an exclusive interview with a man that hates your guts then you'd better goddamn well answer me."

"Are you finished?"

"Don't push your luck, Fabian."

The reporter said nothing. He simply stared at her as if debating how far he could push his luck with her.

"Don't push me," she said, answering the question for him. "How'd you do it?"

"I didn't."

"I beg your pardon?"

"I didn't get him to agree," he said with a shrug. "At least not yet."

Catherine's anger threatened to boil over. "You just went on live television and told our viewers that you had him!" she shouted. "And now you're telling me that's a lie?"

"Not a lie. Per se," Catherine. I'll get him. After tonight's broadcast his bosses will be all over him to sit down for an interview with me. He won't have any say in the matter."

"You'd better be right," Catherine started.

"I am."

"Because if you're not," she continued as if he hadn't spoken. "If John Bartlett isn't sitting across from you on Sunday night then, hot shit or no, I will fire your ass! Is that understood?"

His only response was an arrogant smile as he watched Catherine DePlana walk away.

# # #

"Good night, Atlanta. And God bless."

Janice Kilpatrick sighed as she turned off the TV and tossed the remote toward the foot of the bed. She winced at the action. Once the adrenaline of the moment had worn off Janice hurt all over. After a check up her doctor told her that the aches and pains were fairly normal and would pass in a few days.

"Still sore?" Brian Kilpatrick asked from her side.

"I'll live," she said as she snuggled up next to him. "I just hate being this achy. Maybe a trip to the message therapist is in order," she added as she rolled a finger around in his chest hair.

"If you think that'll help," he said. After all she had been through he was just happy to have her home safe and sound.

"You know it's fake, right?" she finally asked.

"What?"

"The sling."

"Oh?"

296

"Yeah," she snorted. "There's nothing wrong with his arm. I swear that man's a publicity whore. I heard him talking with a ghost-writing service today about writing a novel about his experience during this ordeal."

"So?" Brian asked. "Ben's probably writing another book too. Why shouldn't Fabian write one too?"

"Most of our experience was sitting in a car," she said. "And during most of that I was driving."

"Ah, so you're afraid he won't favorable report your driving skills, is that it?" He was trying hard not to laugh.

Janice chuckled. "Knowing Mr. Alexander, I probably won't even be mentioned by name."

CHAPTER 45

John Bartlett felt good.

After two weeks of medical examinations, multiple follow up visits with his doctors, and three weeks of physical therapy followed by some much-deserved rest, he was almost back to normal. The bullet that tore through his shoulder only did minimal damage and his doctor told him that he would make an almost complete recovery. The doctor also told him that he had been very lucky. Bartlett couldn't argue the point. His right arm was in a sling, but he could use it if he had too as long as he didn't mind a little pain.

The concussion from the blows to the head was a bit harder to manage, but he was expected to make a full recovery from that as well. The dizzy spells had been rough, as was the nausea they sparked, but passed within the span of a week. During that time he was relegated to a wheelchair, which he did not like at all, but there was much nagging from his friends and medical staff so he acquiesced in the vain effort it would shut them all up. Once the dizziness stopped he was able to leave the hated wheelchair behind. While the dizzy spells had passed, the headaches remained. He was popping several Advil Migraine pills a day as per doctor's orders. They helped, but not completely. He was scheduled for a follow up in two weeks to make sure there was no more swelling.

Unfortunately, once he was discharged from the hospital there was a whole stack of problems to deal with. As a police officer involved in a shooting incident, he was immediately taken off active status while Internal Affairs Division conducted their investigation. He had been through a similar investigation before. There were also review board inquiries, mandatory post-incident psychiatric sessions, not to mention even more questions left to be answered. That meant going over his initial report and adding any information that he might have forgotten to include at the time either due to his injuries or the influence of medication. He also tried to catch up on the backlog of paperwork that was always waiting for him back at the office. There wasn't much excuse for not catching up with everything because he would be riding a desk for the foreseeable future while Internal Affairs conducted their investigation.

His current case log was shifted over to other detectives in the precinct. Normally, his partner would have continued on with a temporary replacement partner, but since Detective Lomax had also been involved in the Morehouse estate case, he too was relegated to desk duty while IAD reviewed his involvement.

All of this was mostly routine, of course. There had been a lot of bullets fired in and around the Morehouse estate and each and every one had to be accounted for so the investigators could paint a complete picture of the events that transpired there. It was not an easy task, and John for one was glad wasn't his job to sort it all out. He was cooperating fully with the investigating officers despite the normal animosity between detectives and IAD.

Captain Miller told him not to expect any problems. All of his interactions with the investigators told him that there were enough witnesses and corroborating evidence to back up everything he had told them in his report. There would be no formal charges filed against him regarding the men he killed. He also told him that the state would not be pursuing charges against Benjamin West either. Bartlett's report had been a big help in making that determination. West's growing media attention probably hadn't hurt either. He had become something of a media darling of late.

The captain was also excited by news he had heard regarding the governor of the state of Georgia wanting to present him with a medal or some type of award. It was the last thing John wanted, but he also knew that if the Governor's Office pushed it then the Police Commission would push it and Captain Miller would make it an order. He had been down that road with them before and he was just too tired to argue with them. If they wanted to parade him in front of the cameras and give him a medal then he would put on his monkey suit, smile, and accept it.

He was doing that a lot lately, he realized on one of the sleepless nights where he stared at the ceiling. He had given in to Shan and Laura and his doctors and now the governor and his boss. For a man who was so accustomed to being contrary, he seemed to be mellowing. He wasn't so sure he was happy about that. *I'll have to watch it*, he thought. *I've got a reputation to protect.*

He had also attended the funerals of Francis Chalmers and Philip Jason Hall. Although he didn't know Mr. Hall, he felt responsible for the attorney's death nonetheless. He wanted to attend and pay his respects. He wasn't quite up to driving so Laura Sellars offered to drive him. Surprisingly, she had visited him almost every day in the hospital and they had become good friends in the aftermath of the ordeal they shared. It didn't take long for him to start looking forward to her visits.

John had known Francis Chalmers for several years. They were friends and the warden's death hit John harder than he had expected. There had been quite a turnout for his funeral as government officials and law enforcement officers from around the state came to pay their respects. Shan and Laura rode with him to the funeral. It had taken quite a bit of haggling on Laura's part to convince him to let Shan drive. John wasn't comfortable depending on others, the control freak that he was, but Laura was a lawyer so she easily matched his stubbornness with her own. She won.

Janice Kilpatrick and her husband, Brian, had accompanied Benjamin West and his girlfriend, Sarah to Francis' funeral as well. It was the first time John had met Sarah so West introduced them. She seemed like a good fit for West and seemed to keep him on a short leash too. He didn't hear the first smart-assed comment from the reporter while she was within earshot. He had even let her talk him and into joining her and West for dinner. He agreed on the condition he could bring Laura along. He had witnessed firsthand that she too was able to keep a tight reign on West and the thought of the two women making him behave made John smile. One day he would look back on that dinner as their first official date.

Once he was well enough to move around on his own, John went to visit both Michael Coombes and Judge Hughes at the hospital where both were being kept under guard just in case Morehouse had any other surprises in store for them. The Atlanta PD and GBI had put details on each of the recipients of Morehouse's will, just to be on the safe side. John had noticed an increased number of patrol cars cruising past his house throughout the day.

The FBI had been brought in on the case because it crossed jurisdictions and with international list of names contained in the evidence Bartlett had retrieved from Morehouse's briefcase, the case had quickly become a federal matter. The odd circumstances surrounding how the Atlanta PD detective had obtained the evidence didn't seem to matter to them. The thought of raining down multiple indictments on some of the high profile names mentioned on the list had the Feds salivating. Scuttlebutt had it that they would start making arrests by the end of the week.

Judge Hughes had cracked his hip during the car crash as they tried to escape the estate. It required surgery, but was more or less a simple operation. The judge was not a good patient and gave the hospital staff all kinds of grief during his recovery. The good news was that the judge was set to be released in a day or two, which was what he wanted anyway. He wanted to go home and was not shy about letting anyone within earshot know it. His discharge would also keep the nursing staff from killing him because he was getting on all of their nerves.

The thing the judge seemed most pleased by was that he had beat the odds. Morehouse's video had told him that he would die, but he didn't. Despite his games, Darrin Morehouse had failed and Judge Hughes thought it was incredibly funny.

Mike Coombes was still in serious condition and had not yet woken from the coma he had lapsed into while lying wounded in the woods where Sheriff Myers men had found him. He was med-evaced to the nearest trauma center where he was stabilized for transport to a private hospital on the city of Atlanta's dime since he was injured in the performance of his job. Like Francis Chalmers, Mike Coombes was a friend and it hurt John to see him in this condition.

He and Laura spent several evenings sitting with Michael's wife and four-year-old daughter at the hospital. While she was optimistic that her husband would recover, Jennifer Coombes could not stop crying. Her young daughter, Bethany, while still too young to fully understand what was happening, could tell that something was wrong because she kept repeating, "What's wrong, Mommy?" whenever she saw her mother's tears.

Hearing the daughter's words broke John's heart.

And if that weren't enough headache to deal with then came the media and their requests and pushy behavior. He had given God-only-knew how many interviews since his release from the hospital. He had actually lost count of how many. At the forefront of the reporters beating down his door for the story was Fabian Alexander. Grudgingly, he agreed to a one-on-one sit down with the news anchor after the police commissioner asked him to do so as a personal favor for him.

"You're asking a lot," he told his boss.

"I know," the commissioner replied with a knowing smile. Bartlett assumed that meant the boss now owed him a favor, which could come in handy as often as John managed to get in trouble.

It had been nearly a decade since John Bartlett had first heard the name Darrin Morehouse. Finally, he could mark the Morehouse case closed.

It was finally over.

I beat you, you bastard. I won.

True to his word, Morehouse had messengered over a package that contained the location of the grave where Elisabeth's body was found. John had taken some personal time and traveled with the body to Virginia where she was buried in her family's plot with only a small ceremony attended by family and a few close friends. Thankfully, they had allowed John to stay as well. It was the first time John had spoken to her parents since before her disappearance. They had always blamed him for Elisabeth's leaving, and rightly so. He had once believed they were simply lying to him about knowing where she was, but now he realized that he had misjudged them and that they were hurting over her disappearance as much as he had been.

Knowing the truth about what happened to their daughter would offer them a small measure of closure, but John knew that they would never get over the loss they felt because he felt it too.

With the shadow of Morehouse no longer hanging over him, John Bartlett was free to move on with his life and he planned to put the whole mess behind him and do just that. He had been living with the pain of his ex-wife's disappearance and Morehouse's constant hounding for almost a decade and he was tired of it. For the first time in years it felt as though a weight had lifted from his shoulders. Not only had he finally excised the guilt he'd been feeling since his wife left, but he had come to terms with the fact that she was never coming back. In his mind he had always known she wouldn't return, but his heart had held onto a sliver of hope.

As with everything else he had been dealing with the past few weeks, Laura Sellars was there to help him through it.

Only one nagging question remained.

What had happened to Darrin Morehouse's body?

This one detail left the stain of doubt in Bartlett and West's brains. Although West no longer spouted his belief that Morehouse had faked his death publicly, he still believed it. Bartlett hoped that his assertions were wrong, but that kernel of doubt remained. He tried to tuck it away in one of the far recesses of his mind.

If Morehouse was alive, and he had to stress that it was a slim possibility, then he would eventually come after them again. He would keep playing his twisted games until he won.

And if he really was dead, then *game over*.

John could live with that.

Now that everything was taken care of, life could return to normal, or at least what passed for normal in John Bartlett's world. He had finally gotten a good night's sleep the night before and arrived in the office awake, alert, and ready to get on with his life. He had also shaved, which surprised a good many people. It had been a long time since anyone had seen him without several days worth of stubble.

Although he wasn't cleared to get back on active duty just yet, plus the department shrink wanted him on half days for a time after he did return, he took the opportunity to catch up on the backlog of paperwork that threatened to crush his desk beneath its weight. After two days he finally had it down to a somewhat manageable level.

"That's it," Bartlett said as he pushed his chair away from the desk. "I'm done."

"Done?" his partner asked.

"Yep. All of my files are labeled, transcripts completed, reports signed and filed, and my inbox is empty. And it's about damned time too," he added with a laugh.

"That wasn't so hard, was it?" Shan Lomax asked.

"I wouldn't go that far."

Lomax chuckled.

"We should celebrate."

"Really?" his partner questioned. "All you did was clean off... your..." he let his voice trail off as he looked at Bartlett's desk and realized it was probably the first time he had actually seen the desk calendar that was there. "You're right. We should celebrate this momentous occasion."

"You bet. First round is on me."

#

"To a job well done," John Bartlett said.

John and Shan clanked the necks of their beer bottles together before taking a first drink. The were sitting at the bar of The Rusty Mug Pub and chatting with John's friend and former training officer, Mac Sperling, who owned the pub. The Mug was a cop bar through and through. All of the staff were either former law enforcement officers or were directly related to one.

Stella had just placed the boy's third beers on the bar when the bar's door opened. Bartlett froze when he heard the bell above the entrance chime. A strange feeling of deja vu washed over him.

"How you been, West?" he said without turning around.

"How'd you know it was me?" Benjamin West asked from the door. "You got eyes in the back of your head or something?"

"Spidey sense."

"Right," West said as he slid onto the stool next to Bartlett.

"This guy bothering you, John?" Mac asked.

"You have no idea." He took another sip of his beer.

West ignored the jib. "I'll take whatever you've got on tap," West said as he dropped a twenty dollar bill on the bar. "Their next one is on me too."

Mac swiped the bill off the bar with one hand as he sat a frosty mug in front of the reporter with the other.

West took a drink. "So?" he asked after a moment, dragging out the word.

"Haven't we had enough togetherness for one lifetime, West?"

"Are you kidding? John, you're big news all over again. You and I are going to be seeing a lot more of each other."

"Oh crap. Does that mean...?" Bartlett couldn't bring himself to finish.

West smiled. That was all the answer the detective needed.

"What?" Lomax asked.

"He's writing another book," Bartlett said matter-of-fact.

"Really?"

West smiled. "Signed the contract this morning. My publisher is excited. Thinks it might be another bestseller."

"Congratulations," Lomax said and hefted his beer in a salute.

"Don't encourage him," Bartlett said before taking another sip of his beer.

"Come on, John. What's the harm? I think it's great that he's writing another book."

"That's because you'll probably be in it."

"Maybe," Lomax said with a smile. "What do you think of Samuel L. Jackson playing me in the movie?"

"I think you better get used to disappointment, partner."

West snorted. "Come on, John. I just want to get some of your thoughts on what happened. Especially after we split up and those goons captured you."

"West, why can't you just leave me out of it?"

"Are you kidding?" the writer grunted. "You are the story, John. Besides, you owe me, remember?"

"I remember," he said. "Not that you'd ever let me forget it."

"You got that right."

Bartlett closed his eyes. He knew he was going to regret the words he was about to say. "What do you want to know?" he asked.

"Everything," West said excitedly. "This is going to be great."

John Bartlett sighed and surrendered.

He'd been doing that a lot lately.

CHAPTER 46

FBI Agent Adam Parker made sure no one had followed him.

As soon as he was certain that he was alone he got out of the black town car and took a second look around. Security precautions were tight, but they were also necessary. His FBI training came in handy on days like this. The information he was carrying was of vital importance and time sensitive. He couldn't delay its delivery. He pulled a briefcase from the passenger seat before closing the door.

Agent Parker made his way to the old run down factory with a purposeful stride. The factory had been closed five years earlier and sold at auction. The new owner was a corporate concern that promised to remodel the buildings in an effort to revitalize business in the area.

Five years later nothing had changed.

On the outside.

Agent Parker typed in a five-digit code on the keypad by the door. The light turned orange and he swiped a simple white card over the reader. The light changed to green and the electronic lock released and he pulled open the door.

This was not Agent Parker's first time there and he knew exactly where to go.

The room was sparsely furnished. A small conference table sat in the middle of the room with six chairs even spaced around the edges. Along the far wall were three large paned windows that overlooked the factory floor when this plant had been in operation. Today, however, it was dark on the other side of the glass except for a scattering of low powered ceiling lights that cast a strangely brownish orange glow on the conference room.

The conference room was likewise dim. Except for a small light on a cabinet against the wall to the right there were no lights on in the conference room. Agent Parker reached for the light switch with his free hand.

"I prefer it dark," the room's lone occupant said. She was standing in front of the cabinet, her arms folded in front of her as she stared at a small urn sitting directly beneath the wall-mounted lamp.

"As you wish," Agent Parker said as he dropped the hand to his side.

"I take it you have something for me?"

"Yes, ma'am." Parker walked to the conference table and placed the briefcase there. He flipped open the top and removed a small flash drive. "Everything you requested has been digitized and copied onto this," he said as he placed the flash drive on the table.

"That's everything?"

"As requested. Your suspicions were correct. The Bureau expects to start making arrests within a week's time. You've got a bit of a head start."

"I appreciate your efficiency and your discretion in this matter, Agent Parker."

"Of course, ma'am."

"The amount we discussed has been transferred to your account," she said after making a few taps on her smart phone. "Plus a little something extra for taking care of this matter so quickly."

"I appreciate that," Agent Parker said as he checked his account balance on his phone. "If there's nothing else," he added, letting the sentence trail off.

"That will be all. Thank you, Agent Parker."

"Feel free to call again if you need anything, ma'am," Agent Parker said before heading out the door.

Once he was gone she turned back to the object she had been so fixated on when Agent Parker arrived. The urn was small and rather plain looking. It was a final act of revenge, knowing that the man whose remains rested inside would have hated to know that his final remains were being held in a vessel that was so ordinary looking.

"You always did underestimate me, honey," Vivian Morehouse said to the ashes of her late husband. She did not bother to hide her contempt. "I know this isn't where you expected to end up. You thought you had taken care of all of the arrangements, but as usual you underestimated me. Rerouting your body and having it cremated is easy enough when you've got a couple of FBI agents on the payroll." She smiled. "Wouldn't you agree?"

There wasn't an answer, of course. Nor did she expect one.

"Of course you do," she answered for him. "I wonder if you thought you were really going to get away with killing all of those people, with killing me." She shook her head and smiled. "No matter. We both know which of us was the last one standing."

Darrin Morehouse was gone, but without a body there would always be some small semblance of doubt by his friends and enemies alike. Vivian had a plan to use that doubt to her advantage. She was going to give her late husband the one thing he had always wanted.

She was going to make him a legend.

She walked over to the table and picked up the flash drive. It was hard to believe that the whole of Darrin's empire had been compressed onto the tiny piece of plastic and aluminum in her hand. Everything her husband had built fit snuggly in the palm of her hand. The image made her laugh. The urn would remain hidden away in the building where no one would ever think to look for it. After all, there was nothing that could tie this building back to Vivian Morehouse.

Starting today things were going to change. Everything that had belonged to her husband was now hers. And thanks to the FBI, the only people who stood between her and total control would be arrested within a few days time.

Things couldn't have gone better had she planned it.

"Goodnight, Darrin," she told the ashes before she turned out the light.

"I hope you burn in hell."

ABOUT THE AUTHOR:

From his secret lair in the wilds of Bethlehem, Georgia, Bobby Nash writes. A multitasker, Bobby is certain that he doesn't suffer from ADD, but instead he... ooh, shiny.

When he finally manages to put fingers to the keyboard, Bobby writes novels (*Evil Ways; Fantastix*), comic books (*Fuzzy Bunnies From Hell; Demonslayer; Domino Lady vs. The Mummy; Lance Star: Sky Ranger "One Shot"*), short prose (*A Fistful of Legends; Full Throttle Space Tales Vol. 2: Space Sirens; Green Hornet Case Files; Yours Truly, Johnny Dollar; Zombies vs. Robots*), novellas (*Lance Star: Sky Ranger; Ravenwood: Stepson of Mystery, Night Beat*), graphic novels (*Yin Yang; I Am Googol: The Great Invasion*), and even a little pulp fiction (*Domino Lady; Secret Agent X; The Avenger*) just for good measure. And despite what his brother says, Bobby swears he is not addicted to buying DVD box sets and can quit anytime he wants to. Really.

Bobby's work can be found at www.bobbynash.com, www.lance-star.com, www.facebook.com/bobbyenash, and www.twitter.com/bobbynash, among other places across the web.

ACKNOWLEDGEMENTS

There's a lot of history behind this novel. Originally planned to be the follow up to my first published novel, *Evil Ways*, *Games!* as it was originally titled, began its life much like it's predecessor, in Harriette Austin's Creative Writing Workshop at the University of Georgia. Unfortunately, after a few starts and stops, plus other writing gigs coming in, the novel fell temporarily by the wayside for a couple years while I worked on other things. This story never really left my train of thought fully. I often found myself coming back to work on *Games!*

In *Evil Ways* I had created this wonderfully fictional community of Sommersville, GA so it only seemed natural to return to that sleepy little farming community at some point. I already knew that the sequel to *Evil Ways*, called *Evil Intent* (coming soon, I promise) would follow the exploits of FBI Agent Harold Palmer and would not take place in Sommersville so when it came time to write the showdown at Darrin Morehouse's estate I couldn't think of a better place for it to be than Sommersville. That's where the connection to *Evil Ways* was supposed to end. I had no intention of writing in any of the characters from that novel into this one.

Of course, as so often happens when writing, certain characters just wouldn't stay out of the story. Bringing back Sheriff Tom Myers and his deputies opened up the story in ways I hadn't expected, but at the end of the day you'd think I planned it that way. That's one of the joys of writing. No matter how much you plan or plot, eventually you just have to follow the characters and see what they're going to do.

Go figure.

I really like the characters of John Bartlett and Benjamin West. Who knows, maybe I'll revisit them someday.

Although sometimes it feels like it's just me and the keyboard racing against deadlines, the truth is that no novel is written in a vacuum. And *Deadly Games!* was no exception. There are a few folks I'd like to thank for their invaluable support, expertise, inspiration, and motivation.

As always, my family has been the greatest support staff one could hope for. A big thank you very much to Bobby (R.O.) Nash,

Margaret Nash, and Wes Nash for keeping me inspired and for keeping my ego in check.

Harriette Austin, Mike Gordon, Bill Cunningham, Jeff Austin, Rob Davis, Van Allen Plexico, Tommy Hancock, Ellen C. Maze, Howard Hopkins, Mark Maddox, Jeff Allen, Cathy Carter, and Frank Fradella all provided invaluable feedback and information that helped shape the final product you hold in your hand. And also Ron Sperling, who graciously allowed me to use him as the template for one of the characters in this tale.

A big thanks also goes out to Kurt Allen for his assistance with the covers and for posing for the front cover image. I learned a good bit about making fake blood spatter from Kurt too. That was an education.

I'm sure there's someone I'm forgetting and if so no slight was intended. Sometimes my brain hides valuable information from me until it's too late.

And finally, thank you to those who have purchased this novel. If you've reached this page then you've read, and hopefully enjoyed, the story of **Deadly Games!** Or you skipped ahead to the end, in which case I say, "Don't do that!"

Thanks again and I hope we can get together like this again real soon.

Best Regards,

Bobby Nash
Somewhere in Bethlehem, GA

So... What's Next?
Keeping up with the latest Nash News is easy.

BOBBYNASH.COM

DAILY UPDATES

www.bobbynash.com

NEWS, REVIEWS, INTERVIEWS

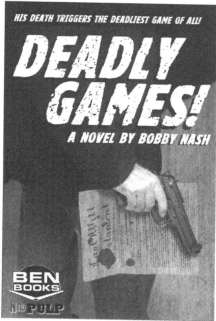

DEADLY GAMES!

53526539R00190

Made in the USA
Columbia, SC
17 March 2019